# Tell Me Who You Are

# Tell Me Who You Are

## Louisa Luna

MCD ⊗ FARRAR, STRAUS AND GIROUX NEW YORK

MCD
Farrar, Straus and Giroux
120 Broadway, New York 10271

Title-page art by korkeng/Shutterstock.com.

Library of Congress Cataloging-in-Publication Data
Names: Luna, Louisa, author.
Title: Tell me who you are : a novel / Louisa Luna.
Description: First edition. | New York : MCD / Farrar, Straus and Giroux, 2024.
Identifiers: LCCN 2023050747 | ISBN 9780374612795 (hardcover)
Subjects: LCGFT: Psychological fiction. | Thrillers (Fiction) | Novels.
Classification: LCC PS3612.U53 T45 2024 | DDC 813/.6—dc23/eng/20231027
LC record available at https://lccn.loc.gov/2023050747

Designed by Abby Kagan

Our books may be purchased in bulk for promotional, educational, or business use. Please
contact your local bookseller or the Macmillan Corporate and Premium Sales Department at
1-800-221-7945, extension 5442, or by email at MacmillanSpecialMarkets@macmillan.com.

www.mcdbooks.com • www.fsgbooks.com
Follow us on social media at @mcdbooks and @fsgbooks

10  9  8  7  6  5  4  3  2  1

*For JP and Florie, finally!*
*I'll set up the Parcheesi . . .*

# Tell Me Who You Are

# Dr. Caroline

You can tell me anything.

When you're in this room, and we're sitting across from each other, and your mind is reeling with all the bad things you've done to people and all the bad things they've done to you, you can let it all out into the air between us. All the weird sex stuff, the compulsive jerking off, the period blood staining the gym shorts when you were thirteen, the infidelities, the regret about having kids or not having kids. You can tell me about the time you did mushrooms and made out with a window for three hours, or that time with your dad's friend, that time you felt a stranger's boner press against you on the subway, how you wish your mother would just die already, how you accidentally screwed that IT girl in the conference room, how the rape scene in *Deliverance* turns you on, how you obsessively think about sex or food or death, how you should get more sleep and make more money, how you should eat more ugly foods and buy more reusable bags, how you lied about voting for Obama. How you wish you were a better person, a better spouse, a better parent, a better worker, a better citizen. How there is something else you should be doing, how you feel trapped in this life and in this body and every day it's like you're living and reliving that Talking Heads song. *Well, how did I get here?*

You can tell me any of it; you can make a list ahead of time or just barf it all up when you sit down, and I will never tell anyone.

Imagine weighing yourself on a bathroom scale, and all the little black lines represent all the things you can tell me—the dial can bounce up and down as many times as you want, and your secrets will be safe with me. There's only one red line we have to worry about, only one little tick mark where the dial has to land in order for me to break my promise, and that would be if you told me you were going to kill someone.

My anorexics love this metaphor.

And yes, of course, if you were going to harm or kill yourself, I'd have to make a call, but if you're telling your shrink in person you're planning to do yourself in and didn't happen to stash your chosen weapon in your purse, chances are you are open to being talked out of it.

My patients call me Dr. Caroline for a couple of reasons. One, because the goal is to make them comfortable, to convince them I am like their smart, impartial friend who has their best interests at heart. Two, because of the Marvel thing. There is a superhero, Doctor Strange, who travels through time/space and knows physics, I guess? I've only seen a couple of those movies with my family and don't care for them. All that Sturm und Drang, so much emotion and wrestling with life choices. I get that day in, day out, eight-thirty in the morning to eight-thirty at night, so when I go to a movie, I just want to see cars blow up and perhaps a nice pair of tits I can admire wholesomely from afar.

I live in a wealthy neighborhood in a wealthy city. Where Botox meets craft butchery, and even the homeless people can do a mean upward-facing dog. It's Brooklyn, so there is still a little edge here and there—the tall, thin vape twins who can barely keep their eyes open even as they blow smoke into your face as you pass them on the sidewalk; the guy with the elaborate facial tattoo asking for coffee money in front of the pediatrician's office; the lady who sits on a tuffet of garbage bags in the bank vestibule. I like this about where I live. I grew up in a sleepy Wisconsin suburb where the most exciting thing that ever happened was two rival dentists got into a fistfight at a sports bar once. When I came to New York City for school, I never looked back.

My patients are primarily from the privileged masses: Prospect Park soccer moms and aging hipster dads, anxious gainfully employed millennials and their oddly relaxed unemployed counterparts.

The lot of them were silenced for a few weeks by the collective sonic boom of the pandemic. In the beginning they resisted the Zoom sessions, but then they caved one by one, and those first appointments were cacophonies of panic; whatever trivial transgressions they'd experienced or caused in their former lives were crushed like a kombucha can under a Prius tire. Very few of them got the virus or knew anyone who'd died, but still, their wild fear seeped through the screen, and I was there to absorb it.

I felt extra-useful in those days, shepherding them from one day to the next, so many of them moving through the most precious realizations (*I should spend less time on social media and more time with my kids!, I should listen more than I talk!, I should stop forcing people to look at my dick!*). But then, after a couple of months, they realized they would probably not die, that they were safe in their little corner of the world, so they went back to old habits and old complaints, running out our time together wringing their hands about emotional affairs with their work husbands, or how Dad had yelled too much, and I'd send them off with a virtual pat on the head and a prescription for their Lexapro/Klonopin refills.

So it's not triage in the ER, who cares? This is my job, and, not to put too fine-tip a point on the scrip pad, all those complaints and meds paid for the brownstone where I live with my family on the parlor and upper levels and meet with patients in the ground-floor office.

I still get a flutter of excitement when I see a new patient, because it really is like a blind date in many ways: will we gel; will we click; will he recognize me as a fellow human and show me something. But between you and me, it doesn't matter if he decides to show me anything, because I'll see it anyway. I watch the hands; I watch the legs crossing; I watch the gazes toward the window. I listen for the vocal modulation when he's speaking about money/sex/Mom/Dad. Give me an hour, I'll tell you who you are.

Second thought, make that fifty minutes.

It's a steaming June day after arguably the worst year humans have seen in a good long while, and a new patient is coming without a referral, which is even more exciting, a blind-leading-the-blind date.

There is an internal staircase leading from my home down to my office, but I walk outside and down the stoop and enter through the door under the stairs just so I can see what he will see: in front of the windows, a cream-colored couch with a small cylindrical table at one end where he can place his phone and water bottle. Also on the table are a box of tissues and a dimmable-display alarm clock, which is for me to keep track of the time. He will also have an identical clock to look at, on another cylindrical table next to my wood-framed chair, an office chair that isn't supposed to look like it belongs in an office. But he has a choice—on the other side of his table is a plush swivel chair.

Where he sits will tell me the first thing. Most people will take the couch because it is more directly positioned in front of me. They're not thinking too much about it. But those who choose the swivel chair don't mind sitting at an angle, or they enjoy swiveling, or they don't want to feel like a patient; they've been taught to associate couches with shrinks and they don't want any part of that. So if they choose the swivel chair, they're making a little statement, crossing their arms and digging in their heels: *Nope, not gonna tell you anything.*

There are two doors behind my chair, one leading to the kitchen, where I keep a Nespresso machine for myself, and the other to a half bath that patients can use. There's a full-length mirror hung on the door of the patient bathroom, and how long they spend in there after the business is done, scrutinizing, muttering, fixing hair, and checking teeth, also tells me a great deal.

I don't use the patient bathroom—for that I'll go upstairs to my home—but I do like to review myself in the mirror. I wear a white suit for my sessions every day. Alexander McQueen wool blends—single-button blazer with boot-cut pants. The white is for both of us: for them, to see me as a blank sheet of paper on which they can write whatever they want; for me, an extra boundary. I've known therapists who wear distressed-hem jeans and cowl-neck sweaters with their patients, who sit cross-legged on beanbag chairs, and that is just not for me. It's not a fucking square dance; it's work.

The patients need the boundaries, even if they buck against them. And some, I would say most, end up appreciating them. Where will Nelson Schack fall?

I position the two linen-covered pillows, one to either side of the couch. Only certain patients use the pillows, always for support—clutching for emotional, tucked behind them for lumbar.

I adjust the temperature on the split AC unit by one degree. Some patients expel their sadness through sweat instead of tears, I've found, so better cool than hot.

I check myself in the mirror once more. The suit is pressed, but the silhouette is simple—I don't look like I'm going to a Wall Street hedge fund or a wedding. Every morning I blow out my hair and style with a rotary brush; the result is natural but controlled, which is the goal.

Then come the three tones of the digital doorbell.

I open the French double doors into the hallway, where there is a single chair and a small table with recent *New Yorker* magazines in a fan. I answer the front door, and here is Nelson Schack. An inch or two taller than me, slender. Hair almost buzz-cut-short but not quite. Swimming-pool-blue eyes and clean-shaven except for a spot missed under the nose. Collared polo shirt, sweat circles in the pits. Khaki pants with slanted lines crisscrossing at the knee, ironed haphazardly.

"Hi, Nelson," I say. "I'm Dr. Caroline."

I hold up my hand in a still wave. Even though he and I have sent each other copies of our vaccination cards via email, I don't need to put anyone through the pros and cons of a handshake with a stranger.

"Hi," he says, only meeting my eyes for a moment.

"Come in," I say, warm but professional.

I hold the door open for him, and he walks past me, giving off a scent of a musky deodorant with a little BO spike.

He stands in the hallway as I close the door, and then turns to me for instruction.

"Please, have a seat," I say, gesturing toward the office.

I know he'll take the couch before he takes the couch. He's nervous; he's never done this before; he won't even think about it.

He sits on the couch, the middle cushion, and crosses his arms over his chest, his fingers cozy in the twin saunas of his pits.

I slide the double doors shut and take my chair.

"Before we begin, I need to make you aware of one thing," I say.

He gets a caught-raccoon sort of look, so I don't keep him in suspense.

"You can tell me anything," I say, turning my finger in a small circle. "This is a safe space."

Then I smile, and he smiles, relieved.

"What brings you here today, Nelson?"

He laughs and puts his hands on his knees, then says, "It's a couple of reasons, Doc. I'm just not sure which one to talk about first."

I nod, because I know. Their first time in therapy, they don't know where to start. *How did my life end up this way?* is a big old rabbit hole to fall into, every rock you hit another loved one to blame.

"Why don't you try just saying whatever comes to the surface first?" I ask, as if I've never suggested it to a patient before.

"Yeah, that's a good idea," he says.

His voice is unexpectedly high, as if he's leading up to a question. Then he pats his knees with an air of decision and says, "Well, here goes."

I give him another smile meant to convey the tell-me-anything rule, and he must truly understand it, because then he says something that I never could have predicted he or any other patient would ever say to me, not in my thirteen years of primary and high school, twelve years total in undergrad, med school, residency, and eleven years of private practice:

"I think I'm going to kill someone, Doc," he says in that strange high register, his eyes scanning the corners of the room. Then he looks straight at me and says, "And I know who you really are."

I'll tell you a little bit about narrative omission in therapy. All of us—you, me, your mom, the dry cleaner—we all rewrite the stories of our lives as we tell them to other people. Sometimes we change things, but more often than not we just omit. We tell our listeners what they need to know, and nothing else. We do that because it's human nature to get to the point, and to a lesser extent not bore the listeners. Why? Because we want them to keep listening to us.

No one cares that a Paleolithic-era caveman took a dump in a hole or was on the receiving end of a nut-cracking BJ from the missus. We care that he killed the bison, and somehow, even with his underdeveloped Neanderthal brain, he recognized that, so that's what he painted on the wall.

My patients do this all the time; however, there's a slightly more devious edge to it. I have a patient, let's call her Meandering Marjory. Marjory drinks too much and pretends she doesn't, which makes her as unique as half of America. So sometimes she'll come in and tell me all about her day leading up to our appointment, how she got coffee in the morning and dropped the kids off at school and went grocery shopping and walked the dog, and it takes her twenty minutes to get through this much of the story and she keeps blowing air out, her upper lip flapping like a doggy door, and adopts a street accent arbitrarily ("You feel me, girl?"), and yet it takes me about thirty seconds to get her to admit that she also drank a pint of dark-and-stormies before showing up.

If you have been in therapy, you have done the same in some way. Sometimes you do it to cut to the chase; sometimes you do it because you don't want your therapist to know something.

Here's a hot tip: we know.

But rest assured, we do it, too. Because we're all cavepeople together! All of us shitting in holes and performing/receiving fellatio, and yet we only pick up the charcoal to draw that pesky bison.

So when I said I grew up in a sleepy Wisconsin suburb where the most exciting thing that ever happened was a fight between two dentists at a sports bar, that wasn't the whole story. Dr. Brower and Dr. Nowak did get in a fistfight at Gator Sam's, but the town is known for something else entirely.

It made national news at the time, but Jeffrey Dahmer had been caught only two years before, and people on the coasts can only take so much news about the goings-on in the middle, even if it's bloody. But in the Upper Midwest it was a big deal for a while.

In late June of 1993 in the village of Glen Grove, Wisconsin, a man murdered his family with a pair of hedge shears. The wife was thirty-eight at the time of her death; the children sixteen and thirteen. The blades on the shears were eleven inches long.

About now you're rushing, skimming, skipping—you want to know it all, don't you? You're desperate for details—how did he do it with the shears, did he stab them, cut off their fingers or their heads? Or worse, you think, did he cut out their hearts . . . did he cut out their hearts and eat them whole, did the police find a pentagram drawn in blood on an altar in the basement?? No, wait, did he . . . no, it's just too awful, he couldn't have . . . *did he have sex with their headless fingerless hollow corpses???*

We all think we'll be the ones so mature and self-realized that we won't look at the car accident, but of course we look; we hope to see something horrible in order to capture the relief that it didn't happen to us. It's natural! Don't beat yourself up about it, but really, satanic-inspired cannibalism and necrophilia are not that prevalent, despite what some swaths of the intellectually damaged population would tell you.

Yes, the Glen Grove murders were gruesome and gory and worse than the worst images from the first slasher movie you saw, which have burrowed into your unconscious so deeply you sometimes wonder if you didn't actually imagine them yourself—Jason chopping off his mom's head, Freddy gutting Johnny Depp (before he was Johnny Depp).

And I happen to have a personal connection to the event, which is not exactly a secret but also not exactly broadcasted, and so when Nelson Schack offers this pair of confessions, I think it best to focus on the one that feels more urgent.

"How long have you been thinking about killing someone?" I say.

He laughs, but not nervously. He seems delighted by my question.

"This one?" he says. "Not long."

He touches his face, fingers to lips and around to the back of the neck. They are the moves of an anxious person, but again, he does not project anxiety. His eyes flicker like candlelight, and his smile, though slight, is genuine. Someone with a wonderful secret. He dropped "this one" thinking I may not notice. This one, as in there have been others. Though I'm always driving, I sometimes like to let my patients think that they are. It occurs to me that Nelson could use a sudden turn.

"Have you decided whom you're going to kill yet, this time?" I ask, casual as can be, as if I were asking one of my older son's idiot friends which extracurricular sports he's doing in the fall.

He stops moving his hands around, and they stay at the back of his neck. Something doesn't please him. Loses the smile.

"Yes, I have."

I realize now would be the time for me to get nervous, if I got nervous. Which I don't. Nelson Schack may be a few inches taller than me but doesn't look like he works out like I do. I can't make out his biceps, but from what I see of his forearms, I doubt he'd make it through a single resistance class at Pure Barre. The way his clothes hang suggest he's not carrying a weapon, and if he is, it's slight and ineffectual. Likely similar to his genitals and/or prefrontal cortex activity.

"Is that information you'd like to share with me?" I ask.

"Uh, no, not yet."

"Okay," I say. "We can pause on that. Have you decided the method of how you're going to kill this person?"

"Oh yeah," he says, as if a familiar song has just spun from the playlist. "Pretty sure I'm gonna just let her starve."

"Hm," I say, because if it wasn't Twenty Questions before, now it is. "So does this person live with you?"

He grins. "No."

"Is this person a relative?"

"Uh-uh, no. She lives in the neighborhood, and I've been watching her awhile. You know her, too, Doc."

He certainly likes a challenge! In residency I treated a handful of real grade-A antisocial personality disorders—people you would call sociopaths and psychopaths. What they all shared was an absence of remorse, a tendency to lie, and, more specifically for the psychos as opposed to the socios, a pattern of manipulation and aggression. But then there are those I call the fanboys. These are the ones who've gobbled up books about the Zodiac Killer and Ted Bundy, who obsessively watched and rewatched *The Silence of the Lambs* and possibly *Manhunter*; maybe even kicked back with a High Life on Wednesday nights to watch *Criminal Minds*, but that really is scraping the bottom of the serial-killer-narrative barrel.

Nelson Schack reads more fanboy than psycho to me. His intention is to provoke, daring me to join the game. He might have done some cursory research about me, but he doesn't know enough about me to know that I have won nearly every game night my family has had since my sons were old enough to fit the little plastic wedges inside the Trivial Pursuit piecrusts.

I say nearly, because I've had to throw quite a few games. Child psychologists will say it's important to let your children lose because it prepares them for coping with failure in the world, and ultimately I agree, but sometimes they just need a win. Boys especially. And yes, I let my husband win some, too.

Because I also like to get laid.

So okay, Nelson, I've got the empty pie, my seven letter tiles (all consonants, by the way), a full set of chess pieces, and a fire-engine-red gingerbread boy from goddamn Candy Land. Winner goes first.

I smile and say, "I know a lot of people. You mind narrowing it down for me?"

He brushes his chin with his fingers and says, "You know who she is but you might not know her personally."

"Is she a local celebrity?"

Quickly I flip through the mental Rolodex of famous and semi-famous in our neighborhood, which may be larger than you'd think. Mayoral candidates, actors, musicians, restaurateurs, writers. Once I saw Padma from *Top Chef* at the roller rink in Prospect Park. She was nine feet tall on skates.

"No. Some people know her name."

"You could say that about anyone, I think," I offer.

His face sinks and sags. Suddenly he looks jowlier than he did when he first sat down.

"You don't believe me," he says.

"What makes you say that?"

"You know, the way you're joking around."

"Nelson," I say. "All I know is what you're telling me, and I take everything you're saying very seriously. However, I notice that you're only telling me a little bit at a time, which implies you'd like me to take some guesses and make some observations."

He nibbles his lips into a pout, and whatever might have been edgy about him dissolves. He's like every other one of my patients, especially the men, awaiting the kitten licks to whatever fragile wound is throbbing just beneath the surface. It will take me, as always, being the bigger person.

"I'm sorry I've misunderstood you," I say. "If you like, we can start over. You can even leave the room and come back in," I say, waving in the direction of the door. "We can pretend we've never met."

He smiles now, charmed by the idea and my apology.

"Do people do that?" he says, letting his head down so that it's almost resting on his shoulder. "Start over?"

"Of course. Getting off on the wrong foot is part of being human. I can't tell you the number of times a new patient has decided to come through the door for the first time twice."

I will tell you the number of times: zero.

He lifts his head and appears to be thinking about it. Even though I just came up with the idea, it's fairly irresistible: To reset. Wouldn't we all like it, even if it's just from this morning, would we waste less time reading garbage on the internet, would we eat the muffin, would we call our mothers? The answer for me for all three would be no, but I'll agree that at least to have the option is intriguing.

"Okay," he says.

"Okay?"

"Yeah," he says, brushing his fingers over his chin again. "I'd like to do that. Go out and come back in."

"That's great," I say, standing, as if this is all pro forma.

He stands, and he stares blankly past me, no longer engaged.

"Please," I say, gesturing toward the door.

"I just go out and come back in again."

"That's right, Nelson. Just start over."

Something about that lands right where it should, because he brings his focus back to me, blue eyes lighting up. Could he be attractive? Not in his current state, to be sure, but maybe some baggier clothes, a tattoo here or there, hair a little longer—he could be a moderately cute bartender.

He heads for the double doors and pulls them open, and I follow, still surprised we're doing this little bit of sitcom staging. Then he passes through the hallway and goes through the front door.

"Thanks, Doc," he says, fully outside now. "For all the great advice."

"You're most welcome."

I shut the door and wait a minute, don't watch him through the peephole so he can't see the glass grow dark.

He doesn't buzz or knock. I finally look through the peephole, and he's gone.

I open the door and walk through the small paved yard, through the front gate, and look left, then right, and I see him, arms heavy at his sides, trudging toward the corner. I stand still, waiting, but he doesn't make a move to return or even turn his head back to look at me.

I cough up a closemouthed laugh. The turn of events is refreshing. Well done, Nelson. Good job sticking the landing on Gumdrop Pass.

I have at least a half hour before my next appointment, Churlish Charlotte, since Nelson didn't take his whole slot. I give all my patients little nicknames, as alliterative and Garbage-Pail-Kids-like as possible as a means to remember them, of course, and maybe also keep myself amused. Churlish Charlotte runs a yoga-studio-slash-custom-tea-shop, and has been a patient for four or five years. For someone who should be blissed out on endorphins from pigeon pose and turmeric-cinnamon blends, she's generally pretty whiny and pissy. Even during the darkest pandemic days she found something petty to obsess over in every session, like how Whole Foods kept running out of the chickpea pasta she has to have because whole grains give her gut-bloat.

I walk up the steps of the stoop and press the passcode into the keypad, go inside. The parlor level of my house smells like rosemary and mint, from a spray I instructed the cleaning lady to spritz in the air and on the chairs and couches. The living room is furnished in what I would call modern-but-not-statement: a curved sectional with tapered legs, an Eames chair, a cowhide ottoman. There is also some art.

My husband is Jonas Eklund the sculptor, and he is well-known in certain circles. He sells two or three pieces a year, which, for a working artist, is considered very successful. He also has pieces in the permanent collections of the Whitney and the Tate. If you are not familiar with these circles, you might think this success pays for our lifestyle significantly. I would say instead he contributes in a quaint way to our household income.

I walk through the kitchen, which is an open plan and was a nightmare of renovation (how many mistakes, how much half-assery, can one contractor commit? the answer is a lot) but now is so beautiful with the white quartzite countertops and mosaic marble backsplash imported from Italy that I barely think of that dark time when plaster chunks covered the floor and every surface was wet and gluey. Now I just want to touch everything.

I didn't grow up poor but I didn't have much, so now I truly take nothing for granted. I believe there is nothing wrong with relishing the bougie-ness I've worked my whole life for. I don't practice any kind of organized religion, so I will pray at the altar of my Bosch oven and anoint myself with a single dot of Amber Aoud behind each ear.

Through the kitchen windows, I see my husband sitting on the deck, wearing his summer uniform: white drawstring wide-leg pajama pants, no shirt. His hair, still more blond than gray even though he's five years my senior, is wet from his daily swim and shower at the Y. He is striking even when he doesn't try to be, tall and tan and lean and looks every inch a Swede, which he is. Effortlessly hot. Women fall at his feet and always have. I had to step over quite a few to get to him.

I slide the glass door open and step onto the deck, and Jonas looks up from his phone and his small paper cup of espresso, one corner of his mouth pinched in a smile.

"Your new patient ended early, Doctor?"

It's a joke in our family—everyone calls me Doctor. It started with Jonas teasing me whenever I curbed toward bossiness, and then the boys picked up on it when they were little. Now we have a selection of stories to tell at functions and events, such as when our oldest, Elias, was in kindergarten and insisted that the second Sunday in May was actually called "Doctor's Day."

"Yes," I say, sitting in the chair opposite Jonas at the patio table. "He was a little something different."

"Ah," says Jonas, not listening. His smile grows as he views the screen on his phone. Then he hands it to me. "Elias is doing tennis again."

I scroll through the pictures. Both of our sons are at sleepaway camp in Vermont for four weeks. We give the people who run the camp thousands of dollars, and in return they send us a steady stream of pictures of our kids doing fun things.

Elias is thirteen and looks and acts like Jonas. He had his first girlfriend at age nine. In the photos, he is smirking as he waits for the ball in a neutral stance, long limbs sprouting out from his white shirt and shorts, blond hair falling over one eye.

"Any of Theo?" I ask.

"Oh yes, keep looking."

I swipe until I see our younger. Theo is eleven, tall and blond like his brother and his father, but emotionally more like I was as a child:

forever analyzing and therefore a little nervous. But I figured out how to balance the two, and I have confidence he will as well. It just may take some time.

In Theo's pictures he is holding a small clay coil pot in one hand and a wire-head loop tool in the other. He's concentrating hard. I zoom in on the pot.

"Those coils are a mess," I say.

Jonas sips his espresso, says, "I didn't see."

I flip the phone around so he can see.

He lets out a snort of laughter. "He'll fix it up," he says.

"If you say so."

I place the phone on the table and slide it to him. "What are your plans for the day?"

He stretches his arms behind his head. "Studio for some time. Then David Layton has an opening-signing thing at Sapirstein in West Chelsea."

My husband goes to one or two exhibition openings a week. Sometimes he knows the artist, and sometimes he doesn't. He says he goes to support his friends and also meet potential buyers. "Art is connection," he has said, in every meaning the words can have. Of course I believe him, but I know he also likes to go and drink cheap rosé and flirt with twenty-five-year-olds. And that is fine, too. I know who I have married, and he knows me. Considering how many of my patients come in and whine about the lack of understanding in their relationships, I have come to see it as a rare thing.

We talk for a minute more and then look at things on our phones. I pull up Nelson Schack's intake form he'd emailed ahead of time. His address is not far from mine, in Sunset Park. I check to see that his deposit hasn't budged on Venmo. I google him, but there is a Peruvian economist with the same name and he takes up all the search space.

I think about calling the police.

I've actually never had to do it before. I've heard countless musings of suicidal ideation and homicidal fantasies—I would argue these are normal. The urge to not have to wake up at five forty-five and go to work every day and live in your pesky body with all its aches and flabbiness is strong for most people at least some of the time. Or fantasies about your ex-wife dying—maybe it's by your hand or maybe she gets hit by the street sweeper on the way to her candle-dipping class or whatever. Normal.

As it turns out, I'm guilty of a little narrative omission myself, you see—next to the big red line on my bathroom scale indicating a necessary breach of doctor-patient privilege, there are actually three skinnier rosy pink lines: the expressed thought that a patient wants to harm himself or another specific person ("I want to kill my mother"), an articulated plan to commit the act ("I'm going to kill my mother by poisoning her tea"), and obvious intent ("I'm intending to kill my mother by poisoning her tea tonight"). If you tell me anything like that, I would have to make a call.

But nothing so detailed from Nelson Schack.

So I forget about him. My job takes total compartmentalized focus. If you're on my couch (or in my swivel chair), you have my attention.

I go back downstairs to fluff the pillows for Charlotte. She is five minutes late and complaining about the CVS pharmacy line that caused her to be late (she would never actually apologize for being late, you see), and drinking from a gallon jug of water with motivational messaging printed at every eight-ounce-mark ("You've Got This—Keep Chugging!"). But her hour starts and passes, and I don't get anything new from her in this session except that she thinks she might have a UTI but hasn't had it checked out; apparently she's been meaning to find a new ob-gyn because her current lady has "weird alien fingers."

Charlotte leaves, and next is Sad Sober Rahul. Still sober, always sad. Every time I see him we talk about meds, how they might change things for him, how we could start on the lowest dose, but Rahul is adamant about being on nothing, no drugs, no meds. Doesn't even take a multivitamin. I find his commitment admirable, but there comes a time when you can say, *I think today I would not like to be so miserable.*

After Rahul we have Amanda Demanda. What does Amanda Demanda do? you wonder. Well, she demands. And asks, and pleads, and whines: *Why can't things be easier? Why is it all uphill, why does it feel like I never get picked first for kickball?*

Funny thing, she has valid reasons to ask these questions. She's had some tragedies, some loss, some pain like most of us, and, hell, after the last year we can probably expand that "most" to "all." But you have to do more than simply demand, more than give your desire a name and admit you're angry or sad. It's the same for all of us, now more than ever—our demands, our prayers, our pleas—they're nothing, as weightless and invisible as the cotton-candy-scented smoke from the vape twins' pens. So I try to impress upon her in the kindest and gentlest of ways, your hope should not be that conditions improve but that you find the strength to meet your own demandas, dear Amanda.

After Amanda, I run upstairs to grab a snack of grapes and almonds and then hurry back down for Dig Doug. Doug works for the Parks Department and is still in the mire of grieving his brother, who died when they were kids. He rarely indulges in self-pity. I'm not a neurologist (though I knew quite a few in school and, boy, are they a quirky bunch), but I believe that when someone is grieving for so long, the pathways of sorrow are burned in the brain so deeply it's nearly impossible to pull him out. I've tried all the thought-pattern tricks, pulled every cognitive behavioral rabbit out of my shrink hat—nothing has stuck for poor Doug. But still he shows up, so then, so will I.

My day would not be complete without a weeper. Today it's Weepy Jasmine. She does not get a more creative name because if you met her at a party or worked with her (she's a middle school teacher, God help her students), your only takeaway from the interaction would be that she cries at everything. When she's happy, when she's sad, when she's angry, when she thinks something is hilarious. She has spent whole hours with me barely getting words out past her sobs. I nod and hand her the tissue box, which she cradles on her lap like a sick cat. She pays me my rate whether or not she speaks, so she can spend her hour however she chooses.

This is when people think being a mental health professional is easy—I could listen to someone cry for an hour, you think. I give my girlfriends good breakup advice and was really nice to that guy I met on the ski lift that time.

Let me tell you something: It takes a particular sort of person, not to mention years of studying and practice, to be able to listen. Just listen. Just be in the room and not share anything from your own life or offer a suggestion, to actively listen to another human being *be* is nearly impossible for an average person to do. As I've said, I did a ton of work with a more acutely disturbed section of the population, people who score literally off the chart on the Psychopathy Checklist, who would have exploded the bathroom scale in my analogy to bits with all the dark shit they thought and said. Do these people ever get better? Some, maybe. With a lot of coaching and a lot of meds, maybe a couple of days a week they don't feel as stabby as they do the rest of the time. In the end, though, when it came time for me to build my practice, I chose the people who just needed someone to actually hear them.

And who could cover my full fee before hitting their out-of-network deductible.

After Jasmine's hour, as is my habit every time she leaves, I empty all the discarded tissues from the small wastebasket. I dump them, like a flock of flightless snot-ridden birds, into the larger garbage can in the kitchen, and then my door chimes, and I'm taken aback.

My last appointment, Bambi Ben, isn't due for another hour. Ben is a wisp of a fellow, gay and southern, with the dewiest doe eyes you've ever seen. He's different from most of my patients because I think he is actually interested in change, committed to the work of being happier. He brings a large coffee to our sessions and will take notes, gliding over the traumas of his gay southern childhood as things that happened and were terrible but are over now. I sometimes wish I could drag him in front of my other patients and say, *You see? It's possible. You don't have to move on but you can move forward.*

But Ben never gets the time wrong and is never this early.

I go to the front door and squint through the peephole and see two strangers standing there. I open the door, and they show me their badges.

Then we begin.

# Ellen Garcia

**M**y tongue is huge, like it's from under the glass at Katz's Deli, swollen and dry and pasted to the roof of my mouth.

I cough and spit on the floor, because that's where I am lying: The floor. A floor. Pitch-black room. I lift my head, and it pounds in the back, and I touch the bump and yelp at the contact. I push myself to all fours, and the pounding ticks up, and I think I'm going to vomit but I just cough again and start to crawl.

The floor is grainy, an unfinished basement, maybe? But I can't even see my hands when I hold them out in front of me. I remember being at Disney World on the PeopleMover with Chris and Bella three years ago, and there's a part where you pass through total darkness and I had the sensation of not feeling my body, and I thought, Is this what death is like, air-conditioned, weightless peace?

Except this isn't peace so can't be death. This is pain. And it's hot, and not being able to see is making me dizzy. My stomach makes a sound I'm not sure I can call a growl—more of a death moan.

As I crawl I try to remember the last thing. Recycling? I brought it to the curb, and then there was that guy who dropped his backpack, or that was what I thought, but then he just sat down on the sidewalk with his legs splayed, wheezing, and he looked scared, so I said, "Hey, you okay?"

"I don't know," he said. "My heart rate's going a little crazy."

He showed me his watch, and he was right—the number was spiking, 140, 150.

"Do you want me to call 911?" I said.

He shook his head. "I think I just . . . need a hand?"

I gave him my hand. I pulled him up to standing. He looked confused but not about to pass out.

"You sure you're okay?"

"Yeah, thanks so much."

I thought of how I'd pitch our exchange for the magazine, a post-COVID vignette, neither of us with masks on the street, not skittish with the contact of hands. Neighbor helping neighbor. I would describe his somewhat feminine features, difficult to make out under the rim of the baseball hat, his uneasy smile.

I said something, either "No problem" or "Don't worry about it," and then turned to go inside the front gate, and—

That's it.

He must've hit me. Now I stop crawling for a second and sit and pat myself down. Still wearing clothes—denim shorts, nylon running shirt, flip-flops, and nothing weird happening in the vagina area, so it's doubtful I've been sexually assaulted. I run my hands over my arms and legs and then under my shirt. Damp with sweat, but that's it. The only source of pain is the back of my head.

Sonofabitch. Really, dude, you're going to assault and kidnap a newly divorced mom after the worldwide shit show of the past year? Fuck that and fuck you.

I start to crawl forward again, and then I come to a wall. I stand slowly and almost lose my balance, legs wobbly, head screaming, hands going up the wall; it feels rough but not dusty like the floor. I follow the wall and walk sideways. I only take three steps before I come to a corner, then six and I hit another corner, then two, and the fingers of my right hand find a light switch, and I flip it.

In the light I see a gray industrial metal door next to the switch, and I leap at it and try the knob, which has barely any give in either direction, locked. I turn and lean back against the door. It's a small room, like a storage space, about six-by-twelve, floor-to-ceiling is probably eight feet. No windows; a naked light bulb on the ceiling. No bucket for pee. No tray with food for the hostage. No saw. No basket with lotion.

The bump on my head is pulsing hard, so I slide down and sit, and the ache eases up just a little. Hold my hand out in front of me like a diving board, and it's shaking like someone just jumped off.

I try to do some math. I can't have been out for that long—an hour, maybe? Which makes it Sunday night, and when I don't answer any emails or texts from Neditor about rewrites tomorrow, he'll know something's up. Although it's possible he'll just think I'm powering through edits.

It'll have to be Bella, and thinking of her face when I don't pick her up at Jitterbugs shreds whatever's left of my heart. But that will be the game-changer, because they'll call Chris, and Chris will come and get Bel, and then he'll try to track me down (even though he's still pissed about everything, he sure as shit doesn't want me dead), and he'll text Neditor, and my parents and my sister, and then Chris will come to my apartment and find my phone and my laptop and wallet, and then he'll call the cops.

Unless I've been out for longer, but that's even better, gets me closer to the tomorrow afternoon pickup time at Jitterbugs. I make myself slow down with the breathing. I've seen this movie before. Best to stay calm and save energy.

Then I notice something in the far corner of the room. Fabric—a curtain, but it's the same color as the walls, so my eye didn't catch it at first. I try to stand again, but it's tough; I can see lack-of-oxygen sparks bursting in my peripheral vision.

I take small steps around the room, holding the wall for support, and I pull the curtain back and see that it's a mirror, full-length, and I stand in front of it and look at myself.

What I take in but doesn't seize my immediate attention: me, pale and wet from sweat, lips desert-dry, a stain on my shorts that I am guessing is dried urine.

What I stare at and continue to stare at as I realize Monday afternoon has come and gone: written on my forehead in black marker are the words IT'S BEEN LONGER THAN YOU THINK.

# Dr. Caroline

I show the detectives in.

The woman is Makeda Marks—Black, plus-sized, navy blue suit with a black T-shirt and black sneakers. Her partner is Miguel Jimenez, Latinx, a little shorter than Makeda and not as sharply dressed, in jeans and a blazer.

After we agree we are all okay with no masks, they sit on the couch, and Makeda's eyes sweep the room. She sits leaning forward with her knees apart in a way that makes me think she is a lesbian. I'm not sure if there is a set of criteria in the gay-lady community to assess the distance—knees three inches or closer, straight; knees four inches apart or more, gay.

You think I shouldn't even speculate? What right have I, the whitest and straightest of white straight women, to imagine if the Black woman in front of me is gay or not gay? I will tell you why: Because there is no judgment in my observation. Because we do it, all of us, every day, and because Makeda just did it herself when she examined my office, pricing out the furniture, and now she's dissecting me, too, her line of vision starting at my shoes and coasting up to my face.

Miguel seems less self-assured than Makeda. He's not quite sure how to sit comfortably on the couch, leaning back and then forward and then finally matching his partner's posture.

"How can I help?" I say.

"We're looking for a missing person," says Makeda. "A woman named Ellen Garcia."

Saying that the name rings a bell is hardly accurate, because I know exactly who Ellen Garcia is, and because two detectives are sitting right here in front of me, they must be aware of the connection between the missing woman and me as well.

That doesn't mean I won't make them work for it.

"Maybe you've seen it on the news?" says Miguel.

I shake my head, which is an entirely authentic response. Who on earth watches local news?

"Do you recognize the name?" says Makeda, soft-spoken.

I exhale thoughtfully. "Yes, I think so, but I can't place it exactly." Then I shake my head, self-deprecating. "I'm sorry, I meet a lot of people in my work, so sometimes the names come and go."

This is the first outright lie I tell them. My memory is not photographic, but it is still extraordinary. I nap whenever I can, and have since I was a teenager. I will usually take two or three twenty-minute naps a day, and something about that gels things for me, imprints everything I've heard from patients, along with grocery lists and sizes of my sons' soccer jerseys, right in my brain. For a time, when I was younger, it was problematic and verging on narcolepsy, how easily and suddenly I could fall asleep, but that phase eventually passed, and I became able to control it a bit better. Now I've come to see it as a great advantage, as have all the sleep disorder experts who tout the benefits of napping for adults—focus-sharpening, mood-boosting, fatigue-reducing.

"Okay," says Makeda, who is not sure she believes me. "She definitely knows who you are, so that's why we're here."

Then she nods at Miguel, who quickly takes out his phone, swipes the screen, and flips the device so I can see it. I lean forward and squint, but I already know what he's showing me. I can recognize the masthead, the logo of a sun setting behind the Brooklyn Bridge.

"Ellen Garcia is a staff writer at a magazine called *Brooklyn Bound*. Are you familiar with it?"

"Yes, absolutely," I say. "They have a lot of good restaurant reviews and interviews with local business owners, things like that."

"Right," says Makeda, nodding at Miguel once more.

He flips the phone around so he can see it again, swipes, and types.

"Two months ago, she published an article about the worst doctors in Brooklyn," says Makeda. "You made the list. Are you aware of this?"

Of course I am aware of this. Of course I read this article, and found a typo almost immediately.

"Oh yes," I say, as if it were so silly of me to have forgotten. "A friend forwarded it to me."

Another lie. I have Google Alerts set up for myself.

Miguel finally pulls up the piece and flips the phone again. I nod at the screen, and he rests the phone on the couch next to him.

"Yes, that's it," I say. "I've never even met Ellen Garza, though."

"Garcia," says Makeda. "Ellen Garcia."

"Yes, sorry about that. Ellen Garcia. I don't know her personally. But she's missing, that's awful. For how long?"

"Almost seventy-two hours," says Makeda.

I rewind the clock to three nights ago. Jonas was at another opening, so I took out the recycling and garbage.

"That seems like a long time," I say.

Makeda smiles, but it isn't really a smile, more like she is engaging in some kind of lip-stretching exercise.

"You wrote a pretty substantial letter about that article to the editor, who was it—Ned Lee?" she says, nodding at Miguel again.

Suffice it to say their relationship consists of a lot of her nodding, and a lot of him struggling to find documents on his phone.

"I did," I say. "I didn't think the journalist did enough research, ultimately. She claimed she spoke to two sources, and I didn't think that was enough to warrant a smear on someone's career. But," I say, sweeping my palms against each other as if to wipe them clean, "free speech. Both directions."

Miguel leans forward and shows me the phone again. It's my emailed letter to the editor.

"Yes, that's it," I say to him encouragingly.

"Free speech," repeats Makeda. She taps her index finger against her bottom lip and then tips it toward me in a little point. "So before, when I mentioned Ellen Garcia's name, you did know who she was?"

Oh, Makeda. You'll have to do a little better.

I smile but am careful not to make it a smirk. It's a kind smile, a let-me-assist-you-in-understanding smile. Now it's my turn to nod to Miguel.

"You'll see in my letter that I don't mention the journalist's name—to be honest, I didn't focus on it when I read the piece. My goal was to communicate to the person in charge that he should be concerned about the integrity of the material he publishes."

Makeda doesn't quite give me a nod but raises her chin the slightest bit, which tells me she gets it. Seeing me as just another Karen who wants to speak to the manager is not a stretch here. I'm happy to inhabit the role if it suits me.

"Forgive me," I say. "I'm still not sure I understand how I can help."

Makeda sits up a little, tugs on the center front of her blazer to straighten it.

"We have a list, Dr. Strange," she says. "People who don't like Ellen Garcia or might harbor a grudge. You're on the list."

"Me?" I say, adding a laugh. "I didn't care for her writing, but I would never . . . I don't have anything to do with this."

Makeda smiles, and this time it's real, but I sense it's born of resignation instead of joy. C'est la vie.

"Because we have to ask, can you account for your whereabouts this past Sunday evening?"

I admit, I'm a fan of the "because we have to ask." It's one of my favorite lines of dialogue from TV, the implication being, *We don't want to ask, we know you'd never even swat a moth, you, the real father of the victim's baby/jealous ex-wife/dissociative identity disorder patient, but just to cover our bases do you happen to have an alibi?*

"I was here at home," I said. "I live upstairs."

"Was anyone here with you?"

"My husband was at an event and got home around midnight, I think. Also I ordered food at some point. I'm sorry, should I be concerned?"

"Not at all," says Makeda right away and yet somehow unconvincingly. "As I said before, you're on our list, and we're working our way through the list. If you could email us the details of that take-out order, we'd appreciate it."

She pulls a business card from her inside jacket pocket and hands it to me.

"To check the box," I say.

"That's right," says Makeda. "To check the box."

I examine her card for a moment—the words *Makeda Marks, Detective, 78th Precinct*, alongside a drab print of the shield-shaped insignia. The NYPD doesn't allow for a lot of flare, it seems.

"Do you need to speak to my husband? He's not home right now, but I can ask him to call you."

"Not right now. We'll reach out if we need to."

I smile warmly and nod.

"Uh, Doctor?" says Miguel. "Do you have any other information you'd like to share with us? Anything that might be relevant to our case?"

Well, well, well, looks like Makeda should give Miguel a little more to do than just serve as her own personal Ask Jeeves.

I let out a short sigh.

"Now that you mention it," I say. "I wouldn't bring this up, but this is feeling like an unusual circumstance. I had a new patient today, a man who claimed he planned to kill someone, and that I knew the victim."

You have to take my word for it that you would shell out all the bills in your wallet if you could see Makeda's face. Not made for poker, this gal. Miguel looks to her, somewhat apologetically, like, *I didn't mean to open this box of exploding dog shit.*

"You mind saying that again?" she says. "That last part?"

"About the new patient?"

"Yeah, that's it."

"Yes, of course. I saw a patient for the first time earlier today, at noon. His name is Nelson Schack. S-C-H-A-C-K," I spell, looking at Miguel, who takes the hint and picks up his phone, begins to type. "He told me that he was going to kill someone, and also that I knew the victim."

"Did he say Ellen Garcia's name?" Makeda asks.

I have to hand it to her; she only allowed herself to be shocked for a few seconds. Back to business quick, which I find admirable.

"No, and that's what made me think he wasn't serious."

"You have any patients before confess they have intentions to kill someone?"

"Not explicitly, but I have plenty of patients who say things they don't mean for plenty of reasons."

Makeda tries to sit up straighter, but it's difficult to do on a moderately soft couch. I sense she would feel more secure if we were in an interrogation room at the station.

"What made you think he was one of those?"

"He seemed to relish in the lurid."

Makeda stares at me. Does she know what I mean? Does she

know what the words mean? Miguel is busy giving his poor index finger a workout with all the swiping and tapping.

"He was a show-off," Makeda says finally.

"Yes, exactly."

"So you didn't believe him."

"No, I didn't," I say. "He was delighted in trying to provoke me, so I played along as a strategy."

"What type of strategy is that?"

"By pretending to indulge him, I showed him I didn't buy what he was selling, in short. He wanted to shock; I showed him I'm unshockable. Which also happens to be the truth."

"Because you've seen it all?" says Makeda, sounding unimpressed.

"Yes, like you," I say enthusiastically, trying to cram in some camaraderie.

She pauses; her slender eyebrows raise for a second, then glide back down.

"This isn't him, right?" says Miguel, flipping the phone so both Makeda and I can see the Google Images results page of the Peruvian economist.

"No, it's not. The Nelson Schack I saw has a *c* in his last name after the *s*. Not spelled 'shack,' like a little house."

"You have contact information for him?" says Makeda.

"Yes, I'll forward you everything he sent me," I say, picking up my phone from the side table.

"Address?"

"Address, phone, email. Venmo information. A copy of his vaccination card, too, if that's helpful?"

"Whatever you have," says Makeda. "Did he say anything else about his plans?"

"Let's see if I can remember exactly."

Now I'm having a little fun, because of course I remember. I cover my mouth with my hand, indicating how hard I'm thinking.

"I asked if this person lived with him, and he said no. He said this person wasn't a relative and that some people know her name, but again, I assumed he was just being provocative."

"Vague," says Makeda.

"Yes, another sign of bluster, I thought. He hadn't planned that far ahead, hadn't expected me to play along so wasn't about to be specific."

"Did you ask him any other questions?"

"I asked how he planned to kill this person, and he said he was pretty sure he was going to let her starve."

Makeda thinks about that.

"Starve," she says. "That was the word he used?"

"Yes, starve. Implying she was already in his care. Or neglect, I suppose, is more accurate."

We all take a moment with this. Even Miguel looks up from his ineffective internet searches. It does sound like one of the more unpleasant ways to die.

"And tell me once more why you didn't call the police? As soon as he left your office?" says Makeda, her tone somewhere between patronization and accusation.

I don't care for it at all.

"Because I'm required by law to report if a patient has an intention to harm himself or others and communicates that intention to me unequivocally. Anything short of that, and it falls under doctor-patient confidentiality. Like I said, people say all sorts of things to me—that's the job. I have to make assessments all the time, every day, about their intentions, and usually I get it right the first time. So earlier, my assessment was that Nelson Schack was another young person who could benefit from therapy and possibly antidepressant or anti-anxiety medication. But when you mentioned Ellen . . ." I say, and squint, pretending to remember her last name. "Garcia, yes?"

Miguel nods emphatically—so helpful he is.

"I reassessed."

"Right," says Makeda. "I guess that's how our lines of work are different. We can't much afford to reassess. We don't have the time. We reassess, somebody dies."

She pauses, and I'm not sure what she's waiting for. Slow clap, maybe? The *Law & Order cha-chunk*? Actually, I do know what she's waiting for. The same thing all my patients are waiting for: someone to finally say, *Oh my goodness, you are very important!*

"Of course," I say. "My assessment, as of now, is that it will ultimately be worth it to give you the details of Nelson Schack's therapy session. However, if it turns out he has nothing to do with any of this, I could lose my license, and he could sue me in civil court."

"So I've potentially put myself at risk for losing my job and all that comes with it by helping you do your job and connecting the dots for *you.*"

I almost want to add a Meandering Marjory, *You feel me, girl?* but don't.

Makeda doesn't look or say sorry right away, but that's okay. She doesn't have to. She regards me with a stiffly polite smile, which I can only hope masks a sliver of humiliation.

"Appreciate that," she says, as if I've pointed out where this store keeps the kitty litter. Then she stands and says, "We won't take any more of your time, then."

She heads for the exit, Miguel a second behind. Makeda lets herself out, and Miguel follows, and Makeda turns to face me as I stand in the doorway.

"You'll let us know if Nelson Schack contacts you?" she says.

"Absolutely," I say. Eager to help, eager to please.

"Thanks very much."

"My pleasure."

Miguel utters, "Thanks," and waves, and then they leave. I shut the door and hear the front gate open and close.

I only have a few minutes before Bambi Ben arrives, so I go to the kitchen and drink a glass of water, touch the button on the Nespresso, and hear its warm-up gurgle.

As I wait, I return to the office and check the mirror. I don't look tired, even though the day turned out to be more draining than I'd expected. But despite that, I feel good for being able to help.

Even though I didn't tell them everything.

# Gordon Strong

The first week of being unemployed feels like a party. The first day, in fact, we all head to Gator Sam's at eleven in the morning, after we pack up our offices. I call Evelyn from the booth in the back and I tell her what happened, how Rieger went through the whole department, one by one, and didn't even have the decency to vary the kill speech. "Without sales, we don't need distribution," he said, like I missed supply-and-demand day in school. Evelyn makes those understanding sounds, "Uh-huh" and "Oh," and I know she's trying to make me feel better, but I can't stand those sounds; it's like she's talking to the kids. It makes me want to make it seem like it's not so bad.

"It's really not that big a deal, Evelyn."

"Oh sure, it'll all work out."

Then she changes her tune and tells me to have fun with the guys, not to worry, and I believe her. She knows I busted my ass and kept my mouth shut through every one of Rieger's dressing-downs about the wrong delivery or the missing list. I made some mistakes but no more than anyone else on the team, sure as shit not more than any of these guys. Maybe Remy pretended he never screwed up, all that hand-raising and volunteering in the weekly catch-ups, but we all got the ax in the end, didn't we? I leave the booth and join the table, and they've already ordered a round of Jack shots and two pitchers of beer from the brewery that just canned us.

Remy makes the toast for the shots: "To freedom," and we shout and toast and drink, but it's sort of half-assed because, looking at the team's faces, I can see everyone's sad and scared shitless knowing what's coming: combing the want ads and making phone calls to Miller and Pabst and Schlitz and even Leinie's up north to see if they need anyone in distribution or to answer phones or take out the damn trash.

Soon we order burgers and fries and more pitchers, and we're taking turns toasting, to that "sack of horseshit, Rieger"; to the bartender, Sally; to no more toilet clogs in the far-right stall in the second-floor bathroom. When it's Jason's turn, he says, "A toast to the women but especially Evelyn, 'cause she's fine as hell!"

Everyone whistles and cheers, and any other day that all might piss me off, him getting horny about my wife, but today it makes me feel big, like some kind of guest of honor, because everyone knows he's right. She *is* fine as hell. She works at it, too, really strict about her diets and doing the workout videos in the basement. I just had to say that one thing to her last year that maybe she'd want to skip the frozen custard at Kopp's, and she got the message.

Sally gets us another round of pitchers, and we keep toasting, and then some stuffed shirts come in, bankers or something, and one of them stops by our table and says he overheard us talking and wants to buy us a round of shots, so he does, and the bankers join us and we all toast to retiring in twenty years and going fishing in Florida. Then someone showers the table with boxes of cigarettes from the machine, and we're all smoking. I haven't had a cigarette in fifteen, twenty years, but it's fine, hysterical, actually, all of us smoking, most of us coughing.

Then more shots, tequila this time, and Sally comes over with her purse and sunglasses on and says her shift is up, and Mike pulls her onto his lap, and she's a good lady, Sally, she laughs and says he deserves a spanking, and so Mike stands up and sticks out his ass, and she does it—she spanks him, and we go wild. Then she blows us kisses, and she's gone.

Dennis and Tasker are behind the bar now, and they buy us a round of pitchers to keep us going, and because it's officially dinner hours, the waitress is on, a hot young thing named Missy, and she seems kind of dumb but real sweet, too, telling us she's never drinking another Kinzer just on principle. It's like everyone is rooting for us, and it took getting fired to find that out, isn't that something.

And we never realized what good friends we were, me and Remy and Mike and Jason. It took all this to show us real friendship—I make a toast to that, and they say, "You should be a writer, man, the shit you say."

At some point I go to the bathroom, and I'm washing up, pumping the lever on the soap dispenser, and the whole thing comes off the wall in my hand, pink goo everywhere, and I just drop the whole dispenser in the sink and rinse my hands.

I come back to the table, and someone's ordered about twenty baskets of wings, and I'm starving all of a sudden, so I dig in. We all do, all of us, our fingers and faces painted red with buffalo sauce—it's making the skin around my mouth so hot it's like I have a real specific sunburn just in that area. Then we're making piles of the empty baskets with all the bones inside, and it's a gruesome scene, all right, just piles and piles of bones. Whoever's next to me hands me a wet wipe inside a foil pouch and I wipe my face and my fingers best I can, all the skin stinging, and throw the wipe in the top basket.

Then people are pointing behind me and turning their chairs to face the TV because the Brewers are on, and I remember thinking this morning that I'd watch this tonight and have a beer, and Brendan might watch with me if he's not still pissed. We don't talk a lot these days unless we're fighting, due to him being a teenage shithead, and this morning he knocked over the whole quart of milk at breakfast, and I told him if he'd shut his damn mouth and focus maybe he wouldn't be so clumsy.

At least the Brewers and Green Bay still hold us together. For a second I think maybe I should try to get home in case he's there, on the couch in the living room, but then as soon as the game gets going I forget about everything else, because the Brewers just play their motherfucking hearts out.

By the time Jaha hits it home in the top of the seventh, we're all screaming and jumping and doing more shots. My friends, they're hugging me, and Remy says, "This is probably the best day of my life," and any other time I would say, my wedding day, the day we closed on our house, when Brendan got his first base hit in Peewee League, but right now I have to say yes to Remy, he's right, there is some magic happening here.

I never saw a win like that—ten–zip, just this monumental miracle, and it gives me hope; it makes me think maybe losing my job is meant to happen so I'll find something else. Become something else. Become the thing I'm supposed to be.

When the game is over, it's almost midnight, and Dennis, Tasker, and Missy are assigning rides because they're not about to let us drive. None of us can argue—Mike is sitting on the floor at this point like he's in a nursery school circle, Jason is trying to hit on a woman at the bar, and Remy's half asleep.

Tasker drives me home. I don't remember much about the ride, but I apparently give him the right directions because he brings me to my house, asks if I have my keys, and I pull them out of my pocket and dangle them. Maybe I say thank you, and I get out, and Tasker drives away as I walk across the front lawn.

Then I see someone in front of the neighbors'. For a second I think it's my girl, Savannah, but it's not. It's her friend Caroline, taking out the garbage. Someone has already brought our garbage to the curb. Probably Evelyn—she never puts her foot down with the kids.

"Hey, hey, Caroline," I say.

She stares at me. I wouldn't say she's cute, exactly. Sort of a long face, with thin hair and braces.

"Hi, Mr. Strong," she says.

She's always real calm, this kid, almost too calm. A little creepy.

"S'real nice a you to take out the garbage for your folks," I say.

She nods and then hustles inside.

I forget about her in a second, because I'm heading toward the front door, happy to be home, bones aching, stomach making sounds like a bull pawing the dirt, and I get up the three steps, but before I reach the door I just have to sit a second, so I kneel and then sit, and then lie down, and I fall asleep right there on the top step of the house I paid for.

# Dr. Caroline

I come downstairs at a little before eight in the morning, and Jonas is passed out on the couch. He's lovely even when he sleeps, one lanky arm stretched over his head, one leg hanging off the cushion, his face the picture of peace. He wears his clothes from last night, and there is a thin twill blanket draped over him. I lean down to kiss his forehead and smell what can only be female perfume coming off his skin and hair, cheap and tangy like someone emptied a Pixy Stix into a bottle of piss. Also I notice sparkles— a dusting of body glitter on his cheeks and chin.

I'll have to address that later. Right now I have work to do. I make a quad espresso and then head down the internal staircase to the ground floor, shut the door at the bottom of the stairs, and go into my office.

My first patient isn't due to arrive until nine-fifteen—Jacked-Up James. James used to be the poster boy for borderline personality, meaning he had some trouble regulating emotions, to say the least. Likes included cutting himself, breaking glass, and Everclear grain alcohol. Dislikes included stressful situations, confrontation, and dreams about his dead mother. I took him through all the dialectical behavioral steps, but it's challenging to teach mindfulness to someone who thinks of self-harm like a lover. So we found a nice Goldi-locks mix of Paxil and Wellbutrin a couple of months ago that allowed him to move through his days without the urge to punch a mirror. The only side effect, or really we can call it an "additional effect," is that James is bursting with energy. He does not stop talking and mov-ing from the moment he comes through the door until the moment he leaves, which is great, considering he used to be the saddest clown at the garage sale. I've given him some Xanax to help him sleep at night, and usually the honeymoon period with any medication lasts two or three months tops, so his condition may not be permanent. But I have to be at the top of my game to keep up with him, so four shots for me this morning.

First, though, I want to call Nelson Schack. I've rolled over my chat with Detective Makeda a few times in my head since last night, and it occurs to me she may be a little too confident in thinking he'll talk to her. I'm not sure of her strategy, and my knowledge of police procedure in general comes largely from television, so I have no idea if she can just get a search warrant with probable cause or arrest him on suspicion of guilt based on my information alone. But something tells me she doesn't have enough on him, not yet.

I sit at the desk and open up his file on my laptop, type his number into my phone, and create a contact for him. Then I tap the call but-ton and put the phone to my ear. I don't imagine I'll be lucky enough for him to pick up, but if it goes to voicemail, maybe I'll be able to pick something out from the way he speaks. It goes to voicemail a moment later, and it's just the automated recording of "You've reached 347- . . ."

I leave a message: "Hi, Nelson. It's Dr. Caroline. I realized we didn't have a chance to confirm next week at the same time, so I will assume you'll be here next Wednesday unless I hear from you other-wise. Hope you're well. 'Bye, now."

My goal is twofold, of course. To show him that I'm not rattled by our last meeting and also that he has no reason not to come back, because nothing is wrong. And, really, is it? Even though Makeda seems to think there's a connection, it is possible to see only a coincidence. If you don't live in New York City, or the borough of Brooklyn, or the neighborhood of Park Slope, this may sound crazy, but when you live here long enough, when your children go to school here, when you shop at the stores and eat at restaurants and drink at bars and go to music venues and comedy clubs (Jonas went through a phase where he'd drag me with him to open mic nights—horrific), the big city shrinks to the size of a Lego Town Center.

But I won't know anything for sure about Nelson unless I can talk to him again. I want to help Makeda and friends, but I also know I can do a better job than they can.

Here now, however, is Jacked-Up James. He is in fine form, sits in the swivel chair to take advantage of the swivel, and tells me about his week, filling in details about the smells of the subway under his mask and how his bathroom never steams from the shower. I appreciate the granularity; before, when he was depressed, and when we were experimenting with the meds, I'd be lucky to get a one-word answer about the weather.

After he leaves, I check my phone. Only one missed call and voicemail from Giraffy Abby, canceling her appointment for tomorrow. Abby is a relatively new patient, and she is tall. She's also been experiencing some malaise. That's about all we've covered so far.

Because it's Thursday, I actually have almost two hours for a lunch break coming up today, and typically in that slot I'd go to one of the newly reopened gyms I belong to, but instead I decide I'll take a stroll over to Nelson's apartment, see if there's anything the street can tell me.

Two more patients before that, though. Copycat Caroline, doomed to be so called just because we share a name, and Bilious Byron, who never caught COVID but has been sniffling and sneezing his way through his sessions for years. Twenty minutes until Caroline arrives, so I tilt my chair back and shut my eyes. I never need to set an alarm; my internal clock is more reliable than anything battery-operated. It's always been a gift, my ability to drop into sleep and not wake up until my circadian rhythm dings the bell. I don't sleep long enough to dream, but when I wake up I am remembering Nelson Schack's face—a perfect oval.

My patients come and go, and I'd be lying if I said I wasn't a little distracted. "Under my skin" is the right phrase, even though I find it disgusting—it makes me think of tick-borne disease, but there is something to be said for it, because that is exactly where Nelson's confession is burrowing, nipping at my blood vessels.

After Byron leaves, coughing into the crook of his elbow, I change from heels into white sneakers and leave my jacket draped over my chair. I take my purse from the closet near the door and put on sunglasses, head out into the sun.

Sometimes the neighborhood feels like a movie set, and it's been that way for about a month now. Like a director has called into the megaphone, "Cue Brooklyn summer," and here is the blue sky with cotton-wisp clouds, the Puerto Rican granny with the curlers in her hair on her stoop, day camp kids in swimsuits returning from a run in the sprinklers. Outside the masks are off, and people are no longer treating each other like they're coated in bird shit.

I walk along Fifth Avenue, watch the scenery change, fewer sit-down restaurants and more take-out storefronts, fewer hipster bars and more cheap chains—frozen yogurt, bargain shoes. The gentrification moves slower than you'd think. It still moves, but even all the working-from-home people with money, any money, don't want to be too far from Manhattan. You ask them why, they'll say, *I didn't come from Kansas/Boise/Peoria to spend all my time in the outer boroughs.* They've set the whole story for themselves, decided that moving to New York will be the crest of their transformation. It is cute, really, but if there's a through line for my patients, if there were a single piece of advice that would be applicable for every one of them, it would be, "Manage expectations."

I come to the street in the Low Forties that Nelson has listed in his contact information, and I cross Fifth Avenue, then down to Fourth. A little more seasoned, these houses—the lean of the slope more obvious than on my block. People I interact with socially will make comments about the foundations of their brownstones and town houses being slanted, the walls uneven, making reflooring and lining up tile on a backsplash challenging. I suppose I do, too. It's not lost on me, the joy of the manageable complaint. There is a luxury in it I don't take for granted. As I've said, I grew up with enough but not a lot. Now I have a lot, quite literally, and it's seventy-by-eighteen feet.

Between Third and Fourth Avenues the houses are more dilapidated, narrower, their frames perched crookedly on concrete bases. I'm surprised at the number of iron cellar door hatches in the front yards, surrounded by garbage cans. Usually it's a thing I see on the avenues, outside commercial properties. New Yorkers are split, I think, on if they're safe to walk over or not. Some will walk quite out of their way on a crowded street to avoid stepping on the doors. I do not. I have walked over maybe a thousand and haven't fallen in yet.

Which makes me think of a patient I used to have, Jinxy Megan. There are superstitious people, who are silly, and then there are obsessive-compulsives, who mask their obsessions and compulsions with superstitions, which is sad. Megan was actually the latter. If I'd said to Megan that I haven't fallen in yet, I'd get an earful about how right now, today, I would step on a cellar door and fall in, down the stairs, break my neck, and knock my front teeth out. Maybe get paralyzed. All because I'd given the thought air, said it out loud, put it out into the "universe." People have funny ideas about the universe. The universe is space and particles and vacuums, and if we really must anthropomorphize it, I guarantee you, the universe wouldn't give a fuck about you or your superstitions.

What I do think when I see all these closed cellar doors is that it would be nice to have a real basement for storage. We only have a drop-ceilinged not-quite-crawl-space, about six-by-eight, beneath the ground floor, with boxes on cinder blocks because all the brownstones on the slope flood at the first summer thunderstorm. I rarely look inside. We also pay rent to an old man for a temperature-controlled windowless room in Gowanus to keep Jonas's old artwork. To keep it in a big-box self storage facility we would have had to pay all sorts of insurance, so Jonas found the old guy through another artist colleague, who said in no uncertain terms that we could keep anything we wanted down there as long as it didn't bark.

I suppose I should have Google-Mapped the address first, because as I walk to Third and then Second, I realize the address Nelson provided is on a block where there don't seem to be any single-family homes or apartment buildings. It's all industrial: garages with signs boasting AUTO DESIGN, and brick storefronts advertising CUSTOM KITCHEN CABINETS (CALL FOR ESTIMATE).

I am sweating quite a bit from my walk now, and I finally come to the building listed on Nelson's intake form. It is another two-floor and brick, three roll-up steel doors on the facade with a weathered sign reading COMPRESSED AIR & FLUID, and another, larger sign: FOR RENT.

And reading the address on a file on my phone didn't mean anything, but looking up at it now, printed in faded green lettering on an awning of the smallest steel door, I realize where I am: 117 Forty-First Street. My birthday is January 17, and I am currently forty-one years old.

What a cozy little universe we have.

# Ellen Garcia

I don't think I've been asleep, but there's some kind of transition where I slowly become aware that I am awake. I'm on the floor next to the covered mirror, my mouth so dry I don't want to open it to lick my lips, afraid exposing my tongue and gums to the air will suck out any moisture that's left. I lift my head, the pounding now a pulse that shakes my whole body.

I turn my head toward the door, and now I'm certain I'm hallucinating, just like Bugs Bunny does in the cartoons after he makes the wrong turn at Albuquerque, how he sees an oasis and palm trees: I see a giant bottled water and a plate with bread. This can't be a mirage, though, because it's just one slice of sandwich bread, and if I were dreaming, if my mind were making it up, it would be a stacked everything bagel with lox and onions and cream cheese and tomato, and there'd be coffee with half-and-half and sugar, and two or three Nathan's hot dogs for dessert.

Without thinking I open my mouth and suck in some air, and the movement stings my lips, but I guess I'm hoping the water from the bottle will fly through the air like a fountain stream into my mouth if I inhale with enough force.

I'm just not thinking straight.

I know I have to get to the bread and water, but I'm tired, boy; before, I figured I'd been here for at least twenty-four hours, but he must've drugged me right off the bat after hitting me on the head, because I was out for so long at first. I bet if I searched my arms and legs, examined my neck in the mirror, I could find the tiny red dot somewhere—the point of the needle's entry—but really that's more of an activity for someone who can lift her head off the floor and who's not covered in dried pee.

It reminds me of a flu I had in my twenties when I didn't eat for three days, and I wasn't drinking, either, because I just couldn't keep it down and my body was just too exhausted to keep going through the motions of vomiting. In such a case, what I learned is if you go without food and water long enough your senses start to dull, vision goes blurry, hearing becomes blunted like everyone is talking to you in the *Peanuts* adult voice. And you can't stand without passing out.

I know I have to crawl, but I can't imagine using my legs for anything. They feel impossibly heavy. I think of baby Bella, how she used to pull herself along with her arms on the floor before she figured out the legs could help. Chris called it the "Terminator" crawl.

Bella. I'm a shitty mother, and I know that about myself. Half the time I'm with her I'm working, not because I'm such a great writer and I can't stay away from the work, but because I don't enjoy mom stuff. When she was little I didn't like playing with Play-Doh, and now I don't like pretending to be interested in whatever crap she finds on Netflix and the weird little dolls with the giant heads.

"You have to fake it better," said Chris in one of our final fights. "With her and with me."

Way harsh, Tai.

I can't fake it, that's the truth. But I can't do the worst thing and die on her. However she hates me in the future, however I fuck her up and doom her to years of therapy, it will just be little rabbit pellets of poop compared to the truckloads of horseshit that she'll have to carry around if I die when she's seven years old.

ELLEN GARCIA

I hold my breath and try to rock side to side. My head kills; if this feeling is not proof that the brain is just floating in skull goo, I don't know what is. I take a deep breath and turn on my side, my tongue going with gravity, spilling out of my mouth toward the floor. I manage to rein it in, and I plant one palm on the floor, then the other, and I push up, grunting.

I don't make it, though; my arms buckle at the elbows, and my chin hits the floor, rows of teeth cracking against each other.

I pant, croak, "Come on."

Don't leave baby Bella with the horseshit, I think, and I try again. Push up on both hands, and it works, I don't fall, and I start to pull myself along. Even the legs start doing their part, bare feet out of the flip-flops scrabbling along the concrete floor like I'm on a rock-climbing wall.

I'm moving faster now, the water and the bread getting closer. The exertion has pushed my vision to double, and my head is rattling so much it's making me nauseous even though there's nothing down there, but I keep pulling and scraping and scratching, and finally I make it.

I know I have to sit up, can't risk any of the water dripping out once I open the bottle. I push up a little more on my hands, arms shaking, and inch my legs underneath me so I'm on my knees.

My heart's really jumping along, right up in the top of my rib cage, and I think maybe some vomit is coming, so I turn my head away from the water and bread and spit a little puddle on the floor. It is shocking to me that I have any liquid left in my body, but I'm pretty sure that was the last of it.

I land my hands on the bottle. Twisting the cap off takes a minute, the plastic edge cutting into the side of my index finger, and I bring the bottle to my mouth and suck right at the top of the neck, not sure how I know or remember bottles have anatomical descriptions for their parts—neck, shoulder, body.

At first there's nothing, no water, nothing on my lips and tongue, and the panic in my throat starts to overflow in its place, but then I squeeze the bottle, and the water spills over the top, and I realize I am too weak to drink properly, so I lick the drips off the sides, and I can taste it, and it's real.

I know I can't take it too fast or it'll all come back up, so I take a sip, only a little bigger than the first. I hold the water in my mouth for a second, trying to let it soak in like my tongue's a sponge, and then I swallow. Then another, and another.

I know I have to pause, and I can't even think about eating the bread yet or else it'll get stuck in the desert of my esophagus, so I examine the bottle and see that it's the kind from Starbucks—Ethos with the mission statement and the torpedo shape. Then I realize there's a label on one side, toward the bottom, a sticker from a mobile order with the customer's name right there in black-and-white: *Caroline*.

# Dr. Caroline

Pouty Petra is not a bad person; she's simply wedged herself into a bad marriage to a verbally abusive real estate guy and has a mouthy teenage daughter who frequently skips her fifty-k-a-year private school.

The problem is Petra delivers all this tragedy in a high-pitched baby voice and punctuates every sentence with a nervous giggle. She even talks about how she was once fired from a nonpaying internship because her boss said listening to her answer the phone every day made him want to shoot himself in the face.

I don't engage in suicidal fantasy for the sake of humor or otherwise, but let's just say Petra's former boss and I have things in common.

I can't let her Smurfette affect get in the way of me doing my job, so I gently bulldoze it to the side in order to focus on dismantling her larger sandcastle of dysfunction. And what can you say when everyone in a person's life is pretty horrible, even if the person might ask for it just a little bit?

"It's not your fault," I say. Over and over again.

I've been seeing Petra on and off for about two years, and she still thinks it's her fault, and I keep telling her it isn't, but what I can't say is, *Your voice is actually really fucking annoying, and if you tried to speak in a normal adult register, people might like you more.* I have to leave that kind of practical work for a life coach.

We make it to the end of yet another hour, and Petra leaves looking cheery, surging out into the world to grate on the nerves of the poor soul she sits next to at the nail salon or who happens to deliver her Seamless order. She is what I call an aggressive engager—make eye contact for a nanosecond too long or send a courteous smile her way, and you're done for; you'll hear all about Dad and Hubby and Daughter and how she should not have had that extra cup of tea this morning because, boy, does she have to piddle.

After I close the door behind her, I stand there and take a nice gusty breath and close my eyes, press my fingertips against the spaces under my eyes, where there might be bags if I didn't sleep so soundly.

I check my phone and see I have three missed calls from a number I don't recognize. One voicemail. I tap and listen. It's a male, his voice low, not quite whispering.

"Uh, hello? Dr. Strange? My name's Billy Harbin, and I'm, uh, I think I need to talk to you?"

That's the whole message. It's not the weirdest voicemail I've received. People, especially new patients, call me for the first time in all sorts of states—weeping, yelling, unnervingly calm.

I have a few sources of referrals. Word of mouth from other patients is the most effective. There's also a local doctor Jonas and I are friendly with, Dr. Kevin, whose kids go to the same school as our boys. He's a primary care physician with Pro-Medical, which is a mega-chain of medical offices for people with a little extra money who don't like sitting in waiting rooms. Basically you pay a monthly fee, and you get the pleasure of having the doctor see you at your actual appointment time. No greasy magazines, no extra moments in the exam room with your ass hanging out of the gown. You might think this wouldn't be such a revolutionary business model, but Pro-Medical thrives. Why? Because you can pay for time. Time is the boss of us all, so when you actually have the opportunity to turn that particular table, if you can take it, you would. That is time you can spend making money for your family or playing with your toes—it actually doesn't matter what you do with the time, only that it's yours.

Anyway, Dr. Kevin and Jonas spent an evening doing bumps of coke in the men's room at the school auction a few years back, and since then Dr. Kevin's treated us like we were all in Vietnam together or something. So he refers any patient who complains about the slightest downcast mood or sour feeling to me, and then if he discovers they really have serious money to spend, he tells them about Jonas's pieces.

Impossible to tell, of course, from Billy Harbin's brief message who's sent him; all I can sense is that his voice is deep but his tone tentative, like he's recently gone through puberty and lost his choirboy falsetto. Like, yesterday.

I tap the number to call back, and there are a few rings, then a disconnect. No voicemail prompt.

A few seconds pass, enough time for me to wonder what Jonas and I will have for dinner and also consider how I can torture him for rubbing up against some millennial sugar baby long enough to get her perfume on his skin.

And then Billy Harbin calls.

"This is Dr. Caroline."

"Hi, hello?"

"Yes, hello. Is this Billy?"

"Yeah," he says, relief in his voice from being recognized. "You got my other message?"

"Yes, I did," I say. "How can I help you, Billy?"

It's a tired phrase that has unfortunately been rendered meaningless by its overuse. When every chirpy store clerk, bored government employee, and outsourced operator hacking his way through stilted English asks how they can help, you tend to stop believing they have that ability at all. I feel I can only communicate how serious I am through the gravity of my tone, hoping Billy can hear what I'm really trying to say. "How can I help you?" is really, *Let me help you.* A plea, not a question.

"I, uh . . ." he says. "Could we meet?"

"Of course. Are days or evenings better for you generally?"

"No," he says right away. "I mean, sorry, I just wanted . . . I think I need to talk to you now."

"I'm afraid I'm not free to speak right now," I say. "And before we meet, I'll need to send you an intake form and we can exchange some information. But in the meantime, if you let me know when you might be—"

"No," he says. "I don't need a doctor. I'm just, I'm calling you, I have to ask you—have you . . ."

He pauses. It sounds like he's walking outside. I can hear city sounds behind him. Car engines and human chatter.

I wait, picking up a couch pillow that has been molested by Petra. I shake it out like a beach towel. I notice I can't hear the background noise anymore on the line, and I think perhaps Billy has hung up.

"Billy?"

"I'm here."

He sounds like he's talking from the bottom of a well, but with no echo, just desolation.

"So am I," I say. "You were in the middle of asking me a question, I think. Have I what, Billy?"

His breathing becomes audible, speedy sniffs and huffs.

"Have you met someone named Nelson Schack?"

I drop the pillow. I think quickly.

"I'm afraid I can't answer that either way," I say, knowing full well my response provided the answer. "Anyone I may meet in a professional context is privy to doctor-patient confidentiality."

"That doesn't . . ." he says, sounding flustered and frustrated. "Look, that doesn't matter. I have some . . . information about him."

Then he pauses, which, whether or not he knows it, means he wants me to take control.

"Billy, would it be all right if we met in person?"

"Yeah, please. Yes," he says immediately.

I tell him to meet me by the Lafayette Memorial off Ninth Street in Prospect Park, and then we hang up. I send a text to Jonas upstairs—"Going for wine"—and then I slip out of my heels into my sneakers and leave.

I skip through some scenarios as I head up to the park. How does Billy Harbin know Nelson Schack? They must be fairly close, if Nelson's sharing that he's seen a therapist. Really close, if he went out of his way to mention me by name. Brothers, roommates, boyfriends. Some combination of the three. Or if Nelson didn't share the information voluntarily, then Billy came by it either by accident or via snooping. Maybe coworkers?

Still, an implied level of intimacy tracks if Billy knows Nelson well enough to contact me, if Billy knows something he thinks I should know, if he's scared of what Nelson might do, but if that's the case, why not call the police? I'm sure Makeda would jump over her Office Depot desk as soon as she heard there was a potential informant on the line with information about Nelson Schack.

I cross Eighth Avenue and can see the entrance to the park ahead, the bas-relief of Lafayette visible. It's another movie-set-ready afternoon, the air cool and not humid, the sun starting to head for cover behind the snaking BQE.

My phone buzzes with a text, and I pull it from my inside pocket. There is a message from Jonas: "We have lots of wine. What the hell kind of excessive shit is this?"

I smile. Jonas doesn't really talk like that. This comes from another family story of our kids saying adorably inappropriate things: once, when the boys were small, Jonas went on multiple rants about how it was a crime that Americans start decorating for Christmas right after Halloween, how it was yet another sign of heartless commercialization, how back in Sweden they put up decorations only in December and buy the tree three or four days before Christmas Eve. I got used to rolling my eyes and nodding politely, because, really, who cares, it's not like we believe the focus needs to be back on baby Jesus and the wise men and all that, so if the dollar store on the corner wants to push tinsel wreaths and tree skirts from China, fine.

The rants had been mostly for my benefit, but we hadn't realized the boys had been listening (the kids are always listening, by the way—they are like little CIA agents; they are listening to you talk and fuck and passive-aggressively argue about the future), Theo especially, who was about four, and at some point in November, not even Thanksgiving yet, we were all strolling down Fifth Avenue in our neighborhood and passed an elaborate window display in a toy store— lights and hanging snowflakes and action figures—and Elias was enraptured, nose against the glass, but Theo just pointed and said gruffly, "What the hell kind of Christmas shit is this?"

Cue the delighted laughter of surprise.

And so, since then, the phrase has been used to express confusion with a soupçon of outrage, albeit for laughs: "What the hell kind of *blank* shit is this?"

I make it to the park. The Lafayette bas-relief is about ten feet tall by twenty feet wide, with a wraparound stone bench at the base. Currently the bench is covered with people: some tween-teens holding skateboards and phones on one side, and what appears to be a family of only one adult with three babies on the other. I sit on a bench nearby, facing the side of the memorial. I'm able to see all the people entering the park from Prospect Park West and from Ninth Street as well, where I came from. I can also see the crowd exiting the park onto the sidewalk.

I scan the faces of the people emerging from the paths and heading into the park from the street. Joggers, cyclists, picnickers, parents with strollers. Young people, old people. Varying skin tones, hair textures. Who could Billy be?

I admit I'm a little off my game; I'm not used to meeting patients, especially new ones, outside my office. My office is contained, and I know where things are, not just in the physical sense: The relationship is clear for the patient and for me. They are coming to my space for help. Out here in the world, well, everything is looser, and both of us are at the same disadvantage of being distracted.

I imagine what I'll say to Billy first to draw his focus: *What brings you here, Billy?*; *How do you know Nelson Schack?*; *You've done the right thing.*

I like that. *You've done the right thing.* It will make him feel like he's already accomplished the impossible. We all love rewards, from the time we're in preschool with the scratch-and-sniff stickers. But even more than rewards, we love thinking that the hard part is over. Which is, of course, a little bit of bullshit. The hard part is never over.

I see a man approach along Prospect Park West from the South Slope direction—a boy, really, probably early twenties, wearing jeans that look too big, and ratty Chucks, and a Knicks T-shirt. Sniffing repeatedly, touching his face. Nervous. I try to catch his eye, scoot my butt to the end of the bench, start to lift my hand in a wave.

"Caroline!"

I lower my hand quickly and see Georgina Melios, the mother of one of Theo's friends, emerge from the park. She is, of course, in athleisure, because she has no job. Her husband is in finance, a stout Greek guy who looks like Super Mario and is clearly the breadwinner. Georgina is involved in all the school fundraising events—the Spring Auction, the Fall Fest, the Holiday Ball, the Mid-Winter Carnival—so I suppose that is what drives her? Making money for an already money-saturated school. I don't resent her too much—I mean, better her than me, but she is also a super-sized chitchatter, and while I can certainly keep up, I seldom want to. Now especially, as I watch the kid in the Knicks shirt getting closer.

Georgina makes the phone gesture with her hand to the side of her head and mouths, *Are you on the phone?* and I'm not sure why she asks that at first, and then I realize I might have been talking to myself. Sometimes I practice before sessions with patients, just to hear how the words sound. I'm confident, but there's always room for improvement, a way to make my questions seem less intrusive and to make the conversation seem spontaneous even though I'm driving every inch of the road.

I shake my head no. Not on the phone.

"I haven't seen you in forever!" she says, standing a respectable distance away from me. God bless COVID. If it weren't for pandemic rules, she'd be leaning in for a faux-Euro kiss-kiss.

"How are you, Georgina?" I say, keeping one eye on the boy with the Knicks shirt, who passes the Lafayette Memorial and my bench without pausing.

Either he's not Billy or he was scared off—it doesn't really matter which; either case means the sooner I get rid of Georgina, the better.

"Good," she says after a moment of thought, as if she's really considering it, which means trouble. It means she's going to tell me more. "We sent the kids to Greece for the summer."

"Great."

"Oh no, their numbers are spiking," she says, looking grave.

It seems I've answered incorrectly. Already this conversation is too much work.

"Are they with your family?" I ask.

"Yes, Steve's cousins in Thessaloniki. The numbers are higher in Athens, which is south, so they'll stay clear of there."

"There you are," I say. "Plenty of worse places to wait out a pandemic than a Mediterranean paradise."

Georgina smiles tentatively. I'm not sure how I got into the position of consoling her, but I'm not surprised. Once people find out I'm a therapist, they start fishing for free life advice even if it's in the form of generic encouragement.

"And what about Theo?" she says, her face brightening. "He's at sleepaway?"

"Yes, in Vermont with his brother," I say, allowing my sight to wander in search of Billy candidates.

"Amazing," she says with a sigh. "It sounds like that's just what Theo needed after the misunderstanding last month."

I plant my eyes back on Georgina. Replay that sentence slowly in my head.

"It's been very restorative for him," I say. "I wonder if Stavros has ever been through something like that."

Her face flares up at the mention of her son, a bloated tick of a boy often picked last in sports.

"No, Stavros doesn't . . . he wouldn't even know what the word means," she says. "He seems much less mature than Theo, he still plays Pokémon."

She laughs, and I do, too, impressed that she's somehow made a self-deprecating sort of comment at her son's expense.

"I wanted to touch base with you about it but never saw you at drop-off—I wanted to say I thought you and Jonas handled the situation just so appropriately."

And now she, Georgina Melios, crowned royalty of schmooze, can't look me in the eye, which implies that whatever the hell she's talking about that involved my son and husband is either embarrassing or shameful or both. Really there are few topics that can cause a brazen extrovert to curl up like a dried brine shrimp, and I would say all of them have to do with sex.

"Thank you, Georgina," I say. "I can't tell you how much that means."

She smiles, encouraged by my humility, which must throw her off course, because then she literally, actually, IRL and not in a soap opera or as a joke, looks at the smartwatch on her wrist and laughs and says, as if it is a surprise, "I'm so sorry I have to run!"

"No worries at all," I say. "So nice to see you."

"Oh, you, too! Have a wonderful rest of your summer!"

I wish her the same, and she bounces away as if talking to me were just another planned pit stop in her fitness journey.

I'm not sure what bothers me more—that people in my family have hid something from me or that Georgina pretended to be in a rush to end our conversation.

I take out my phone to call Jonas, my husband of the cool head. I sometimes think he gets his ice off by staying calmer than me. I have never seen him lose it, throw things, scream. Early Christmas decorations bring out the worst, which is overall fairly mild.

I, on the other hand, have lost it numerous times in our marriage, broken glasses and plates and screamed myself hoarse, and part of me thinks he's relished that—out-chilling the shrink.

I tap his name, and there is one ring before he picks up.

"Doctor?"

"I just ran into Georgina Melios," I say, watching a boy in his high teens walking a bicycle around the memorial.

The boy stops and gazes up at the bas-relief, pulls his phone from his messenger bag, and takes a picture.

Could Billy be a *Hamilton* fan?

"Poor doctor," says Jonas.

"Yes, poor me."

The boy with the bicycle ambles in my direction, glancing around. Then he looks at me for a moment. His manner is relaxed, limbs loose and lazy, and while I would not have pegged Billy to appear so calm, it's not impossible to conceive of. Sometimes surprises are nice.

But then someone suddenly enters my peripheral from the left, fast and twitchy like he's just been dropped off a helicopter rope ladder, and he says, "Dr. Caroline?"

I turn to look at him, this man, and I stand up, the phone still at my ear, the boy with the bicycle rolling past because, it's clear now, he's not Billy.

This is Billy, right in front of me, sweating, head jerking to the right as he rubs his neck, the stench of untended anxiety and a day or two of shower-skipping coming off him, and I can see by the way he's looking at me—expectant, but genuinely unsure—that he thinks he's never met me. This is Billy.

Only problem is, it's Nelson Schack.

"I have to go," I say to Jonas, and I hang up. "Billy?" I say.

He nods.

I stare at his face, waiting for him to recognize me, but it doesn't happen. I gesture to the bench for him to sit, for both of us to sit and talk, because what else can I do besides pretend this is business as usual, even though all I can think is, What the hell kind of Sybil shit is this?

# Gordon Strong

First couple days, I check the want ads, make some calls. I remember Dirk Grayber, who used to work at Kinzer back in the old days, is now high up in the line at Miller. I didn't know him too well, but I got nothing to lose, so I call, and I get disconnected four or five times and have to negotiate with his bitchy secretary, who keeps giving me the same line about how busy he is, like she knows I just lost my job, and the idea of being busy at work with a paying job is a cold, thick steak on a hook dangling in front of me while I'm pacing in the cage.

I tell her I can wait all day, because I know that's what this takes. This morning before Evelyn left for work, she kissed me on the top of the head and said, "Good luck with the job search," and I put up this jack-o'-lantern smile and said thanks with my mouth full of Mini-Wheats, because it was a dumb thing of her to say. I can't blame her, exactly, she was just trying to make me feel better, but none of this is luck. It's a damn boxing ring. Who can take the most hits and stay standing.

Finally, I get through to Dirk, and he gives me a big welcome.

"Strong-man!" he shouts, like we're old friends, and sure we are—I mean, that's why I'm calling, but being honest, we were just friendly in the break room and at Christmas parties. We never saw a ball game together or had a barbecue.

But I think, hell, if I ever needed a friend, especially one who might help me get a job, it's now, so I can be friendly as the family dog on a TV show.

"Hey, Dirk," I say, trying to remember if he had any nicknames, but I'm blank. I keep thinking Dirkenator but am pretty sure I just made it up. "How've you been?"

"Fine, just fine," he says, and I believe him.

Co-Distribution Manager—North America, is his title, and I know all that means is America-America plus Canada, but it just sounds bigger. Continental.

We catch up for a few minutes, and I wish I could say I enjoy it, and I'm trying my damnedest to make it sound natural, covering the bases about kids and wives and weather and sports, but underneath it's like I'm starving, sweating, glad he can't see me because I'm pacing in my socks in front of the picture window in the living room.

But I knew this was part of it going in, the small talk—that's business. Business is personal, that's what no one tells you when you're starting out, that all the parts of your life actually relate to each other.

There is something nice about it, the connection. I remember back in high school having those five-subject spiral notebooks with the coil that always ended up buckling and stabbing you in the palm—the idea was to keep all the classes separate—your math, your English, your history—but why not mix them up, let them overlap because it's all related, you know?

Just like how the small talk with Dirk is actually big talk—this casual hallway friendship could end up saving my ass.

"I got an idea why you're calling," Dirk says after a few minutes, and I have to say, even though I'm swearing at myself for not calling sooner, knowing someone else already got to him, I'm relieved I don't have to lay it all out.

"You heard, then?"

"Yeah, Tony Ruggiero called me a couple days ago," he says. "A few other guys from the old days."

I shake my head, glad again Dirk can't see me. Tony Ruggiero's the type of guy who'd shit in the toilet tank just to watch everyone go crazy from the smell.

"Jeez, I'm sorry," I say.

Then he laughs, and I can't tell what kind of a laugh it is. I mean, it doesn't sound like he's making fun of me, but like I said, Dirk and me were never that tight, so if he was having a laugh at my expense, I might have no idea.

"The hell you sorry for?" he says. "I'm glad you called. To tell you the truth, ever since I heard about the layoffs, I've been hoping I'd hear from you."

"Yeah?" I said, not believing it at first, because now it seems this is going too much my way too quickly.

"You probably don't remember this, Gordon, but when I just started at Kinzer, I had no idea what to do with those quarterly aggregate forms—they'd explained it to me in training, but it just went over my head." He laughs again and says, "Irony is that's all I do day in, day out now, but back then no one gave the time of day to a new guy—Jim Kambach, Remy Parsons, Mike Lotke, even Tony said he was too busy—but you did, Gordon. I remember you stopped whatever you were doing and showed me how to get the numbers coming in from the boards, showed me what to put where."

I'm smiling as he's talking, although, to be honest, I don't have a shred of memory about this blessed event that was apparently the smartest thing I ever did, so only for a second do I think about saying, *I gotta tell you, Dirk, I don't remember that at all.* Because maybe it happened—I mean, usually I kept my head down and did whatever I had to do to get to five o'clock, but I might've taken a break to help out a new guy.

Dirk keeps going: "I thought about it, and I realized I never thanked you for that. You have no idea how much it meant to me, so thank you."

He sounds almost like he's getting choked up about it, and I'm a little embarrassed for him, but he's the one with the keys to my future, so I play along.

"Hey, don't mention it," I say. "That's how I was raised."

"That's what I'm saying!" he booms. "It's integrity! You can't learn that stuff—you either have it or you don't."

"You're preaching to the altar boy here, Dirk," I say, and he laughs again.

I laugh, too, again and again, trying to think of a way to bring the conversation back around to the favor, when I'll be damned if he doesn't do it for me.

"Look, Gordon, I might have something for you. I'm not positive it'll be in distribution. It might be in a different department—would you be amenable to that?"

"Dirk," I say, hoping he can't hear the squeaky relief in my voice. "I'm not picky. I want to work." Then I add, "You know me," because it really sounds like he does. I've never been a big fan of fate, but this whole conversation may have sold me on it, makes me think everything I've done, how hard I've worked, it's all coming together; I was just laying the foundation up to now.

"Yeah, I do," he says.

We shoot the breeze a few more minutes. He tells me he's got to talk to some people in his department and upstairs in management; he's got to have some conversations aboveboard and some off-the-record to feel out the situation and he'll get back to me in a few days.

When I hang up, I sit on the couch and hold the cordless to my head for a couple of minutes, thinking, Thank you, thank you, thank you. Or at least I think I'm thinking it, and then I realize I'm saying it out loud, and then I laugh because I'd look nutso to anyone who walked in. Lucky I'm alone.

I toss the phone on the couch and head for the door, figure I'll cut the grass and clip the hedge before Evelyn gets home, but then I see her, home early, outside on the narrow pavement path that runs the length of our block. She's talking to Chuck from next door. They're laughing, and she's putting all her weight on one foot, the other sort of up on the tiptoe, and she's looking down while she's talking, and it seems like the pose of a teenager, like something I'd see Savannah doing.

And Chuck, he's laughing, too.

# Dr. Caroline

Dissociative identity disorder. I have some thoughts.

The condition formerly known as multiple personality disorder was made famous in the seventies by a psychoanalyst named Dr. Cornelia B. Wilbur and her patient, "Sybil," who was apparently the proprietor of sixteen separate personalities.

"Apparently" is the key word.

MPD became a fad after that and well into the eighties. Suddenly everyone had at least a few personalities tucked away in their crowded psyches. Therapists would throw parties for their patients, "multiples mixers," where all their fractured personas could come out and have pigs in blankets together. Also there were a few more high-profile cases—criminals who claimed they suffered from the condition as their legal defenses. *No, Your Honor, I didn't rape her/kill him/chop down that cherry tree—it was one of my alters.*

A convenient condition, you could say. One that guarantees the sufferer plenty of attention and possibly a homicide acquittal.

You don't hear about it too much anymore, I think because society at large is over it. Just like the mass panic about baby-gobbling Satanists, these waves come and go but all start the same way: with overly imaginative patients and their overly suggestive therapists.

The jury is still out, so to speak, on DID. Some mental health professionals cling to the idea that it's a valid diagnosis, putting out dissertations and notes and articles, claiming Patient X is the real deal, but the rest of us, after reviewing the research and utilizing, I don't know, common sense for grown-ups and the bare minimum of analytical thought, have come to the inevitable conclusion that DID is a Hefty bag of bullshit, that those who claim multiple personalities are in fact garden-variety borderline-personality-types or antisocials, the more violent of whom use DID as an excuse to carry out their vicious crimes. Then there are the sadder ones, like Shirley Mason, on whom the famed Sybil was based, who likely found comfort in the idea that all the jagged pieces of her soul actually fit into a whole that made sense to someone. At one point she'd confessed it was all fake, the personalities, that she was simply a broken girl from years of debilitating anxiety and repression, exploited by Dr. Connie, who wanted more than anything to be taken seriously as a doctor (and didn't mind the money or notoriety, either).

Don't get me wrong, I carry a similarly sized Hefty bag of sympathy for that. No matter what Beyoncé says now, it's James Brown's lyrics, unfortunately, that still hold water: it's a goddamn man's world.

And yet, and yet, would I fabricate a condition to solidify my career? Well, maybe.

Not the issue at hand.

Billy Harbin, as he's asking to be called, is nervous in a way Nelson was not. He runs his hands up and down his thighs in a constant motion as if trying to wipe off excess hand sanitizer. He jerks his head in one direction, then the other, like he's hearing sudden noises from every side. There is fear in his voice when he speaks, whereas with Nelson there was only disappointment from his inability to shock and then pleasure when he felt like he had a crack at it. And Nelson gave the impression that he embraced his twitches and sudden movements, while Billy appears to be held hostage by them.

So either Nelson/Billy is a talented actor and con man, or he is the real deal. At this point, there's no use in confronting him; in that way it's like any other session. First I get the history; then we talk. Confrontation comes later.

"Thank you for meeting me," he says, sounding out of breath.

"Of course," I say.

I angle my body toward his so I can see his expression and body language, but we're both mostly facing forward, sitting side by side.

"I, uh, I don't know where to start," he says, sniffing, wiping his nose.

"You've already started," I say. "You've come this far. Why don't you tell me what's at the very top?"

I hold my hand near my forehead like a salute.

"The surface," I add. "The very first thought that comes into your head, and if they're all jumbled up—"

He nods vigorously.

I continue: "Then just say some words, and we'll fit them together."

"Like Legos," he says, wistful.

"Yes, like Legos," I say, happy that he's given me a skeleton key even if he doesn't know it yet. "Did you play with Legos as a boy?"

·"Still do," he says, nodding. "They're expensive, though, if you buy them separately from the sets. There's a store in Fort Greene that sells them even though it's illegal, I think. It's a very licensed thing."

"I had no idea," I say. "What do you build?"

Personally I think adults playing with children's toys is the height of self-indulgence, although, being married to an artist, I've seen full installations of nothing but Play-Doh and Lite Brite boards, so I can appreciate that there may be some skill involved. Or at least I can pretend to.

He shrugs, says, "Gardens. Green baseplates with trees and shrubs."

"Do you have any pictures?"

"No," he says, sounding surprised. "They're not that good."

"They don't have to be," I say. "If it's a thing you enjoy doing."

70

He glances at me, intrigued by this idea.

"Yeah, I guess you're right."

We're both quiet then, watching the babies crawl on the ledge around the Lafayette Memorial. The evening air has lost the heat of the day, and now it feels like a soft breath on the skin.

"Nelson wasn't always around," says Billy.

"Oh?"

He inhales sharply through his nose, shakes his head, says, "Devil brought him when I was twelve."

Another hot tip for you budding shrinks: even when a person tells you the most shithouse-rat-crazy thing, accept the new information as if it's absolutely normal and also a topic you're curious to know more about.

"And what did he say exactly?" I ask innocently. "The devil."

Billy wipes the sheen of sweat off the lower half of his face, starting below his nose and sweeping his palm over his lips and chin.

"I woke up and he was there, in the middle of the night. He told me he wanted to help me, so he was giving me a friend named Nelson."

And this is the moment, if I were the star of my own reality show, when I'd cast my eyes above the camera at the producer and mouth, *Get me the fuck out of here.*

But this is real, and I'm a professional, and I'm good, so I'm going to pick out the most crucial part of what he's telling me.

"What did you need help with, Billy?"

He flinches, says, "I don't want to get into that."

"Okay, we don't have to," I say. "Do you want to tell me more about what the devil said, how he was giving you a friend named Nelson?"

He nods, continues: "Devil said anytime I need him, just call him up."

"Call him up?" I repeat. "How would you do that?"

"Well, back then, I'd say it like in the Red Rover game. Red Rover, Red Rover, send Nelson right over, and he'd come."

"And now?" I ask.

He turns to face me. He's not the most bronzed guy to begin with, but his pallor is extra-pale right now.

"He sort of makes me say it. Like he's coming anyway even if he wasn't invited."

"What does that feel like?"

He faces forward again, gazing up toward Lafayette.

"It's like you're driving, and then somehow you're in the backseat and he's driving."

"Are you aware of the things he does?" I ask. "When he's driving?"

"Sometimes."

He wipes his mouth and chin again as if there's more sweat, but his skin looks chalky dry.

"Why did you want to tell me about Nelson, Billy?"

He hunches over, clasps his hands, says, "I think he's done something really bad this time."

I look at his hands, fingers tightly knotted. His head is bowed. This is a man who is ready to confess.

"Billy, what has Nelson done to Ellen Garcia?"

He shakes out of his pose, jolts up from the bench.

"I—I—I have to go," he stammers.

"Billy," I say, standing quickly.

I reach my hand toward his shoulder but know better than to make physical contact.

"I'm sorry," he says, and then he takes off, hurrying past the Lafayette bas-relief and the ice-cream vendor and the people ambling in and out of the park.

He rushes across Ninth Street, heading west at the last blink of the don't-walk hand, and cars honk in their obligatory way.

I take exactly one second to scold myself for the too-much-too-soon. If the session had taken place in a controlled environment like my office, I never would have pushed so hard. But I could have sworn he was ready to tell me anything. My mistake to fix. Even though Billy's not technically my patient, and neither is Nelson, seeing that we only had an introductory consult, I still feel a degree of responsibility. I also have a needling determination to figure this out, so I'm compelled to heed what some consider the second creed of being a doctor, right behind do no harm: where your patient goes, you follow.

# Ellen Garcia

There is nothing but pain in the brain, but still I try to force the old girl into servitude. I imagine an electric prod poking at the mass of wet, quivering wrinkles, although who am I kidding? That little raisin is so parched from years of anxiety and margaritas it's a fucking miracle I can put three words together.

But still I try.

I'm on the floor in what the French might call la position fetale. I should be doing push-ups or side planks, something to keep my strength up, but my stomach, guts, intestines—basically everything between my neck and crotch—are burning. I know it's because I ate the bread and drank the water. Followed the instructions, just like Alice.

I don't think I've been poisoned at this point—why go through the trouble of kidnapping me and doing the whole escape room thing just to kill me off right away without a little recreational rape and torture beforehand?

More probably: It's the rush of calories hitting my system, which isn't tip-top to begin with, and I tried not to drink the water too quickly and inhale the bread, but I always eat fast anyway, not because I want to get it over with—it's the opposite, I love it. If I weren't running all over the city picking up temp work and interviewing people for stories and taking Bella to karate twice a week, if I were some kind of stay-at-home *something* with a trust fund or a husband who brought home the literal and figurative bacon, I would eat and eat and eat just like the ladies on the TV who can't leave their bedrooms because they're too big. Even during the worst of the COVID bullshit, I was running, just in my apartment and a surrounding one-mile radius, scrambling to make money and setting up socially distanced playground playdates and fighting with my husband, so when I finally got my hands on some food it was like some kind of pagan consummation ceremony, a union between me and my greatest love, mayonnaise. Or rice and beans and pork from the Cuban place, or pancakes or whatever, and because I'd always be so hungry by the time I ate, I'd scarf it all, and if it was night or maybe sometimes even not, I'd wash it down with three or four light beers.

What I'm getting at is it was enjoyable! It may have been to service me out of or into numbness, but I liked it.

But this bread and this water I didn't even taste. If there was any flavor, I couldn't discern it. I just wanted them in.

The empty water bottle is about a foot away, on its side like me. I can still make out the label: *Caroline.* Who is Caroline?

Does Psycho Killer have a female accomplice? Does he go by Caroline? I try to remember his face. I think and I think and I think, and my thoughts turn into a Dr. Seuss poem. She thought and she thought and she couldn't think any longer. What a shame, such a shame she couldn't get any stronger.

His eyes were blue, I remember that much. His skin smooth, sweaty, not dripping but glossy, like he'd applied it with a makeup brush. That's how I'd describe him if I were writing him into one of my stories.

Which makes me think, when I write about this whole experience for the magazine, I'll open with the landscape: post-COVID, the city opening up again, I try to help my fellow human, and look what happens . . . again. That bitch Lucy yanks up the football and again I fall on my ass.

I'll write about my state of mind, how I'd just consumed my nightly beers in an effort to both feel a thing and not feel a thing, how maybe this pandemic shit did take a toll on me even though I'm lucky. How many times have I heard that warped record: I'm lucky, I'm so lucky, I didn't die, I'm so lucky my kid didn't die; if all that whole shitty year-plus did was force my husband and me to accelerate our hate for each other, well, isn't it ultimately better that we know that? Lucky lucky lucky. Hashtag motherfucking grateful.

Then I'll write about the hunger, the smell of piss, the Sharpie on my forehead, the shrouded mirror, the invisible needle-prick, and then I'll write about the fear, how it's a good thing it's dulled by the pain, and then it occurs to me, maybe that *is* the pain. Maybe that is the heat under my skin, the lawn mower blades churning in my organs: fear.

I start to cry, streams heading south, sideways over the bridge of my nose onto my temple and then the floor because Jesus God I am scared, maybe for the first time in my life. I'm sure it's not; of course I've been scared before, one thousand times before, but being in this room has turned me into some kind of fear virgin. All I can think is, Please let the thing I'm writing in my head just be a feature article and not a full-length book. And please don't let it be written by someone else.

# Dr. Caroline

I'm difficult to miss. I'm five-eight, have a cascade of caramel-colored hair with auburn lowlights (my colorist says the shade is "mulled wine"), and am dressed head-to-toe in white. I'm striking. "Attractive" is also a word that I've heard, but I think "striking" is more accurate and my preference. Even Jonas says the first time he saw me across the room felt like a direct hit, an attack from above, and then he was drawn to me, pulled in as if by a tractor beam.

I guess I'm some sort of alien spacecraft in this metaphor, and that's fine. How lovely and mysterious they are, even in their blurry likenesses. That was almost sixteen years ago, and I think I look better now in many ways—I certainly pay more attention, because now I have to.

I work hard to look like this: exercise, diet, hair appointments every six weeks, teeth whitening, powder dip manicures, eyebrow threading, bikini and underarm waxing. I love the skin care products from Goop. They go on smooth and don't smell medicinal. But I don't buy into the rest of that ethos. Everyone loves a vagina, but no one likes a show-off.

Yes, it's work, and not unenjoyable, but I also need to take a little credit for just being me under all the trappings. I'd look good in a barrel with suspenders.

I'm just saying, it's a bit hard to stay hidden now, far enough behind Billy so he wouldn't see me right away should he look over his shoulder. At the same time I have to keep him in sight, which isn't the easiest thing when half the Brooklyn population is wandering around stoned on the perfect weather.

It shouldn't be underestimated, the power of late spring and early summer, the way it brings people together, families and young singles—breeders and ballers, so to speak. The poor and the rich and the in-betweeners, CrossFit crazies and frizzled druggies.

Speaking of, I see the vape twins as I follow Billy taking a left on Fifth Ave. And even the twins are laughing through their opioid nods, the warm, fragrant air caressing their acne-nicked faces.

Billy continues south, his dull navy blue shirt melting into the crowd. I speed up, prep what I'll say if he catches me before we reach his destination.

I'll use the same tools as I did with Jonas the night we met, except Billy doesn't need to find me attractive; he just needs to be attracted to me in the most literal sense: like he's in the UFO beam. *You don't have to run, Billy. I can help you. Maybe you've heard that before from people who ended up hurting you, but I promise I won't do that. I find your pain a precious thing.*

We are on Fifth Avenue moving toward South Slope now, and it occurs to me that he could actually be heading to Sunset Park and eventually the COMPRESSED AIR & FLUID building, the one that he, or Nelson rather, gave as his home address. The one made up of my birthday and current age.

Which I haven't been thinking too much about because coincidences are real and they are just that and nothing more. My more paranoid patients might see trickery writ large, again that devious universe and all its menacing forces conspiring against a single truth-teller who sees things as they really are. And I ask again, what makes us tiny twiddle-bugs so special?

I suppose it just comes down to individual strengths that very few are born with. Some, like my husband, seem to drift through life in a perpetual state of being rewarded. He is a good artist, not a great one, but that hasn't stopped him from selling pieces, because he acts like he's great. Except to him he's not acting. In addition to some cultural entitlement and the whole man's-world thing, he also has a blind and unfailing self-confidence. He is the kind of man other men hate when they find they can't pull off the same thing.

As for me, I've never spent a whole lot of time being jealous of other women. I wasn't born smart or pretty or rich, but I figured out how to do all of it by myself, so what's there to be jealous of? Some ditzy socialite with a trust fund or a cadaverous supermodel with hollowed cheeks—sure, might have been nice to kick life off with a little step up, but I didn't have any of that. Not in Glen Grove. Not with Chuck and Lil.

I didn't look like this back then. I was as awkward as a girl could be, bony shoulders and hair I couldn't pull a brush through and always wearing the wrong bra. I guess things started to change at the end of middle school. There came a point when I made some decisions.

Now a blast of hot air comes at me from the left, and I'm out of Glen Grove and back on Fifth Ave, the B63 bus rushing past me, and I see Billy jogging to the bus stop across the street.

I start jogging, too; running, actually—quickly realizing I have to give up the spy game if I have any hope of making a connection, or at the very least seeing him and/or Nelson again.

Firm up the core and sprint, fat ass, I say to myself. As a mental health professional I caution against negative self-directed talk, but sometimes, just between me and me, a little degradation goes a long way and can, in fact, serve as motivation.

I run on the balls of my feet, dodging dawdlers, and I see the bus come to its lurching stop, outgassing as the doors open, and the front section of the cab sinks to let passengers on.

People begin to board, and I see Billy from the back, last in line, pulling a paper nonsurgical mask from his back pocket. Push, I say to myself, and I pump my arms and almost run into three different people but slip between them. I should really go running more, because what a damn feeling it is to be fast.

Billy steps onto the bus, wearing the mask now, and pulls himself up by the railing. When I say his name, he'll jerk and jump but recover and flee, and I could of course follow him, but then, we're on a bus, surrounded by people, and the cortisol will be coursing through his system and he'll be far more likely to feel the darkened windows and the four sides closing in. So it comes down to two things: if I want to keep this conversation open, I have to keep him on the street, and to stop him from actually moving onto the bus I need to make physical contact. Touching patients is a no-no except for the initial handshake, but this is what we would call an exigent circumstance.

I reach out my hand and say, perhaps louder than I intend, but my heart rate is up and my breath is huffing out in bursts, "Billy!"

My hand lands on his shoulder, and he jerks and jumps like I knew he would. He turns to me, shocked, and I see right away that his eyes are brown, and he has facial hair under the mask, and I look down at the rest of his body and see a tattoo of a snake on his arm and a Yankees logo on his shirt.

I retract my hand and say, "Sorry. I thought you were somebody else."

# Gordon Strong

I decide to make myself useful and do something with the front lawn. Evelyn can't work the mower, which isn't her fault—she's not a big woman, and we never got around to buying a motorized one, and now, well, it's not the time for spending.

Right now she's at work, Brendan's at his summer job taking orders at Cousins Subs, and Savannah's at the Field House for day camp. I'm all alone, again.

I've got a beauty of a headache, had a little too much last night, I guess. It was one of those times you don't realize it—I was just watching the Brewers and having some beers, and by the ninth I guess I'd put away a sixer, and as soon as Wegman gave up another run, I swore at the TV, something like, "Dumbass motherfucker," and Brendan, who'd been watching it with me while he fiddled around with his Game Boy, stood up and said, "Chill." Then I remember I told him to try saying that to me one more time, and I turned and saw Savannah and her friend from next door, Caroline, and I didn't even know they were sitting at the counter. They both stared at me, and then they left through the back door, Caroline going first, and Savannah, she turned around before she left and said, "God, Dad!" Maybe it sounded all choked and maybe she had tears in her eyes and maybe

Caroline was looking at me like I was some sludge she scraped off the bottom of her shoe.

Evelyn had been in the bathroom, or the bedroom; wherever she was, she wasn't there to give me a bunch of shit for swearing in front of the kids. But straight talk—you can't tell me that's anything new to them, especially now that Savannah's officially a teenager. I mean, they hear worse on the radio.

Savannah, I swear, I love her, but the crap she and Caroline listen to would make your ears bleed. They go into Savannah's room and crank it up and thump around—I guess they're practicing dance moves. The B-word, the S-word, the F-word. She doesn't say that stuff at school in front of her teachers, so what do I care? And if I'm having a beer and watching a game in my own house, and Wegman's pissing the bed, why should anyone mind if I let a little blue streak fly?

Long story short, I had a few more beers and fell asleep watching highlights. Woke up around four with a skull-pounder and a dry mouth, went upstairs and took some Advil, crunched a few Tums, and got into bed next to Evelyn, who was curled up on her side, so small up by her pillow like a hermit crab. Then I passed out again and woke up when everyone was gone.

I can't do much with the landscaping, but neither can anyone else on the block. We all have the same little square, so there's not a whole lot of keeping up with the Joneses. Chuck Strange next door lets the grass get pretty high, wild almost, and when I came outside this morning with my coffee I thought ours isn't much better, but dammit, why not? Now I have the time, why not make a lawn that would make Chuck jealous? Maybe make his wife, Lil, say to Evelyn, *I wish our lawn looked as nice as yours,* or even, *Can Gordon give Chuck some gardening tips?*

Easiest thing is to start with the grass, because all it is is back and forth, brush off the clippings, and start again. The grass at this point is so high, I have to do two cuts. Then I get the shears and start on the big hedge, which is in even worse shape than the lawn. Scraggly and overgrown boxwood, not that there's anything boxy about it—at this point they're just wild bushes, so I figure I'll work on one side, the side that faces away from the house, clip the branches so that side is flat, and then maybe tomorrow I'll do the top, the next day the side that faces the house, and keep going until we have nice clean sides all around. It doesn't take up the whole length of the property, but altogether it's probably thirty feet, separating our property from the road. Between us and the neighbors on the other side, Bob and Cheryl, is a line of giant hostas, but they're on Bob's side, so I don't think about them too much. There's a fence between us and the Stranges' place, used to be white but now it's just the brown wood underneath with a few white specks. The hedge has been there forever, since we bought the place when the kids were little, I guess the previous owners' thinking was privacy and making neighbors jealous with the precision of it, the sharp edges.

Around noon it's hot, low eighties. I'm sweating, arms and lower back are starting to ache, but it feels good. Feels like I've earned it. I take a break and go inside, make a ham sandwich, and take a minute when I look at the beers on the bottom shelf on the door, and Evelyn's two-liter of Diet Coke right in the middle, and I grab two beers with one hand, go back outside.

I get through about six feet of the hedge, clipping up and down, some of the branches stubborn and I really have to chew through them with the shears, the handles tearing into the skin on my palms. I finish my lunch and my beer and run back inside, get another beer. Nothing hits the spot like a Kinzer. That was a campaign they had a few years back. I still see faded signs with that slogan in South Side bars. I used to get a jolt of pride looking at them. Sure, I'd laugh it off— "Can't get away from the office to save my life!" But inside, it gave me a satisfied feeling, like I worked at some famous place.

I'm on my knees, still making my way with the street-facing strip, when I see a bike wheel and a pair of white sneakers out of the corner of my eye. I look up and see Savannah's friend from next door. Came out of nowhere; didn't even hear her coming.

"Hi, Caroline, where'd you come from?" I say, trying to make it sound jokey, even though it's a little creepy how she lurks.

She shrugs, says, "Just riding around."

"Field House let out already?"

"I don't go to the Field House."

"Oh yeah?" I say. "Why's that?"

She shrugs again, doesn't answer but doesn't really move. She's not the friendliest kid to begin with, but she doesn't seem to want to be in the conversation, so I'm wondering why she doesn't just leave.

I take the last swig of my beer and glance up at her. She forces a smile back, mouth full of metal.

I remember last night, swearing at the TV. Not that I'd forgotten it, but if I do something with my hands it's easier not to think, so I go back to clipping. But, seeing Caroline again, I remember how shocked and grossed-out she looked, how disappointed and embarrassed Savannah was.

Then I think, maybe Caroline's expecting an apology? Hell, even if she's not, maybe she'd tell Savannah if I did. And maybe it would be like a little payment, a little money in the bank toward forgiveness.

"Hey, Caroline?"

She looks down at me, one foot spinning a pedal.

"I'm sorry about last night."

She scrunches up her eyebrows. Poor kid's got these mannish eyebrows—black strips like her father's.

"When I swore at the TV?"

She's still got a look like she doesn't have a clue what I'm talking about, so I keep going, trying to jog her memory.

"You know, the baseball game? I yelled at the TV?"

She shakes her head again. Still not ringing any bells. Or she's pretending she doesn't remember.

"Well, I acted sort of childishly, and I'm sorry for that. For my language."

She doesn't look as confused as she did a minute ago, but she's still not making this easy on me. Would it kill her to throw me a bone of an *It's okay, Mr. S, don't beat yourself up about it. You should hear my dad during a Packers game!*

But she doesn't say anything, and that makes me think I should just keep talking.

"I got a little carried away. It's just being a dad, you know?" I say, trying to make her laugh. "I'm sure your dad gets into watching sports, too."

"Sometimes," she says, squinting at me.

I laugh, not because anything is funny; truthfully, I'm just glad she spoke. I turn back to the hedge and keep clipping. Still, she doesn't seem to be going anywhere.

"So what's your dad doing for work these days?" I ask.

Memory serves, Chuck worked at a hospital as an orderly. But I haven't had a conversation with him in a while, so who knows? Though, if his lawn looks like it does, and he can't even afford the monthly swimming pool fee and equipment pass for Caroline to go to the Field House in the summer, maybe he's doing worse than me.

I couldn't explain it if somebody asked me, but suddenly I really want to know how badly Chuck Strange is doing.

"He works at Aurora still as a nursing assistant," she says. "But he's going to school at night to be a paramedic."

"Oh," I say, pretty surprised. "Really?"

I knew that orderlies knew CPR and stuff like that, but a paramedic sounds like the real deal, like he'll actually be saving lives on a daily basis. It sounds important.

"How long's he been doing that?"

"About a year, I guess," she says, rubbing her nose on her wrist. "Soon he'll start clinical rotations in ambulances."

"Well, that's . . ." I pause, lay down the shears for a second. "That's great. Good for him. No wonder he doesn't have time to cut the grass."

As soon as I say it, I know I've made a mistake. I meant for it to sound funny, but Caroline doesn't seem too amused. Her little nostrils flare and pink circles spread on her cheeks, and she blinks a few times, like she's holding back tears.

"Aw, no, Caroline, I just meant he's so busy with his studies and working, he doesn't have time for this stuff. Like me, it took me losing my job to mow the damn lawn, you see what I'm saying?"

She looks away from me and nods.

"And your mom, I'm sure she's just like Mrs. Strong, too small to work the manual mower, isn't that right?"

She shrugs and nods at the same time, which I think is a yes. Wipes the corner of her eye with her shoulder. Being honest, Lil Strange might be short, but she's not thin, not like Evelyn at all, actually. When they first moved in a year or so after we did, she was pretty cute, always wore these tight jeans and T-shirts tied in a knot at the waist, but year by year she put on weight, and now, for a long time, really, she's been big. Really big. About a month ago I saw her in a pair of khaki shorts that were a little too small for her, and the seam running up the middle of her stomach divided her fat into two chunks. It reminded me of that scene from the old sci-fi movie when the blob oozes through the movie theater and gets split by the doorframe on the way out.

This is never stuff I'd say to anyone! Lil's nice enough. She and Evelyn used to be closer, but not so much anymore. Come to think of it, when the kids were little, we did have a couple cookouts with them, helped out with the others' kid's birthday parties, stuff like that. I'm trying to remember when it changed, and I can't.

"Hey, do you remember having cookouts with us?" I say to Caroline, opening another beer.

She seems surprised, dark eyebrows shooting up, and I guess I did change the subject, but now it's bugging me and I really want to track it down.

"You remember, when you and Savannah and Brendan were little, we'd come over to your house for cookouts, or you'd come to ours?"

"I think so."

I take a sip and try not to react to how good it feels to drink a cold beer with the sun in my face.

"I'm trying to think of the last time," I say. "You and Savannah and Brendan played that game when you make a chain holding hands and run into each other? Shoot, what's that called again?"

"Red Rover."

Then comes a thing I really can't remember seeing—Caroline smiles, but genuinely this time. I mean, the kid is still not exactly attractive. I know I'm being unfair: I'm comparing her to Savannah, and Savannah's my kid, but everyone says how pretty she is, because she looks like Evelyn, and Evelyn is and will always be a knockout, especially when she's staying away from sweets. Sorry to say, Caroline is taking after her dad, with an egg-shaped head and thin lips, both of them tall and thick. But everyone looks better when they smile, even Caroline, braces sparkling in the sun.

"Right, Red Rover. You need more people for it, usually, but you kids managed to do okay."

She nods, then says, "I remember my dad teaching Evelyn how to flip a burger."

I know I'm not the most modern guy, but it rubs me the wrong way when kids don't call their elders Mr. and Mrs. I let it slide because I have a lot of questions—I don't have any memory of Evelyn learning how to work a grill, much less get a barbecue lesson from Chuck.

"Yeah?" I say. "When was that?"

"Oh, I don't know," she says. "When me and Savannah were eight or something."

I take a bigger swig from the can than I plan to—it rushes down my throat like I'm shotgunning at a tailgate party. I sputter, and a little beer dribbles onto my chin. I watch Caroline's eyes follow the stream and wipe it off with the back of my hand, mumbling, "Sorry."

I pick up the shears and turn back to the hedge, try to focus on snipping a dried-up zigzagging branch, but all I can think about is Chuck Strange and my wife.

"So he, your dad, taught Mrs. Strong how to flip a burger?" I ask.

Then I think maybe I sound too serious, like I'm accusing her of something, so I add a laugh and say, "I just don't remember that."

"Oh, I'm pretty sure it happened, because I remember him standing behind her and, like, holding her hand on the spatula, and then they flipped one onto the ground by accident, and we all laughed—me and Savannah, and my dad and Evelyn."

"What about me?" I say, and now I don't much care how I sound, angry or bossy or even a little tipsy. "Was I laughing, Caroline?"

She rolls her bike forward a few inches, toward her house. Away from me.

"I don't really know," she says. "You, everyone, all the adults, you were all drinking a lot of beers and wine coolers and stuff."

"Right, sure."

Then she smiles again. It's small, but it's real.

"My dad was still working third shift, so he'd have to leave at nine at night usually, but I guess he had that night off."

"I forgot your dad worked third shift."

"Yeah, still does. Up until two or three years ago, before he started school, he was at home during the day. Just him and all the other moms on the block who don't work."

I'm not looking at her anymore, just trying to get through this bitch of a branch, the blades of the shears gnawing at it, skin chafing and peeling on the pads of my fingers.

Evelyn only started working three years ago, when I stopped getting raises and bonuses. Company said sales were flat and their hands were tied, which everyone knew was horseshit, but what were we supposed to do? I'm sure all the stuffed shirts got their payoffs for their new lake house boats and golf club memberships, and I was pissed at the time and stressed out and upset, thinking, How are we going to get through, how are we going to pay for soccer jerseys and birthday party favors and ballet shoes? And Evelyn just offered to get a job, said it was no big deal, the kids were older now, why should all the pressure be on me. I know some other guys' wives would bitch and moan and never let them hear the end of it, but not mine. She just up and volunteered.

Almost like she was trying to make something up to me.

"Well, gotta go," says Caroline suddenly. "See you later."

She starts to roll forward on her bike.

"'Bye, sweetheart," I say.

I don't think too much about it—I'd call Savannah the same thing, and I'm sure I or probably Evelyn have called Caroline "sweetheart" before, or "honey" or "cutie," but now her shoulders arch like I just dropped ice cubes down her shirt, and she takes her left foot off the pedal and plants it on the ground. She turns her head to the side and tilts it, and I realize she's studying the section of hedge I've already clipped.

"This looks kind of uneven," she says. "Like a slide, you know?"

I chuckle, trying to keep it light.

"I don't think so, Caroline," I say, lining my head up next to the hedge so I can look at it straight on. "Looks pretty straight to me."

"Hm," she says. "I'm just saying here, from where I am, it's all uneven."

Then she waves a limp hand in my direction, gesturing me to stand.

I start to rise, and it's embarrassing and weird to say, but I feel a little lightheaded and have to kind of lean on the hedge as I stand up, and I take the couple of steps over to her and look down, the way she's looking down. And I'll be goddamned if she isn't right. If you're looking from above, the whole bush is sloping down, wider at the bottom like a wave about to crash.

"You're right," I say, and then without thinking: "Shit."

She doesn't react in any way to me cursing this time, though. Instead she taps my hand gently, and I look down, realize I'm still holding the shears.

"I think you just need sharper blades, Gordon."

# Dr. Caroline

When I get home it's just before eight, and Jonas is sitting at the island in the kitchen, drinking white wine and nibbling on a cracker. He's set out a cutting board for us: his standard supper of thin dark rye bread, smoked salmon, a container of Icelandic yogurt, almonds, and some sliced apple. "Doctor."

I've worked up a little sweat chasing Billy and am experiencing some aches and pains in my glutes and hamstrings due to my lack of stretching beforehand. I don't acknowledge Jonas and wash my hands at the kitchen sink, take a glass from the cabinet, and pour some wine.

"I thought you were buying more wine," he observes.

I sit on a stool at the island, at a right angle to him.

"I was not," I say, taking a sip.

It feels like my tongue absorbs the wine before I can taste it—a sign that I need water right now more than alcohol, but I haven't the slightest interest in rehydration.

"I was meeting a patient."

Jonas raises his eyebrows, picks an apple slice from the board.

"Georgina Melios?" he says.

"No," I say. "Not Georgina Melios. A new patient."

He chews. I drink. We do this for a couple of minutes.

Finally he speaks: "I have a feeling you know something."

"Your feeling is correct."

His eyes light up in a way that is familiar to me. A little shot of dopamine rushing through his brain. Since he doesn't do anger, his typical response to me becoming upset is predominantly arousal.

"Georgina opened her lovely large mouth," he says.

"'Lovely' is debatable, but yes, she shared some things with me."

"Ah," he says, grinning.

He really can be an asshole, my husband whom I love.

"You may have questions," he says, leaning forward, elbows on the island.

"No, Jonas, I don't have questions," I say, setting my glass down a little roughly. "That's not how this works. You are keeping a secret and so it is up to you to offer the information to me. Your wife. Mother of your boys."

He draws a circle with his index finger on the cutting board and sighs like this is an inconvenience, but he still has an expression like a cat, sneaky and pleased.

"Yes, I suppose you're right," he says.

I pick up my glass once again and tilt it in his direction as a toast. "That's a good start."

He picks up the wine bottle and tops off his drink. "I picked up Theo from school on a day Elias had lacrosse, and the mother—the one with the . . ."

He points to his right eye, wiggling his finger.

"The strabismus," I say.

He looks puzzled. Of course I know he doesn't know what strabismus is (truth be told, I didn't, either, until I met Allison Vaughn and googled it, and how pleasant it is sometimes to discover a medical term you didn't know existed), but I enjoy knowing things he doesn't know. And I enjoy him knowing that.

"The wandering eye," I say, impatient. "Allison Vaughn."

"Yes, Allison," he says. "She pulled me aside and said that the day before Theo had called her daughter a name, and that they didn't want to go to the dean. 'Make a big stink,' she said. But if Theo apologized to the girl . . ." He pauses, searching for the name.

I make a big production of sighing and say, "Bronwen."

"Bronwen. If Theo apologized to Bronwen, we could all move on, and it would be water under the bridge."

He sips his wine, looks at me as if to prompt any clarifying questions.

"Please go on," I say.

"I say to Theo, do you have something to apologize to Bronwen about, and he said yes. Then I said why don't you apologize, and he said okay. And then he apologized, and Bronwen said okay. And Allison said thank you."

He picks up a piece of dark rye from the board and begins spreading yogurt on it. I watch him layer a piece of salmon and place a sprig of dill on top. As he takes a bite I realize the whole story is done.

"And that's it," I say.

"That's it."

"And you didn't think too much of it because it was just between you and Allison Vaughn. And Theo and Bronwen," I answer for him.

"Mm," he says, his mouth full, offering a single-shouldered shrug.

"Then how did Georgina Melios know?"

Jonas swallows, washes his bite down with some wine. "I'm sure the women talk. No one told the school, so what does it matter?"

He finishes the shrug, tosses an almond into his mouth.

"And why didn't you tell me about any of this?"

"It didn't seem like a thing to bother you with," he says. Then he flashes a smile with his almost-perfect teeth, only the left canine crooked. It's my favorite tooth, and he knows it. "The doctor is busy," he adds.

"I am," I say. "But Theo didn't tell me about it, either."

Lying has never come naturally to Theo. He gets sick to his stomach if he lies, and therefore was never able to join his older brother in subjecting the neighbors to Ding-Dong Ditch or sneaking downstairs after lights-out for cookies. Elias, however, has no issue, can lie right to your face, then turn around and tell a different lie to someone else's face. Thankfully, he doesn't do it that often. Not yet anyway.

But Theo is incapable of keeping a secret. Any secret. So if he refrained from mentioning this incident to me, there's really only one explanation.

"I may have told him not to bother you with it," says Jonas, barely containing a grin.

"I don't see parenting as a bother."

"Of course not," says Jonas. "I'd never think you would. It's only that this seemed so insignificant at the time."

"So it's even more insignificant now that what—a whole month has passed?"

"Exactly," he says, pleased.

"No, not exactly," I say, feeling my throat tightening with rage. "To you, darling, you've spared me from an unnecessary stress, but to me, you've coerced our son into conspiring to keep something from me. So you see, there are two ways of looking at it. Like Johns's faces and vases."

He laughs. Not because he's so impressed; he just thinks it's cute how I bring modern art into the conversation.

I continue: "And this isn't something in the so-distant past since it's pretty fresh in Georgina's mind, not to mention she and Allison Vaughn aren't even friends."

"Now, how do you know that, Doctor?" he teases.

"It's the boy-girl divide," I say. "At this age the boys don't interact with the girls socially until it starts to turn sexual, so the parents are divided the same way."

"Really?" he says, absolutely never having thought about it before.

"Yes," I say, sounding exhausted for his benefit, as if I'm deeply worn out by explaining everything to him. "So that means quite a few people know about this, if we play six degrees of Georgina Melios."

Jonas looks at me quizzically but is still excited for me to play teacher. Sometimes American pop culture is lost on him.

"Six degrees," he repeats.

"It works like this," I say. "Allison Vaughn, mother of Bronwen, tells Hope Chee, mother of Chloe, since Bronwen and Chloe have been best friends since third grade. Chloe Chee plays after-school soccer with Lily Aaronson, so Hope tells Astrid Aaronson as they peel the mandarin oranges for snack."

I pause and reach for some almonds. Now I'm enjoying myself a little bit and don't want it to pass too quickly.

"We still haven't crossed the boy-girl divide," says Jonas, wagging a finger at me.

"I'm getting to it," I say. "Astrid Aaronson is also the mother of Jake, who plays trombone in the band and sits next to the second trumpet player. Who is . . ."

I hold my hand out, as if I'm waiting for Jonas to place his answer gently on my palm.

"Stavros Melios?" he says.

"Correct."

"So the Aaronson children—they're fraternal twins. That's how you cross the divide!" he says, absolutely thrilled.

"Yes."

"Amazing how they all tell each other everything," he says.

He's right and he isn't. The rich gossiping mom is a cliché for a reason; however, I think nine of ten rich gossiping moms are doing it not out of avarice but instead out of anxiety. It starts when the kids are little, with rashes and tantrums and weird poop rituals; then the kids get older and are they just sensitive or do they have sensory issues; ADHD or just impatient; and then just when they have all that figured out the kids hit puberty, and all bets are off; then the haunting refrain reaches a fever pitch: Is this normal? Is my kid normal? Will he be okay? Will I be okay?

It doesn't surprise me in the least that whatever went down between Theo and Bronwen Vaughn has made its way across at least half of his fifth-grade class.

But that doesn't mean I like being the last to know.

"And now all of these women are talking about Theo, and us, and I've had no idea," I say, tapping the nail of my middle finger on the countertop.

"You're making too much of this, Doctor," he says, baring his teeth again in an effort to charm me. "I don't believe any of them have given it as much thought as you are."

"I don't believe it, either," I say. "But that's not the point. As soon as Allison Vaughn finds a new plant-based meal service or Georgina Melios manages to successfully superimpose her acupuncturist's face on her husband's as he's slogging away on top of her, they'll forget all about Theo and Bronwen and the incident. They have distracted divergent minds—"

"But you're not judging," says Jonas, cheeky.

"I'm not judging, smart-ass," I say, the skin on my neck getting hot. "Good for them that they can move so swiftly through life, allowing themselves to be bothered by a thing only as long as it's dangling in front of them and then poof. Gone."

"But it's not like that for you."

"No, it's not like that for me."

"Because it stays with you."

"Because I remember everything, Jonas. And I don't like someone, especially those women, having something on me or Theo that I'm not even aware of."

"Perhaps you should try to let the whole thing go," he suggests blithely, knowing exactly how I'll react.

"Let the whole thing go?" I repeat. "That would imply some kind of resolution."

"Ah, an apology," he says. "I'm so sorry."

He doesn't look sorry. He looks delighted. And, like any man who's really a child inside, he is only sorry he is caught, and even then, not so much.

"I accept your pitiful apology."

"Are you angry with me?" he asks, not expecting a direct response but praying to some Swedish god of eroticism that the answer is yes.

"Meaningless and pitiful."

"The way you talk, Doctor," he says, his voice growing huskier.

Arguments usually serve as foreplay for us. It doesn't make us special. After having been married for so long, it actually feels fairly tame. We've never gotten into the rough stuff, unless you count some of the truly fucked-up things I've said to him that get him going. And seeing him get going gets me going. So we go together.

But now there is a barrier, and I'm trying to put my pinkie on it.

"What was the name?" I say.

"What name?"

"What Theo called Bronwen. What started all the drama?"

This softens his arousal for a moment, as he thinks.

"I don't know," he says. "I don't think Allison told me."

"And you didn't ask?"

"No," he said, nodding at me, back at the game. "Was I wrong?"

He's hoping I'll reprimand him again, and I definitely will, but my enthusiasm is tempered because I'm truly disappointed. Theo came late to language, not late enough to warrant occupational or speech therapy, but for the longest time he would just point at a thing and grunt sweetly, like a baby Frankenstein. Now he's ahead of grade level in reading but just behind the curve in writing and speaking. I've already made the decision to hire a tutor as soon as he starts sixth grade in the fall, because he still seems to have challenges finding the words. Even at home, Elias will rattle off a story or a joke from school, and Theo tries to keep up verbally, interjecting details here and there, but I can see him struggling.

So you see I'm not immune to it, either. Is this normal? Is my child normal? Will he be okay? The difference is I would never discuss my children's development with the other click-clacking mother hens.

My point is Theo doesn't swear, in front of me anyway. He doesn't come up with snappy comebacks or sick burns like his brother or some of his friends, so how could he have tormented Bronwen Vaughn? Your mother's got strabismus?

"Of course you were wrong," I growl. "Now I have to call Allison and find out."

Jonas seems surprised. Turned on, but surprised.

"I don't think you have to?" he says.

"Yes, I do, Jonas," I say, leaning way into the anger. "If you had somehow seen through your Cava hangover clearly enough to ask her yourself, I wouldn't have to."

He smiles.

"And maybe if you weren't sleeping it off until noon today, you might have had a chance to wash the fucking glitter off your skin. What'd you do—go down on Tinkerbell?"

That makes him laugh. He stands up from his stool and comes around to my side of the island. I stand up, too, so we're facing each other, about a foot of distance between us.

"You know it is only you, Doctor," he says in what might be considered the throatiest, sexiest voice of any man with a foreign accent, but there's no way I'm giving in without having some basic demands met. Luckily he's not dumb and adds, "How can I make it up to you?"

"You have to make me come twice," I say, holding up two fingers. "Clitoral only. None of that poking-around, blind-man-in-a-whorehouse shit."

Now he takes a step forward, places his hands on my hips.

I push them off and say, "No hands yet."

"Yes, Doctor."

He presses his lips on my neck, hands behind his back. It feels okay. His hair smells like clove shampoo; his day-old bristles scrape my skin. Maybe better than okay. I tilt my head toward him, my chin and cheek against his hair.

One of the reasons I married him, quite possibly the primary, is that he is the only man I've ever met who can take me out of my head. It usually doesn't last too long. We don't have those seventy-two-hour tantric Sting orgies. It's a matter of seconds here or there when he first touches me, or right when I'm about to come, in the delirium of anticipation, that finally my mind is blank. Even the midst of a climax is already too late for me, neurons already firing about the next thing and then the next and the one after that blasting full-force into my consciousness.

But there are times, like now, right now, for a moment I'm liquid.

Then my purse on the island begins to hum, the ghost light of the phone inside glowing. What if it's Billy? Liquid me will have to wait. Brain always wins.

I give Jonas a gentle shove off me. He's taken aback but not shocked, glancing toward the light and the noise.

"Who is that?" he asks, because he's used to me knowing the answer.

I don't answer him, lean over to the island and yank my purse toward me, unzip, open. Due to the law of ringing phones, the phone has stopped ringing as soon as I have it in my hands. But I am granted a reprieve—it begins to hum and light up again.

The name *Makeda* scrolls along the top of the screen, and I allow myself only part of a second of disappointment before picking up.

"Hi, Makeda."

She pauses, I suspect still bristling because I don't call her Detective. Here's how to get to square one of Dr. Caroline-Land, Makeda—know that I do everything for a reason!

"Hi, Dr. Strange," she says.

I hear her inhale, preparing to speak, and I speak instead: "Is there any news about Nelson?"

"Yes and no," she says. "We have a few more questions for you. Hoping you might come to see us at the station."

I have seen this show: I go down to the station. They say I don't have to, but I'd probably be more comfortable there. They say I'm not under arrest; they simply want to ask a few questions. I gasp, *Wait, am I a suspect?* Then they—Makeda and Miguel the water boy—exchange a look. Looking at them looking at each other, I stammer, *I think I need a lawyer.* Makeda sighs, her plentiful bosom rising and falling with disappointment. Cut to commercial.

The main difference, though, between me and all those poor *Law & Order* stooges is that I'd actually love to tell the police more. I have a lot to share and nothing to hide. Nothing they need to know, anyway.

"Of course," I say. "Is now a good time?"

She pauses again, no doubt surprised by my offer of cooperation, but she recovers quickly.

"Yes, it is. We are here."

She gives me the address, which I don't need to write down, just repeat after her to seal the information in my memory. Then we both say thank you and goodbye, and we hang up.

Jonas has retreated to his stool and is chewing more almonds, attempting to snack his erection out of existence.

"Precinct?" he says, intrigued.

"I'll tell you about it later," I say, pulling the car key fob from my purse. "It's about a patient."

"It always is."

There is nothing in his tone to suggest he is offended by where he ranks on my list of priorities, because he quite simply isn't. He's never experienced jealously, as far as I can tell. It's something I admire in him. It also makes me want to bone the plumber on the quartzite countertop in front of him just to provoke a reaction. I mean, not *our* plumber—he's in his sixties—but a plumber, the porn plumber of frustrated housewife fantasy.

But the dearth of jealousy comes in handy now as he offers his cheek to me for a kiss and tells me he loves me before I go.

The police station is more DMV than *Law & Order*. Everything is a shade of beige in the reception area, from the chipped counter to the speckled floor to the worn vinyl chairs. The air is stagnant and warm, and it smells like someone has sprayed a fart-scented air freshener seconds before I came in. There is not, however, any background noise of phones ringing or typewriters tapping out warrants, but why would there be when all our New York City tax dollars have gone a long way in bringing the NYPD out of the eighties?

Makeda appears on the staircase next to the reception desk and waves her hand at me when she reaches the bottom but doesn't come any closer. She's wearing a mask, like I am, so I can't tell if she's faking a smile. Her big eyes are static.

I follow her up the steps and into a surprisingly tidy office with unsurprisingly smudged glass walls. It would actually be a decent-sized space except that it's clear Makeda shares the office with Miguel, two desks flush against each other like in an old-time newsroom. Miguel springs up from his seat when he sees me and offers a wave.

Makeda closes the door behind her, points to her mask, and says, "It's required in the hallways and bathrooms, but if we're in here and you're okay with it, it's fine."

"As long as you're okay with it, I'm okay with it."

The three of us glance at each other for a couple of rounds, each of us making sure the other two are okay with it, and then Makeda and I remove our masks, and Miguel tucks his back into his pocket.

Makeda gestures to a single folding chair against the wall and says, "Please."

I sit, and she pulls her chair around her desk so she faces me, as does Miguel. It's the same setup as it was in my office, and I would say that they have home-court advantage, but frankly, their office is so unimpressive I don't feel threatened in any way.

However, I'm aware enough of how my past affects my present that I can recognize when I'm triggered, and anything having to do with police that's more immediate than me watching them on TV does the trick every time. I can remain calm, keep my heart rate steady at forty-four BPM, but it's impossible to come into one police station and not think of the other time I was in one, when I was thirteen, describing all the horrific things I'd seen.

# Gordon Strong

I tie one on with a sailor's knot the night the Brewers lose the last game in the Yankees series. I have to go out to the garage to get the rest of the twelve-pack, which is hilarious considering the fridge out there's been busted for three months. But Evelyn told me there's only room for one six-pack in the kitchen fridge, so the couple extra cases of Busch I got on sale at Bev-Town had to go in the garage.

I drink a few of the warm beers and watch the Brewers break my heart. I'm yelling at the screen again but don't swear, not too much anyway, and when the game ends I feel like calling every guy in the outfield a nutless wonder and throwing the remote through the screen, but instead I just say, loudly, "Oh well, you win some, you lose some."

It seems like such a fair thing to say, such an adult thing to say; as soon as I say it I feel pretty proud of myself, and I turn around to see the expressions on Evelyn's and the kids' faces, but they're gone. Up to bed, I guess. I'm alone in the living room, and I'm wondering for how long.

I get up from the recliner, and four or five empties roll off me and the arms of the chair to the carpet. I lean down to pick them up and feel something tweak in my lower back, like someone just took aim with a slingshot full of marbles. Then I try to stand up straight, and it's like the bones in my back are sawing welder sparks, and there are noises, too—cracks and creaks.

I walk through the kitchen, hunched over, get the Advil that Evelyn keeps on the bottom shelf of the spice cabinet with her vitamins. Pop the top and swallow four. Then I remember something: in the back of the cupboard on the floor to the left of the sink is where we keep the liquor.

We don't drink too much of the stuff, Evelyn or me, mostly keep it around for when we have people over, but shit, I can't remember the last time we had people over in a social way, unless you count Savannah's sleepovers or Brendan's video game marathons with his friends in the basement.

I squat a little without straightening my spine and I open the cupboard, take a quick inventory: gin, vodka, Kahlúa with a crusty cap, and half a fifth of Jack Daniel's. I reach for the Jack.

My back doesn't like it when I come up from the squat. Feels like a door hinge desperate for WD-40. I don't think I can open a cabinet for a glass; even the mug tree where my KING OF THE CASTLE coffee cup hangs is set too far back on the counter for me to reach.

I tighten my grip on the neck of the bottle and shuffle back to the living room. First I head in the direction of the recliner, but then I see the phone on the side table next to the couch, and I think maybe I'll call Remy, since his wife, Eileen, is a nurse.

I unscrew the cap off the Jack and take a small sip. It burns my throat, and I'm thinking does bourbon go bad, but then I remember why I don't drink the hard stuff. Smelling it on my old man's breath growing up was enough to swear me off it for life, but truthfully I just don't like how it tastes.

Right now, though, I know it's medicine, probably the only thing that's going to numb the back pain without a prescription, so I tilt the bottle up and gulp a couple times like I'm on a Mountain Dew commercial. For a minute I'm a little stunned, my back still throbbing and thrumming, but then another minute passes, and another, and I take one more big gulp, and another, and then suddenly my back doesn't feel so bad anymore. My stomach, maybe, but my back is better, pressure relieved.

I feel like I can finally take a deep breath, so I do, and I take another healthy swig of the Jack, the taste just fine now, and I can appreciate the woody sweetness of it. I pick up the receiver and dial Remy's home number, get the machine.

Then a few more sips, and it's working, and I feel good, better, actually, than I did earlier, before my back snapped. I don't know why, but I decide to give my old man a call. I haven't talked to him in a while—I try to remember when's the last time, maybe three years ago, when he had the stroke. Figure maybe it's time to check in. I look at the receiver in my hand, and that song goes through my head: "I just called . . . to say . . . I love you."

My old man and I don't say that to each other, but still I could tell him what's going on, tell him what grades the kids are in school, et cetera.

I dial him up, and he picks up right away, like he's waiting for my call.

"Pop, it's me," I say. Then I figure I better get more specific, since it's been so long. "It's Gordy."

"Gordy," he says, and he sounds exactly the same. Not the same like he did three years ago but the same as he did when I was a kid. Young and pissed off. "What the hell do you want?"

"Just wanted to see how you're doing," I say.

"The same," he says, like he's reading my mind. "I'm the same. You're the same, too."

I can't tell if he's drunk. Let me fix that: I can't tell *how* drunk he is. He's got to be at least as drunk as I am, but strangely, considering how much I've put away, I don't think I'm that drunk. He's definitely not less, I'll say that.

"How's your health?"

"Same, same," he says. "What d'you do for work, again?"

He's not kidding when he says "same." My old man's known I worked for Kinzer for twenty years. He likes to play a game where he pretends he doesn't remember, but I know he does—he just likes to give me an impression that he couldn't care less.

"Funny you should ask," I say, and it's like I'm hearing those particular words in that order for the first time, because there's really nothing funny about it. Funny can mean a lot of things. Funny and strange. Funny in the head.

The old man's quiet. I can't even hear him breathing, much less his trademark lung rattle from sucking down two packs of Lucky Strikes a day for fifty years.

"They actually canned me."

"What's that?" he says, smelling blood in the water.

Now he's pretending again—this time, that he can't hear me, so I have to say it again. So I have to hear it again. It's not like I ever forgot, but talking to him makes me remember: It wasn't what he did to you; it's what he made you do to yourself that was the worst thing.

"They fired me, Pop," I say. "The whole department, so it's not like they singled me out."

"You lost your job?"

"Yeah, I lost my job," I say, louder. "Along with the whole department. They cut us all loose without any kind of warning."

I do this every time I talk to him, run my mouth on and on, because I'm nervous about what he'll say, so I keep filling up the space with chatter. It's a thing I know I do, but that doesn't mean I'm not goddamned sick of it.

I take another big gulp of Jack and wedge the bottle between my thighs, keep my hand steady on the neck. The old man's still quiet.

"What, Pop?" I say. "I know you got an opinion on it, so why don't you spit it out?"

I picture him in his old recliner with the threadbare arms where he's spent almost every minute since he retired fifteen years ago. He was passed out and pissing himself in that very chair the night my mother walked out on us and never looked back.

Then I hear him laughing. It starts out a small chuckle and then it booms, and the inside of my stomach starts to curdle like bad milk. How many times did I hear that growing up—me and my siblings hiding in the basement from him, and him guffawing as he stumbled down the stairs to beat the shit out of us.

My hands are shaking, so I wrap them both around the body of the bottle and take another few gulps. I pull the bottle away and see I've almost finished it, maybe two fingers left. At least my hands have stopped shaking.

The old man's finally stopped laughing, too.

"I knew it," he says. "You couldn't hold down a job if your life depended on it."

"You're wrong, Pop," I say, pointing at the phone like he can see me. "I worked there for twenty years."

"Who cares?" he says. "I never lost my job. And I went to work blind drunk twice a week."

He's proud of this. It's like some kind of fucked-up Boy Scout honor for him to brag about. The drunk-at-work badge. Of course, he was a guard at the Green Bay Correctional Institution his whole life, so the inmates weren't exactly in a position to complain.

"My job was different than your job was, Pop," I say. "Kinzer's a big company, and sales are down across the board."

He yawns, makes a big deal about it. How I'm boring him with my excuses.

"They keep who they wanna keep," he says at the tail end of his yawn. "If you did your job better than anyone, they woulda kept you."

"That's not how it works there," I say, realizing as I say it there's no point. Arguing with the old man goes nowhere, ends with me punching a hole in the wall.

He ignores me anyway, says, "You tell the little woman?"

"Yeah, Pop, of course I told her. She's behind me a hundred percent."

"Sure she is," he says, and I can tell he's gearing up for something. "She's backed the crippled horse for so long, the hell's she gonna do about it now?"

"She's a good woman," I snap.

"I'm not arguing with you, boyo," he says. "She'd have to be a goddamn saint to stick around."

Maybe it's the Jack, but I'm not as worked up as I used to get when he'd tear into me.

"You're right about that," I say. "She happens to be a goddamn saint."

"Yeah?" he says, and I can tell that took the wind out of him.

I take a victory sip and think maybe this is the only way to talk to my dad, drinking bourbon and getting down in the mud with him. Maybe that's the only way I can stand hearing his voice.

"I ever tell you about Murph?" he says.

"Huh?"

"Murph. Poor sap used to work at GBCI with me. His wife was the cutest Betty Crocker you ever saw. Always cleaning house, baking cookies, rubbing Murph's feet when he got home. Did I mention he worked the night shift?"

The old man doesn't wait for me to answer, keeps going: "What he didn't know was as soon as he pulled out of the driveway, she was up off the couch, out of the house, and going down to Mackey's Pub to pick up some new stud every night of the week and twice on Sundays. Let 'em drill her right in their bed, too, with the kiddos dreaming of sugarplums in the next room. Poor fuckin' sap, Murph. Never had any idea," he says, laughing.

Since I can't shut my ears off I shut my eyes. I know I should just hang up, but I can't—I can't let him win.

"Why're you telling me this, Pop?"

"Why?" he says, shocked. "You dumb cunt. No woman is that good. They always got their eye out, boyo. And one that looks like your wife does, especially."

"That's enough, Pop," I say, trying to put some fire in my voice. But the only fire in me is from the booze sloshing around in my gut.

"You got a good-looking milkman? Paperboy?"

I feel the fire rising, in my chest now.

"You don't know shit about my wife, old man," I say.

It sounds and feels like a warning, but it just makes him laugh harder.

"Sure I do! She's a woman. She's got half a brain and a sneaky little snatch. Now, you think hard—maybe it's one of your boy's buddies? Mailman? Next-door neighbor?"

Fire's live. I burst up from the couch and I'm screaming. First I'm screaming at him, about how he's a sonofabitch and an asshole and how he's wrong and doesn't know shit about my wife or my life, and I wish he'd died three years ago when he had the stroke.

Then I'm screaming because of my back. It feels like the muscles at the base of my spine got shredded up, all the edges seared on a grill. I fall backward onto the couch, and it hurts too much to sit straight, so I pass out right there, wake up with puke on my chest, the bottle in one hand, phone receiver in the other, the disconnect tone bleating its way into my dreams.

# Dr. Caroline

It suddenly smells terrible in Makeda and Miguel's office. If this were *Law & Order*, maybe the detective would say, *Something stinks in here, and it's not the fart-scented air freshener.*

They must smell it, too, but they are business-as-usual, both of them leaning forward on the edges of their chairs, Miguel holding a tiny spiral notebook like it's his first day in AP English.

"Nelson Schack's vaccination card is a fake," says Makeda. "Also the home address he provided you is a commercial business, and the proprietors don't know anyone by that name. Phone number doesn't exist, either."

She says it all with a practical sort of gravity. Like, *I know you know you're in serious doo-doo, but let's pretend I just have to list all the facts for now.*

"That doesn't surprise me," I say.

"No?"

"No," I say. "I've done a bit of research on my own, and I now believe that Nelson Schack may be a fake name."

"What makes you say that?" says Makeda.

Good girl, keep up, don't flinch.

The irony is I want Makeda and Miguel to do well. I want them to get their man. But I can't escape the feeling that I could simply get him faster. And, being honest, it pains me a little to know this. Intelligence is mostly a burden—there have been countless studies on how some of the most brilliant minds, the highest achievers, the most demonstrably, inarguably smart people are also the most anxious, the most depressed, have the highest rates of addiction. They simply know too much.

But as much as I'd like to keep my encounter with Billy to myself, I think it's best to share that tidbit. If it had been him whose shoulder I put my hand on as he boarded the bus, I would have said, *Come with me, Billy. Let's figure this out together.* And he would have come with me. And when Makeda called me I would have delivered him to them in the sweetest of suspect gift bags. But no.

I don't allow myself regret generally. What I tell my patients is, allow yourself to regret something for five, ten minutes max, then dump it in your mental recycling bin, turn it into action for next time.

The downside, right now, is that it doesn't make sense for me not to come clean.

"A few reasons," I say. "But chief among them is that I think his name is actually Billy Harbin."

Miguel looks up from his notebook, shaken and stirred from the new information, but Makeda keeps it cool.

"What makes you think that?" she says.

"Because he told me, Makeda," I say. "Would it be helpful for me to tell you the whole story?"

"Please."

So I tell them the whole story. The phone call, how I ran into someone I knew before meeting him in the park, how he ran away and I lost him in the crowd. It's all the truth, except I throw in a sore ankle on my part to make it sound more realistic that I couldn't keep up with him.

"The friend you ran into in the park—what was her name?" says Makeda.

"Georgina Melios," I say. "M-E-L-I-O-S."

"Do you think she saw him, Schack . . . or Harbin, right?"

"I don't think so, but you could certainly ask. I'm happy to give you her contact information," I say, dreading the future one thousand conversations that I will have with the faculty, staff, and parent-student community at my sons' school on this topic.

"Billy Harbin's the name?" says Miguel, pulling his phone from his jacket pocket, tiny notebook disposed of.

"Yes, that's right. I'll give you the number he called me from, but I have a feeling it's a prepaid cell."

Makeda sits back in her chair, and I can tell she's thinking hard, her eyes fixed on some point in the distance.

"You think he has a split personality?" she says.

"It's called DID," I say. "Dissociative identity disorder. And whether or not Billy has it remains to be seen."

"Nelson-slash-Billy," says Miguel, visibly proud that he's kept up.

"That's right," I confirm, smiling my approval.

"So he might not have it?" asks Makeda.

"It's my medical opinion that the condition likely doesn't exist," I say, slipping into a more professorial tone. "I believe those who claim to have it do so because it's convenient for them."

"So he's pretending to have it?"

"I think so," I say. "Although I admit, he's a talented actor if it is, in fact, an act."

"So, wait, he might have it?" Star Student Miguel pipes in.

"Correct," I say, and then I decide to downshift into humility. "DID isn't my area of expertise, so I'm afraid I can't say for certain, but if the condition is fake, and he's faking it, he still may believe it to be true on some level. So it's best for us to treat it as truth as well. For now anyway."

"A lot of William Harbins," says Miguel, gazing at his search results.

"You say you lost him around Ninth Street and Fifth Ave?" says Makeda.

"Yes, it was very crowded."

"Before that, when you and he talked, did he tell you any other information about himself—either Billy or Nelson?"

"We spoke for a few minutes," I say. "It's the general consensus among mental health professionals that DID, if it exists, manifests as a result of severe emotional and physical trauma, and that tracks with what Billy told me."

"How so?"

"He said Nelson first appeared when he was twelve years old, and that the devil brought him."

"The devil?" asks Miguel, but he's not as shocked as I would have imagined.

Makeda, also, doesn't blink. I am a little impressed, but then again, they are cops in Brooklyn. They have seen a few things. Not as much as I have, but a few.

"Do you recall his exact words?" says Makeda.

"Yes, he said, 'Devil brought him when I was twelve. He told me he wanted to help me, so he was giving me a friend named Nelson.' I'm inferring he, Billy, underwent some kind of abuse and then created Nelson as a defense mechanism."

"But you also think he's faking it?"

"On some level," I say. "He may have convinced himself a long time ago that Nelson was real, but there is some degree of awareness on his part. Again, that's just my theory."

Makeda rests her elbows on her knees and folds her hands.

"So the answer to the question, Does he really have a split personality—DID," she says, correcting herself, "is irrelevant."

"Correct," I say. "Trauma generally informs antisocial behavior later in life, if not full-blown psychopathy, so his whole story makes a great deal of sense, actually."

Now Miguel has moved past the mild shock and into more of a stoned surfer look. Makeda appears quizzical.

Then she asks, "But someone who's antisocial may not necessarily be a psychopath, right?"

That gives me pause. I'm surprised and a little pissed not to be able to flex my knowledge base.

She continues: "Antisocial is the path; psychopathy is just one of the destinations?"

I think the thing that really gets to me is that Makeda is decidedly not trying to impress me—her face exhibits no hint of a boast.

"That's exactly right," I say.

"So whether Nelson, aka Billy, has DID, is a sociopath, a psychopath, or merely antisocial isn't the question we need answered right now, you agree?"

"Yes," I say, doing my best to hide the realization that perhaps I've truly underestimated Makeda. "I think, really, we only have one: Where did he go?"

"I have some other questions, too," she says.

Then it occurs to me, not that it was ever far from my mind, that she called me into this smelly little office not to show off everything she's learned from the *American Journal of Psychiatry* podcast, but because something about my original story didn't stand up.

"So do I, Makeda," I say. "A lot of them, but until we find Billy Harbin, there's not much else I can do."

She thinks about that. She doesn't like me dodging the prospect of being interviewed again. Too bad, so sad.

"When we locate him, we'll look forward to your psychiatric assessment," she says, recovering quickly. "But if I understand what you're saying, if we're working under the assumption that if Billy Harbin does have DID, then he is aware of his alternate identity as Nelson Schack, or vice versa, then that takes us back a few steps to why I called you here in the first place."

"You did, didn't you?" I say. "But now, since we've all discussed that, what could be left?"

I keep my tone calm but firm to stress the practicality of my resistance. My tone says, *Can't you see we have more in common than not, Makeda?* I mean, I really don't buy that, but she's forced me into this corner, so I have no choice but to drop the big one, the magic words of working women everywhere:

"We don't want to waste each other's time."

"No, we certainly don't," she says. "Which is why I'll keep this brief, and then I'll let you go."

I don't think she says this by accident: let you go. Implying that right now I'm caught.

"You didn't mention your backstory before," she says.

There's a jaunty lilt in her tone I don't much care for.

"I didn't feel my personal history was particularly relevant," I say. "I still don't."

"I might disagree with you there," she says.

In so many ways, I'm rooting for Makeda's success, but now that she's deliberately trying to poke her stubby fingers around my hippocampus, I'm inclined to put up a brand-new wall, brick by brick.

"First of all, it isn't a 'backstory,'" I say with the air quotes. "It's my life. Secondly, it's not something I discuss with people whom I don't know very well."

"I can appreciate that. But I have to ask you to appreciate that my job," she says, hand on chest, "is to draw lines, see patterns, make connections. Just like yours."

She seems so proud of herself with that line. Gestalt me later, sweetheart.

She continues: "Schack comes to you, confides in you that he's going to kill someone. Maybe he did his research on you ahead of time and figured you had experience with that."

"Experience with what—hearing confessions?" I say, smoothing out a wrinkle on my pants leg. "Obviously. He wouldn't be the first patient to treat me like a priest."

"No," says Makeda, shaking her head gently. "Not a priest. A murder witness."

She's all wide-eyed and feigning naivete, like these are just the runniest-of-the-milliest questions that she would ask anyone.

"So your theory is the man calling himself Nelson Schack decides to kill someone and googles 'therapist with murder witness experience,' which leads him to me. It's just a civilian's opinion, but I'm afraid that sounds like a tenuous connection at best."

Makeda maintains a cool half smile. I can tell she's pleased that I'm trying to evade her line of questioning. Oh, how satisfying it will be to rip a gash in her sails. She puts her hands together like she's about to pray. You better start praying to someone, you feel me, girl?

"My mistake," she says, full of grace. "So why do you think he picked you? Out of all the therapists in Brooklyn?"

Now it all clicks: I'd neglected to share with her the second piece of Nelson's confession, the one that went, "I know who you really are," which would imply that the stretch is not a stretch after all. But I'd never told Makeda that, and here she is, sniffing it out like it's her truffle in the dirt.

"He didn't tell me," I said. "But if I had to venture a guess, it's because he's kidnapped Ellen Garcia, and she's the key to all this."

I stare at them, both seemingly dumbfounded.

"Isn't it?" I say. "Somehow he knows Ellen Garcia, probably fetishizes her from afar. One day he finally screws up the courage to hit her over the head with the lead pipe in the dining room and torture her for kicks. He reads all the trash she wrote for *Brooklyn Bound* and thinks it would be great fun to aim the spotlight on people she's maligned."

"To frame them," says Miguel, apparently still awake.

"To divert attention," I say. "And, yes, to frame them."

"So how does he settle on Ellen Garcia again?" asks Makeda,

giving off a playful shrug. "Sorry, just sounds like a pretty specific obsession, wanting to frame her enemies."

She continues to work a little game with me. I realize she thinks she's won a round in driving me to lose my patience, and maybe she has. But it ain't over till it's over, Makeda. You know who said that? Both Yogi Berra and Lenny Kravitz. One talking about baseball and the other singing about love. Savannah Strong and I used to listen to that CD on repeat and imagine making out with Lenny Kravitz and how crazy our parents would go if we dated a Black guy. Even if he was light-skinned and rich.

In her room, it was either Lenny or House of Pain or Stone Temple Pilots. Savannah had a Rubbermaid bin of CD singles that we made mixes from and spun for our little dance parties. I always brought *Check Your Head* by the Beasties when I slept over, listened to it every morning and every night. Something that Spotify can't do is elicit the Pavlovian response of excitement from cover art or even the actual CD. My heart rate quickened every time I saw the rich velvet red of *Check Your Head*, the Grand Royal logo across the top.

But Makeda doesn't need to know any of that.

"Why Ellen Garcia?" I say to her.

"Yes, why her?"

I let out a middling sigh, genuinely becoming frustrated, and say, "I don't know. He thinks she's cute, likes the way she looks in a caftan? Maybe she's on his FedEx route or maybe they're neighbors?

"I realize I've only met him briefly twice, but if I can suggest a direction, maybe stop the pointless lines of questioning and start homing your lens on people who live or work closely enough to Ellen Garcia to stalk her."

"Because our guy's likely obsessed with her," says Makeda, and I can't tell if she's agreeing with me or just regurgitating whatever I say.

"Yes," I say.

Miguel is hard at work on the phone again, and right now both he and Makeda seem so many steps behind me, I think he's probably given up on the case and is just tapping all the boxes with streetlights so he can get back into his Zappos account.

"Could be," says Makeda. "Or he reads all about you and your past online, kidnaps someone who's recently done you wrong, then comes and tells you about it, pretends to have a split personality to keep you guessing. Starves out his victim as an offering . . . to you. Or to frame you in some way, I don't know, you've only met him twice."

Now she has the balls to sigh, as if she's exhausted that it's taken me this long to figure it out.

"So if we're looking at it that way, seems Ellen Garcia is just another pawn on the board. He's not obsessed with her at all," she says, raising her eyebrows in a dare. "He's obsessed with you, Dr. Strange. You're the queen."

# Ellen Garcia

**E**yes open. There's a smell. It's not the piss on my shorts or the sweat above my lip or the scent of the room where I'm trapped, which took me a minute to get used to—the right-after-the-chalk-dust-settles-from-the-eraser-clap smell. Something new now: woodsy and sweet and familiar, could be a cleaning product, but it makes my crispy, dry eyes weep and tugs at my nose hairs, and that's how I know: perfume. I can stick my nose into a canister of bleach wipes and not feel a thing, but if there's a dowager in the same train car as me with Chanel No. 5 dabbed behind her ears I start sneezing, even with a mask on.

I sneeze and actually appreciate the moisture it brings to my mouth. There's been no more bread and water since the first time. I'm still staring at the empty bottle. I've already licked and sucked and fellated the top of that thing for any last drop, and as I swipe the dry sponge of my tongue across my lips I realize with relief: I have to pee.

This is a thing everyone knows, that you can drink your own pee. I mean, it's a problematic bit of phrasing: When do you have access to *other* people's pee? But this is a thing, tried-and-true. Right now, for me, it's a question of mechanics. I'm not superconfident I can even sit up straight, much less cup my hand underneath my chochita and pee into it successfully. But if I could aim into the water bottle I'd have a chance. The bottle labeled *Caroline*.

And who the fuck is Caroline? Girlfriend, wife, mom? Is Psycho Killer a woman? Is he Caroline? Are they Caroline?

I know I have to try this; the need overwhelms the hesitation; I have the urge to scratch the skin on my neck, I'm so thirsty. I push myself up to sitting, and there's the pounding in the head, the cadence speeding up and slowing down like ping-pong balls in a raffle basket. I unbutton my shorts, and I know I have to lift my butt to slide them off. Used to be a wriggle, but hey, great diet plan here in the locked room, must have lost some weight, because the shorts are loose on my hips. Don't be discouraged, ladies—you, too, can reach your fitness goals; just get yourself abducted and watch the pounds melt away.

That means strength-summoning. I am not great at summoning strength in a normal type of situation. I'm pretty skilled in weakness-summoning. If there's a weaker option, I will take it. If I have a choice between marathoning QVC from the comfort of my couch and the free Zumba class in the park, I will choose QVC. If helping out a fellow reporter means I don't get the angle, I will not help the reporter. If lying to my husband about maybe sharing a sloppy kiss in a bar bathroom with said fellow reporter is easier than telling my husband the truth, I will lie every time.

Not that I have done any of those things.

But baby Bella, source of light and warmth, my hand on her cheek of velvet—that is the prize, and that fuels whatever drive I have left. I place my right palm behind me and straighten my arm, push and push and push, lift my ass up toward the ceiling. This has got to be some kind of butt exercise from the Jane Fonda days: *Let's go, ladies, squeeze those cheeks, shove a Barbie right up there and just rip her little head off.*

My arm shakes, but I'm working quick. I tug my shorts down with my left, hook my thumb over my underwear, and pull those, too, just enough, just over the sad sack that is my ass. Then grab the bottle and aim best I can.

When I was in labor, after they gave me the epidural, I had to hover over a bedpan to empty my bladder, squatting on the edge of the hospital bed, but I had Chris holding one arm and a nurse holding the other, and I was laughing because it was silly and also because I was so, so stoned, and I am missing all four of those comfort factors now: drugs, Chris, the nurse, joy at the absurd.

I swap out my right hand for my left in the tent-pole position and grab the empty bottle with my right, and the pee just comes; I don't even have to push anymore these days. I guess it's the fate of being a lady of a certain age who's squeezed out a baby at some point—it's like a Pavlovian pee response now; as soon as I see anything that gives my bladder a cue—it doesn't even have to be a toilet; it can be me seeing the front door of my apartment as I'm fumbling for my keys and my bladder somehow knows there's a toilet inside, so it just releases whenever, like, eh, close enough.

She's a wild stream, uncontrolled, unbridled. Warm rivulets spilling over my fingers and the bottle's neck, but some of it is making it in; I can feel the bottle getting a little heavier, even though it's hard for me to see exactly how much. And then I'm done.

I push, trying to eke out a little more, but then feel the sting of a nascent UTI, so I stop, because that is the last thing one needs. Not a lot of Macrobid available in this underground pharmacy.

I let my butt fall to the floor and set the bottle down next to me, shaking the drops off my fingers. About half an inch of fluid inside. I pull my underwear up a little and wriggle into my shorts—they're only at half-mast, but it'll do. I may be in an extreme situation, but I'll be goddamned if I'm going to help this guy achieve his perv goals.

I pick up the bottle again, lift it to my nose. A fine bouquet. Piquant, front notes of cedar and pine. Now or never, like the kiddies sing in *High School Musical*. I pinch my nose with two fingers and take a sip. It's tea, it's lemon water at a spa, not rank urine from my deteriorating body.

Still, I almost cough it up. Brain still beats the body, it turns out, but I manage to get it down. One sip anyway. I know when I unclamp my nose I'll get the full taste of it still clinging to my tongue and the roof of my mouth. I give myself a little countdown. Five, four, three, two, one. Fingers off.

I cough. I smell it; I taste it; I wretch and dry-heave, remember the fear when I had COVID back in the beginning, March of '20. I mean, maybe I didn't have it—I couldn't even get a test then—but I had a cold and a cough and couldn't smell or taste my coffee for a week and told Chris, who'd already asked me for a trial separation at that point, that he better keep Bella at his place until I was out of the woods. If I could will just the anosmia back, I would, because if I couldn't smell the piss on my breath I'd be fine, but now that I can, the stench is making my stomach roil, the acid creep up my esophagus, my eyes burn and water.

But then another thing happens that jerks my attention away from my nausea: the door opens.

My instinct is to run, but that project starts and ends pretty quick. I try to stand but can't even get to all fours, my arms and legs buckling as I squint into the doorway and see him, except he's just a shadow, backlit by a bright yellow light, and my eyes are leaking like busted rain gutters, tears spilling out over the lids and lashes.

I try to stand again, thinking, Bella Bella Bella. The mantra makes its way to my muscle groups, pumps the blood, and I'm up to all fours, then kneeling. I lean my weight into my right leg and foot, and I'm dizzy and nauseous, but I keep going. Bella Bella Bella, and then I've got it—the strength of ten bad mommies plus two. I'm up, I'm standing, I'm facing him, and he's not moving, just standing there watching me. He's tall and thin, wearing a surgical mask and a baseball cap, jeans, and a gray trainer hoodie and white sneakers. It's time to go.

I lurch forward, don't think about it; in mid-stumble I think, He's not that big or broad, I have a shot, but then he's coming at me fast and throws something the size of a file folder at my chest. It's not heavy, but it shocks me, and I try to catch it and lose my balance, fall back on my butt, and then my head snaps back and hits the floor.

There's heat radiating from my skull, and I taste blood in my mouth where my teeth must have clamped my tongue with the impact. My fingers are still clutching what he threw at me; without looking, at first I think it's one of those coloring books for adults and so nice that my kidnapper's invested in my mindfulness journey.

Then I look down and see that it's a *New York Post*—I'd recognize the bold font and barely veiled fascist propaganda anywhere. Blood drip-drops from my bottom lip onto the paper and slides down the cover, just-fed-vampire-style.

The guy comes toward me, and I drop the paper and push off the floor with my hands and try to scoot back, away from him, but I can barely get any traction so only move an inch or two. Then he leans down over me and his face is in my face, and I wince because it's all I can do, the only shield I have left is to shut my eyes, but something tells me to look at him, so I look in his eyes, and they're actually pretty, blue and clear, with crinkles at the corners, and I think he probably got cheated on by a girl in the eighth grade or his mom did a number on him and I think, Fuck you, dude, you're not taking me down to the depths of your misogynistic cathartic shithole, save that brain trash for your shrinky-dink, so I reach my hands up and grip the fabric of his sweatshirt with both my fists and say, "The fuck do you want?"

I mean to yell it, scream it, shake the walls, but it's just a sad little croak.

He doesn't answer, just shoves the paper at my chest, and I see his hand, think what clean, clear nails he has, for a murderer, and I fall back to the floor, and then I can't see his eyes anymore, he's holding

ELLEN GARCIA

a phone in front of his face, takes a picture with the flash on, which gives me the spins, makes my eyeballs roll in my head.

Then he leaves, quick as he came, as blood fills my mouth, and my head pulses, eyelids fluttering, and it hits me—I think I know him.

# Dr. Caroline

I wake up in the car parked a block away from home, realize I shut my eyes for a few minutes after my chat with New York's finest.

The note from Jonas under my half-empty wineglass in the kitchen reads: *Gone to sleep . . . rain check.* Then I see he has sketched a small umbrella with faint slanted hash marks above it, meant to be raindrops. I pick up the glass and finish the lukewarm wine in one sip. Makes me think of urine.

There was a guy I knew from Histology and Pathology in my first year at med school who was fond of the scent. It took me a couple months of dating him before I realized he could only get hard if he could get a whiff—I could give a walking tour of Morningside Heights bar bathrooms and tell you which had the most stable wall-mounted sinks. I've googled him since then in moments of boredom and curiosity, as you do. Once a handsome, dark-haired Jewish med student, now a schlubby, balding Jewish ophthalmologist. Nothing on LinkedIn on whether he still digs pee-play.

I take an unopened Vinho Verde from the fridge and head down to my office. Sit at my desk and unscrew the cap, give myself a generous pour. Tap the keyboard to wake up the desktop.

I search for "Nelson Schack William Harbin," which produces gobbledygook. Which was a phrase my dear old mother used with some regularity. "Nothing but gobbledygook," she'd say, scraping the remains of a piece of chocolate cake that she'd mashed up with her fork into the garbage disposal. But she wouldn't run the water or flip the switch, you see.

The search results are even less rewarding than garbage cake. Not even the Peruvian economist comes up, just old census reports and in-memory-ofs, but after a few clicks I see they're all red herrings—I can't find any page where both names appear together.

I take a sip of wine. It's so cold, with that little spark of minerality, a fizz that dissolves in less than a second on the tongue. I've never kept a gratitude journal, even though I recommend it to certain patients, either those who need the focus amid their depression hazes or those who are just a little bit spoiled and need to imagine what it would be like without these everyday jewels. Personally, I don't need to imagine anything—no one in the neighborhood where I grew up knew what a Vinho or a Verde was; the only wine they knew had Seagram's or Boone's on the label and tasted like a dirty fruit snack. All to say I've never felt the need to keep a record of things I am thankful for, but if I did, cold Vinho Verde would be number one today.

And then, with that lovely bubbly spark, I know what I have to do next. I won't find Billy by actually looking for him. I need to imagine I am him.

I google "Survivor" and add "Strong family murders."

And there I am, in black-and-white. Next-door-neighbor Caroline Strange.

Only a few hits, mostly from the *Journal Sentinel.* Typically, news outlets withhold the names of children, bound by legal standards and/ or ethical obligation, but when the vans showed up at our house, my mother got her big old butt off the sunken couch cushions and offered to sign whatever release forms they waved in front of her. *Can we use your thirteen-year-old daughter's name/age/height/weight/astrological sign? Can we say she's at that awkward in-between mid-pubescent stage? Can we say she was clearly destined to be the wingman to the year-round-tanned, no-makeup-needing, kind-to-all-creatures Savannah Strong?*

Okay, maybe they didn't write all of that, but it certainly seemed to be the underlying suggestion. Darling Mother actually didn't need to be talked into any of it.

Then came the long slog of eighth grade, where I was the object of pity and disgust, crushed and choked by the negative space created by Savannah's absence. Difficult to grieve when you're busy being garden-variety unpopular. Not to mention the sleep thing—my narcolepsy-lite was partially inherited but largely manifested by post-traumatic stress and caused me to fall asleep at odd moments, to put it mildly. Once on the girls' locker room floor, once while sitting on the toilet in the bathroom at the graduation dance. As hard as it may be for you to imagine, this did not endear me to my fellow middle schoolers. Of course, it all changed the next year in high school. But a fat lot of good that did thirteen-year-old me.

I read through my old quotes. Savannah's best friend, in the house for a sleepover, slumbered through the entire ordeal. "I just found them like that."

It's the truth, and even though it happened almost thirty years ago, it's right here in front of me: the memory, the feeling of stumbling down the hallway with the rubber runners. I can breathe it; I can smell the smell. In fact, anytime I'm at a cookout, if I'm sitting closely enough to the steaks right in that moment before they go on the grill, it all comes back. Because it's the same smell. Blood and dead meat. You'd think it would've turned me vegan, but no, my family ate McDonald's two or three times a week, and it was a habit I carried through college and med school.

And now I only let myself have a steak about once a month, to control my fat intake and the cholesterol, and when I do, I enjoy it, but it will never not take me back to the upstairs hallway in the Strong house that morning, the whistling of the box fan in the bathroom window circulating that smell.

I keep scrolling. I haven't looked at the news stories about me in a long time, and I suppose I might have inflated and multiplied them in my memory, because there really aren't that many. The *Journal Sentinel*, and some CNN, a one-on-one interview with Helene Garelick from Channel 5, Wisconsin's Oprah knock-off, and the *48 Hours* special for which my mother once again signed away any scrap of privacy I might have had; she practically wrote the script for the slug-brained producers. She'd watched enough of those shows to know every beat and cliff-hanger right before the cut to commercial; all she had to say was, *You can use my daughter's story as the twist. The sole survivor of the Strong Family Massacre.*

She was right, and she was wrong. I'm not even referring to the ethics of the thing, because there's no doubt she was wrong, the shit-tiest of the shitty. I'm sticking purely to the semantic accuracy; it was evident I was still alive, walking and talking and eating McDonald's three times a week, but the problem is with the word itself: "survivor." To be a survivor you need to have been either a target or a victim—of a shipwreck, a war crime, a murderer. And I was none of those.

I didn't escape through the broken window at the last minute, only to have the shoelace of my K-Swiss hook on a stray rusty nail; didn't try to yank my leg away while whisper-crying, *Come on, come on*; didn't kick goalie-mask-wearing Gordon Strong off me as he grabbed my ankle, only to end up holding my empty shoe as I fell to the grass below, banged up but alive.

Nope. I was asleep in Savannah's brother Brendan's sleeping bag on the floor of Savannah's room the entire time. I loved that stinky old sleeping bag because I secretly loved Brendan Strong, and the bag smelled like him: boy-BO, campfire smoke, and a hint of skunk spray from a long-ago Cub Scout trip. My stunted horny mind went wild with the possibilities of what he'd done in that bag—I could only hope it had involved hours of furtive self-stimulation.

I survived nothing, and as a result had no survivor's remorse. I once had a client who was a survivor of an active shooter incident, a young woman who barricaded herself in the copy room of her office along with a few of her coworkers while someone's jilted lover sprayed bullets into the air outside, killing seven and injuring twelve. The girl didn't know it at the time, but her instinct was the thing that saved her life—a killer like that, he's not going to bother with doors and locks; any bird flying by at the turkey shoot is just fine. She had a shit-ton of survivor's remorse and would ask me quite plainly, Why them and not me?

I said all the therapist answers: There is no sense to a tragedy like this; You haven't done anything wrong; Now you have an opportunity to honor their memories. What I never said but what is the bald truth: *You lived because you happened to make the right decision. Because you were smart in the split second when it counted.*

She had earned her guilt, and it added up in the algebra of mental health. I, on the other hand, never had it because the answer to the question was obvious: I didn't lock myself in Savannah's room and hide out in my Brendan-scented cocoon to survive—I was asleep, wearing my Sony foldable headphones with the cushy ear pads, *Check Your Head* tracks playing on the loudspeakers in my dreams. Sometimes I still wake up humming the opening Jimi Hendrix/Curtis Knight guitar sample from "Jimmy James."

Plainer still: Gordon Strong didn't give a fuck about me, couldn't have cared less if I lived or died. When the fissures in his psyche finally gave way in those early-morning hours and he convinced himself the only solution was to kill his family before hanging himself in the basement, he wasn't thinking about me.

He wasn't my parent, after all. It wasn't lost on me that I should have been thankful for Chuck and Lil. I mean, at least they weren't psychotic murderers; they had that going for them. Honest truth, I did love my father—I actually came to respect him quite a bit, how he bettered himself, training as an EMT midlife, even if he worked so much and such long hours that he often fell asleep in the middle of a conversation. I'm sure that's where I inherited my ability to conk out both at will and not, though his never appeared stress-induced. As a result, I learned how to speed-talk through my emotions, even if I were simply lodging standard adolescent complaints, before he passed out from exhaustion. In retrospect, I can see now it aided in my journey to becoming a mental health professional, as most of what I do is distill patients' internal chaos into a few well-worded sentences and a single snappy diagnosis. So I suppose I owe him that.

But Mother, no. I owe her not the smallest of things. She was a shittier wife than she was a mother, which tells you a lot. At any time she could've gotten a job after she lost hers as a receptionist in the hospital where they met, but she claimed she couldn't, that she was too "nervous" to be around people. So all she could do was sit on the couch and aggro-eat and offer up her daughter to newsmagazines.

And she didn't do it for the money, either, that's the kicker. Local news outlets didn't hand out money for eyewitness quotes and interviews, and the 48 Hours interview was a onetime payout. She wasn't in it for the notoriety, of which there wasn't much anyway. She was rightfully ashamed of her appearance and also her undiagnosed agoraphobia.

There's really only one answer. You see, the reason she never flipped the switch for the garbage disposal, after scraping the mashed-up chocolate cake or leftover scrambled eggs or the remnants of a honey-baked ham sandwich into the sink was because at night, when my father was either working or in bed, and I was supposed to be asleep, my mother would return to the kitchen and eat all the day's food out of the drain. Even if the milk had curdled and the cold cuts were lukewarm, she'd scoop the mess out with her fingers and eat it all, swallow it without chewing.

I know because I caught her. She didn't see me, but I could clearly see what she was doing. The next night I stayed up and went downstairs at the same time, saw her doing it again. And the next night.

Then I stopped. Once would have been a fluke; twice a coincidence; but three times was a pattern. I was even more disgusted with her than before, a thing I didn't think possible. My mother literally ate our family's garbage, and not because she was such a big believer in food sustainability, but because she was a pig. And even actual pigs don't eat actual garbage—and they might even incorporate whole grains into their diet, something I don't think my mother ever did.

So it's a metaphor and it's not—she thrived on what I rejected, on what was distasteful or revolting to me, to us. She gorged herself on it.

Another way in which I'm not a survivor: a common result of the guilt is wishing you'd died too. I never wished for that, though I did often wish that somehow my mother had found herself in the path of Gordon Strong's shears.

# Gordon Strong

I 've been on the couch two days now, getting up to use the toilet but that's it. Every time I sit up or stand, my lower back goes into spasms. The pain's so intense tears jump to my eyes without me even thinking about it.

I've watched the kids come and go, and Evelyn, too—both days she's laid out a sandwich on a plate under a sheet of wax paper, and a bottle of lemonade on the floor next to me. I've maybe been a little rude to her in the mornings, but it's only on account of the pain. The second day I plan to make it up to her as soon as she comes home, tell her she looks nice, but when I hear the front door open, I hear her and a man's voice. Too old to be Brendan. I realize who it is just before they come into the living room.

Goddamn Chuck Strange.

Evelyn looks like she does when we've been on a pontoon boat—seasick and yellow—and I'm glad. She should know better. I glare at her, and she looks away.

Chuck's wearing blue scrubs, pretending to be an actual doctor.

"Well, hey, there, Gordon," he says, cheery. "Having some back problems?"

I almost say, *Gee whiz, Chuck, how'd you figure that out?* but Evelyn pipes up: "I thought maybe Chuck could take a look at you. Since he's in the medical profession."

"Medical profession," I say, feeling spit gathering in the corners of my mouth. "Say, Chuck, aren't you an orderly? Like a security guard?"

Chuck chuckles. He's a regular walking tongue twister: Chuckling Chuck Chuckles.

"That's what I said to Evelyn, truth be told," he says.

Where's a grown man get a phrase like that—"truth be told"? Sounds like a little old lady at her bridge club.

"He's not just an orderly," says Evelyn. "He's training to be a paramedic."

Chuck shrugs, all humble pie, which is bad enough, but then that sonofabitch has the balls to blush.

"'Training' is the key word there," he says. "I'm not sure I can help you here, Gordon—you probably need a chiropractor."

"That's okay, like I said," chirps Evelyn. "It would just be such a favor to us if you could take a look and, you know, give us your opinion."

"Take a look?" I say. "How exactly is he supposed to do that, Evelyn?"

Then they glance at each other, like this has already been discussed.

Evelyn touches the tips of her hair—her split ends, she calls them—and rubs them between her fingers, which is a thing I know she does when she's nervous.

"Yeah, maybe he could examine you," she says quietly.

"Examine me?" I repeat, not because I didn't hear her. Out of disbelief. "Like he wants me to bend over and cough?"

Chuck laughs like I made a grand old joke.

"I don't think you have to do that, Gordon," he says. "But if you're able to physically, you can turn on your side, and I can put a little bit of pressure on certain parts of your back, see where the hot spot is. Then I do know a guy at work—an orthopedic specialist. I could ask him what he thinks. Informally, you know?"

Evelyn gasps with relief.

"Oh, Chuck," she says. "That would just be incredible."

I roll my eyes, but since they're staring at each other, they don't see it. Incredible, amazing Chuck. Who knew we lived next door to a superhero?

"We'd only have you move as far as it's comfortable," he says to me, trying to sell me on it.

"That's just it, Chuck," I say. "This is the only position I can be in without it hurting like a motherfucker."

Evelyn winces at the profanity. Sometimes her fragile-flower act gets to be a little much.

"Got it," says Chuck, running his eyes from my feet to my head and back down again. "Let's try something, if you're game, Gordon. If it hurts, we won't do it. How does that sound?"

How does it sound, Chuck? It sounds like a hundred wet farts from a hundred fat pigs in the slop, that's what it sounds like.

Evelyn's almost yanking her hair out at this point.

"Gordon, please," she whispers.

It's not her begging that makes me say yes—that pathetic act makes me want to vomit—it's that I want to prove to her how stupid her idea is.

"Is this gonna be like one of those Christian southern revivals where you lay your hands on me and I go dancing down the aisle?"

Chuck laughs, and as much as I try not to, I laugh, too, because the sonofabitch is genuinely acting like he thinks I'm some kind of comedian.

"I don't know about that, but who knows, huh?"

Who knows, Chuck?

I glance at Evelyn, and now her hands are clasped, and I think wouldn't it just stick it to her if old Chuck jacked my back up even more, like for good? Then I'm thinking, maybe I could even sue him—I got no idea how rich or poor the Stranges are. I mean, their lawn looks like shit and who knows how many mortgages they have out on their house, but Lil can afford not to work, and they did get a new Mazda a couple years back, and come to think of it, Caroline's bike looked pretty shiny, so maybe they do have a few coins between the couch cushions.

I bet Savannah'd love a bike like that.

"Sure thing, Chuck, that sounds fine to me," I hear myself say. Weird how sometimes I don't even recognize my own voice.

Evelyn exhales and shuts her eyes for a second, and I can tell she's saying thank you to God in her head. She should really be thanking me, but now that I think about it she's been pretty short on thank-yous the past few years.

"Okay, then," says Chuck, still all smiles.

He squints at me, thinking hard. Then he says, "Evelyn, could we use a pillow? Not one of these," he says, pointing to the square couch pillows I've tossed to the floor. "A little longer—like a pillow you'd sleep on?"

"Yeah, sure thing," she says, and she hurries out of the room, just thrilled to have an assignment from old Chuck.

"My idea is we put the pillow under your knees," he says, "then your lower back will press down, into the couch. It'll take some pressure off those muscles."

I stare at him. I'm not smiling or nodding, not giving him the satisfaction.

"I got a friend at the hospital—he's a physical therapist. He says most times if you pull a muscle, it just needs some heat or ice and a little rest, but the pain's actually coming from the muscles surrounding the one that gets pulled." Chuck makes a fist. "They seize up. Usually just need a little pressure released."

"You don't say," I say to Chuck. "Tell me something, Chuck, did Evelyn call you up and ask you to come over here?"

Chuck rests his hands on his hips as he thinks about it, like it was so long ago.

"No, she rang the bell. I just finished my last class for the day, thought I'd come home and get some dinner before heading back to work." He laughs and shakes his head. "I gotta tell you, I'm burning the candle at both ends these days, Gordon."

I don't laugh along with him. It's like he knows I'm out of work and don't have a damn cent to pay for any kind of night school.

"You're a busy guy," I say.

"Yeah," he says, running his hand over his buzz cut. "It's a nutty time. But, you know, the crazy thing is that I'm actually kind of enjoying it." He laughs again, like he's heard another great joke.

Evelyn finally comes back with the pillow. It's one of ours, from our bed, and she hasn't even taken the pillowcase off. I get embarrassed about Chuck seeing my damn pillowcase; then I get angry thinking he and Lil probably have clean white sheets like they do at the hospital and not some flitty flower pattern.

He doesn't seem to notice, though, and takes the pillow. "Thanks, Evelyn." Then he kneels next to me, asks, "Okay, Gordon, do you think you can bend your knees at all?"

"Problem's with my back, not my knees," I say.

"Right you are," he says. "But it's all connected. Like that old song, you know? Leg bone's connected to the knee bone, so on."

Evelyn's grinning now, but her eyes are still wrinkled and worried, and it's pissing me off, her whole Mother Teresa act. It's like she's done something wrong and now she's trying to make it up to me with all the hand-wringing. A big part of me can't wait until Chuck leaves so I can lay into her about how idiotic this all is. My mouth almost waters at the thought of her shame.

"This might hurt when I'm sliding the pillow under," Chuck says, keeping his line of sight fixed on my lower back. "But it'll just be for a second."

I bend my right knee, and it feels there are a few hundred toothpick-sized bones creaking and crackling in my back, but I'll be damned if I'm going to give Chuck the satisfaction of seeing me in pain, so I keep my expression straight.

I must be pretty good at it, too, because he says, "That okay?" and I nod like it's no big deal.

"Great, let's try the other one."

I bend my left knee, and now the spasm starts, like an electrified belt curling and snapping against my spine, and I can feel the poker face melting off because I can't hide how much it hurts.

"Gordon—" says Evelyn, and in her eyes now is pity.

I've seen her look like that before. Never with me, but once when we were just kids dating, we went up camping with a bunch of friends in Door County. I hit a beaver with my car, and the thing died in front of us. I grew up in a rural area, so I've seen plenty of them, but Evelyn never had, being from Madison, so didn't know they were that big. Or that cute. Or dumb. And now that's how she's looking at me.

Chuck's sure as hell not looking at my face, still staring at my back shaking and quivering, and I think, Great, boy, you keep staring and doing nothing and I'll have that much more ammo when I sue your ass.

But then he pushes the pillow under my knees and right after slides his hands under my lower back, and suddenly the pressure's off my back completely; it sinks down onto Chuck's palms, and tears burst from my eyes again, but from relief this time.

I gasp without meaning to, and Chuck moves his fingers just a little, massaging the muscles around the spasm gently.

"You okay, Gordon?"

I nod, unable to speak.

"Good," he says. "It's real important you tell me if what I'm doing is hurting in a bad way."

I try to laugh, but it comes out a cough.

"How'm I supposed to know if it's a bad way or a good way?"

Chuck smiles. "That's one of those things they don't even teach you in medical school," he says. "You just know."

I look at Evelyn, and she's not looking at me like a dying beaver or a healthy man. She's not looking at me at all. She's looking at Chuck. He's right about one thing: I just know.

# Dr. Caroline

First up is Deluded Delia, who showed up to our first appointment three years ago in a non-PETA-approved real fur coat and leather pants. She is sad because her husband works a lot to pay for all her shit, and she wonders if he does it because he doesn't like her. Which reminds her of how she used to wonder the same thing about her father, who also worked long hours to pay for all her shit.

I've counseled many of these finance/tech/media wives whose husbands make absurd amounts of money and live in condos that make my little brownstone look like a shoebox fairy house. They're mostly lonely because they have two or three nannies for the kids, and they have their brunchy girlfriends, and they have their personal trainers, but what's it all about, right?

If I knew Delia as a friend or even an acquaintance, I would say, *Either you get to see your husband every day or you can barely see him and cry about it curled into a ball on the floor of your massive walk-in closet.*

But for Delia, my patient, I have to take a different tack.

She, of course, shops to fill the void. Furniture, mostly, because I guess she has so many clothes and accessories already it doesn't give her the coveted dopamine gush. So now she spends her time at show-rooms and online with craft builders in Germany, Italy, Japan—the triple axis of interior design—spending tens of thousands of her husband's possibly hard-earned dollars.

Still, she doesn't know why she does it; when I push her to make the connection, she can't see it. I can almost hear her thinking, like the lonely drip from a busted faucet.

Also, being honest, she's just not the most emotionally aware.

"It's not a good feeling," she says, big blink from the sunken dry eyes.

So I try to help. That's why I'm here.

"Delia, when is a moment you're satisfied?"

Plucked brow furrows. Make it simpler.

I try again: "What's your favorite food, Delia?"

"I have this beet-and-greens smoothie at Juicy Lucy twice a week," she says right away.

I smile politely to indicate I've heard her, but then continue: "Did you have any cravings when you were pregnant with your kids—pancakes with a lot of syrup, salty chips, milkshakes?"

"Oh, with Emmy I loved grilled cheese," she says wistfully.

"Grilled cheese," I say. "Let's say you're pregnant and you're craving a grilled cheese and you eat one—how do you feel?"

She thinks. "Full?"

"Full," I say. "Is it a good feeling?"

More thinking. "Yeah, I'm not hungry anymore."

"Because you're full," I say, pointing at her.

"Yeah," she says, smiling and nodding.

"And there's an element of peace there."

She nods again.

"So how is that feeling different from the feeling you have after you click the mouse on the *Buy Now* button or swipe the credit card at the showroom?"

She squints.

I continue: "When you eat that comfort food, and you're satisfied, you're . . ."

I let it dangle, hoping against hope she can fill in the blank.

"Full?" she says.

"Yes. Full," I say. "And that's different from the other feeling, the bad feeling, because then you feel . . ."

I let it hang again, but she doesn't grab. There could be a retro-Vegas sign flashing above my head, one letter lighting up at a time— E-M-P-T-Y—and she still wouldn't get it.

"Shopping isn't like grilled cheese," she says finally.

"No," I say, masking a sigh with a tiny cough. "It's not. We have to pause here, so we can pick up with that next time."

When she leaves, it's only noon, but I'm exhausted. I was up until one-thirty printing everything I could find about myself on the internet. My goal was to test out Makeda's theory, put myself in Billy's shoes. Let's say a person was obsessed with li'l old me, how would he piece together such a puzzle?

The sheets sit stacked next to the printer facedown. That is apparently what I'm reduced to: thirty or forty hits. I have a few minutes before my next patient arrives, so I take the stack of sheets along with a roll of double-sided tape and go into the kitchen.

I stare at the blank wall opposite the sink and fridge for a moment, perhaps like an artist does. Not Jonas, though. A more gifted artist. A Kusama, a Basquiat, someone on fire. No offense to darling husband. His talent is comprised mostly of confidence, which most people in the art world just gobble right up. It's not like what I do, where one can't fake it.

I begin taping up the sheets of paper: every quote of mine from the *Milwaukee Journal Sentinel*, my LinkedIn profile, my Columbia medical page, the donors' list from the boys' school, my articles in *Psychiatry Today* and *Thought Process and Research*, the transcripts from panels at Johns Hopkins and UCSF, talks I gave at the University of Michigan and Stanford, top ten "ones to watch" of recent psychiatry program grads, and, of course, Ellen Garcia's piece in *Brooklyn Bound*. Number two out of the top ten worst doctors in the borough. I'd be lying if I said it didn't bother me to not make number one. To at least be the absolute worst.

I've actually read the article a number of times. It's not poorly written, if you excuse the shoddy research and creative conclusions. I have committed a few turns of phrase to memory, but now I reread the most salacious bits in an effort to see them fresh, the way Billy might have:

"A former patient who wished to remain anonymous told me Strange ridiculed her for not admitting she was at least partially responsible for her own sexual assault."

Allow me to explain.

I know exactly who this anonymous source is, first of all. It's Tawdry Twyla, whom I saw professionally for about a year. If Ellen Garcia had asked her any meaningful pointed questions instead of doubtlessly leaving the door wide open for Twyla's interpretation, Ellen would have quickly discovered that Twyla liked to engage in rape-fantasy narratives with her biker boyfriend, so I merely suggested she should perhaps take some responsibility in Big Drake or Big Jake or whoever getting rough with her. I did so because she explicitly asked him to get rough with her. As consenting adults do.

Twyla didn't like me for the same reason all quitters don't: they aren't interested in the truth. When she broke it off, she said apologetically, "I just don't think I'm getting a lot out of this," which is an excuse I've heard many times before, and my response to Twyla should have been, *Of course you're not. You're an obstinate child who wants things to change but has no interest in doing anything differently.*

Ellen has another source, and this one is more slippery. A quote: "She makes you call her Dr. Caroline. Like what is this—kindergarten?"

She goes on to say how I infantilized and patronized her and made her feel unsafe, which bruised her fragile sensibilities and reminded her of her bossy mother, the very demon she'd come to me to exorcise, which, frankly, could be the chief complaint from at least half of my female patients.

BrooklynBound.com gets an estimated two hundred thousand readers per month, and while it's hard to say exactly how many of those readers might have skimmed a portion of Ellen Garcia's article, or simply glanced just below the title, where the names of the ten worst doctors were listed, bolded and bullet-pointed to make it easy on the tired eyes of the pandemic-fatigued reader, the rag is whoringly exhibitionistic with its analytics, posting a "click counter" at the bottom of every piece. And "Top Ten Worst Doctors in Brooklyn" got upward of forty-eight hundred clicks.

Almost five thousand people read that trash about me. What I didn't tell anyone, not even Jonas and certainly not Makeda, was that I lost patients over it. I mean, I can't be certain the article was the definitive culprit, but the coincidence in timing seemed suspicious. They all doled out excuses that I've heard before and that many times are true (money, schedule, "just don't think I'm a therapy person"), but I doubt it was the case for any of these ship-jumpers.

It didn't cripple my income but it stung in sneaky ways. Now, if there's some quack with an online degree on Eastern Parkway hoodwinking patients with essential oils and theremin sounds, then yes, such a person deserves to be called out. And I know I can't speak for anyone else on the list—dermatologists, ENTs, orthopedists—but I know I'm trying to help people, and this is where Ellen's sloppy work fails. If she had spent an hour talking to some of my other patients, or even if she'd asked Tawdry Twyla a few more questions—she might be dumb, but she's still smart enough to know that she feels better leaving my office than she does when she comes in—Ellen would've seen how much I can do for people. And if I were on the best doctors list instead of the worst, then those forty-eight hundred users might think, I could use a doctor like her, and they would have found actual genuine support and solutions instead of a quick chuckle over their coffee.

It turns out if I *had* wanted to find Ellen Garcia to ask her, *Who the hell do you think you are ruining people's lives writing this shit for which you barely get paid?* I wouldn't have had to look very hard.

First I looked her up in the archives on *Brooklyn Bound* to see what tickled her poison pen before the "Ten Worst Doctors" piece. Most of her stories were puff pieces; the only somewhat meaningful story was about an exiled group of squatters in Sunset Park—it made the reader root for them, while also unexpectedly portraying the management company as not complete capitalist pigs. I thought it an impressive trick and wondered why she couldn't have applied such an even hand to the "Ten Worst Doctors" piece.

But I didn't wonder for long. The squatter story click counter read, "267"—a shriveled weenie of a number next to the hulking dick that was "4,811" clicks for the Ten Worst.

A baity story that bashed a person's reputation was just worth more.

I may have also seen some of her posts on *South Slope Rant*, where she and her neighbors routinely complained about a city contractor who wouldn't clear a nearly block-long line of dumpsters. It only took me one or two walks during a canceled patient appointment time to find such a block.

And she'd provided enough detail in her comments for me to narrow down her building (she described her view into a nearby dumpster as "peering into a black hole of scrap metal topped with a sprinkling of construction dust"), so I easily found the dumpster and deduced a few houses where she could potentially live—all of them those beaten-up row-style South Slope specials. Up the stoops I went, and on my second try I found what I was looking for—the name printed on a sticker from an office label-maker next to a buzzer the size and color of a black licorice square: GARCIA.

I've said it before: it's small, this world, and the people in it. I could find Ellen Garcia in an afternoon, and Billy could find me, so why would Makeda or anyone be surprised when connections happen between supposedly disparate people?

My next patient is an actress. At first I called her Soppy Sophia—in her thirties, did all the right things, got an MFA, worked the Shakespeare festivals. Now she does voice-over work for commercials, although she had to move back home with her parents during COVID, because there was no work, period. Let's all take a moment to mourn the struggling artists who couldn't even foam lattes for tips during the shutdown. Now she is back in town and auditioning and sometimes working, although her true craft is disordered eating, achieving a nearly superheroic level of obsession, and so she has earned the revised name: Dysmorphia.

I find myself having respect for her commitment, thinking if she put half the energy into preparing for auditions as she did for pinching the nonexistent skin around her waist and ruminating into self-distortion insanity, she could probably be the next Meryl Streep. Or at least the next Blake Lively.

We go around and around, and toward the end of our session the door buzzer rings, and she jumps, her frail bones disturbed by the disruption, and I swear silently at UPS or FedEx because, yes, they're heroes for working through the pandemic, risking their lives to bring us dried fruit and dish soap, but Jesus God, do they not see the sign that is hard to miss right over the doorbell that reads PLEASE DELIVER ALL PACKAGES UPSTAIRS?

Dysmorphia recovers and gets a little glassy-eyed as we wrap up—a lot of patients do, not necessarily because they're sad to leave, but because they're already thinking of the next thing; they're already planning how they're going to ignore everything they've learned in treatment and go about their day and business as if we've never spoken. Even though we've spent an hour discussing healthy patterns and habits, Dysmorphia's literally counting the calories in the seven Tic Tacs she's going to have for lunch in her head.

But hopefully a word or two, or even a whole sentence, will stick, like those money booth arcade games where the players have to grab the dollars flying by. Maybe Dysmorphia will catch one, and that will be the one that saves her. Maybe it will be me saying I knew she'd have a nice long life; or maybe it will be when I said she could have anything she wanted, all she'd have to do is decide. Maybe she'll think about one of those things and for that one day she'll say, Okay, I'll have a slice of bread and a string cheese and an apple, and tomorrow I'll go back to the Tic Tacs and the Diet Coke.

That is what breaking an addiction is, by the way—grasping one or two words flying by each hour of each day, on and on.

Sometimes I think I could have gone into high-end rehab, lived in Aspen or Jackson Hole or Santa Fe, run a clinic on top of a big red rock. Sunrise yoga and macrobiotic local food. Group therapy and individual therapy and mud mask therapy. It would be like my own little cult except I would want the members to leave so new people could come and pay through their coke-blasted noses.

When Dysmorphia leaves, I check my phone and see that I have a voicemail. I have fifteen minutes before Cracker Jack Carl shows up. He's made a mess of his life again and again—relationships, jobs, finances—and it's all because of his parents, who treated him quite nicely by his account, divorced when he was seven, and had the nerve to co-parent amicably. So he earned his nickname from me because underneath all that sticky stuff there's just the flimsiest little temporary tattoo and no greater prize of a tragedy. Not yet, anyway.

On my voicemail, an unknown number.

I tap.

"Well, hey, Doc, you know who this is by now, don't you?"

I like to think I'm mostly in control of sensations that come and go in my body, but the chills spreading on the crown of my head are unexpected.

On the voicemail, he laughs.

"Hear you met Billy. That kid—I'd let him out more, but he just won't listen. You have kids, Doc, you know how it is when they do shit that's against their own good."

I can hear him sigh.

"Too bad you didn't pick up. I would've let you talk to Ellen. Oh well," he calls in a singsong, and that's it.

I stare at the screen, my hand shaking, and I tap the voicemail again with my thumb so I can listen again, but then Jonas calls and I try to tap decline but instead, somehow, I click the little red garbage can and delete Nelson's message.

"Fuck," I yell, and I press my index finger deliberately on the accept button. "What is it?!"

Normally Jonas would chuckle or gently rib me for answering so brusquely, but his voice is so cold and disengaged it makes me realize something's not normal.

"There are three people here to see you," he says.

But then it becomes clear that it's not just unusual, it's extremely wrong, when he adds, "You should come right now, Caroline."

Caroline.

I run up the stairs. Makeda and Miguel are in my living room, along with a white guy who can't be older than twenty-two, black jeans and black muscle-man T-shirt, black latex gloves, and a forearm tattoo of a wolf or a tiger or some other animal that's supposed to tell me he doesn't take any crap.

"He just called me," I say urgently, holding my phone out to them. "Just now. Nelson . . . Billy."

Miguel glances at Makeda and seems excited, as he should be, but Makeda's face is straight up, no chaser, as my dad would say. No-Crap-Taker blinks at me above his surgical mask. We're all just standing around the living room looking at each other, like we're about to play Twister.

"Okay," says Makeda, pulling an envelope from her inside pocket. "Dr. Strange, we have a warrant signed by a judge to search your electronic devices. Officer Colling," she says, gesturing to No-Crap-Taker, "can perform the search here if you prefer, or if not, we can remove them from the premises and return them to you tomorrow."

I take the envelope from her hand and pass it to Jonas.

"Here," I say, handing my phone to Colling. "I am literally surrendering my phone to you. Start with the last voicemail. I might have deleted it accidentally, but it's got to be on there somewhere. Nelson left it for me during my last session, which means within the past hour."

"Caroline," Jonas says.

He's a calm person, and he trusts me. He's also a natural exhibitionist and frequently walks naked in front of uncovered windows, but like most of us, he's a little grabby about his shit and doesn't necessarily want people messing with it, especially seeing photos of his pieces before they're finished.

"It's all right," I tell him. "A woman is missing, and a patient who came to see me for a consult may be involved." Then I turn back to the police and say, "That's all you'll need. The message, it's there."

Officer Colling is just a pair of dull blue eyes above his mask. He hasn't made a move to get into the phone.

"Okay," says Makeda. "But we'll also need any laptops, desktops, tablets that belong to you." She has a stern but somewhat pleased look.

"That's fine!" I say. "I'm telling you, it's fine. I want you to look at this. If you find that message, if you find all of them, from Nelson and Billy, maybe you can trace them to an IP address," I say to Colling.

I remember having to identify an IP address for a library computer in med school. Do they still exist?

"Caroline," says Jonas.

"It's all right," I say to him again, over my shoulder. "Let them look. I want to get to the bottom of this, too, as much as you do," I say to Makeda. "Maybe even more."

I don't mean to sound spiteful, but it creeps out. Because I realize I do want it more than her. Finding Ellen Garcia to her is just a job, a file the sarge dropped onto her desk. Suddenly it feels more urgent than simply beating her to the punch—for me, now, it feels like it's my purpose.

"Caroline," says Jonas again.

"What?" I say, turning my head in his direction.

He hands me the paper he's removed from the envelope, and I scan it quickly. Warrant of the Southern District Court of New York, Honorable Gina T. Solomon. There's a crooked case number, and then I see what Jonas has been trying to tell me. It's in the description of the affidavit, what Makeda wrote to get the judge to grant the warrant in the first place:

"Affidavit having been made before me by Detective Makeda Marks of the 78th Precinct, who has reason to believe that on the premises known as . . ."

Our address is listed then, and then it reads, "there is now concealed property, namely digital records, laptops, smartphones, desktop computers, which contain potential documentary evidence relating to Ellen Garcia, missing person."

Then there's some more language about how they only have ten days to perform the search, how they have to leave me a copy, so I can stick it on the fridge next to the DONUT FORGET DONUTS magnetic shopping list.

I turn the sheet of paper over to see if there's anything else.

"That's it?" I say. "There's nothing about Nelson or Billy, who just called, just now."

I point to my phone again in Colling's hand, in case they've missed the point.

"Perhaps your husband can retrieve the devices, and you and I can keep talking if you like," says Makeda.

Placating me. Like I'm the patient.

"If you find that message, if you trace the numbers, you'll find him," I say slowly. "Your suspect."

"Caroline," Jonas whispers, something damaged in his tone.

I finally turn to face him.

"What is it?" I say through my teeth. I almost feel the need to add a cursory, *Can't you see I'm in the middle of something?*

I notice the paper in his hand is moving, as if a fan is blowing gusts right at it, but then I see it's Jonas who's moving. Shaking. He once carved out three hundred perfect eyes with a scalpel on a bar of soap. The sculpture was called *Comfort*.

"It's you," he says, like we're the only two people in the room. "The suspect is you."

I can feel the cortisol spiking from my adrenals, my kidneys practically glowing with it, as my tongue dries up and shrinks. "Mr. Thirsty," my children's dentist has named the tube that sucks the moisture from their mouths when they get their teeth cleaned. Right now it's like Mr. Thirsty has made me his bitch ten times over.

I turn back to face Makeda. She seems pleased and is actually not trying too hard to hide it. I swear I see her plum-shaded lips curling at the corners in glee.

"You're not a suspect, Dr. Strange," she says. "You're what we call a person of interest."

We all let that one sit in the air for a minute. Then Makeda turns her head the slightest bit toward Miguel and Colling and gives a nod.

"If you can bring any portable devices to them here, that would be helpful. Assuming it's okay if they perform the searches at your counter?" she says, pointing to the kitchen. Miguel and Colling head that way. Without receiving a response, she continues: "If you have desktops, Colling can examine them wherever they're located."

I hear Jonas begin to move behind me.

"There are iPads upstairs," he mutters. "Our sons'."

"That'd be great!" I hear Miguel chirp, like he's been offered a goddamn lemonade.

Makeda and I stare at each other.

So many breakthroughs, so close together. If a patient were experiencing this in a session, I would encourage her to engage in some thoughtful journaling when she got home so that she could remember everything.

One—Makeda is smarter and more duplicitous than I gave her credit for.

Two—I don't know what specific documentary evidence she's looking for, but sure, if it's a spindly little search history and drafts of the emails she already has, she'll be able to see them all.

Three—She thinks I've done something terrible.

Four—She doesn't know the half of it.

# Ellen Garcia

Something happened with that flash. I know I haven't eaten in a while (has it been an hour or six hours or twelve?), but I keep remembering this guy who's abducted me—I think I have seen him before.

I put out a story a couple months ago about the ten worst doctors in Brooklyn. It was pretty fun and easy to do the research—you'd be surprised, or maybe you wouldn't, about how many people want to talk trash about their health care professionals. Some of them are genuinely awful, most of them male doctors making female patients feel like they're blowing up their own symptoms, classic misogynistic gaslighting. But a couple of women made the cut, and boy oh boy were they legendary.

I was proud of it, and I wasn't proud. I'd worked like hell on the Sunset Park story in late 2019. I talked to everyone, chased every lead, wrote late nights after Bella went to sleep and early mornings before she woke up, but I didn't feel tired because I had this thing, the turning worm of journalistic integrity spiking optimism and creativity through my fingers to the keyboard, generating thirty-five hundred words of pure Pulitzer gold dust. Because it was about everything; it was the squatters' story; it was the management company's story; it was the neighbors' story; it was Brooklyn's story. It was about how they, how we, were all connected whether they wanted to be or not.

And then seven people read it.

It was a downer. It didn't make anyone laugh. It was meme-less. It was written for a pre-COVID audience, but there was no place for it post-COVID, either.

So, sure, I say to all the forces plotting against me and my Pulitzer, you want clicks, you want hits, you want something funny that'll get retweeted? You got it.

Back in November 2020, I'm out at Mission Dolores with Dulcey, crying on her shoulder, thankful that we can even be at a bar, even if we're sitting outside and it starts to rain and we're pulling our masks up between sips (at least during the first drink; at some point the lack of mask-wearing becomes proportional to the amount of alcohol consumed—classic COVID math), but we're not moving—no one in the little courtyard's moving—because all any of us want to do is cry into our masks on each other's shoulders and drink in the rain, and I'm saying to her who the fuck asks for a divorce during a pandemic, and she's like half the population; the other half proposes.

Then a couple comes in, and she knows the guy, and they do an air fist bump, and she invites them to sit. They worked together at Reuters ten years ago; his name is Jonathan or Jackson or Jimathan—is that a name, Jimathan? And he's with a woman who's sucking down vodka tonics no fruit at a respectable pace, whom I'm enjoying talking to largely because she's providing a decent distraction from the anxiety of my pending divorce and the mashed-potato mountain of logistics involving my kid pulsing behind my eyeballs. But then she proves to be interesting.

Interesting in the way journalists find interesting, or, more specifically, exactly in the way I need someone to be interesting at that moment in time. Like as if the gods of bougie culture and style rags gazed down upon me in that rainy courtyard as I wept about tanking my own marriage and was trying to pin it on my ex, and bestowed the single greatest gift a journalist could pray for: a source.

She asks if I know any therapists in the neighborhood. At first I'm thinking physical therapists, because everything in my body hurts at all times, all the writerly pains from the home office setup, crammed into a corner of my non-eat-in-kitchen, laptop flipped open between the toaster and the coffee machine—hips and upper back and neck wrenched, forearms sore from typing with them slightly raised off the counter, and then my hands and fingers—don't get me started on the ballad of the strained pinkies, the most overworked little digits, always striving, constantly reaching for the *a* and the apostrophe.

I start to tell her about the Chinese massage on Seventh Ave, where the guy beats the crap out of you for thirty minutes for forty dollars and you feel maybe as if you've gained a few months of your life back when you leave. Not necessarily a new person but in slightly newer packaging.

"No, not that kind," she says, and by the way she swills the rest of her drink, I get it.

"Oh, *therapy* therapy," I say, and she nods with her mouth full of ice. "I can't help you there; I haven't been in a while."

She shrugs kind of sadly, like, *Lucky you.* Now I feel like I want to make her laugh. I have this thing; Chris says it used to be a thing he loved about me but came to view as a major personality flaw: I'm a people-pleaser. I want to make them laugh, but not because I get off on the attention—I want *them* to feel happy.

"You want to know why?" I say.

She shrugs again. Sure.

"They're all out-of-network," I say, throwing my hands up.

She laughs. And then she begins to talk, the words sputtering forth like a Bellagio fountain stream. She's unhappy, something about PTSD and feeling stuck in her job and is a big procrastinator and really is in want of some benzos to just gnaw the edges off before bedtime, and a few months before the pandemic she was referred by a friend of a friend to a shrink in Park Slope, a woman who handed out sedatives without a lot of explanation required, like a priest holding up a Valium and placing one on the tongue of each member of his congregation. *This is the body and the blah-blah, but really it's just, this is what you get for showing up, my child.*

My new friend tells me it isn't just for the drugs that she's seeking therapy, even though I assure her, I am in no place to judge. Live and let fucking live is my motto, and frankly die and let die for those who want to go that route.

She was sad! Is sad! Always been sad. Something shitty happened when she was a kid, and she still thinks about it, the thing she saw and how she felt, the fight-or-flight is like stuck inside her and tells her to do things, or more accurately tells her not to do things, like her inner child, this little knot of dysfunction with a voice like Elmo: *Me no like engaging with other people* . . . That's more Cookie Monster, but you get it.

And she wanted to finally get some help with it and, yes, maybe also some pills, so January of 2020 she goes to see this lady and says she's wearing all white like a televangelist with four-inch heels, impeccable makeup, and styled layered hair like she's just had a blowout. She notices the office smells like a particular perfume. Turns out my new friend works in cosmetics marketing, naming lip glosses, actually (which coincidentally is a job I think I'd be good at, especially for a late-thirties/early-forties drunk divorcée demographic: "Dance of Desperation"; "Gummy Bear Breakfast"; "Coffee Breath"). Apparently if you're on this particular career path you get samples of everything, all the little vials and foil pouches, and my friend recognizes the scent in the shrink's office because apparently it's that distinctive—Amber Aoud. Seven hundred bucks for three and a half ounces, and she, my new friend, feels a little intimidated. Like maybe she doesn't feel like barfing up her soul and begging for drugs to this one-percenter who probably secretly voted for Trump because she wishes he wasn't such a meanie but justifies it because she's portfolio-forward.

Long story short, my new friend takes it as some kind of flex, like, *You, too, can aspire to break out of your pathetic little life to one day be like me of the highlighted hair and pricy fragrance.*

So then comes the best part—Shrink with the Good Hair says to call her Dr. Caroline; that's what all her patients call her.

"Like what is this—kindergarten?" says my new friend.

"Right?" I say, taking a shot of Don Julio. I keep talking: "I've been to a few shrinks in my life . . . I don't remember calling them anything, like I'm talking all about myself, when do you even refer to them by name?"

"Totally!" she says, scrolling down her phone, looking for the contact info for this Dr. Caroline to give to me.

"It's not like you're with her at the club on the weekend introducing her around and are like these are my friends, Ross, Rachel, and Dr. Caroline."

"So true!" says my new friend, snorting with laughter.

Then it hits me—I blame the liquor for it not hitting me sooner—for the piece I've been focusing on physical medical care, mostly general practitioners. MDs only. I hadn't even thought of therapists, and my mind explodes with the idea of a spin-off piece—"The Ten Worst Mental Health Professionals in Brooklyn"—but for now, for this piece, I'm thinking pretentious Dr. Caroline would be perfect.

I buy another round of shots, and she starts telling me about her mom, and then about how she tried to adopt a pandemic dog with one eye, and then she asks if I trust Instacart. The frequent subject-shift tells me she's good and sauced, so I pop the question: Can I use her as a source?

She slurs, "Only if I can stay anony-mybous."

I'm, like, of course, my dear, and then I ask if I can get the contact info for the friend of a friend, the one who referred her to Dr. Caroline in the first place, and she sends it to me—I'm swishing my third shot like mouthwash as I watch the text pop up on my screen with the name *Twyla*.

Eventually we all part ways. I get home and pass out on the couch, which also happens to be my bed. Since splitting from Chris, I have a one-bedroom, and the bedroom isn't much to look at but it has a door, and I wanted Bella to feel like she could shut herself in there and talk to her little ponies and big-head dolls and create little narratives for them with a modicum of privacy. She doesn't need me listening in or offering commentary about her storylines. No one likes to be edited.

So I sleep on the couch, even on the nights when Bella's at Chris's. It's actually fine for me, because I sleep like shit wherever I am no matter what I've had to eat or drink, so I'm hashtag-grateful to be so consistent in that regard.

I wake up around six, ready. Feeling like I'm made of eggshells, but ready.

I call Twyla later that morning and leave a voicemail. I like to make calls for the initial contact as opposed to email or text. People are afraid of not responding to a phone call. Emails and texts are easier to delete and lie about not knowing they exist. On my voicemail I briefly describe the piece, explain how my new friend gave me her information. Less than five minutes pass before a text comes through that wakes up every hormone in my dull hungover body: "Yes would love to talk. She should not be practicing!!!!"

Four exclamation points. What could merit more than the predetermined over-the-top enthusiasm of three exclamation points?

When we speak later on, Twyla says of the doctor, "First of all, she's a total slut-shamer," and she tells me how she went to therapy in the first place to talk about her being sexually abused by her boyfriend, and then she says something really fast about how they dabble in some lowercase s&m. But there's a little street noise behind her, and she says it so quickly I don't really hear it.

So I don't write it down.

And now I have my two confirmed sources, which is enough for Neditor and more than enough for me, anony-mybous or not, and Dr. Caroline Shrinkie-Dearest Victim-Blamer gets the silver, second only to Dr. Fungus/Flesh-Eating Virus.

I start researching Dr. Caroline online, and it turns out she has an absolutely bananas backstory, but I think how Neditor would tell me once again about his triumvirate of acceptable content: "True? Yes. Clicky? Yes. Relevant? No." I know I have to keep focus, and there's actually plenty to work with.

I find a few photos of her, and she's attractive, clear skin with defined cheekbones, or maybe she just knows how to contour with makeup. Good hair, quality highlight job, and definitely not the Féria special I do for myself in the bathroom with the flimsy plastic gloves that come in the box.

There is a professional-looking color headshot I study for a few minutes, in which I can see the color of her eyes. Blue—not quite tropical, but paint-can turquoise like the bottom of a suburban swimming pool.

I call her office number and listen to her outgoing message: "Hello, you've reached Dr. Caroline Strange. If this is an emergency, please hang up and dial 911 or proceed to your nearest emergency room. Otherwise leave a message at the tone, and I'll get back to you as soon as I can." She's got the standard nice-and-steady therapist voice. I love how they all recommend dialing 911, seeing as the last place you'd want to be if you're experiencing any kind of suicidal or homicidal thoughts is a Brooklyn emergency room.

Then the electro-spin of my mind turns back, and I remember how in the interest of totally serious subject research, I decided to get a whiff of Dr. Caroline's signature scent: Amber Aoud. I made an appointment at Saks because that's what you had to do to get through the door—gone were the days when you had to dodge the painted ladies spritzing you with unwanted scents. Now I had to go in at my appointed time to meet a dedicated sales associate (Alisha, wearing a shade of gloss I would call "Mature Carnival") and try to inhale through my mask what two hundred an ounce smells like. Which, as it turns out, at first sniff, is really fucking strong. Like smoke from a musky campfire that I can feel in the back of my throat. But then I smell it again, and somehow it's turned sweet, like the woods but without the shitty mulchy part of the woods and just the essence of the woods, of nature, of life. Even though it makes me sneeze like all perfumes do, I think I could see myself spritzing my wrists and around my hair every day with this stuff, might keep it in one of those crystal bottles with a squeeze bulb and a little tassel like Miss Piggy backstage.

You think I'm exaggerating, well, I would, too, if I hadn't smelled it myself. Because you and I can't afford that kind of distilled transcendence. We have to settle for our Designer Imposters Body Sprays and maybe a CBD-infused essential oil now and again.

I put it in the first draft, and it was such a damn good detail, but Neditor zapped it anyway (*Objection! Relevance, Your Honor!* read his comment in the margin). I'd responded to his comment super-aggressively with the approved three exclamation points: *Shows how she flaunts her wealth in the patients' faces!!!* No dice.

That smell from the other day (or hour? this morning? yesterday?), I thought it was perfume. The manicured hand, the eyes. Did I see a glimpse of the ankle when I hit the concrete—shaven and white?

Then it hits me, the realization so potent it forces my sandbag head up about an inch off the floor as I say aloud, "Shit."

Because how dumb of me not to think of it before, to know that Neditor was dead wrong—that everything is relevant, everything, and Dr. Caroline's backstory-now-with-extra-crazy actually makes a ton of sense, because maybe it had more of an effect on her besides just in-spiring her to embark on a life of service in the mental health field.

Maybe seeing the work of a psychopath up close actually turned her into one.

# Dr. Caroline

I tell Jonas everything as we stand huddled on the top of our stoop, just outside the front door. He smokes a Swedish cigarette he rolled himself, a habit he indulges in when he's drunk or nervous. We glance through the living room window to the kitchen, where Makeda and Miguel and Colling examine my laptop. They have Jonas's as well but are demonstrably not as interested in his. It sits off to the side along with the boys' iPads.

I've put in a call to a lawyer I know, Reggie Ginsburg, whose son was tight with Theo when they were littler. They seem to have grown apart as they approach middle school, but Reggie is quite well known in the space, having successfully defended a state senator last year for laundering just a teensy amount of his campaign funds. The guy still went to jail for a few months, but it was one of those cushy jails with the five-hundred-thread-count towels and tennis courts, not so much the cigarette trades and soap-dropping.

"They think you're a team?" Jonas asks me. "You and who's-it—Harbin?"

"I honestly don't know what they think," I say, although I have some ideas. "All I know is that I've been completely forthcoming about everything."

"Not everything, Doctor," Jonas says, as nonconfrontationally as he possibly can.

"I've told them what they need to know," I say. "I don't want to cloud the process with extraneous information."

"O-kay," he says, drawing out the second syllable with a skeptical note.

I sigh. "They don't *need* to know about my history; they don't *need* to know I took a walk to try to find him . . ."

My thought drifts off. I did tell Jonas I tried to find him and he'd clearly given me a fake address, but I didn't tell him that the street and building numbers were the same as my birthday and age. Because I didn't want to cloud his process, either.

Jonas lets go of the line anyway and goes back to Billy Harbin.

"So you believe there are two personalities in one man—that he has the disorder?"

"No," I say. "I think the diagnosis is bullshit. But he's convinced himself of it, so it is actually a six-of-one thing."

Jonas turns away from the window and points his cigarette toward me.

"You don't think anyone has it?"

"No," I say. "It's a trend diagnosis. Gets popular and everyone thinks he/she/they have it."

"It might be real," Jonas muses, shrugging. "Like in that movie . . . you remember that movie?"

"What movie?" I say, beginning to get pissed that he would disagree with me on this. "There are a hundred movies, but they are movies, Jonas. With screenplays and sets and costumes. They're not documentaries."

"No, I know that, but this one I saw on cable, it was quite believable. It made a good argument. The guy is bald and he has many personalities, and one of the bad ones kidnaps three girls. It sounds like what's happening with your Billy. *Spilt*, I think it's called."

"Spilt? As in milk?"

"Yes, *Spilt*. Directed by that guy—you know, the Nightman."

"What the *fuck* are you talking about?"

Sometimes Jonas's English-as-a-second-language thing is adorable, sometimes hot, and sometimes just absolutely maddening. But we're so caught up in the discussion, we don't notice that Makeda has come to the door.

We stop talking immediately, conspicuously, and Jonas throws his cigarette to the ground like Makeda's going to bust him for smoking.

"We're all done for now," she says. "Just need a minute and then we'll be out of your way."

Jonas and I glance at each other, then at her.

"Would you . . . like to come back inside?" she says.

You mean to my house that I paid for. Yes, Makeda, I would love that.

"Yes, thanks," I say, and we follow her in.

Colling is packing up his stuff, his phone and cords and USBs, into a black messenger bag, and Miguel is lining up all our devices on the island in a nice little row. He's got a great future at the Apple Store if all this crime-fighting doesn't work out.

"We didn't find anything," says Makeda.

The sensation of relief is somehow unexpected, but, boy, can I feel it physically. Like being a kid in a suffocatingly hot Midwest summer again and holding a sputtering garden hose at the base of my neck. Then I remember I'm pissed off.

"Are you sure you're supposed to tell me that?" I say.

"We've been fully transparent with you about what we're doing here," says Makeda. "We had to follow a trail. If it ended here," she says, gesturing to the devices, "we'd take the next appropriate step."

"Which would be arresting me, right?" I say.

"More questions first," she says.

"And now?"

Makeda doesn't blink when she looks at me. "More questions."

"I'd like you to know I've called my attorney," I say.

DR. CAROLINE

I can practically feel a breeze from her mental eye roll. I am guessing I am not the first rich white person to say that to her.

"That's fine," she says. "You don't have to answer any more questions if you prefer not to."

Prefer not to. She's trying to Bartleby me, goddammit, and it is absolutely infuriating.

"I prefer to help you find Ellen Garcia," I say slowly. "Isn't that the goal here?"

"Yes," says Makeda.

I'm a little surprised she agrees with me so quickly, but I recover and add, "Did you find the numbers, the unknowns?"

I turn to Colling and Miguel, say to them both, "Did you find the texts from Nelson Schack? Can you trace that number?"

Colling doesn't answer, shoots a look over his mask to Miguel. I guess Colling's the Harpo of this team.

"Doesn't quite work like that," Miguel says. "We found some texts, but they're all to temporary accounts. Burner phones. It's like a phone you get at Best Buy with a prepaid amount of minutes. Mechanically speaking, they don't exist."

"I know what a burner phone is," I say. "I know you can't trace them. But can you get anything from the signature—what generation of burner phone, where he might have bought them?"

I'm fairly impressed with the amount of police work I'm doing right now. But then again, it's not a surprise: their job seems to be about thinking creatively, and if Makeda's most creative idea is to target me, she's not going to get very far.

"Doesn't quite work like that," says Miguel again. "When it's gone, it's gone."

"So you didn't find what you were looking for?" says Jonas, about a minute behind in the conversation.

"No, we didn't," says Makeda.

"Can you tell us what that is? What you're looking for? Maybe we can help," he says earnestly.

He's nothing but earnest when he wants to be. And Makeda might be gay, but Jonas's whole Nordic Don Juan vibe isn't lost on anyone.

"Actually, I can tell you," she says. Then she glances at me: "In the interest of transparency."

She removes her phone from her pocket and taps and swipes, then flips the screen toward us and hands me the phone. Jonas draws in close to me and we both look at the picture.

It's a woman. It's Ellen Garcia, but she doesn't look like she looked in the photos I found of her online: all on social media with friends, colleagues, squished selfies, and a faux-professional headshot of her leaning on a railing next to the East River, the Brooklyn Bridge in the back.

She doesn't look at all like herself in this picture. She looks nearly dead, and since I have seen a few dead people up close, I know what I'm talking about. The first thing I notice is how thin her face is. In all the pictures I saw of her before, her face was round, naturally apple-shaped, with red squirrel cheeks. In the picture I'm looking at, she's lying down on her back, her mouth slightly open, eyes almost closed from the flash. I estimate at least a pound melted from her face alone; even her nose has taken on an aquiline element, the scrappy pugness no longer visible. Skeletal fingers loosely clutch a copy of the New York Post to her chest; the first thing I think is that it's been thrown at her. I can almost imagine her stumbling back from the impact. It's shocking to see, but I keep it together. Jonas, on the other hand, gasps.

"My God," he says, running his hand over his mouth and chin. Then he points to the upper portion of the screen: "What is that written on her face?"

Makeda zooms in: there are words in black marker, it looks like, on Ellen Garcia's forehead. The letters are smeared and jumbled like they've been shaken out of a Boggle cube, but I can make them out.

"IT'S BEEN LONGER THAN YOU THINK," I read.

Makeda and Jonas both look up at me, away from the screen.

"That's right," Makeda says. "Written backwards."

"What does it mean?" Jonas asks her.

"Not quite sure," she says. "She's been missing five days now."

"Maybe she thought it was less, and this is him toying with her," I suggest.

Makeda raises her thin eyebrows just a little bit.

"Maybe," she says.

"Does she have a family?" says Jonas.

Makeda smiles at him, says, "A seven-year-old daughter, ex-husband."

"Have you spoken with him, the ex?" I say.

Makeda pauses, says, "We have."

"Did they have a contentious relationship? Maybe he knows something," I say.

"He doesn't appear to have anything to do with it," says Makeda.

"Seven years old," says Jonas, shaking his head sadly. "Ours are thirteen and eleven."

Makeda smiles and nods kindly. Both of their schticks enrage me, Jonas's sensitive artist and Makeda's cop with a heart of gold.

"Do you have kids?" Jonas asks her.

She nods.

"I can't imagine," he says, looking once more at the screen.

I glance at the image again as he hands the phone back to Makeda. Then I remember the wording on the warrant: potential documentary evidence relating to Ellen Garcia, missing person.

"I'm sorry," I say. "You thought you were going to find *that* picture on my computer? As if I'm the one who sent it?"

"We didn't know," says Makeda. "Have to run down all the leads."

"Where do you think I'm keeping her, exactly? Our crawl space?"

Jonas places a hand on my upper arm. Makeda sees it, takes it in. She knows it means stop talking. But yet she doesn't appear surprised.

I yank my arm away from him, my throat burning, sweat suddenly streaming down the small of my back, soaking the waist of my pants.

It occurs to me Makeda got that warrant to search the devices because it's the only one she could get. It would have been for more, my office, the house, if she could have convinced the judge to sign off. But Honorable Gina T. Solomon, the stickler for detail, needed some actual evidence.

"They're ruling things out. Isn't that right?" Jonas asks Makeda in a way that recalls a parent speaking to his child in front of a teacher.

"That's right," says Makeda. The teacher.

I glare at my husband. *Don't help, darling.*

I say that again in my head: *Don't help.*

I turn my focus to Makeda.

"Am I still a person of interest, now that you haven't found anything?"

"Not legally," says Makeda right away.

"But you think I am, don't you, dear?"

"I like information," she says. "It's how I work. From what I've seen in my career, people are the sum total of what has happened to them plus what they have done since. So I look at all the information available. Unlike you, for example, who works just from what people tell you."

I know she is referencing my past and at the same time slighting my profession, and actually both are fine with me. Everyone, even in New York City, has an opinion about shrinks and mental health treatment in general. There's still a stigma that it's either for neurotic Woody Allen types or straitjacket-wriggling madmen only, and that the rest of us should just be able to white-knuckle it through life without ever speaking freely to another human being.

And as for my past, well, everyone can use a computer, can't she? Police detectives and psycho kidnappers alike, and Makeda is clearly not alone in researching me.

"I like information, too," I say, calm. "If you don't want my help finding Billy, that's fine. But I can't stop him from reaching out to me, and if he, say, wants to meet with me again, I'll do that."

"I don't recommend that," she says. "If he contacts you, please call me."

At least we're still at the "please" stage, she and I.

"Tell you what, Makeda," I say. "If I find out where he is, I'll let you know."

"I appreciate that," she says.

I'm so much more centered than I was a few minutes ago. It's not from relief, necessarily, because I'm savvy enough to know Makeda still doesn't trust me as far as she can throw me—which actually might be a fair distance, a big girl like her, and me the paper waif.

But I'm thicker than I look, and there's even more to me than her box-checking cop brain can handle. So, while I'm not exactly relieved, a sense of calm has come over me, because now I see the whole game, and she and I are locked in a race to the last square: the candy kingdom or the confidential envelope or Retirement (hilarious that you win the Game of Life with that instead of Death—I guess a little too dark for the *Laugh-In* sixties). Makeda may have done her little Google search, but she sure as hell doesn't get that I won this one while she was probably still in diapers. Not too many rules on the flip side of the box; just the object of the game, which is simply: Find the Hidden Killer.

# Gordon Strong

I guess I'm thankful. My back's almost normal. Chuck Strange didn't cure me or anything—he's not some magical witch doctor—but after the massage on the couch, I was able to stand without too much pain and get to a chiropractor, who told me exactly what goddamn Chuck had said, that I'd had some kind of spasm, and all the muscles had locked up. The doc pressed and cracked my lower back, told me to come back in a couple of weeks and maybe once a month after. That's how doctors get you, though, they keep you coming back for "maintenance," gobble up all those co-payments. I told him I'd come back if I needed to.

I'm working the hedge outside again. I owe it to Evelyn. I know I've been hitting the bottle a little hard—to be honest, I don't have a lot of memory of most nights. Last night, for example, I know I went down to the basement and called my old man again and ended up yelling at him. I don't even remember what we were arguing about—I just remember Evelyn trying to take the receiver from me, her face all puffy and weepy, saying, "Please, Gordon, please stop."

Then I can't remember if I pushed her off me, but I'm pretty sure I laid into her and called her some names. I remember Savannah standing at the top of the stairs, pretty sure she heard the whole thing. They were all gone before I woke up, so I didn't have a chance to say sorry.

My old man always said since he paid the bills he didn't have to apologize for anything. He reminded me of it last night in fact. Only pansies apologize to women, so if you're saying sorry, you must be a pansy, too. And I guess since you ain't paying the bills, that makes a hell of a lot of sense.

I think I got the top line on the hedge that separates our property from the road pretty even. I try to remember if we have a level somewhere, or even a yardstick. Figure I'll go look in the garage, and if I come up empty, maybe there's a ruler in one of the kids' rooms. I stand up, blink away the sweat. Then I hear a noise, like a cat mewling after a fight, but quiet.

I look in the direction of the Stranges' place, and I see Caroline on the porch in the corner of the stairs, face in her hands, crying.

My first feeling is not to get involved, go about my day, back away slowly and find the ruler and make sure the top of the hedge is straight. And there's something about that kid that sticks with me the wrong way.

I look around, over both shoulders, see if by any chance her mother's car is turning the corner, or even silently hoping Savannah's home from camp early so she can talk to her friend, but no dice. There's no one but me.

Then I think of Savannah, remember how she looked at the top of the stairs last night. She somehow still has her baby face with those big brown eyes and also looks like a young lady, like Evelyn, actually, when she's happy and when she's sad. Last night she was sad. Because of me. Again.

She and Caroline talk every day and night, in person or on the phone. Caroline sleeps at our place every weekend. It hits me again that if I do something right with Caroline, it'll get back to Savannah, maybe shift the scales back a little bit in my direction. Even though, to be honest, the last thing I want to do is talk to this kid.

I rest the shears on top of the hedge and get up to the fence that separates our place from the Stranges'.

"Hey, Caroline," I say, quietly as I can but loud enough so she can hear me.

She shakes out of her pose; her streaky face pops up from the cradle of her hands.

"I didn't see you," she says, wiping her eyes with her knuckles.

"Sorry," I say. "I was behind the hedge."

She glances over at the hedge, sort of suspicious, like someone else might be hiding back there. Then she nods.

"You okay?" I say.

She shrugs, keeps rubbing her eyes.

"You want to, uh, you want to talk about it?"

Her hands drift away from her face, her lips stuck in a frown. God help me, she's a weird-looking kid. Sort of frog-like. Not like I spend a whole lot of time thinking about how other guys look, but I know Chuck's not ugly, and before Lil put on the weight she was pretty attractive, so not sure what happened with Caroline. She's not doing herself any favors with the way she's done her hair, yanked back into a tight ponytail. It's like her face doesn't have anywhere to hide.

She glances at her front door behind her and then stands, shuffles over to the fence, about a foot away from me.

"It's my parents," she says. "They fight a lot."

"Yeah?" I say, and now that thing pricks up in me—happiness at someone else's bad luck. It's not like I'm the only one who does it, everyone feels it, right? Maybe not Evelyn, but it's a human thing. And hearing Chuck Strange isn't perfect helps. I bet Caroline's felt it—she seems like the kind of kid who might try to cover up a smile when another kid trips. "Yeah," she says. "It's getting worse, too."

"I'm sorry to hear that," I say. I could not be less sorry, but I keep thinking of a conversation she might have with Savannah later, both of them sitting cross-legged in Savannah's room in their pajamas, Caroline saying, *You're so lucky to have a dad like that.*

"Grown-ups say a lot of things when they're arguing," I say. "Sometimes they just say things to hurt each other, and they don't mean it at all. You'll see someday, Caroline, when you're a mom—"

"Gordon?" she says, interrupting me. "I found something."

"What do you mean?"

She shakes her head and takes one more step so she's right in front of me. She's so much taller than Savannah, thicker, sturdier. Seems to be taking after old Chuck so far, and I find myself hoping, for her sake, she doesn't take after Lil. It's easy for a guy to go through the world like a tank, you can pull off that whole played-ball-in-school stuff, but damn tough for a woman.

She looks over both shoulders and then stands on her toes and looks over mine, making sure no one's around. Then she pulls a photo from her back pocket and hands it to me.

It's Evelyn.

She's in a red bikini that I have no memory of her owning. And it's not like she's at the beach or the lake or a water park in the Dells— she's in front of the mirror in our bedroom, holding the camera to the mirror, taking a picture of herself.

"What is this?" I say, bringing it closer to my face.

"I found it in my dad's clothes when I was doing the laundry," she says. "You haven't even seen the worst part. Turn it over."

I don't realize my hands are shaking until I turn it over to see what Caroline wants me to. There's a heart, drawn in black marker on the back, blurry over the Kodak logo.

I flip the picture over again in my hand, to the image of my wife in the swimsuit, and then back again to the black heart. I do that a few more times—Evelyn, black heart, Evelyn, black heart.

"When . . ." I say, not even sure what my question is.

"When did she give that to him?" Caroline says, filling in the blank for me. "I don't know for sure. I was loading up the washer this morning, and it was in the back pocket of his jeans from yesterday."

I race through every memory I have of yesterday. All I can think of is yelling on the phone at my old man last night, Evelyn trying to pull the phone away. Before that—I was watching the Brewers lose again, drinking beers. Not paying any attention to what she was doing behind me. She might not even have been at home. She might have been doing a striptease for Chuck on the lawn, for all I know.

I shake my head. This is Evelyn. My Evelyn. She might be frustrated with me, and, hell, maybe she's hurt and she's angry, but she wouldn't do this.

"Maybe your dad took this," I say, handing it back to Caroline.

"You mean stole it?" she says, and I realize I probably offended her, but I'm not a hundred percent sure I care if I did or not.

"Yeah," I say, more confident about it now.

Caroline lifts her thick shoulders up to her ears and drops them.

"I guess," she says. "I guess I'm just wondering where he would find it, you know?"

I stare at the back of the picture, the heart, and suddenly it becomes my heart, black and inky and dripping in my chest. Suddenly I can hear it in my head, rattling my eardrums. I know she's right. It's not the kind of picture you peel out of a photo album.

"Yeah, I don't know," I say finally.

"I know my mom's got problems," Caroline says, wiping her eyes with the back of her hand. "But she doesn't deserve this."

"Hey," I say. "We still don't know the whole story here. We don't know how this ended up in the laundry. And even if it's, you know, the worst thing, even if Evelyn g-gave . . ." I stammer, and then I pause.

Caroline's fixed her steely eyes on me. She's not buying it. I'm starting to wonder why I'm even trying to make myself buy it.

She reaches her hand up and snatches the picture from my fingers. It happens so quick, I don't even have a second to think about holding on. She stares at it again, and then her face goes soft.

"I don't think you deserve it, either, Gordon," she says quietly. "You're a good person. You've just had some bad luck. But that's all it is. Just luck. Which can change in a second."

Something about what she's saying hits me right in the chin. Here I've been feeling sorry for myself, letting everything just happen, just letting the waves hit me and not even trying to swim to dry land.

"You're right, but you can also change your own luck, I believe that," I say, waving a teacherly finger toward her.

She stares at my finger, her eyes going a little cross-eyed.

"How do you mean?" she says.

"I mean we could take control of this situation a little bit," I say. "You and me."

She screws up her forehead and her eyebrows, confused. I'm guessing that's exactly how she looks in math class when her hand shoots up. Goddamn, it must be the shits to be a teacher; you have to put up with every kid, even the ones you don't like.

"I don't understand," she says, a whiny tinge to her voice, and now I realize I'm going to have to make it real simple for her.

"You don't want your parents to get divorced, right?"

She shakes her head.

"And I don't want to get divorced from Savannah's mom," I say. "So maybe we can help each other."

"How?"

"Well," I say, realizing I haven't exactly thought this through. My eyes wander to the picture in her hand, and I point to it. "This is a good start. Stuff like this. You see anything else funny, you let me know. And if I see anything funny, I'll let you know."

"But that's just us, like, noticing things. We're not *doing* anything."

"Yeah," I say, knowing she's right again.

"I think I'm going to try to talk to my dad," she says. "I'm going to tell him I found this."

Then she starts crying again a little bit, and a tear runs down her cheek and lands on the picture, right on Evelyn's face.

I get a flash of the conversation, Chuck with his open understanding face. *Tell Daddy what happened, sweetheart.* And she gets into how she and I talked all about it, and now he thinks I put the idea in her head. Now I'm the bad guy.

"Hang on a second, now," I say, trying to make my voice soft. "Maybe there's something else we can do."

She blinks, and a couple more tears fall, her eyes red.

"Like what? I don't see anything else we can do unless we . . ."

"Catch them," I say, finishing her sentence.

The cartoon light bulb goes off, but it's bigger, like at my old job when the line managers used to flip the switches on the factory floor, and the fluorescents would light up, row by row in a rolling wave.

Then she shakes her head and winces. "We have to get it all out in the open. That's what my dad always says when there's a misunderstanding. You just have to all sit in a room and talk it out. He and my mom, you and Evelyn."

She looks so desperate now I almost want to say, *Sure, honesty's the best policy. We just all need to make like Washington with his cherry tree and ride off into the sunset.*

But I see it on a movie screen in my head—three, two, one, the color washed from Evelyn's face as she knows she's been caught. Chuck's fucking understanding peacekeeper act. *Gordon, I can explain . . .*

I slap my hand against the side of my head to chase the image out.

Caroline shudders and stares at me.

"Sorry," I say. "Mosquito."

She nods slowly, wipes her nose on her forearm.

"My dad . . ." she begins. "He'll have an explanation, I know he will."

Her mouth does that terrible thing that Savannah's does, too, when she's trying not to cry, the corners twitching as they turn down. Poor kid. I have to hand it to her, she's a hell of a lot more trustworthy than I was at that age. Hell, even Savannah tries to squeeze fibs by us, tries to convince us we forgot to give her her allowance if she needs a little extra that week.

"Wait a second, now, Caroline," I say. "Let's just think about this. You might be a little young to know this, but grown-ups, everyone, if you back them into a corner, you don't know what they'll do. Your dad, he's a good man, you know that, but if you show him that picture, it'll be real easy for him to make up some story to explain it away. Either that or he'll get upset about it, maybe take it out on you, which you don't deserve."

Even before I see the panic in her eyes I know I'm being manipulative, but I have to look at it like collateral damage at this point. And something about her alarm starts me up, not in a perverted way, but it gives me a boost like a car getting a jump.

She nods sadly. "What do we do, then?" she says, plugging one nostril with her knuckle and sniffing hard. "Try to . . . trap them?"

I shake my head. "We're not trapping them, hon. We're finding out the truth."

"Just so we can know for sure?"

"Exactly!" I say.

"How would we do it?" she says. "You know, if we wanted to do it."

I know I can convince her now, and cap the urge to laugh, I'm so relieved.

"Well, I'm not sure," I say. "We'd have to get them in the same place at the same time."

"My dad's not home very much."

"Third shift, right?" I say, remembering. "So he's home from, what—five to eleven?"

"Yeah, and he sleeps in the morning for a few hours."

I think, shit, when would they find the time, but where there's a will there's a goddamn way. And as much as I don't want to imagine Evelyn having the will, I look at that picture in Caroline's hand and realize how stupid I've been. Then I think back to last night. I must have passed out around nine. And she must have been pissed off and upset, and Chuck's got that nice broad shoulder to cry on. Thinking about it, I've been passing out around nine a lot these days.

"Hey, Caroline," I say.

"Yeah?"

"Did you, uh, do you know where your dad was last night, before he went to work, say, between nine and eleven?"

She thinks.

"I don't know," she says. "I was watching TV with my mom."

"And you found that when—this morning?" I say, pointing to the picture.

She nods.

"I need you to think about this, now, do you remember, lately, seeing your dad around that time at night? Between nine and eleven?"

"Sometimes he watches TV with us," she says, shrugging. Then she thinks about it and adds, coughing out a laugh, "But usually when he's studying to get peace and quiet, he goes and sits in his car."

"Okay, that's good," I say. "Tonight, you and me, we're going to make it easy for them. We need to give one of them a sign from the other."

"Like a note?"

"Yeah, good thinking, a note."

"Wait!" she says, excited, and she runs off and disappears into the house.

I stand up straight, pull my shoulders back. I didn't even realize I was hunching.

Caroline bursts through the screen door not a minute later, carrying a shoebox. She sits on the top step and opens the box, starts flipping through papers. Cards and photos. She pulls one out and opens it up, reads for a second, and then thrusts it toward me.

"Here," she says.

*On Your Birthday*, reads the front. A bouquet of blue flowers underneath the words. I open the card, and there's a poem that I don't read, and then below, written in my wife's cursive: *Happy Birthday, Caroline!!! Love, Evelyn and Gordon.*

"I don't even remember this," I say.

"You guys give me one every year with five bucks inside," she says, taking the card from me.

"Yeah?" I say.

It's a nice thing Evelyn does, remembers everyone's birthdays, sends gifts to my brother and his family on Christmas, even mails cards to my old man on Father's Day. I'm not sure I've ever thanked her, but I've always been glad she does it. But now it's making me think, what else is there that I have no idea about?

Caroline has the card open on her lap, tracing Evelyn's signature with her finger.

"Maybe I can copy her handwriting?" she says.

"You could write your dad a note," I say.

She nods, thinks about it.

"Telling him to meet," I add.

My back starts to ache. Not as bad as before, thanks to goddamn Chuck, and don't think that irony is lost on me, but now there's a skinny needle jabbing me at the base of my spine, so it turns out he's not capable of producing miracles of modern science anyway.

"In his car, right?" she asks.

I feel that one in my throat. A beanbag. I swallow hard and say, "Yeah, that's what we write. Meet me in your car. Ten o'clock."

"I'll put it in the mailbox," she says, pointing to the box at the curb. "My dad always checks it first thing when he gets home at five."

"Good thinking," I say.

She beams at my compliment. She's not a bad kid at all, I think. Just got a raw deal with her folks. Like most of us.

"I can definitely fake my dad's handwriting," she says. "I've done it before."

I decide not to ask details about that one, and pat her on the shoulder.

"You can write Evelyn a note, too, then—I'll put it in our mailbox. She always picks it up when she comes home from work."

"Yeah, saying the same thing—meet you in your car at ten to talk."

"Then you watch," I say, pointing at her upstairs window, "and I'll watch."

"And then we'll know," she says.

"That's right."

Then she gets sad again, the eyebrows fall. Two limp mustaches.

"But like you said before, if we corner them and if they're innocent, won't they be really angry that we tried to trap them?"

I pause. Because, yes, they will, of course they will; even Saint Evelyn loses her shit, and even if she and Chuck are the most blameless Mr. Rogers's neighbors, they're still human, and no one wants to be accused of something they didn't do. But I got this tickle I can't quite locate, somewhere in the back of my head, that tells me I'm right. I don't need to get into that with Caroline, though. I just need to convince her.

"Maybe, but the difference is if they're guilty, they won't be able to lie about it. The truth is important, Caroline," I say. "It's worth us taking a little heat."

She thinks about this for a second but still doesn't seem convinced.

"Now, you listen to me," I say, quieter and gentler now, "what you and me are doing, we're doing the opposite of what they're doing. If they're doing what we think they are, they're trying to break this all apart," I say, gesturing toward her house, then mine. "Me and you, we're trying to hold it together."

"We're the tape," she says, and she smiles.

"That's exactly right," I say. "We're the Scotch tape, Caroline. We're helping everyone."

She gets a proud look on her face, and why shouldn't she? It feels good to help people.

# Dr. Caroline

For most people, Saturday is the day they feel the freest, the map of the weekend unfolded before them. For me, it's another workday but also an opportunity to charge twice my usual rate. But today I cancel all my appointments.

*Hello, blank, this is Dr. Caroline. Many, many apologies for the short notice, but a family issue has arisen that requires my immediate attention. I'll count on seeing you at our next scheduled appointment but please let me know if you'd like to meet sooner, and I will find time for us to connect.*

I leave nine messages. Not one of them picks up, because they're scared of talking on the phone. Most people are. Too much of a confrontation, but what they usually don't realize is avoiding confrontation is itself a form of manipulation. *I don't want to face you, so it's up to you to find me.*

Luckily, I don't have a problem with either: confrontations or phone calls. So, next I sit at my desk in my office and start by calling the numbers in my Recents, from either Billy or Nelson. As expected, they all end with robo-voices, telling me the numbers are no longer active.

I scroll through my initial emails from him, the fake vax card, the impostor contact information. I stare at the address he chose: my birthday and my age. Which is interesting. I'm not on social media (it's obviously a big no-no for shrinks—no one needs to see her therapist with the family at the Grand Canyon or drinking out of a coconut with the girls), not even LinkedIn. I walk into the kitchen and stare at the wall where I've taped all the sheets of paper—my articles, Ellen Garcia's story, the *Journal Sentinel*. Only the latter mentions my age, in 1993, so that's how Billy captured that piece, but how did he find my birthday? Employing a background check service would leave a detailed paper trail, so I doubt he would've taken that route.

The buzzer buzzes, and I glance at the clock: 10:37 a.m. This hour is Josiah the Jock's appointment time, but if he hadn't gotten my message he likely would have shown up at 10:00. He's a personal trainer and is generally on time. Talks a lot about his father. Powerlifts to avoid aging and death. Good luck with that.

I walk back into the office and peer above the bottom-up accordion shades on the front window and see someone with a helmet. Likely a delivery guy.

I grind my teeth, swearing at Jonas; it's probably a fucking almond cappuccino and apple cake from the Swedish bakery in Bay Ridge— his comfort food that he likely ordered since he was up half the night stressed from the police visit.

I hurry to the door and open it, and it's not a delivery guy. It's a kid. I don't recognize her at first because of the helmet and the mask. Tank top, shorts, roller skates. A fringe of purple hair on one side of her face.

"Hi, Caroline!" she says, holding up her hand in a wave. Then she pulls her mask down for a second so I can see her face. "It's me, it's Florie."

Before Theo went to private school he went to our neighborhood hippy-dippy pre-K program, where they baked kale chips for snacks and decided what books they would read at circle time through a democratic vote. Theo fell in love with little bright-eyed Florie, and they still hang out now and again, even though they go to different schools.

"Florie," I say. "You're so big."

She smiles and pulls her mask up over her mouth and nose.

"Theo's not here, though. He's at sleepaway," I say.

"Oh yeah, I know," she says. "I talked to him last night, actually."

That takes a second to land. At my children's camp, the kids can call once or twice a week if they choose. Elias never once called, even at eight years old. Two years ago, during his first summer, Theo called quite a few times, sometimes homesick and sometimes just filling us in on the minutiae of his day. But so far this summer, nothing. Which, frankly, is fine by us. We are paying for them to be entertained and occupied. We are paying to have a break from their every thought and worry.

It had simply not occurred to me that Theo would use the opportunity to call anyone else. For a moment I'm not sure if I'm jealous or relieved. Then of course I realize I am both.

"You did?" I say, then quickly add, "How great."

"Yeah," she says. "So I told him I'd send him Jolly Ranchers, but my parents said I should ask you first and make sure it was okay."

"Florie, that's so thoughtful," I say. "Yes, of course it's okay. He'll be thrilled to get candy in the mail. Who wouldn't be?"

Her eyes widen, mask stretching over her smile.

"Your mom and dad could have texted me, though," I say. "You didn't have to come out of your way."

"Oh, I don't mind," she says. "I like to talk to people in person."

"I think that's very mature of you," I say, and then Georgina Melios's face swirls into my consciousness, and I realize I have a little unexpected window. "So how is Theo doing?" I say, adding a chuckle, trying to hide the fact that an eleven-year-old might know more about my son than I do.

"He's having fun," says Florie. "He's made a couple of friends. He says he gets homesick at night when he's tired."

"Everything's worse when you're tired," I say.

"Yeah!" she says with enthusiasm, as if this is something she has noticed, too. "I think I'm also going to send him a couple of my graphic novels. They're good to read at night, to distract yourself. I have some about the Greek gods that are so good. The Hades one especially, because—did you know that Hades isn't really a bad guy? He just picked the short stick, and Zeus was just like, guess you're in charge of the underworld, bruh, and Hades was like, cool."

"So he's not just pure evil?" I say.

"No, not at all."

Then she raises her shoulders and drops them with a sigh.

"Well, I should go," she says. "'Bye!"

"'Bye."

Off she goes, skates clacking on the sidewalk. It's a little maddening, how well adjusted she is. It makes me think we could have saved a shitload of money and just sent the boys to the crumbling public elementary school around the corner, and Theo would be going to the skate park with Florie over the summer chatting about Greek mythology. And as a nice little bonus I wouldn't have to deal with private school parents, but I suppose public school parents have all their own little dramas, too, that I'd be drawn into. I don't remember too much about Florie's mother, she of the stained shirts.

I return inside, to my desk, thinking of Theo on the porch of the cabin where they lay out cell phones for call hour, picking one up and deciding to phone a friend.

And then I think, what if Billy asked someone else about me, someone who knew my birthday and who knows maybe other things, too? If he read what was available about me, whose names would he see?

Jonas isn't mentioned in anything online about me, but my name shows up in a couple of articles about him. But he didn't go through

Jonas, obviously; it has to be someone else. I scroll through the hits on me—my colleagues at Columbia, doubtful, they all resented me because I was at the top of every class; the chances of them knowing my birthday are slim. Further back: the *Journal Sentinel* stories from the nineties, who is mentioned—the Strongs, the cops, my parents.

Can't be dear old Dad, dead for almost ten years now. The spindly fingers of grief grip my throat as I think of him, slumped over the steering wheel, head against the airbag. On purpose or by accident? No one really knew, although if I had to live with my mother, I know which one I'd choose.

My mother, the last one standing.

I pick up my phone, tap the contact. It rings once, twice. By the time the receptionist at the front desk answers with, "Golden Brook Living," I make another decision and end the call.

I grab my purse and check for my keys, thinking maybe me and bold young Florie have a thing in common: we like to talk to people in person.

# Ellen Garcia

I wake up again at some point, some time, some day or night, and there's more bread and another bottle of Starbucks water. This time it's next to my head, so I take a couple of dusty breaths and turn onto my right side.

My head throbs on all four sides now: front, back, left temple, right temple. It's got to be a concussion. I'm sure my brain's just swelling like a sponge in there, but nothing much to do about it now except add it to my list of grievances. Not like an MRI machine has been installed in the room while I slept.

I read what's typed on the sticker, every word: *Item: 1 of 1. Items in order: 1. *Caroline* Ethos Water. 17-June-2021. Mobile.*

So it's the seventeenth, or was the seventeenth not long ago. I try to remember what day it was when I took out the recycling and got nabbed. The twelfth, the thirteenth? So four days I've been here, five? How long does it take someone to starve? Random, possibly inaccurate facts I've learned spin on a game-show wheel in front of me. You can live two weeks without food but only one without water. You can live ten days without food but only five without water. You can live forty days and nights without food but none without water.

How long was Tom Hanks on the island in *Castaway* before he found water? What about Jennifer Lawrence in *The Hunger Games*? Christian Bale in *Rescue Dawn*. The little boy in *The Black Stallion*. The boy on the boat with the tiger in *Life of Pi*. The *Lord of the Flies* kids, the *Swiss Family Robinson* kids, the *Blue Lagoon* kids. I don't recall it being an issue for any of those last three. They were too busy killing each other, riding ostriches, and boning, respectively.

No obvious conclusions emerge from any of those sources. I lift my head about an inch off the floor but the throbs are too intense, not exactly like my skull's trapped in a steel vise—maybe a Happy Meal version with puffy plastic jaws. But still, it's too much.

I lower my head back down, figure I can tip the bottle and catch the water in a stream. But first I have to open it. I hold the base of the bottle with my right hand and try to unscrew the top with my left. When did they make these plastic caps so tight—that little perforated ring around the neck clinging to the piece above it? I take a break, wipe my left hand on my shirt, trying to dry it out. Then I start again, and finally I hear a little crack, and after a few more twists and drying my palms on my shirt, I'm able to get the damn thing open.

I tilt it toward my mouth, careful not to tip the whole thing. Reminds me of the big bucket at Kalahari, me and Bella standing under it in our swimsuits, listening to the *tick-tick-tick* as we watch the bucket fill up and tip and dump all those gallons of water on our heads. Right now my tongue smacks against the roof of my mouth as I think about water, any water, even water park chlorine pee water.

I hold the bottle with both hands and pour a splash into my mouth, but then I lose my grip and it falls on its side for a second. I raise my head as a reflex, but ye olde braine doesn't care for that, and pain pinballs off the four sides inside my skull, north, south, east, west. Pinpricks of light cloud my eyes, and I reach for the bottle and stand it upright, before my head sinks back down.

Only a little has spilled, a tablespoon or two, maybe, not that I was ever great with culinary-type measurements. I angle my head to the floor and lap at the wet spot. It's not bad—a little chalky, but there is moisture there, and I know I need the hydration for energy. To say nothing of the bread.

It's weird what has happened—the way I really don't feel hunger anymore, just thirst. I don't even really want the bread and its doughy dryness, can't imagine it making its way down the rusty flume that is my esophagus. It would probably get stuck and choke me anyway.

Which is maybe the point?

It's occurred to me that I am being watched, somehow. Or listened to, maybe. If there's a teeny-tiny camera in the mirror in the corner, or a microphone in the doorknob or buried in my hair like a little lost mosquito, I could actually communicate.

I focus on the bottle. *Caroline.* If it's her. If she went straight off the diving board into the insanity pool when she read my story, if that detonated the explosive inside her that was lit so long ago by that nutjob in Wisconsin. If she had a clean psychotic break, and the loudest voice in her head said, *Yep, this is the thing you gotta do. You just gotta kill little old Ellen Garcia, and all that stuff that happened to you won't matter anymore. You'll be free of it.*

One way to find out. One more sip first. I take a sharp breath through my nose and lift my head. Pounds and throbs and drumsticks beating, pulsing down through my jaw, which I grind. I tilt the bottle and push the neck into my mouth, lift it, and swig. I cough a little, but most of it goes down, and my throat actually feels slick, which was the goal. Hydrated enough to talk. I roll onto my back like a potato bug, figure I can get more air out that way.

"Hey," I call, and I cough. My voice is hoarse but audible. I can hear it, anyway. Voice still works, ears still work. "Can you hear me? I don't know if you can hear me. My name's Ellen, and I think I know who you are. Dr. Caroline, right? That's what patients call you. Look, I'm sorry I wrote that story about you. I didn't even want to write it. I have this editor, and he assigned it to me, you know? But, look, you seemed pretty successful when I read about you, so, like, why would you worry about what some hack journalist thinks about you? Like I

188

don't even have a bathtub, you know? And my car finally died last year, but before that I had to get in through the trunk because the front door locks didn't work.

"What I'm trying to say is that I'm nothing, you know, like I don't even register on anyone's radar for any reason. I'm not that good a writer. I'm no threat to you. And that story, stories like that, people click on them for a week if we're lucky and then that's it. No one's digging through the archives to read crap like that."

I'm not sure I thought it was possible, but it seems even quieter in the room than it was before. I try to picture Dr. Caroline's face, and I can't quite land on it, but I close my eyes and see her sitting in some kind of awards show director's booth, watching me on a black-and-white screen. What would she want to hear?

"I'm sorry," I say. "I'm sorry I wrote it. The whole thing. It was the lowest-hanging mango, and I should have stuck to my guns and said I wanted to write something more important. Not that health care isn't important, but not anything that ruins anybody's career."

Then I get an idea. It's small and maybe worthless, like most of my ideas, but there's a little spark there. Maybe this is what she's wanted all along. Maybe she wants me to make it right.

"I could write that whole piece over," I say. "Make it about every doctor on the list and interview the patients they've helped, the ones that they've saved. I'm sure you have patients like that, a lot of them. I only interviewed two; there must be a hundred who'd tell me what a great psychiatrist you are, how much you've helped them. You could even tell me which people to use for it.

"I could make it about how much you've overcome. I read about you. What happened to you when you were a kid, and I can't imagine going through that. I know everyone probably says that to you when they hear about it—*I can't imagine*—but I mean it, I literally can't. Sure, I read about it—the *Milwaukee Journal Sentinel*, right? Usually I can get pretty creative, especially when it comes to anxious thought cycles, but something in my brain stops me when I think of what you saw, like a little trauma bouncer in there, he's in front of the velvet rope and he's like, *Sorry, that is not getting in here.*

"I got some trauma, too, not like yours—I don't think anyone's going to beat you in that rock-paper-scissors, but I had a thing happen to me that wasn't great. It was just me, and I was thirteen, and I was dumb and found myself in a situation with these three older boys in the woods."

I sigh, unimpressed with how boring my story is compared to hers.

"It's not like they beat me up or anything. Hell, I even dated one of them later. But you know—I don't know if you know, I don't know if you've ever been through anything like that specifically, but something shitty happens, and you do the thing that you think will make you feel less shitty about the original thing. So for me I thought maybe if I actually date one of them, and we go to dances and shit and fall in love, it'll make me feel better about what happened in the woods."

I laugh, and it's a weird feeling—the choppy air coming up from my chest dries my throat on contact, makes me cough.

"News-fucking-flash: it didn't."

I cough for another minute or two, maybe twelve, I don't know. Then I laugh again.

"It's amazing any of us make it through. Women, actually. Girls who grow up. I mean, we're born, right? And maybe we have parents who have jobs and can feed us and give us clothes, and maybe we don't, but we make it through early childhood, right? Manage to go to school, manage to make a friend or two, manage to, you know, show up. And then puberty comes, and it's like they can't wait to get their hands on us. Or maybe they don't even wait for us to grow jellybean boobs, they just catch us whenever they can.

"I've never told anyone this, but when I found out I was having a girl, in the ultrasound place, I was like, Shit, because I hadn't realized I was thinking about all of this, that I secretly had been hoping for a boy with a bossy little penis, because they can do whatever they want, and as their parents you just have to help them dial down, which is a hell of a lot easier than building up a girl. Like, fortifying the walls of a girl.

"Of course, Chris—that's my ex—he saw the expression on my face, he knows me really well. He'll see my eyebrow twitch, and be like, *You're unhappy in our marriage.* Anyway, he saw me, and I tried to explain it to him, and we got in a fight about it. He was like, *This is a fucking miracle of creation why are you pissing all over it?*"

I think about it for a second, remember Chris's face. Hurt plus anger.

"I didn't have an answer for him. It was just a thing inside me I couldn't control. I wanted to be happy, but I was scared to death. I couldn't explain all this to him, about girls, how we spend our whole lives doing evasive maneuvers away from what happened to us in childhood just to make something. Write something. Make a career like you have."

I turn my head to the side, and a couple of tears roll down. It's shocking to me, actually, that I have any water in my body left to generate.

I lick my lips, say, "Like I said, your thing makes my thing look like a fucking day at Six Flags, but I'm just speaking generally. So we try to have our careers and our marriages and our kids, we try to, you know, have it all, really nail that work-life balance, and we also have to work out and get our hair done and acrylics glued and hair ripped off our bodies in sheets of hot wax—that actually, that's a good metaphor. You've got all the hot strips on—your legs, your ass, your chocha, and you know the pain is coming, you're just trying to guess where it'll be first."

I start laughing again, and it's like a Dust Bowl tornado in my throat.

"But, like, seriously, between you and me, after a fucking day of writing and trying to juggle for my editor and bringing my kid from here to there and making sure she has her change of masks and her

hand sanitizer and reading the news and getting enraged and nauseous with worry, I've got to be real with you, I don't feel like getting
on the goddamn elliptical. I want to swallow a pizza and have five
shots, because I need a break from myself more than anyone else. I
want to be off the clock from babysitting my own goddamn mind."

I swallow, or rather the muscles in my throat mimic swallowing,
but there is no liquid left. A drought has hit the creek bed once
more, and I know I have to do the whole dance again with the water
bottle, but not yet.

I realize I've talked more about myself just now than I have in
years, and I don't have any more energy to laugh, but if I did I would
because it turns out this Dr. Caroline—she's a pretty good listener.

# Dr. Caroline

As soon as you escape the glamour of Staten Island and come off the Goethals Bridge, you hit Elizabeth, New Jersey, where my mother lives in a senior care facility. About a year after my father died it became clear my mother could no longer take care of herself, either by choice or coincidence. My parents had me when they were almost forty, so my mother's age combined with her obesity and diabetes 2 diagnosis gave me one option—to move her from the house where I'd grown up in Glen Grove to the tristate area, where I could get to her within an hour if I needed to.

Just to clarify: I would've left her in a nursing home in Wisconsin if I could have, but I could foresee the emergencies, the phone calls, the booking of 6:00 a.m. flights back and forth to Milwaukee when she needed endless procedures done: kidney dialysis, physical therapy, flea dips. As the only child and next of kin, I brought her to the East Coast to make it easier on me.

Sure enough, she had a stroke (or two or three—they couldn't really tell) within the first few months of the move. Since then she's been fuzz-brained, her memory erratic, but at least she stopped calling me. They keep her busy there, certainly. A few months before COVID hit, she appeared in a story in the local free weekly along with some of the other inmates. The management sent me a copy, and I chuckled when I saw the photo of her doing water aerobics, the baggy skin from her arms floating on the pool's surface. See how nice it is to get your picture on the front page, I said to myself right before tossing the paper into the recycling bin.

I try to make it out to see her once every fiscal quarter now. I don't bring Jonas or the boys; we don't visit on holidays; the boys don't call her Grammy or Maw-Maw. Many people convince themselves they need to be connected to their parents as they age and near death, even if they are terrible people. That somehow parents should be absolved for their unapologetic wrongdoings just because they can't remember your name anymore. I am happily not one of them.

Golden Brook looks less like a hospital and more like a Victorian-era resort. Specifically the Overlook Hotel from *The Shining*, only instead of sitting on a sprawling mountaintop in Colorado, it's spitting distance from the off-ramp in Jersey. But all these factors contributed to choosing it for my mother—the proximity to the turnpike, the quality of care, the chance that she might stumble across a guy in a bloody bear costume on her way to Craft Choice Time.

I park in the visitors' lot and put on a mask, open the small cooler I've set on the passenger seat and take out what's inside, place the item carefully into my tote bag. Then I get out, walk across the lot to the polished front desk, through the automatic doors, into the main reception area. As grand as it looks from the outside, it's still standard health care status quo inside, with the smell of lemon and bleach and medical personnel in panda-print scrubs.

I tell the receptionist who I'm here to see and hand her my license and vax card. She looks over her bifocals at the monitor in front of her, runs her finger along the scroll wheel on the mouse.

"I don't have you on the visitor log for today, Ms. Strange," she says. "Is this an impromptu?"

"Yes, impromptu," I say. "I was in the neighborhood. Thought I'd stop by and say hello."

"Very nice," she says, grinning, her bifocals steaming up above her mask. "Let me check her schedule." She pauses, scrolls. "Looks like she's just back from the garden, so she should be in her room. Perfect timing." Another grin, more steam.

She taps the keyboard, and a small printer at the end of the desk buzzes, spits out a name tag reading VISITOR—IMPROMPTU—G7—CAROLINE STRANGE—LILLIAN STRANGE.

She hands me the name tag and says, "Did you bring any gifts?"

"I'm sorry?" Add an eye flutter of confusion.

"Anything from outside—we need to check for impermissible items. Standard procedure."

"Of course," I say. "No gifts today. Because of the . . . impromptu," I say, tapping the name tag.

"All right, then, you can go ahead. Elevators on your left to the third floor, G Wing."

I thank her and head to the elevator bank. No, kind reception nurse, even though I am smuggling something in, my mother doesn't need any gifts. This place is her gift, the cool quarter of a million it took to get her on the accelerated wait list, not to mention the monthly payments. Not living out the remainder of life in a place where they let you marinate in your diaper because they're short-staffed or just not interested—Merry Christmas and happy birthday, Mom.

I get out at the third floor, follow the signs to G Wing, walk through what they call the "Big Room," which has a giant skylight for a roof. Here are all the senior citizens who can still walk and talk and for the most part dress themselves. They're playing cards at one table, they're painting watercolors at another. The TV in the corner is off; they have regulated screen time, too. On the second floor, there is H Wing, where the residents are spoon-fed meals and have their teeth lovingly brushed. That's where Mom will go next, when this phase is done.

It makes my stomach lining curl, thinking of getting old like this. Even high-end getting old is still getting old.

I walk under the arch to the hallway where my mother's room is located, find Number 7. The door is open a few inches, and I don't knock, push it open gently.

She is standing at the window, holding up an iPad. I watch her tap the button on the bottom of the screen, taking a picture.

"Mom."

She turns, lowers the iPad slowly like it's a weapon and she just got caught by the authorities. Her face is a blank sheet, and then she squints at me. I remove my mask.

"You're here."

They keep her hair nice, I'll say that. They've dyed it an auburn that could almost be natural, a far cry from the goldfinch-yellow it was my entire childhood. She used to dye it herself in the utility sink next to the washer and dryer in the basement, yellow drops staining the carpet and the wall like gunshot evidence.

And then there's the weight loss. When I brought her here she tipped the scales a little over 350, but now she looks to be closer to two hundred. I refuse to give her credit for this. When I was in the process of determining her health care plan with her facility caseworker, I told them to put her on a diet. They said of course, of course, showed me a selection of plans and menus—does she like fruit, does she like vegetables, does she like chicken, tofu, whole grains. I said no, she likes Pringles dipped in Marshmallow Fluff. Imagine you're packing a lunch for an army of trailer park kindergartners, and that's what she eats. I told them to just pick a low-to-no-sugar diet. It was easy to say it's for her diabetes, of course, we don't want her to have another stroke, we want her to be healthy and active, to do morning yoga and Zumba and whatever the hell else you have available but really, truly, I wanted her to suffer. To take away her medicine, the thing that activates—everyone has a few, and sometimes they're fine, and sometimes they're bad for you. That first sip of coffee or a limey gin and tonic, the boneless ecstasy of a seven-mile run, sweet nicotine smoke entering your pipes, new box cutter slicing zebra stripes up your forearm, fingers scrambling down your throat as you make yourself vomit, watching a stranger remove her shirt and bra in front of you.

My mother's is and always has been food. Any food, really, though after my father died she didn't even make an effort to eat anything with any amount of nutritional value.

I admit I didn't think it was possible, but she's lost weight here at Golden Brook. I thought she would've been more wily and figured out a way to manipulate the staff into bringing her extra rice pudding or buttery mashed potatoes. In the beginning she called me every day to complain, and I stopped picking up after a while. She's got skills, though, dear old Mom; she does have a tendency to adapt, so then she'd have the staff call registering unhappiness on her behalf, and I finally told her caseworker, in just the nicest way, I am paying for this to be your problem now. Then, eventually, the calls stopped altogether. Just like with my boys, if you stop helping them, at a certain point they will figure it out. They'll have to.

So now she's thinner. Not thin, but she can move around without wheezing and wear clothes that can be purchased online at Target in the plus-size section instead of specialty stores that sell only caftans and ponchos.

"It's me," I confirm. Not a dream, not a hallucination.

For a second she smiles genuinely, her tiny mouth revealing her barracuda teeth, and I admit I feel badly. I let the guilt come and go, knowing I should see her more often, look at how happy it makes her. It's human nature to want to make another human being happy, even if it's in service to yourself, so it's only natural I entertain thoughts of planning future visits. But like I tell my patients, let's zoom out, shall we? Don't just show me the curated Instagram post, let's see the whole picture.

She is still my mother. I am still me. There is just no getting away from it.

She seems to understand this, too, because the smile dissipates as quickly as it sprang forth.

"Where you been?" she says, shuffling over to a reclining chair.

"I've been busy, Mom," I say. "I work a lot."

"I know," she says. "Shrinky-dink."

"That's me."

"When . . ." she begins, and then stops, makes fists.

I see the frustration on her face; she doesn't have the words. Must be awful. Sucks for you. As much as I would like to see her stew in her exasperation, I am here for a reason.

"When was the last time you saw me?" I say.

"Yeah," she says, pointing at me.

"A few months ago."

"Months?" she says. Her stroke has turned her into a cartoon tourist: *Vat are zese, "months"?*

"Yes, February."

She nods, playing the part of someone who understands.

"I brought you something," I say.

I go to the door of the room and shut it, take a chair from the corner, and position it a couple of feet away, facing her. I open up my tote bag, and she peers inside, expectant. I reach inside and pull out the gift.

It's a large white carton dripping condensation on my palm but softened by the heat, just from the minute it took me to walk from my car to the front door.

"Ice cream," she says, eyeing it.

She moves her mouth around; I can tell saliva's gathering. I reach inside the tote for the biodegradable spoon I brought.

"Better than that, Mom," I say. "Frozen custard."

She blows air through her lips in dismissal. "They can't make custard out here."

"I think Shake Shack does okay," I say. Then I start to put the spoon back into the bag, just to fuck with her, and say, "But if you don't want it . . ."

"Give it here," she says, leaning forward in the chair, stretching out her arm.

I take the top off the carton and stick the spoon into the chocolate mush, hand it to her. Shake Shack's the only place you can get frozen custard in New York City, which is basically ice cream but with egg yolks for extra fattiness—it's a Wisconsin delicacy, and you can buy it by the pint or quart at shops on every street corner. Leave it to those midwesterners to find a dessert with an even higher fat content than ice cream. Living there is like being at a state fair year-round, where there's a constant competition to find the thing that will give you a heart attack the quickest.

But here we can only get it at Shake Shack and they only sell it by the shake or by the scoop, so I brought my own quart-sized paper soup container left over from Elias's birthday in the winter when he and his friends made their own ramen bowls, and I paid the nice people at Shake Shack for three double-scoops to fill the carton to the top.

She grabs it like she hasn't eaten all day and shoves a bite into her mouth. Makes a nearly sexual sound, which I heard thousands of times during my childhood when she had the first bite of something that was bad for her. And it doesn't take a psychiatry degree to guess why, either—her relationship with food is simply the most intimate one she has ever experienced. It makes sense that it should provide her with climactic levels of carnal contentment.

She comes up for air after a few shovels, the custard dribbling down her chin, which she wipes away. She is almost panting.

"They don't let me eat this stuff," she says.

"I know," I say. "That's why I brought it."

She lifts the carton in my direction in a toast. "Thanks."

She's warmed up now, both to me and to talking. After the stroke, the speech therapist on staff told me, the more she practiced talking, the better at it she'd be, both generally and even day-to-day, conversation to conversation.

"I have to ask you something, Mom," I say.

She stirs the custard around, gazing into it like it's a witch's brew.

"Ask me something," she repeats.

"Yes. I know it's hard to remember sometimes, but I need you to try. Has anyone contacted you and asked you any questions about me?"

"Questions."

She lifts the spoon to her mouth, the custard dripping off the bottom into the carton.

"In the last couple of months," I say, and then I realize that means nothing to her.

Time, time. Time is an illusion; time is nothing. So we're told by Einstein and Richard Bach, author of a book about a goddamn seagull. But that's why I'm not a physicist or a new-age fruit fly—because they are actually dead wrong. Time is everything—the universal yardstick. Even though my mother might not have the strongest grasp on it doesn't mean she gets a pass.

I realize I just have to give her some signage.

"Remember Easter? They had decorations up, Easter eggs on the door," I say, trying to remember the fluff from the biweekly newsletter Golden Brook sends. "The flowers, all the new flowers in the garden."

"We planted them," she says in recognition.

"That's right. You remember when they came up?"

"Yeah, we went for a walk. All those pansies, and the snappers," she says, pinching two fingers together on an imaginary snapdragon.

"Yes," I say. "Did anyone ask you about me? Any new people call you on the phone or send you a letter? Did you get any letters?"

She shakes her head, chewing the custard as if it's a solid food. Then she sneers.

"No one sends me letters," she says. "You don't."

"No, I don't," I say. "But I visit you sometimes. You're sure you haven't gotten any letters?"

"No," she says, annoyed now. "You don't visit."

"Mom, I visit when I can. And I promise to visit more, okay?"

She bristles, stirs the custard. I realize I have to bring up the big one.

"Remember Mother's Day?" I say. "There were a lot more people here probably, maybe even a few kids—do you remember that?"

"Mother's . . ." she says. Then she remembers. The corners of her little mouth turn way down, almost to her chin. "You weren't here. You didn't come."

"I couldn't, I'm sorry," I say. "I'll come next year, I promise."

The muscles in her face relax a little. My promises mean nothing, hollow like glass ornaments, but I'm betting she won't remember them in an hour. And if on the off chance she does, so be it. So she feels disappointed next Christmas or Easter or Mother's Day when she watches all her pals receive visitors bearing flowers and cards and sugar-free candies, and she, poor old Lil, has none. Oh well.

Then it occurs to me: Golden Brook has a list I gave them of approved visitors. They would have called me if a stranger had shown up trying to see my mother, but on holidays the grounds are visitor-heavy, maybe not as much during COVID, but in the spring during the vaccination rush there must have been at least twenty, thirty non-residents strolling the grounds. Any one of them could have popped his head into my mother's room on his way to the bathroom.

"Mom, did anyone come and talk to you on those days? Anyone you didn't know? Anyone come in and say hi?"

She lowers her face so it's closer to the custard and takes a small lick.

"Crisenda brought her daughter," she says. "She's in finance. I said my daughter's a big doctor, she's coming later. Ha!"

She looks at me with disdain, and I just can't tell you how much it doesn't mean to me. Her disdain is like a pair of Georgina Melios's Eurotrash kisses, dissolving into the air.

"Anyone else?" I said. "Any new people asking questions about me?"

"You," she says, like she just noticed I got here. Something is clicking.

"Did someone ask you about me, Mom?"

My mother stares into the carton. She's devoured half of it already.

"Mom?" I say.

She looks up.

"You sure you didn't meet anyone on those holidays, when there were a lot of strangers around?"

"Nah," she says, her tone annoyed.

She waves me off with her hand, and then seems to forget why she's moving her hand and scratches her ear.

"Everyone's a real jerk here," she says. "Why'd you put me in this place with all these jerks?"

I sigh, already exhausted, realizing she's downshifted from confusion into standard complaints.

"Food's garbage," she says. "Tastes like snot. And they don't clean anything."

That last one makes me laugh out loud. When I was growing up, my mother thought cleaning the house meant making sure her doody made it down the slow toilet drain.

She glares at me.

"The place is spotless, Mom," I say. "It costs a lot of money to live here, you know?"

"You pay for that," she says, adding a snort of laughter.

"Yes, I do."

"Why can't I come live with you?" she says, nodding at me. "I could eat what I want."

The stroke stripped her of any put-upon emotion, her ability to beat around the bush, or nuance—never her strong suits to begin with, but now there's really nothing. A more clever person would try to butter me up, manipulate me, cry, and say how sad she is, how lonely, please don't let me live out my remaining days here. But my mother just barks out ideas as she has them, devoid of any attempt to convince me.

"Sorry," I say, equally devoid of subtlety. "No room at the inn."

"Pssh," she says, turning her lips into a duck bill of disapproval. "You got plenty of room. You got money."

I shrug and smile. *Who, me?*

"I could live in your whole basement," she says.

"That's where my office is, Mom," I said. "Where I work."

"Work," she says, and then she laughs again, liquefied custard spraying onto the carton. "Listen to people complain all day and then give 'em drugs, that's what you do."

"You got it," I say.

"We never needed any of that," she says. "We just solved our own problems."

She digs her spoon into the custard, scoops a heap inside her mouth.

"I guess people out here on the East Coast just aren't as strong as you, Mom."

"Strong," she repeats.

Hearing her say the word presses the corner piece of a jigsaw in my mind.

"Mom, did anyone here talk to you about the Strongs? Savannah? Or Gordon?"

She stares into the carton again, says, "Yeah, the Strongs."

"Mom," I say, leaning forward on my seat. "Has someone asked you about the Strongs? A visitor? Someone on the phone?" I say, pointing to the landline unit on her bedside table.

She lowers the carton into her lap, away from her face, two streams of chocolate running down her chin. She stares at me, almost as if she's just seeing me.

"You did it," she says.

"I did what?"

"You killed them," she says, pointing at me. "Evelyn, Brendan, Savannah. Even Gordon. You killed Gordon, too."

"Mom, that's enough," I say. "Gordon killed his family and then himself. It was a terrible tragedy."

"You did it," she whispers, then covers her mouth in shock at her own words.

I shouldn't feel needle-pricks on my scalp, the back of my neck, running up and down my sides from my hips to my pits. I shouldn't let the nonsensical accusations of a diabetic stroke victim rattle me, but I am after all the only human who had the privilege of occupying a seat in the very front car of the Strong Family Murder Roller Coaster Thrill Ride, now with added loops and corkscrews.

"No. I. Didn't," I say, enunciating, as if the phonetic clarity will give the words a better shot of burrowing into my mother's consciousness. "Gordon Strong killed his family. Remember Gordon, Mom? The guy next door who lost his job and clipped that hedge all the way down to nothing?"

She wears her standard blank expression, but I can tell she's thinking about it, searching for images to match what I'm saying.

"Yeah," she says, remembering. "The hedge—it was like a hill."

"That's right," I say. "Before he destroyed it completely."

My mother shakes her head, bares her teeth.

"You're tryin-a confuse me," she says. Then she stares at me, points her spoon at my face. "You did it, not Gordon." She laughs. "Oh boy, I'm gonna tell everyone the truth."

"That's enough," I snap, as if she's a naughty child. "That is absolute nonsense, Mom. Everyone knows Gordon killed them. I was asleep in Savannah's room the whole time. Don't you know how hard that was for me? Do you realize how traumatized I was? Do you even care?"

She rears back, her head lolling on top of her neck, as if I've knocked her off balance.

"I care," she says. "I tried to help you, and you thought you fooled everyone, didn't you? But not me. I know who you are."

"That's right," I say, gripping her knee and lowering my voice. "And I know who you are, too. Maybe you killed the Strongs, huh? Oh, that's right, how could you do that, you could barely make it up a flight of stairs in that fat suit you called a body. You only had enough upper-body strength to reach your hand up to the Culver's drive-through window. How could you possibly stab a bunch of people? Way to eliminate yourself from the suspect list, Mom."

She realizes I'm insulting her and pushes my hand off her knee, holds the carton close to her chest as if I'm about to take it away. Starts shoveling again. Then quits with the spoon altogether and lifts the carton to her mouth and drinks from it.

"You were always jealous of Savannah and how pretty she was. She got all the attention, and you couldn't stand it 'cause you weren't ever that nice-looking. Kinda big and dumpy, and all those pimples. Ugh."

Now this, being told how unattractive one was by one's mother, this is the sort of thing that might send my patients into spirals, but me, this is like a comfy rec-room beanbag of dysfunction. It doesn't even make a scratch.

"You want to tell me what an ugly kid I was, go for it," I say. "Just add it to your myriad mother-of-the-year moments, along with how you sold me off to every news outlet that asked that summer."

She lowers the carton. Chocolate lines her bottom lip and covers her chin.

She shrugs, says, "No one ever thought about it, but it makes more sense that you did it instead of Gordon. He was just a guy down on his luck. You were a manipulative sociopath."

Now something has changed. This isn't my mother being delusional and demented and cruel. She's never used the words "manipu-lative sociopath" in her life, and it's unlikely she read them, as she doesn't read anything without pictures. So it stands to reason she heard it from someone else.

"Who told you that?" I said. "Who said I was a manipulative sociopath?"

"I did," she said.

"Not right now," I say, the patience trickling out of me like a just-needled water balloon. "Before. Someone said that to you, didn't he? That I was a manipulative sociopath? Who was it? What was his name?"

She scrunches up her face, a mess of frustrated wrinkles.

"Will," she says finally.

The sound of the name gives my heart a little punch, wrings my tongue out to make my mouth dry.

"His name was Will," I repeat.

"Course it is," she says, like, dumb of me to even be asking for confirmation.

"Who is Will?" I say. "Was he a visitor here?"

"Nah, *Will*," she says, as if I'm going to say, *Oh, you mean* that *Will, of course, what a silly goat I've been.*

"Mom," I say, leaning forward, elbows on my knees. "Who is Will?"

She sighs. I am trying her patience. *I* am trying *her* patience.

"He worked in the garden every Friday," she says, pointing to the window. "Cut the bushes and, you know, what-do-you-call-it—pruned. Guy who does it now chops off too much, pulls out the healthy stuff. I told him he's ruining it, but he just smiled like a fool. Probably doesn't speak-a the English."

While she rattles on with her not-at-all veiled racist critique, I try to digest what she's actually telling me.

"Will worked here?" I say. "In the garden?"

"Yes!" she says, frustrated I'm still asking questions.

"But he doesn't work here anymore?"

"No, they fired him. He was my only friend during that Chinky virus shit, 'cause they wouldn't let us near each other." She pauses and laughs. "Not that I wanted to socialize with any of those losers out there."

"When, Mom? When did he work here?"

"I don't know. A while ago. Did you see them out there with their goddamn puzzles? They just do puzzles all day and all night."

"What was his last name, Mom? Will what?"

"Last name?" she snaps, pissed that I've interrupted. "I don't know."

"Was it Harbin with an *H*?" I ask.

"Harbin?"

"Yes, Harbin. Was that Will's last name?"

"Why d'you keep asking me this stuff? How do I know his last name?"

"Because you were best friends forever, apparently," I say through my teeth. "Did you talk to him about me, Mom? Did you talk about me and the Strongs?"

"Sure," she says casually. "I told him everything. He's the only person ever asked me questions about myself. Interested in me. Your father never asked me how my day was when he got home, you know that. Just, Hi, Lil, where's the supper?"

"Well, that might have been because he was working eighteen-hour days, but you don't remember that part."

She opens her mouth to argue with me, but I cut her off: "What did you tell Will about me?"

"Truth and nothing but the truth," she says, her eyes cold, wet pebbles. She sets the carton in her lap and rests one hand over the top of it, lifts the other, holding the spoon high. "So help me God." She laughs, says, "You had them all fooled, too, huh? Told them how you found everyone? And they believed you."

"They believed me because it's the truth," I say. "You think those detectives with all that evidence—Gordon Strong's fingerprints on the murder weapon—you think all that was fake?"

"Keystone Kops," she says, ignoring the question. "Didn't think you could do it."

She keeps laughing. I can see the custard in her mouth, coating her tongue, which I wouldn't mind ripping out like a perforated sheet from a prescription pad.

"I couldn't do it," I say. "Physically, Mom. I was thirteen years old. How could I have that kind of strength—enough to push a pair of shears through Savannah's breastplate and slash the blades across Brendan's neck? And what he did to his wife."

As I've said, I've been to therapy myself; I in no way think I'm above it. I've talked about what I saw. As part of my residency, I underwent weekly psychotherapy sessions with Dr. Ringo (not his real name, but he was from Liverpool) for two years. I've done EMDR therapy and cognitive behavioral therapy. I've gone through hypnosis and role-play, had acupressure and acupuncture. Once, as an undergrad, I went to a psychic who lit incense and cracked an egg into a mortar-and-pestle to rid me of the curse. I've learned to give my trauma some language, to talk about what I saw in a way that won't send my body into lockdown the way it used to.

But still, the image of what Gordon Strong did to his wife lies on the backs of my eyelids like an indelible rubber stamp. Although I can describe it, I know it takes me to a certain place I generally don't care to visit.

"And him, Mom," I say. "Big Gordon Strong. You think I hung him in the basement? He weighed, what, about two hundred pounds, and I wasn't even a hundred, so how exactly would I have done that?"

"People get strong," she says knowingly. "In those moments. I seen it on a show. The bear who lifts the car to get her cub underneath."

"What the fuck are you talking about?" I say. "There's no bear, Mom, it was a human woman they say did that, and the story is likely not true."

How many times have I heard the bullshit hysterical strength theory? Almost as many as I've heard about dissociative identity. But I'm not about to get into the nuances with my mother. Like all idiots, she is highly suggestible. If they let her watch Fox News once in this place, she'd be knitting everyone MAGA sweaters the next day.

She doesn't respond, dips the spoon back into the custard, which is now soup.

I grab the carton from her hands.

"You told him my birthday?" I say.

"Yeah," she says, her eyes following the carton. "Told him how you wouldn't come out, and the doctor said he would've used the tongs like in the old days if he could've."

"What else does Will know?"

"What does Will know?" she repeats.

"What else did you tell him?"

She still stares at the carton, hypnotized.

"Nothing," she says. "Everything."

I know logically I'm not going to get anything more substantial out of her than I've already gotten. The more I suggest, the more she'll agree.

So I figure I'm here so rarely, might as well enjoy myself.

I hold the carton above my head, watch her track it with her eyes. She stretches her arms out like a baby and I stretch my arm back so it's just out of reach. Then she seems to remember she's not paralyzed below the waist, so starts to stand, and I poke two fingers into her chest to push her back down. She's wearing a blouse with a low crew neck, so I feel her crepey skin on my fingertips. She bats my hand away, spits out, "Don't you touch me!"

"What—like this?" I say, tagging her shoulder. "Like this?" poking her in the stomach like the Pillsbury Doughboy. "Like this?" tapping the shore of her receding hairline.

She flails and covers her face.

"Stop!" she yells.

"Stop what?" I say. "I'm not doing anything, Mom. Don't you want to finish your custard?"

She peeks through her fingers, and I hold the carton toward her. Milk-Bone for the doggie.

She reaches her hand out to take it, and right before she makes contact I drop it. It falls into her lap, the goop spattering the front of her blouse and pants, and she grabs at the carton wildly but of course fumbles, and it falls to the floor, spilling whatever's left at our feet.

"Oops," I say.

"You!" she shouts. "You did that on purpose!"

She lunges at me, but if there is a thing I know for sure about my mother, it's that even though she's much thinner than she used to be, graceful she is not. So she falls. I mean, not far, she just sort of tumbles out of the chair and onto the floor, scrambling around in the custard, trying to find footing but stuck on all fours.

She raises her head up like a turtle and yells, "You're not a nice person!"

I stand, sling the tote over my shoulder. "Neither are you."

I open the door of her room and see two female nurses, one tall and the other short, coming to the rescue. Tall rushes into the room, and Short says, "Is everything all right?"

"Yes, she just took a spill. I'm so sorry I couldn't catch her—I think she's very confused." Then I whisper, "She thinks I pushed her."

I put on my best thoughtful sad face, and Short nods in sympathy.

Tall stands in front of my mother and holds both of her hands as if the two of them are about to dance. Short walks into the room and takes a look at the spill.

"I'm sorry," I say. "She dropped the sugar-free ice cream I brought. I was just trying to give her a treat."

Short smiles and nods again, pulls a small black box device from a belt on her hip, and speaks into it: "We have a food-related spill in Room G7. Could you please send staff to clean?"

"There you are," says Tall to my mother. "You're doing well."

My mother glares at me, the sticky sheen of chocolate coating her chin and sprayed all over her clothes like she's an eyewitness to a mob hit. *CSI: Wonka Factory.*

I glance to see that neither nurse is focused on me and place my thumb on the tip of my nose, wiggle my fingers in a neener-neener taunt.

"I'm not doing well!" she crows. Then she points at me, says, "Pure evil."

Short turns to me with another compassionate expression. *It's so hard watching them like this,* say her eyes. I nod at her thankfully, throw in some prayer hands, just so she knows the degree of my gratitude. It is high, and vaguely spiritual in nature.

I look back to my mother and say, "I love you, Mom. No matter what."

Tall turns her head toward me, and both nurses are smiling at me now.

"Nasty, evil girl," my mother hisses, baring her teeth. "You always have been."

"Now, Mrs. Strange, she came all the way here to visit you," says Short mildly.

"That's all right," I say to Short. "It's probably best if I leave. Thank you both so much for your help and for everything you do here."

"You're welcome. Our pleasure," they say.

"Nasty! Evil!" my mother shouts, like she's a malfunctioning, ill-conceived children's toy.

For a moment I think maybe I could ask the nurses if they knew someone named Will who worked in the garden and apparently planted plenty of ideas in the muddled heads of the patients, but I need to elevate my line of questioning. As I return the way I came, through the big activity room, I catch a glimpse of myself in a large wall mirror near where the residents are doing syncopated stretches in chairs.

Lean in, they say, every therapist and self-care expert tells you this, lean into who you are, your "brand." The problem with this is something every awkward teen knows immediately: What if you don't know who you are? That's A, but B is my real question: What if you're a total asshole? Who cares, just lean in, fake it till you make it, everyone's a snowflake, don't overthink it, look in the mirror and say you can do this even if you have no idea what you're doing, even if your portrayal of yourself is a little shallow. As I've said before, I'm happy to play the role if it suits me, and I can't deny it's kind of my brand.

Hi, I'm Karen, and I'd like to see the motherfucking manager.

# Gordon Strong

It's not what you'd call a trap. I wouldn't call it a trap. I'd call it an experiment, like for a science class.

That's what Caroline said, anyway.

She wrote a note to Chuck in Evelyn's handwriting, like we talked about. Did a fair job of it, too, especially with the signature, the way Evelyn makes the bottom of the *y* swing around like a lasso.

We decided it should sound pretty vague, the note, not hot and heavy, just-the-facts-ma'am kind of thing.

*Could we meet tonight by your car at 10? It is important.* —Evelyn.

Then the other: *I'll be studying in my car at 10. Could you meet me there? It is important.* —Chuck.

Then it's easy enough to do the next part. Caroline puts the letter for Chuck in their mailbox, and I put the letter for Evelyn in ours. Then we both go back to each of our own houses and wait for the day to end.

I try to keep myself busy, decide maybe I'll follow up on jobs again, realize I haven't made any calls in a couple of weeks. Throwing my back out really got my routine out of whack, and then, well, I've just been distracted.

I put in a call to Dirk Grayber first and leave a message with his bitchy secretary. Then I call some of the guys from the old job, get Remy on the phone. He tells me he got a part-time job down at Allen-Bradley on the factory floor, and says Mike and Jason both found work at Menards in the stock room, basically doing jobs that high school and college kids do. They all took big pay cuts, and I just can't see myself doing it. Making less. I don't say this to Remy, but I think maybe these guys gave up too soon. Remy's telling me it's just temporary, all of them are saying that, it's just a paycheck until something better comes along, but I know how it goes—you get comfortable doing something easy and decide, eh, maybe I'll settle.

I don't want to hop in the first dusty truck that picks me up on the side of the road. I want the right job, the perfect job, and as soon as I find it, I'll clean up my act, cut back on the booze. Take better care of myself.

And I vow to be a little nicer to Evelyn. But first I just have to know this thing isn't true, that when she and Chuck meet out by his car, both will be confused as hell to be there. I guess she might be pissed at me eventually, and even Chuck the Saint might lay into me, but that's tomorrow's problem. Today's problems first.

Coming on four o'clock. Evelyn's not home yet; Brendan's out with his buddies; Savannah's in her room listening to that god-awful rap shit and talking to someone on the kids' line.

Six hours is a while to wait totally sober, and anyway, part of the plan is to make Evelyn think I'm passed out by ten like I have been most nights lately, so I need to at least have a few beers to make it believable.

I grab one from the fridge and plant myself on my chair in front of the TV in the living room.

Soon Evelyn comes home, looks at me, looks at the beer, looks at the TV. She's holding a grocery bag in her arms and a Target bag dangles from her wrist, her purse slung over her shoulder. I can see a stack of mail pinned under her arm.

"Hey, Ev," I say, trying to sound even-keeled as I can. "What's for supper?"

"I just walked through the door, Gordon. Could you give me a minute or two?"

She'll say I always pick the fights, but sometimes she does, just in an underhanded way. Like by pointing out she just walked through the door, what she really means is she just walked through the door after a day of working so hard at her job, which I wouldn't know anything about since I don't have a job. So she's actually trying to needle me into having a fight.

But she's shit out of luck because I'm not taking the bait. Not tonight.

"Sure, babe," I say. "Take all the time you need."

She doesn't have any smart response to that one and trudges into the kitchen. I keep watching TV and sipping my beer, listening to her put away groceries and turn the sink on and off a few times. After a few minutes, I turn my head just a little so I can see her out of the corner of my eye flipping through catalogues and coupon books, a magazine. Then she stops flipping, picks up a letter, examines the front.

I whip my head back to the TV, almost giddy. It's started; it's working. Any minute now Chuck will be home if he's not already, and he'll see his letter, and then this thing is happening, like a train with busted air brakes.

I hear the rip of the paper behind me, and I pick up the remote and turn the sound down a couple of notches, not too much, don't want to make her suspicious. I wait a few seconds, picture her reading, wish I could see her face, but I can't take the chance. Got to be patient and act natural.

After a minute or two she says, "You want gravy on the top round, or breaded?"

Just for a second I feel like someone's flicked me on the Adam's apple, like I'm about to choke, because, goddamn, she failed the first test. If there was nothing, I mean zero nothing, then when she opened that letter why wouldn't she say to me, *Hey, Gordon, this is weird—Chuck Strange just asked me to meet him in his car at ten o'clock at night? What do you suppose that's all about?*

But she didn't. Now she's keeping a secret. I mean, sure, it's a secret I put there for her to keep, but still, she's already hiding something, and the sun hasn't even gone down yet.

I have some more beers. Evelyn starts cooking dinner, house starts smelling like top steak in butter.

Soon she stands at the bottom of the stairs and yells, "Savannah! Dinner!"

I stand and pick up my empties from the chair, two in each hand.

"Where's Brendan?" I ask.

Evelyn sighs, says, "It's Wednesday—he always plays ball with Matt and Huck on Wednesdays, and then they go to Mayfair for food."

"That's right," I say, like I just remembered, but I don't think I ever knew it.

She brings food to the table—a salad with iceberg lettuce, the breaded top steak cutlets, rolls, and butter. Savannah comes down the stairs reading a magazine.

"Hey, sweetheart," I say.

"Hi, Daddy," she says, her eyes on the magazine.

"Why don't you put that away, we're going to have supper."

Savannah sighs, says, "Mom."

"I tell her she can read it while we eat if she wants to."

I try to think, and I guess I have a fuzzy memory of Savannah reading magazines at the dinner table. For some reason, tonight it feels like I'm seeing everything for the first time. Probably not a coincidence.

"We're all here, we should eat as a family," I say. "Without any distractions."

"Mom!" Savannah cries.

Evelyn stares at Savannah, her jaw tense. She shakes her head in a twitchy way.

"It's fine, Savannah. You can read it after dinner."

"Ugh!" Savannah sighs, shuts the magazine, and sets it next to her plate.

"Come on," I say. "I want to hear about your day."

The phone starts ringing in the living room, and we all look toward it.

"Let the machine get it," I say, waving my hand in that direction. "Go ahead, what'd you do at camp today?"

Savannah picks at a bread roll and shrugs, mutters, "Swam."

We all hear the machine pick up. Evelyn's voice: "Hi, you've reached the Strongs—"

"I'm jealous, it was a hot one today."

"We belong to the pool," says Evelyn to me quietly. "You can go anytime."

Then the beep of the machine.

Then: "Hey-a, Gordon, this is Dirk Grayber over at Miller—"

I jump up from the chair and feel a twinge in my lower back but ignore it, rush into the living room, and pick up the phone while Dirk's still leaving his message.

"I thought we were eating as a family," I hear Savannah say to Evelyn. "Why does he get to talk on the phone?"

"Dirk? Dirk? Can you hear me? I'm here."

For a second I think I've lost him, and I think, Shit, please no, please still be there.

"Yeah, Strong-man, I'm here!"

I laugh, sink into the couch.

"Hope I'm not disturbing supper," he says.

"Nah, not at all."

"Sorry it's so late in the day. I'm just working through my call list now. Been one of those days."

"Not a problem, Dirk. Good to be busy."

"I happen to agree. Look—I'll cut right to the chase. I might have something for you with our global partners."

"Global?" I say, my head reeling.

Dirk laughs, says, "It's actually not as fancy as it sounds. All it means is you liaise with the distribution guys on the other side of the pond, so you'd probably have to shift your hours a little differently than what you're used to because they're in a later time zone. You'd probably have to start work around seven in the morning or so—is that something you think you could swing?"

"Yeah, are you kidding, yeah, of course, Dirk. I'll work any time you want me to work," I say.

Evelyn and Savannah are watching me from the table. The sweetest, smallest smile is breaking ground on Evelyn's face, and I feel like I haven't seen it in a year.

"Hey," I say to Dirk. "Does this mean . . . are you making me an offer?"

Dirk chuckles again, but it's good-natured, not schoolyard-bully.

"Not officially yet," he says. "I just needed to make sure you'd be okay with those hours before I run this up and get the approvals."

"Yeah, of course. I'm okay with those hours. What do we do next?"

"Just sit tight, and let me do what I need to do on my end, okay?" he says. "I'll call you by the end of the week."

Of course I say, "Okay." Then we say thank you and goodbye, and we hang up.

"Who was that?" says Evelyn.

"Dirk Grayber at Miller," I say. "He might have a job for me by the end of the week."

Evelyn's smile gets bigger, and she looks like she might even cry.

"Oh, Gordon," she says. "Miller? That would be amazing."

"Wait, you got a job at Miller, Dad?" says Savannah, just tuning in.

"Well, not quite yet," I say, coming back to the table. "Dirk says he's got to clear it with some people, but yeah, he says it's looking good."

"Go, Dad," says Savannah, and her pride in me is one of those shocker paddles to the heart they use on ER patients.

Evelyn doesn't say anything else, just keeps smiling.

For a few seconds I feel like crap for doubting her. For exactly one second I think about coming clean and calling off the plan. But I keep coming back to the fact: better to know than not to know.

We finish dinner, and Savannah heads back upstairs; Evelyn clears the table, and goes upstairs to watch the little TV in our room. I grab three more beers from the fridge and plant myself on the chair to watch the Brewers. Evelyn's not shooting me any more stink-eye now that she knows I'm going to be gainfully employed in a few days.

The next couple of hours move quickly. Around nine I shut my eyes, which is what I do most nights, except tonight I haven't gotten into the bourbon, so I'm not as gobbed up as usual, but I'm still tired, so it's not exactly a challenge to pretend to doze. I knew it might be a problem, so I put in a fail-safe: I don't take a piss before I close my eyes like I usually do; I know my bladder will keep me up, and it does. At first it's a little nag, but then it gets more and more uncomfortable, like there's a bowling ball sitting on my gut.

I open one eye and watch the time tick by on the cable box: 9:38; 9:39.

About five minutes before ten, Evelyn comes down the stairs. I shut my eyes, try not to squeeze the lids too hard, try to look natural. I think about adding a snore but don't want to push my luck.

I hear her pass behind me, walking in her ballet shoe slippers, think about how they look like little Italian bread loaves. Then I listen as she opens the front door real quiet, and then shuts it behind her even quieter, the softest click.

I wait for a second or two, just in case she comes right back inside, but she doesn't, so I get up, and, boy, do I have to piss. It feels like a dam's about to break, but now it's too late—the plan is happening right in front of me. Runaway train's rolling down the tracks.

I peer through the living room window, separating the blinds with my thumb and forefinger. I see Evelyn out there, zipping up her Packers windbreaker and folding her arms.

I see Chuck, too, in his car in the driveway, just where Caroline said he'd be. I look up toward Caroline's bedroom window to see if she's watching, but all the windows are dark.

Evelyn walks to the passenger-side window, and Chuck rolls it down. They talk. I can't make out either of their faces, but I see Evelyn shaking her head. No. Then Chuck shakes his head. Then Evelyn pulls the envelope from her windbreaker pocket and hands it to Chuck, who looks at it. Then he gives her an envelope, and now they're both reading letters. Then they talk again, and Chuck gets out of the car. Slams the door.

He marches up his driveway and to his front door. Evelyn stands there, looks around, a little nervous. I pull my head back out of sight, but then lean forward again after a few seconds.

Chuck returns, and this time Caroline is behind him, wearing a white pajama top and shorts.

"Shit," I say.

I hurry outside, walking fast with my thighs clenched so I don't wet myself, and as I get closer I start to get it: Chuck is angry.

"Do you have something to say?" he says to Caroline, holding one of the letters out to her.

"What's going on?" I say.

Evelyn turns to me and winces, nods toward Caroline, and says, "There's been a kind of misunderstanding."

"No, Evelyn, I'm sorry," says Chuck, all courtesy. "It's not a misunderstanding. A misunderstanding is when one fails to understand something correctly. I don't think any of us are failing to understand this correctly."

As Chuck talks, Caroline stares at her flip-flops.

"Caroline likes to play around with handwriting. She's done this before," he explains to us. "Caroline—did you write these letters?"

In this second I realize I don't really know what I expected to happen if Chuck and Evelyn were actually completely innocent, like not even a hint of guilt from flirting at a barbecue in the mid-eighties. I know there's a thing I should do. The right thing, maybe? But between all the beer I drank and my bladder burning up, I can't think straight.

Caroline starts breathing quickly through her nose, wipes at one eye with the heel of her hand.

"Chuck, it's okay," says Evelyn.

"It's not okay at all," says Chuck. "Caroline, please tell me and Mr. and Mrs. Strong if you wrote these letters."

Caroline's teeth start chattering, and then she nods quickly, and then more tears come, but no sound.

Chuck holds his hand to his head, combs his upper lip with his bottom teeth.

"Please say you're sorry, and then I want you to go inside right to bed and we'll talk about this in the morning when I'm home from work."

Caroline looks up at me, odd-shaped red blotches blooming on her cheeks and forehead.

"Aren't you going to say anything?" she pleads.

"Caroline, that's enough!" says Chuck.

"No, Dad," she blubbers. "It wasn't just me. We thought of it together, me and Gordon."

"You call him Mr. Strong!" bellows Chuck.

Caroline rears back at the volume. Even Evelyn and I jump a little. I've never heard Chuck raise his voice in all the years we've lived next to each other.

"Me and . . . me and Mr. Strong, we thought of it together."

Then all three of them are looking at me. I glance at them, one by one. Evelyn's still wincing, but now she's confused, too, and maybe even scared. Chuck's staring at his daughter, looking like he's about to blow. Caroline's glowering at me, desperation in her eyes.

Sorry, kid. It's me or you.

"I'm not sure what you want me to say, sweetheart," I say finally.

Then I look straight at Chuck and add, "I don't know what she's talking about."

"Liar!" shouts Caroline.

"That's it," says Chuck, and he takes a step and puts his arm around her roughly, physically turns her around toward the house. "Evelyn, Gordon, I apologize," he says over his shoulder as she keeps talking and crying.

"Dad, no," says Caroline. "It was his idea first!"

"Not another word," Chuck says.

Caroline looks back once more right at me. Her face is on fire now, almost all mottled red, wet with tears and snot.

"That poor girl," says Evelyn. "She must be going through a lot."

I watch them go through the front door, and I can hear Caroline's sobs for a minute even after they're inside.

"I wouldn't worry about her too much," I say, still hoping I don't piss my pants. "She'll be okay."

# Dr. Caroline

I have a string of fruitless discussions with the community life associate, the member crisis manager, and the personnel director. None of them know offhand who Will the gardener is or even what landscaping company Golden Brook uses. Apparently hiring of the grounds-maintenance service providers falls under the purview of the operations director, who works remotely. It would seem to me to be easy enough to Zoom this person, but once the three middle-management clowns hear that someone they employed by proxy was actually engaging with a cognitively compromised resident, they clam up, afraid I'm going to sue. I even throw in some noble weeping: "My mother, she just, she isn't the same person, and it's been very hard [dab, dab] . . . If this young man was able to connect with her, I'd just like to ask him how he did it, to be very honest with you." But it all falls on their willfully clogged ears.

So I leave and call Makeda from the car as I drive back to Brooklyn. She doesn't pick up and I leave a message: "Hi, Makeda, this is Dr. Caroline. Could you please call me back as soon as possible? I believe I've found Billy Harbin."

I let out a breath when I get to the Goethals, and it feels like I haven't taken one in a while. Now this will be easy. I was of course hoping the staff would've been a collection of half-wits and quacks, that I could have convinced someone to pass me a file folder with the name of the landscaping service they use and an accompanying list of employees. Or like in a movie if one of them had been called away for a moment, and I could have snuck around her desk to figure out her password on her computer (Hmm . . . let's see, on her desk there's a framed picture of her dog with the name Lucious on his collar, so let's try Lucious. Password not accepted. Lucious1. Password not accepted. Then I'd bring a finger to my lips thoughtfully. LuciousIsMy-BabyBoy. Password accepted—they always get it on the third try) and then I would've uploaded the file on the USB port I always carry around my neck on a chain.

This is not how it's going down, however. Which, ultimately, is fine. Even though it would have been a lovely moment to serve up a Billy Harbin canapé to Makeda and friends, leading her straight to somewhere he worked will have to do.

Just as I'm coming off the Verrazzano into Brooklyn, my Bluetooth butler announces, "Call from Makeda." I tap the Yes to answer.

"Makeda, can you hear me?" I say.

"Yes, I hear you," she says, a little winded. Maybe from climbing a flight of stairs, although she's a bit of a big girl, so it may not take much movement to strain her breathing.

"Did you get my message?"

"I did, yes."

She doesn't say anything else right away, and I think perhaps she's still catching her breath.

"It's true," I finally say. "I think I found him. Well, I figured out how we can find him."

"Okay," she says.

"Okay?" I repeat. "Would you like to hear the details or anything?"

"Sure," she says, as if she's agreeing to trying the special.

"He was a landscaper at the facility where my mother lives. Golden Brook in Elizabeth, New Jersey. I just spoke with her, and she said there was someone who worked in the garden—a man named Will. She said he's not coming there anymore, but when he was, she told him all sorts of personal information about me and also quite a few lies. She had a stroke a few years ago and is quite delusional.

"Now, she didn't know his last name, and the management was very difficult and refused to give me any information. I'm sure a warrant or a court order will do the trick, so if we can get one of those, we can get the name of the landscaping company. But frankly I think you won't even need to go that far—all it will take is a call from NYPD, and I bet they'll start talking. If we can find the company where he worked, we can get all his payroll information, Social Security. We can get him."

Makeda doesn't say anything right away and then says, "Dr. Strange, I'm in the middle of a few things. Do you want to come to the station, and we can discuss face-to-face?"

"On my way."

We hang up, and I feel something like pride fill my chest. It's better than pride, though—it's like pride with a peppery tequila shot on the side, because I'm not just happy to be helpful with this investigation. I'm happy because I'm the one who's bringing it to the finish line. End zone, home plate? Pick your sports analogy; it all comes down to the same thing: I win. And of course justice will be served, and Ellen Garcia will be found and mended and have the opportunity to write as many half-assed-researched clickbait posts as she chooses for the rest of her life. But also, I win.

I find a spot around the corner from the station and walk quickly through the front doors, greeted by the now-familiar fart smell. I give the receptionist my name but don't take a seat in the waiting area, which is just as well, because Miguel appears in less than a minute.

We say hello, and I follow him up the stairs, and he asks me how it is outside, and I say beautiful and a little humid even though I have been paying zero attention. I don't say, *I've had a busy day solving your case, Miguel, I haven't had a lot of time to notice the weather.*

We arrive at the office, and Makeda is sitting at her desk, wearing thick black-rimmed glasses, staring at something on her monitor.

"Miguel, will you grab my docs from the printer, please?" she says. Then, "Hi, Dr. Strange, please have a seat."

Miguel leaves us alone, closing the door behind him.

I reach into my purse and pull out three business cards, hold them up for Makeda to see.

"These are the people at Golden Brook you should get in touch with. One of them will have the information."

Makeda smiles politely. Fake-politely. I lean forward in the chair and set the cards down on the desk, fan them out Vegas-style.

"I think this is it," I say. "This has got to be him. All the pieces fit, don't you think?"

Makeda doesn't speak, just regards me, a hint of a smile still remaining.

I sigh and continue: "My mother, she fed him all these lies about me, and I'm guessing he was unstable enough to run with it."

My tone is somewhat wistful. I'm playing it up a little, but it is sad, isn't it? Sick people doing sick things?

Mona Lisa behind the desk doesn't appear moved, continues to observe me silently.

Miguel returns holding a few sheets of paper, which he hands to Makeda, who nods at him.

"Will you excuse us?" she says to him.

He doesn't answer, glances at me and then the floor, as if he's embarrassed or about to be, and then he leaves.

Makeda is taking her time reviewing her documents, flipping through the sheets slowly.

"I'm sorry, do you grasp what I'm telling you?" I say. "Billy Harbin, or Will the gardener, was in contact with my mother. That was his entrée."

"I grasp it," she says, still focused on her papers.

"You grasp it."

"Mm-hmm."

"Well, do you maybe want to set down your book report there for a second so we can engage about this and plan our next steps?"

So that gets her attention. She looks up from her reading and removes her glasses, sets them on the desk. Then she stands, ambles around the desk, and leans against it, next to where I've set the business cards. I guess she's attempting to seem casual, but there's something else—she wants to look down at me.

"Officer Colling was able to extract some data from your laptop device. It wasn't the photo we were looking for, but it seemed potentially significant, so I needed to follow up on it. Turns out it is," she says. "Significant."

She pauses again for dramatic effect.

"Are you waiting for me to ask you to please share with me what you're talking about? Okay, Makeda, what are you talking about? What's that you have there?" I ask.

What I don't ask aloud is, *What do you know that I don't?*

"I'll read it to you," she says, putting her glasses back on.

Yay, story time with the NYPD. Hope there are pictures.

"'Dear Miss Garcia, Here is some free advice: Spend less time writing trash and more time watching your back. Sincerely, a friend.'"

Makeda removes her glasses, flips the paper around so I can see the words, and hands it to me.

"That message came from a Gmail account created the day it was sent. By you, on your laptop."

I stare at the paper, black letters on the white page.

"So you didn't bring me here for a discussion," I say, getting it. "You brought me here for an interrogation."

A genuine laugh of disbelief escapes from Makeda now.

"I don't have any questions, Dr. Strange. You sent this to Ellen Garcia less than two weeks ago. I don't need you to admit anything," she says, tapping the paper in my hand. "I have everything."

I relax a little, sling my arm around the back of the chair.

"Okay," I say. "I see you have a precious little theory. This could be evidence, sure, but circumstantial, right? I'm not really up-to-date on all the machinations of universal unique identifiers or firewalls or malware, but I'm sure even Officer WikiLeaks out there would admit there's a dozen ways this email could have been generated from anywhere.

"On the other hand, I have a theory with substantial evidence. And even better than that—an actual lead to an actual suspect. Not just words on a page, a human being. So every second you spend here trying to one-up me with this bullshit, Ellen Garcia is locked in a room somewhere getting starved out, and I'd think you'd want to cut to the goddamn chase, wouldn't you?"

Makeda makes a little frowny face, then strolls back around to her chair, sits.

"We talked to Georgina Melios like you suggested. You said you ran into her right before you met Billy Harbin at Prospect Park."

"Yes, that's right," I say. "Did she see us together? Did she get a look at him?"

It would be the biggest irony of my life thus far if a garden gnome like Georgina Melios contributes something meaningful.

"No, she didn't," says Makeda. "She did notice something, though."

Makeda pauses. Dramatic effect. She could really have a viable side hustle as a magician's assistant.

"She said she saw you talking to yourself. Not a little, either—she said when she looked back at you, you were having what appeared to be a full conversation. A dialogue."

"People talk to themselves all the time," I say. "This is New York. If you *don't* talk to yourself, you haven't lived here very long."

"Could be," she says kindly. "But it's another piece for me. That email," she says, pointing at the paper in my hand. "That's a piece. The fact that we can't locate a Nelson Schack or a Billy Harbin—that's a piece."

"You're not listening to what I'm telling you," I say. "Those are fake names—he's Will, the—"

"Gardener," she says. "At Golden Brook. You mentioned that. You said your mother was delusional?"

"Yes," I say, and then Makeda nods, and I realize I've said the wrong thing. "I mean, yes and no. She's delusional in that she's created a whole alternate narrative about me and what happened when I was a child, but she's not making up a person."

I've learned from years of listening to people and their stories that how they think they sound is often completely divergent from how they actually sound. They may think they're telling me just a totally normal story about their daily lives, but I'm able to hear how absolutely bananas it actually is. Right now I can hear what I'm saying through Makeda's ears, and I'd be lying if I said I didn't have concerns.

"I'll be honest with you, Dr. Strange. If I were canvassing witnesses, I'd probably skip the interview with the senior citizen who was prone to hallucinations," she says.

"She doesn't have hallucinations," I say. "It's delusions. There's a difference. Hallucinations are sensory—things you see and hear that you perceive to be real but aren't. Delusions are beliefs that conflict with reality."

Makeda shrugs, says, "It's not a stretch, though, to say she makes things up generally."

"But not this," I say. "If you'd just get a warrant so you can take a look at the employee records, you'll find him."

"Maybe," says Makeda. Then she looks quizzical and says, "I actually do have a question for you, if you don't mind, Dr. Strange. Do you recall talking to yourself in Prospect Park that day, after you ran into Georgina Melios?"

"Yes," I say, not sure where we're going. "Like I said, I talk to myself all the time like most people. And right then I was practicing, which I sometimes do before I meet a new patient, like an actor would rehearse lines."

"Makes sense," she says. "But you were playing two parts, right? You and the new patient—Billy? It was like you were having a conversation, like Georgina Melios said?"

"Yes, probably."

"Hm," she says, nodding.

And now I see where she's driven us. Right to the edge of a Grand Canyon cliff. Or rather, it's just me with my back to the railing.

"What was it that you said about delusions?" she says. "Beliefs that conflict with reality?"

"Yes," I say. "That's right."

"Dr. Strange, have you ever seen a psychiatrist yourself?"

The thing I hate most about her right now is that she's just so self-assured, so confident she's got me. She's played fair and square, I have to admit, and if it were all over and she won, I'd have to concede. But it's not quite over yet, and her attitude makes me want to claw my way out even more.

"I think I'd like my lawyer present before we say anything else," I say calmly.

She nods, as if she expected this, says, "Now would be a good time to call him."

"I'm not sure he's available," I say. "Could we set up a time for me to come back with him?"

Makeda squints, thinks about it. "I think it's better if you call him and have him meet you here now."

I can feel the threat wrapped in her request, a glowing red cocoon.

"I see," I say quietly, and take a deep breath. "May I use your restroom first?"

"Sure," she says. "One floor down, on your left."

"Okay if I leave this here?" I say, pointing to the tote bag.

"Of course."

I stand and leave the office, follow her directions to the bathroom. Go inside and pee, pump ten squirts of bubble-gum-pink soap on my hands, and look at myself in the mirror. One of the fluorescent tube lights above is flickering, making me appear rather ghostly. I could use a little lip gloss, but now is not the time.

The funny thing about the tote bag is that I could have just left it in the car. I had the Golden Brook business cards in there and didn't want to take the time to remove them, so I just grabbed the tote. But now it's almost like I planned it. Now Makeda sees the tote on the chair in her office, and some part of her, even if it's subconscious, thinks, She would never leave her purse behind if she were to, say, make a run for it. What she doesn't realize is I have a leather card billfold in my pants pocket with my driver's license, a few twenties, my vax card, and a credit card. The key fob to my car and my phone are in my other pocket. Today I left my purse at home.

I brought the tote, however, and it's become a sneakily smelly red herring. I love it when my unconscious does all the work.

I leave the bathroom and scan the hallway—a few people walking around, scrolling or talking on phones. No one looking at me. Makeda likely just where I left her in the office. I continue down the stairs and head for the exit.

Of course, it occurs to me to stay, to call Reggie Ginsburg and Jonas and tell them I believe a case is being built against me and they should come to my rescue. But Will the gardener is out there some-where, and he's going to let Ellen Garcia die unless somebody stops him. Makeda and her clown car clearly can't be relied upon, so, as usual, it's up to me to fix everything.

# Gordon Strong

I don't see Caroline for a couple of days. Savannah tells me she's grounded, and I ask for how long, and Savannah says, "I don't know—like twenty years. She won't even tell me what she did to make her dad so angry."

I admit I feel a little badly about how things turned out with her and me and our experiment, but I have to say, it's almost like I had to go through that to get to where I am with Evelyn, which is maybe better than it's ever been.

Right after the whole mess with Chuck and Caroline that night, Evelyn and I had a long talk. I told her how hard it's been for me being out of work as the man of the house, and she nodded and understood everything. For just one second I thought about telling her the truth, that I'd planned it with Caroline, but the second came and went, and I didn't say anything, and who would it help, really? I mean, I suppose it would've helped Caroline, but, being honest, that just wasn't enough to make me come clean. Then me and Evelyn got close and had some sex, which we really hadn't done in a while, and I fell asleep thinking everything really was going to be okay.

I make some trips to the hardware store, get some spackle and grout, and touch up holes in the garage and basement, clean up the

edges on the bathtub upstairs and around the sink in the half bathroom downstairs. Thinking I better take care of all the housekeeping
business before Dirk calls me about the job. Maybe he'll want me to
start next week—who knows?

I go by Menards to pick up an even bigger pair of shears for the
hedge outside, and I see Jason. I tell him all about the job, and I can
see the envy in his eyes—it's like he's starving and I'm holding the
party sub. I know it's a shitty thing for me to enjoy, but I almost laugh
in his face. He's a friend, and of course I want him to get a good job,
too, but so many times in my life I felt like I watched other guys get
the good luck, and finally it's my turn.

At home I go back to the hedge, still trying to even the thing out.
The side that faces the house I've got flat, but the side that faces the
street is still a mess, and there's still a slope on the top. Part of me
thinks I should have just asked the guy in the landscaping department of Menards—there must be a box hedge tool out there, but I
should be able to do this on my own without screwing it up. I never
did look for the ruler in the kids' rooms, but now I realize that
wouldn't be any help at all—I need a yardstick to measure the height
from the ground.

I'm trying to think if we have a yardstick and where it would be
when the front door to the Stranges' place opens, and Caroline comes
out. Her eyes are puffy, her whole face actually, skin still splotchy. It's
almost like she's frozen in time from the other night. The only clue
that time has passed for her is that she's not wearing pajamas anymore. Also she's carrying a boom box.

I stand up straight when I see her. She sees me, too, looks right at
me while she sets the boom box down.

"Hey, Caroline," I say, and I come around the hedge toward the
fence.

She doesn't answer, presses a button on the boom box.

Music blasts from the speakers, if you can call it music. It's that rap garbage Savannah listens to all the time. Just people yelling non-sense with instruments wailing in the background.

I walk up the Stranges' driveway, say, "Caroline," again, but I can't even hear myself over the noise; I can't imagine she can, either.

She stares at me, sits on her front step. Presses a finger on another button, and the music gets louder.

I wince. That shit will burn my eardrums if it keeps going.

"Caroline!" I shout, waving my hands at her.

She keeps staring at me, points to the speaker, and then points to her head. I can't make out any of the words those animals are scream-ing in the song, but then suddenly they become more articulate, or maybe because I've heard it so much from Savannah's room I can suddenly understand the language, God help me.

I can make out the words clearly, just from this one part of the song—chorus, verse, who knows: "Well I think I'm losing my mind, this time . . . This time, I'm losing my mind."

"Caroline, please turn it down!" I yell again.

She seems to finally hear me, presses another button, and the mu-sic stops completely.

"Thank you," I shout, my volume skewed. Then I say quieter, "Thank you."

She doesn't answer, stares at me.

"Caroline," I say, "I'm sorry about the other night."

She winces, still doesn't speak.

"This is hard to explain. Someday when you're older, when you're married and have kids of your own, you'll understand. That's all I can say about it. I know you're angry now, and that's okay. But what I did will make sense to you someday."

She looks down at her feet, makes a little circle with the tip of her sneaker on the step.

"All of this stuff, marriages and families, this is complicated, you know? And I know we had a plan, you and me, but I knew right away we were wrong. You saw that, too, I'm sure. And it didn't make sense for both of us to get punished, you know?" I catch myself, shake my head. "I mean, I wouldn't get punished, like grounded, but there was no point in Mrs. Strong being upset at me also. Your dad was already upset at you, you know what I mean?"

Now she grinds the tip of her sneaker into the step, like she's killing a bug.

"Look, the important part is we were wrong," I say, smiling. "Everything's okay. Nothing weird's going on. So that part of the plan worked pretty well—we found out the truth. I know being grounded isn't a lot of fun, but that time'll pass, and then the truth part of it will still be there."

She lets out a big sigh, like sized-for-an-adult, looks up at me, and says, "My dad never gets angry."

"Sweetie, I know. Like I said, I'm real sorry about that."

"No," she says impatiently, shaking her head. "You're not getting it."

Even though I know I sort of owe her, it still pushes a button, having a thirteen-year-old get mouthy with me.

But I keep it together, ask real politely, "What do you mean?"

She says again, slowly, "My dad never gets angry. When I was six, I filled the tub with shampoo and dish soap and ran the water, and it overflowed everywhere and they had to get the tiles redone and the ceiling in the basement fixed. He wasn't angry at me. When I was eight, I put a toy mouse in the garbage disposal, and he still wasn't angry at me. When I was ten, I burned his work uniform in the barbecue, and guess what?"

She looks at me like she's waiting for me to answer, but then she says, "Not angry. So why would he get angry about this, Gordon?"

Sweat starts to creep down my forehead and temples.

I try to keep cool and say, "He was angry because of what you and I did. I think his reaction makes sense, honey."

"What about Evelyn?"

"Evelyn? What do you mean?"

Caroline rolls her eyes, and I feel my heart rate rise a little. Her attitude's starting to piss me off, to be honest, how she thinks she knows everything.

"How did Evelyn act after? When you guys went inside? Did she act different than usual?"

"Yeah," I answer, before thinking it's probably not appropriate to get into it with Caroline, but then I remember it all in bursts—the hug, the talk, how she seemed so, I don't know, single-minded with taking off her clothes and my clothes, like she was on a mission.

"Maybe her reaction wasn't normal, and my dad's reaction wasn't normal, because they know we know."

I'm listening to her and still picturing Evelyn that night kissing my chest and my stomach, and then she started with giving me a little bite on the love handles, and then worked her way up to my nipples and back down again—I laughed because it tickled and I didn't expect it, and she giggled, and it was playful, like we were a couple of puppies who just met in the mud pit in the park, but the thing that's sticking in my craw is I can't remember Evelyn ever being that playful in bed. It's like she learned how to be that way somewhere else.

I shake my head, say, "I understand you're angry, but that's not what's happening."

"Oh yeah?" she says, sounding snotty. "I bet they were both trying to distract us the other night, my dad by being angry and Evelyn by being all fake—"

"That's enough, now," I say, feeling a wave of heat crash over the back of my head and neck. "You can say whatever you want about your family, but you better watch your mouth when it comes to mine."

"Or what?" she says, standing up.

"Or I'll have a talk with your dad."

She laughs, points at her house behind her with her thumb.

"I'm already grounded forever. Not much more he can do to me. So, you know, those are some bullshit threats, Gordon."

GORDON STRONG

I guess I never realized what a little bitch she was. So rude, such a know-it-all. Some kids you meet, you just can't wait for them to get out so you can watch the whole world crush them to bits.

"Then I'll tell Savannah to stay away from you, our whole family, to steer clear of yours. All of us—Brendan and Evelyn, too."

The confidence washes out of her face, and her eyes get big, blue veins splintering on her skin like her forehead is a topographical map.

"They're trying to trick us, you idiot!"

"You shut up!" I yell. "You're a mean, nasty kid, you know that? You spread nastiness everywhere, and I let you convince me of all this . . . crazy stuff. I don't know what Savannah sees in you."

Her head rears back, like my comments are hitting her straight on physically. In some way I don't even know what I'm saying anymore. It's just coming out, spit flying like sparks out of my mouth.

"She's gotta just feel sorry for you," I say. "She's this beautiful, popular girl, and she's got a kind heart, and you, you're none of that. You're nothing."

She looks past me into the street, and her eyes fill up, but she doesn't cry. The tears don't actually fall; it's like they're stuck, and she's taking real short breaths.

We stand there for a minute, and everything slows down. My heartbeat gets back to normal, cold sweat running over me in sheets, but it feels like something got released in my glands, like I'm being cleansed.

Caroline doesn't look like a kid anymore; she looks like a sad young woman, like someone you'd see at a bus stop in the snow.

"Caroline," I say.

She focuses on me.

"Caroline, I'm—"

"Sorry," she finishes.

She reaches down and picks up her boom box, turns around to go inside.

"I am," I call after her.

She turns her head to the side like she's going to say another thing, but she doesn't, goes inside.

"Caroline," I say one last time, but the door is closed, and she's gone.

.

.

# Dr. Caroline

Jonas is home when I get there, chattering on the phone, and his hair is messy but not in a stylish way, like he's run product through it to make it look that way. Not-hot-messy. He's also wearing swim trunks and a T-shirt that seems too small and has the logo of our sons' school. When he sees me he says, "Yes, thank you, I got it all . . . Whenever you can . . . whatever the price . . . Thank you, my friend," and hangs up.

"What are you wearing? What's wrong with your hair? Who was that?"

Jonas looks down at himself. "I took the first thing on the top of the clean laundry. That was Reggie, but the police called me ten minutes ago. Detective Marks, looking for you."

"What did you say?"

"I said the truth, that you weren't here—but I'm supposed to call her back. She said to call her back when you get home."

He holds the phone toward me, as if this is a thing we're going to do.

"And you said you would?!" I say.

"Yes!" he shouts. "It's the police, Caroline! She said that you just left an interview, walked out. Did you do that?"

"I wasn't about to stay there and listen to her bullshit accusations while I could be actually out here doing something productive to find Ellen Garcia."

"Caroline, you can't just run away from the police. You are like a fugitive now."

"Don't be so dramatic," I say. "I'm not under arrest. She can't keep me there."

"Well, she said they are coming anyway, here. Now."

"Yes, I figured," I say. "But you spoke with Reggie."

"Reggie," he says, sounding relieved just by uttering the name. "Yes, I finally got in touch with Reggie. He will help us."

"Okay, great. How?"

"He says we should give them everything," Jonas says, eager.

"What do you mean, everything?"

Jonas shrugs, gestures around the house. I see that he's gathered all the devices once more—my laptop, his laptop, the boys' iPads, and placed them all on the island in the kitchen.

"Everything, whatever they want. They can search the house, the boys' rooms, your office, the crawl space." He continues, starts waving his hand around, thinking about other ways for the police to violate our privacy. "They can look in the trunk of the car—we can give them the keys to the storage space—"

"No fucking way," I say. "They don't need to know about the Gowanus space."

Jonas shakes his head in a twitch.

"Reggie said to give them everything. We have nothing to hide, so we give them everything they want to show them you have nothing to do with this."

"That's what Reggie said?" I say, and Jonas nods. "That's the worst legal advice I've ever heard."

"Transparency!" Jonas says, raising his voice. "Transparency is the quickest way out, Caroline."

"Jonas," I say, realizing I have to spell it out for him. "I know you

don't have a lot of experience with this because in Sweden the lawyers probably just have to, like, make a waffle or something instead of
taking the bar exam, but here the lawyers are supposed to protect
their clients, not expose them."

"What is wrong with this idea?" he says, genuinely bewildered. "I
don't care if they see all the pieces in the Gowanus space. They can
have them, if that's what it takes for you to not be a . . ." He stumbles
over the word, then says, "A suspect."

"Jonas, if they get into that space they'll know we're not insured
for it, and we could be subject to all kinds of fines, and the old guy,
he'll have his whole life blown up because it's unregulated."

"It's just money, Caroline," he says. "Who cares? We'll pay off the
old guy. We'll buy him a new building."

"We will?"

"Yes," he says. "We will."

I don't mess with my husband too much about money, don't remind him that I'm the one who makes it and I'm the one who made
good investments and pulled out right before the '08 crash because I
had a feeling. Don't get me wrong—I value art, I think it's real and
connects humanity in a way that more obvious forms of communication can't, and Jonas is quite good at it when he's not being too self-
indulgent. I don't harp on the fact that I have years of education and
training and spend days locked in the psyches of my patients while he
dips newspaper strips in goop and smokes skinny, fragrant joints.

"For you to not go to jail, we will," he adds, just to show that he's
not spending money carelessly.

"I'm not going to jail, Jonas," I say, walking to the refrigerator. "I'm
going to find Ellen Garcia myself."

"What?" he says. "You can't do that. That is the job of the
police."

"And they're botching it."

I take a boxed iced coffee from the fridge and grab my laptop from
the island.

"When Makeda gets here, tell her you haven't seen me. Can you do that?"

"Lie?" he says.

"Yes, Jonas, lie. All you have to do is say I haven't been home."

"I can't lie to the police," he says, shaking his head.

"Fine, then tell them the truth. Tell them I took my laptop and left. They don't know what they're doing anyway, so it likely doesn't matter."

"Doctor," he says quietly, running his hand through the tangled nest of his hair.

"Jonas."

He has bags under his eyes, poor thing. So few times have I seen him scared.

"You would tell me, wouldn't you, if you were in trouble?" he says.

I peer at him sideways. He looks awfully pale. I don't want him to be sick with worry, but at the same time, really, how dare he? Ours is a marriage based on the space between us, not secrets exactly, but we've never understood those couples who text each other constantly, who chatter away about endless complex vacation plans, have date nights when they get tipsy and make teary confessions about minor indiscretions. No one needs to be inside anyone else's head all the time, take it from me. Even the person who is closest to you needs to wait just outside the door sometimes while you do what you need to do.

So there's the truth, and then there are lies, and there's exactly what people can handle when they can handle it. That's an AA thing, right? God only gives you what you can handle? That's the problem with God—he's woefully out of touch with what the average person can handle. Either that or he's a total dick.

But I'm not like that. I only give people what they're ready for. In sessions with my patients, I don't come out swinging right away. I don't drive the awakenings; I just shift the light. Similarly with Jonas, he knows what I allow him to know, and do you know why that is? It's the same answer across the board for my husband, my kids, my patients. Because I really do love them.

Right now Jonas doesn't need to know any more than he already does, and anyone can see that's for the best. Even with just the bare minimum of insight into the situation, he's a nervous wreck, and I want nothing more than to relieve him of this burden. So I look at my husband of almost fifteen years, the father of my children, and I lie right to his beautiful face and say tenderly, "Of course, my love, you know I would."

# Ellen Garcia

I talked for a long time and then eventually I stopped. I lost all my spit, and my throat turned raw from exposure to the air, which has become freezing. In reality, it is probably exactly the same temperature as it was when I got here, but my body heat must be dwindling, because I've started shivering and can't stop. The rows of my teeth are knocking against each other like I'm a Halloween skeleton swinging from a doorknob. Can't stop sweating, either, but it's cold, making me colder. I keep wiping my face with the bottom of my shirt until the fabric's soaked through, then go right back to hugging my arms as hard as I can to create some skin-on-skin warmth.

I could only get a couple of bites of the bread down but at least drank all the water without spitting it up, so maybe that'll give me something down the line, extend me staying awake, or me breathing, or something. But honestly I think it's all coming out in the sweat, all the energy wasted by me shaking.

I'm not fantasizing about food or even water anymore. Now it's a hot tub—not a warm bath but a Jacuzzi with the jets, with the heat jacked up so high my chest would hurt. I picture sliding in, feet first, then legs, then belly, then upper body, just my head floating on top of the liquid heat and falling asleep.

I shake awake, thinking I've heard a noise. A voice. I squint, try to focus. I hear it again, but it's like only one sound, one word from the other side of the door, and then it's over. It's a male voice, unfamiliar to me. I'm well aware I might be suffering an audio hallucination at this point, but it's coming and going, and maybe, I don't know, maybe a hallucination would be more consistent? Like reliably trippy?

Then comes a whole string of words: "Yeah, I don't think I'm in the right place. The door's gotta lock on it downstairs, like a padlock, but it was unlocked."

I don't remember the voice of Dr. Caroline as she normally sounds or playing the role of my kidnapper, but it sounded higher than this person, who sounds like a middle-aged guy right out of Brooklyn-Jersey central casting.

"I can't hear you, you're goin' out," he says.

"Help," I say, but it's not loud, barely a rasp.

I try to crawl, drag myself forward, clawing at the chalky floor with my hands.

"Aw fuck," he says, but not to me. To his phone that's lost service.

Which means soon he'll leave wherever this is to get better service. Which means I probably don't even have a minute, maybe a few seconds.

I breathe deep, push myself up to give my lungs some room, and let it rip:

"HELP!!!"

I start gasping; my eyes water; my throat is thrashed, so dry I start coughing seal barks.

"Hello?" he says.

"Help!" I say, as loud as I can, which is not loud, just hoarse.

"Are you locked in there?" he says.

Then he knocks on the door, and I'm crying. Someone has found me. Brooklyn Joe, Staten Island Mike, my savior. Hope he's single.

"Yes," I say, sobbing. "Yes, please help."

"Yeah, I will. I got shitty service in here."

"Cops," I say. "Call cops."

"I will, I promise, I won't leave you in there. You're gonna be okay."

I keep crying, blubbering, thinking I love Brooklyn. I love New York. Anyone can say whatever they want about how rude people are, but I dare you to find one average citizen of the five boroughs who'll leave you to die in a storage space.

"Just hang on—I'm texting my friend, I got a bar, I think I can get him."

I crawl closer to the door, every muscle in my body glowing with pain, the breath burning my throat and nose as I cough and sputter.

"Please," I say, throwing my hand limply against the door.

"I hear you," he says. "Hang on . . . Shit. This isn't going through. Listen, I'll be right back."

"No!" I screech, both my hands on the door now. "Don't go!"

"Hey, I gotta just run upstairs so I can get some service—and I'm telling you, I'm not gonna leave you in there."

"No," I say, slapping the door with open palms, but I'm so weak it sounds like a kid playing patty-cake.

"It's okay, lady, it's okay. I'll be right back. What's your name?"

I press my face sideways against the door, which is cold, makes my shoulders shudder.

"Ellen Garcia," I say. "Ellen."

"Helen? Okay, Helen, I'm not leaving you in here. I'll be right back." He pauses for a second, and I hear something else. Jingling keys. "Hey . . . hey, there's a woman locked in here. Do you have any service?"

I pull my head away from the door. Someone else is out there.

"Is this your unit?" he says. "What the fuck?"

"No!" I yell, slapping the door some more.

"You can stand there all you want, but I'm calling the goddamn cops!"

Then I hear another voice. High but not too high. It's her, it's him. It's my kidnapper. I can't make out any of the words.

"Get the fuck outta my way!" shouts Brooklyn Joe.

"No," I say, clenching my right hand, the fingers so weak I have to press them into a fist.

I hear noise. Movement. Fighting. My kidnapper is saying something, but it's still too quiet for me to hear.

"What—" yells Brooklyn Joe, heaving and panting.

I beat my limp fist against the door for another minute or two, I really don't know how long. Then I pull it away, and there's no more noise outside.

"Hey!" I call, then cough and wheeze.

There's silence and some more seconds pass. My coughing dies down, and now I only hear my breath. I press my ear against the door, then my forehead.

Then there's a sound. The key in the lock.

I try to push myself up on all fours, but before I can, the door swings open, cracking against my forehead, knocking me backward.

My head feels like it's ballooning, filling with fluid, water streaming from my eyes. The light from the hallway is bright; I can't make anything out except shapes. Someone leaning over, back to me, dressed in white like a mental hospital orderly.

I try to say, "Help," but the word turns to mush in my mouth. Something is wrong with my head, or rather the passageway from my head to my lips.

The person in white backs into the room slowly, and I think I have to get up, I have to get out while the door is open, but my head, whatever's happening is radiating through my body. I'm thinking, Move, goddammit, move, but it's not working. It's like my body's done with taking orders.

My vision is still blurry, but now I see that the person in white is pulling something heavy. Which is another person. The person in white drops the arms of the guy who was supposed to be my savior and perhaps eventually boyfriend and turns to me.

I can't make out the face because of the light, the tears in my eyes, my water-balloon head. The person in white is wearing a mask and a white baseball cap, and after glancing at me turns back around, steps over the other guy, leaves, and pulls the door shut. Then I hear the keys in the lock.

Slowly my eyes adjust to the low light of the room again, and I get a look at the guy in here with me. Mustache, big belly, probably thirties or forties, wearing jeans and a muscle tee, some janky tattoos of women's names with hearts and birds. He's got blood coming from somewhere, pouring out, but I can't quite tell where. Eventually, I move again, scoot myself inch by inch to get closer to him, to see if he's breathing at least.

I finally get there, right next to him, and I put my hand on his chest and then two fingers against his wet bloody neck but don't feel any beat.

It's definitely Brooklyn Joe, and he's definitely dead.

# Dr. Caroline

I wake up from a nap in the driver's seat and feel refreshed. It's been almost an hour already, and my shoulders are sore, proba- bly from my head falling in the space between the window and the seat. Not a day passes that I don't appreciate how I'm able to fall asleep in the midst of a high-stress moment. Like delirious Dorothy in the middle of that tornado.

I've parked on a side street in Gowanus, somewhere out of the way in case, for example, police are canvassing my neighborhood looking for my license plate. But I also don't flatter myself. I am just one person of interest, or, okay, fine, a suspect, in a city full of suspects. Once, for kicks, when we were looking at houses to buy, I accessed the public records to view local registered sex offenders, and our whole neighborhood lit up like the Rockefeller Center Christmas tree. All of Brooklyn, in fact.

I think more likely that it's just Makeda out there looking for me, and even if Jonas crumbles, which I think there's a fifty-fifty chance of, it will still take her some time to track me down.

I pull my laptop from the bag on the passenger seat and flip it open. Go to the Golden Brook website and read all about how Golden Brook is for the golden years. Your loved ones have worked so hard, don't they deserve a nice place to fall apart and shit their pants and die?

It doesn't exactly say that, but that's the subtext of all these places. Let us do the dirty work so you don't have to. Frankly, the promotional materials could read just like that, and I would be in. Sign me up, take my money.

I click on the "About Us" link and then the "Leadership" link and "Careers," and I find profiles of the big dogs—the CEO, the head doctor, the chief of staff, even the personnel director with whom I met—but there are no photos or bios about the little people, the nurses, the dining services crew, the diaper-changers. Nothing about the vendors who empty the trash and wash the windows and yank the weeds.

It occurs to me I shouldn't be looking to the brass for help. "Follow us on Facebook, Instagram, Twitter" reads a line at the bottom, so I click the Instagram logo and begin to scroll backward through seemingly endless pictures of old folks in masks doing their various activities six feet apart for the past year plus. Back in January there's a post celebrating the first round of vaccinations, a shriveled grandpa with a face like an acorn makes a thumbs-up to the camera as he gets his shot.

Back even further through 2020, through all the notifications and updates, reels posted by facility management about everything they know and all the COVID precautions they're taking. We know you're eager to see your loved ones, but for the safety of all our residents and staff, we ask that you refrain from in-person visits at this time.

No problemo, Madam CEO.

After a few more pictures, I find something. The post is captioned, "Many thanks to @jacksonlandscapers for the beautiful work on the autumn garden!" The picture shows a neatly arranged row of orange flowers along a walkway leading to a man-made creek. I vaguely remember the foliage and the water features when I took the tour of the place initially. I generally appreciate a curated green space, but then I was likely only seeing additional dollar signs adding to the total cost in every leaf and petal.

I click on @jacksonlandscapers and do the same rewind, scrolling through a hundred snapshots of boxwoods and manicured lawns, scanning for a post about Golden Brook. Unfortunately, there don't appear to be many pictures of staff in the process of creating these horticultural miracles, only the finished products.

But then I hit the three-cherry jackpot with a post dated December 14, 2019, captioned, "All work and no play makes Jackson a dull place to work! Thanks for a great year, team!" Turns out they threw a little holiday party for the staff at a bar-and-grill in Jersey City. Chicken wings and frosty mugs. I'm thankful on the timing because there's not a mask in sight—I can see people's whole faces.

There are five pictures in the post, and I scroll and zoom, drag my finger around the screen so I can examine each face. Then in the third picture I see him. Or someone who could be him—his face is small, and his hair is longer than when I met him, down below his ears, but I can see the high cheekbones. The color of his eyes doesn't quite come through in the photo—that highlighter blue—but there is a translucence to them that's familiar.

He, Billy, or now Will, is standing at the far right in a line of people standing in front of the bar, most of whom are laughing and clinking glasses, but he is not smiling. He doesn't seem surly, per se, just surprised.

"There you are," I say aloud, tapping the screen.

As I tap, links appear, tags—@xyz. I tap one of them and go to another user—a middle-aged Black guy with some pictures of family and dogs and nature. I realize the savvy social media director at Jackson Landscapers was smart enough to tag his employees if they had Instagram accounts.

I back up to the group shot, keep following the tags—there are about ten on the post: TequilaMan27, GaryBenedict, ESanchezinNJ.

I glance at each account, the profile picture, and then one or two of the posts, just to see if it's Will. But I already got the payoff with the pictures, not quite lucky enough for this guy to have his own account with his full name and contact information.

But the guy standing next to him—young and tan-skinned, possibly Latinx, with vintage Mario Lopez hair. He has an account with his name right there at the top: Mateo Robin. Mateo's got a lot of pictures of him and his busty girlfriend, and him riding various types of motorbikes. I scroll down, trying to find any pictures with Will, but don't see any white people, frankly, but then, July 2020, a selfie of Mateo with a few friends, all in masks, framing a Jackson Landscapers post sign on the side of the road, and I'm almost certain one of them is Will. "Gonna miss you, JL!" reads the caption.

I tap the DM squiggle in the upper right corner. I have an Instagram account for lurking purposes only, also Facebook and Twitter. I can't imagine I'll ever share what's happened over the past few days with my sons, but right now, at this moment, I imagine they would be pretty impressed with my social media acumen.

"Hi Mateo," I write. "I'm trying to find my nephew, Will, who worked with you at Jackson Landscapers. He is experiencing some mental health challenges and has gone a bit off the grid. Just following every avenue at this point. Any information you have would be much appreciated. Thank you, Caroline Strange."

It's a gamble, to be sure. That Mateo knows him well enough to have his email address or a phone number, but not well enough to say, *Hey, Will doesn't have an aunt named Caroline*. And also that he doesn't write back with, "There were a couple of Wills who worked there. What's his last name?"

Back to gambling: The more you play, the more you win. And also lose, of course, but I'm choosing not to focus on that. I go back to the holiday party post, and tap on the tags, send DMs to as many as I can find. Hi Gary, Hi Eloisa, Hi TequilaMan27. More gambles that they don't all speak to each other on a regular basis.

While I'm cutting-and-pasting a message to TysonTiki, a red "1" pops up. I have a message.

I click, and it's Mateo.

"Yes. Do you want to call me?"

I hold the phone up and think, God bless you, Mateo, you kind-hearted landscaper-dirt-bike-afficionado with the bountiful hair and bouncy-breasted girlfriend.

I tap the number in the DM and it rings once. Then he picks up.

"Mateo," he says.

"Oh, hello, Mateo. This is Caroline, I'm Will's aunt. Thank you so much—I'm just so relieved I got in touch with you."

"Yeah, of course, ma'am. I want to help."

"I truly appreciate that, Mateo. Have you by any chance heard from him lately? Usually he checks in with us every few weeks, but right now we can't locate him, and we're all very worried."

"Yeah, I'm sure—who's we, though?"

I think fast. Who is we? I'm the aunt, so it's my sister or brother who is or was the mother or father, but now we fly into a little bit of a sticky strip, because hopefully Mateo doesn't know a lot of details about Will's family.

"All of us."

Keep it vague, cross fingers.

"I didn't know the guy had any family left, glad he does, though."

I take the "left" as a piece, as Makeda would say. Hold on to it for later. Generally if you say you don't have any family left, you're talking about immediate family. Right now I have to assume maybe the parents are out of the picture, so best not to mention them.

"Well, you're exactly right," I say. "It's just me and my husband and my sons—Will's cousins—and some other aunts and uncles and cousins-once-removed."

"Sure, right on," says Mateo. "It's been a minute since I talked to him, though. I had to quit Jackson during the pandemic to take care of my ma."

"Oh, I see," I say. "So you didn't stay in touch with him, by any chance?"

"Nah, not really."

"How long did you work together? He started in, what was it—2018, 2019?" I ask, trying to sound matter-of-fact.

"Huh," he says, thinking about it. "I got there in the summer of '19, and he got hired a couple of months after, I guess. Yeah, he was there for all the fall installations."

I think briefly about the "autumn garden" post from Golden Brook, and then realize the story in the local paper with the photo of my mother in the pool came out in late August. "Lillian Strange enjoys a morning workout routine with friends," read the caption.

"Mateo—did you happen to work on the garden at the Golden Brook senior living facility in Elizabeth? Will always talked about how much he enjoyed the job there."

Mateo pauses, and a tiny kernel of panic lodges in my chest. I'm suddenly worried he'll be on to me, say, *You know an awful lot of details, lady.*

Then he says, "Yeah, I did the lawn there. Will did the cuts and trims—that was his thing, trimming the hedges and boxwoods." He pauses and then says wistfully, "You know?" The way he says it, I know he's remembering, putting himself back there on the lawn at Golden Brook, mid-September sun on his neck. "He seemed to like that job—which made me kind of happy for him, because he always seemed like such a sad guy."

"Yes, sometimes he is," I say, sounding thoughtful. "Is there anything else you can remember about him, anything he said or did that might give us an idea where he is now?"

"I don't think so, I'm real sorry."

"That's okay, Mateo. I appreciate you taking the time to speak with me."

"Yeah, I was always kinda worried about him, you know? After what happened to him as a kid, it just made me want to protect him."

"What happened to him as a kid" echoes in my head. I rewind to my first meeting with Billy, not Nelson, at the Lafayette Memorial. I remember Billy saying Nelson came out to protect him when he was twelve. And maybe Will brought out Billy to begin with.

"Right, when he was twelve," I say. "That makes you a good friend, Mateo, that you felt so protective."

"Ah, I don't know about that. I should've kept in touch."

"You shouldn't beat yourself up about it. It's been a tough year for everyone," I say, trying to figure out a way to bring Will's past back into the conversation, but also make Mateo think I know everything about it. "You must have been somewhat close to him, though, for Will to share what happened with you. It was never easy for him to talk about."

"Sure, we were friendly, but tell you the truth, I kinda found out by accident. I was just, like, making small talk, asking where you from, where'd you grow up, and he said South Jersey near PA, and I was like, my whole family lives in Freehold, what town, and he said Oakwood Park, and I said, oh yeah, where that shit went down, excuse me, that stuff went down when the father took out the whole family but the son managed to live somehow."

It becomes clear I need to turn the AC back on in the car, the air takes on a density around me, like I'm on a plane that's taken a sudden drop in altitude.

"He was the son," I say.

"Yeah," Mateo says sadly. "He didn't even have to say it. Just—his face, you know?"

I close my eyes, see his face. He is handsome despite it all, those eyes, the soft sculpted chin, the runway-ready cheekbones. Something really did happen to him when he was twelve that made him want to inhabit the skin of another human being, maybe two. Like I've said before, whether it's true that he has alternate personalities or whether he's making it up is immaterial. The cause and result are the same: he did it to survive.

"I didn't think twice about it when I first met him, because Pearleater is sort of an odd-sounding name, unusual, like I might have recognized it if he went by Will Pearleater, but he didn't—I just met him as Will Wall."

"Wall," I repeat, careful not to make it sound like a question.

"Wall," Mateo says, sighing. "But, hell, sorry—heck, if I had an auntie with the last name Strange, I'd just take that one. Like Dr. Strange, that's tough."

He laughs, and I do, too, extra-loud so he can hear it over any noise behind him.

"I offered it to him, but he wanted the name he picked," I say.

"Right on," says Mateo. "I get it."

"Mateo, thank you again for speaking to me. Are you sure you don't have any information, an old email address, maybe?"

"You know, I gotta check. When you first asked, I was thinking a cell number, and I've been through like three phones since then, so I know I don't have that, but let me search my Gmail and see what I can find. I can text it to this number, if I find anything?"

"That would just be incredible, Mateo," I say. "Thank you so much again."

"No problem, take it easy, Miss Strange," he says kindly, and then he hangs up.

I stare at the phone for a moment and then drop it into my purse, pull my laptop back onto my lap. Turn on the engine and crank the AC.

Then I type into Google Images, "Pearleater Murders Oakwood Park," and watch the chaos splash across the screen. My hand floats up to cover my mouth, because not only is it horrifying, it's familiar. Even though telepathy is bullshit, I think, I'm coming for you, Will Pearleater, but first I have to see exactly how much we're alike.

# Gordon Strong

It's a rare Friday night when both kids are home, the Brewers are on TV in the background, and we're all eating dinner together as a family, but we hit the bull's-eye tonight. I'm a few beers in but I feel good, everything's been good since that night in the driveway. I barely think about Caroline, because I know she'll get over it. That's what kids do. Bad things happen, and you deal with it, and then they pass. That's how you grow up.

Something changed between Evelyn and me for the better, or maybe it's just gone back to the way it was, and I forgot what that was, but something about it feels new. She kisses me on the top of the head when she leaves the room now, and I snap her behind with a dish towel, and she giggles and waves me away, and Brendan or Savannah say, "Gross, you guys."

Things are pretty great in the bedroom, too. "We have to take advantage of all this energy you have before you start your big job," she'll say, unbuttoning my pants. When she kisses my stomach and tugs on my nipples with her teeth, I have to force out the memory of the conversation with Caroline, about Evelyn trying to distract me. That's just the thing—I'm not distracted, I feel like I'm paying all kinds of attention. I'm listening to the kids tell me about their days. I'm noticing what Evelyn's wearing and saying the color looks nice on her.

I keep the idea of the new job close to me all the time, like a little Zippo flame in the middle of my chest. I'm trying not to watch the clock tonight as the evening moves on. Dirk did say he'd call by the end of the week, but he's an important guy, and shit happens at work, I know that. Sometimes you get a fire drill you have to deal with, so although I'm disappointed I probably won't hear from the guy until Monday, I'm determined not to worry about it.

Evelyn starts clearing the plates from dinner, and Savannah gets bowls and spoons from the kitchen for custard, and then Kevin Reimer from the Brewers hits a home run, out to the deep right field line. Both Brendan and I jump to our feet as we watch it fly, and then we scream and high-five.

"They gotta take Leiter out now," says Brendan. "Dude, the Tigers are idiots."

"Yeah, I don't know what they're waiting for," I say. "They're just gonna keep stealing hits."

"Can we please turn down the game while we finish dessert, boys?" says Evelyn, pretending to be more annoyed than she is.

"Can we listen to music?" says Savannah, perking up.

"Sure," I say. "But we're not listening to that rap crap you listen to up there."

Savannah rolls her eyes, says, "Dad, it's the Beastie Boys, and they're super-dope."

"No, let's put on STP," says Brendan, giving his sister a shove on the shoulder.

"Ugh," says Savannah. "That's on MTV like every other second."

"We are listening to Papa's music," I say, standing up.

Now both kids groan.

"No country!" yells Savannah.

I go to the stereo and put on the Billy Ray Cyrus CD. Before I got fired from Kinzer, Jason would blast it in the break room and sing along, and it's one of those songs, the "Achy Breaky," that's just addictive. You can't get it out of your head once it's in.

The opening chords come on, and the kids are howling now like they're being tortured. I turn it up even more and try to sing along, but I really don't know any of the words except the chorus, so when it gets to that part, I croon, "But don't tell my heart . . ."

"I'm eating my custard in my room!" Savannah shouts.

"All right, all right," I say.

I turn it down and I lean my head toward the speaker and listen to some more of the lyrics, and it's all about this guy's different body parts, and how they react to his woman leaving him. Sort of weird.

Then the phone rings, and Evelyn and I look at each other. I look at the cable box—8:07. A little late for Dirk to be calling, but it's possible.

I turn the music down even more and pick up.

"Hello?"

"Gordon."

"Hey, Dirk!" I say, nodding at Evelyn.

She smiles and clasps her hands together in front of her face, like she's praying.

"Hi," he says. "Look, Gordon, I had lunch with Mike Lotke today."

Right off the bat I have to say Dirk doesn't exactly sound like his chipper self. He sounds like a guy about to deliver bad news, but I'm trying to stay positive. No sense in worrying until I have to.

"Oh yeah? How's Mike doing?"

"He's fine," he says quickly, like that's definitely not the thing I'm supposed to be taking away from this conversation. "He and I got to talking about the old days, and I mentioned how I got approval to hire you for the global position—"

I look at Evelyn and give her the thumbs-up, and she puts her hands over her mouth, and then whispers to the kids and points to me, and the kids are clapping, and Evelyn's shushing them.

"That's just great news, Dirk," I say, before he finishes.

I try not to interrupt people in general, but it's hard to contain myself right now.

"Hang on, Gordon."

I notice a couple of things—he doesn't sound happy, and he's not calling me Strong-man.

He continues: "I told Mike how I've always trusted you since the beginning, when you showed me how to get the numbers coming in from the boards, and Mike says, I, meaning *he*, did that. He's the one who showed me, because he worked in distribution first. You didn't start out in that department, did you?"

"No," I say. "I worked the floor."

"Yes," he says, sounding pissed. "You worked the floor, for a couple years, right? So when I first got there, you weren't in distribution yet. So you couldn't have shown me how to get the numbers from the boards. It was Mike Lotke did that. Not you."

"Dirk, I guess I forgot," I say, my mouth drying up. "Sorry about that. It was such a long time ago."

"Well, to me it feels like yesterday," he says. "And whoever takes on this global role, this is someone I'll be working with very closely, and it has to be someone I can trust."

I feel all the blood drain from my face. It feels like it's leaving my body for good, dripping out of my toes.

"Dirk," I say.

"Let me finish please," he says. "I feel like you tried to pull one over on me, and I don't like that feeling, in my work or in my personal life. So I'm sorry, Gordon, but I can't offer you this position."

My fingers around the receiver have gone numb, and there's a pain shooting down my forearm, but it's strange—I can feel the pressure but not the pain exactly, like when you get a tooth pulled.

"Dirk," I say again. "This is a misunderstanding, I swear. I didn't remember if I was the guy who showed you how to get the numbers from the board, but it sort of sounded familiar, and I wasn't trying to trick you, I swear. I just didn't remember."

"Then that's the thing you say, Gordon," he says, cold. "You say, *Gee, Dirk, I don't exactly remember that.* You don't take credit for a thing you didn't do."

"Please, Dirk," I say. "Give me a chance at this job. I'll knock it out of the park on day one."

"Sorry, Gordon," he says. "I don't have any interest in working with disingenuous people."

"Disingenuous?" I say. "You know I'm a stand-up, guy, Dirk. You *know* I bust my ass."

"I don't know that, Gordon," he says, sounding snotty. "If you must know, Mike had a few other things to say about working with you at Kinzer. How you used to sneak drinks and talk to yourself in the break room."

Dirk sounds real distant all of a sudden. I pull the receiver away from my ear and stare; I can see I'm holding it, but I just can't feel it on my skin, can't feel if I'm gripping it tightly or barely grasping it.

"Good luck with the job search," he squawks.

Then he hangs up.

"Gordon?" says Evelyn. "What happened? What did he say?"

"There's no job," I say, stunned.

"What?" she says, breathless. "But there was a job—he said on Wednesday there was one."

"No," I say, shutting my eyes, realizing that in addition to just living through the conversation, I now have to tell the story of the conversation. "There is a job. I'm just not getting it."

"The job at Miller?" says Savannah. "I thought you already had it. Did you get fired again?!"

"No, dork," says Brendan. "He never had it in the first place."

"Kids," says Evelyn. "Go finish your custard upstairs, okay?"

"I don't get it," says Savannah, and Brendan punches her in the shoulder.

"Ow!"

"Shut up," says Brendan.

"No hitting," says Evelyn, looking pained. "Please go upstairs."

The kids rush up the steps, bickering and knocking into each other.

"Gordon," says Evelyn, making her way over to me. "Put the phone down."

She puts her hand on mine, and together we hang up the receiver.

"What did he say?"

I know it's my turn to speak, but I'm not sure my voice will keep working, so I cough, then tell her everything. Except the part about me in the break room.

Evelyn listens, her hand still on mine. She looks confused, says, "But you didn't lie, you just didn't remember?"

"Yeah, that's right. I mean, when he mentioned it originally, I didn't know what the hell he was talking about, but he was so pumped up about it, I thought, Okay, it could have happened, just agree with him."

"Gordon," she says softly, pulling her hand away and touching the hair on the back of her neck. "So you did lie. You just said it. You didn't know what the hell he was talking about."

"No, that's not—" I say. "I mean, it might have happened, Ev."

"But you don't remember it," she says. "So, from Dirk's point of view, you lied."

I wiggle my fingers, trying to get some sensation back in the tips.

"You agreeing with him?" I say. "Huh, Ev?"

She looks down, gets shy all of a sudden.

"I can see his point, that's all I'm saying."

"You can see his point?" I say. "You taking his side? You don't think I deserved that job?"

"I didn't say that," she says, taking a step back.

"Why're you moving away from me?" I say, taking a step toward her.

"I'm just, I'm still cleaning up," she stammers.

"Yeah, but we're having a discussion right now. You're in the middle of telling me how you agree with Dirk that I'm a liar."

"I didn't say anything like that," she says. Then she gets a look on her face that she used to get with the kids when they fell off their bikes. "Look, this is just a little setback. There are plenty of other jobs out there."

She's smiling now but still seems nervous, and I wish it didn't make me angry, but it does. It's like I can see myself in the future apologizing, but I can't stop it.

"You don't have to tell me that," I say. "I *know* that."

"I know you know," she says, then laughs. Sounds like one of those tracks on the old shows. *Brady Bunch* and *Ozzie and Harriet.* Bullshit happy family shows.

"Not sure why you're laughing. I didn't say anything funny."

She nods and takes a step back again, holding her hands up, like she's trying to block me.

"Stop backing away from me, Evelyn!" I yell. "You're making me feel like a monster!"

"Gordon," she says, her voice hushed.

"What's going on?" calls Savannah from the top of the stairs, Brendan right behind her.

"Go to your room!" I scream, and it's louder than I plan, but something's happening to me. My voice sounds far away, muffled, like it's coming from another side of the house.

Savannah's mouth drops open, and Brendan looks shocked and pissed, and the sight of them should be enough, that's all it should take for me to put a lid on it, let the air out, calm down.

But it isn't.

I look at Evelyn, her hands over her ears, and I know I wasn't that loud. I think she's putting on a little show for the kids.

"Just stop it," I say impatiently, and I grab her wrists and pull them away from her face.

"Dad!"

It's Brendan. He's at the bottom of the stairs now. I look at Evelyn, tears spilling from her eyes, looking like a little trapped mouse on the glue.

"Let her go," my boy says, stern and brave, and I feel proud of him, and that's what does it—that's what wakes me up.

I loosen my grip on Evelyn's wrists, and she yanks them away from me, the betrayal and disbelief clear on her face. She rushes to Brendan's side. I glance up to Savannah, sitting on the top step, hugging her knees, crying.

Why do they all have to make me feel so bad about myself?

# Dr. Caroline

What a relief it is to find out someone else knows what it's like to be you.

Well, it's never quite that simple, is it? But still a relief to know that another human may have had an experience close to yours, may have been close to a terrible thing the way you were close to it, may be haunted by it at 3:33 in the morning the way you are, may have it sneak up on them in the drive-through line or watching an explosion on a movie screen.

I can't say I remember hearing about the Pearleater murders. There are a couple of reasons for this—one, when they happened, in 2010, Theo had just been born, and Elias was two. We had just bought our house and were knee-deep in renovations, and I was working, seeing patients in the unfinished basement with construction noise above us, then running upstairs between sessions to either pump or take Theo from the nanny to breastfeed for a few minutes. That madness only lasted a couple of months. Breastfeeding to me was never a beautiful moment of bonding between mother and child; it, like everything with my children at that age, was something to get done so I could get back to work. So you see, ladies, you can have it all, you just won't *like* it all.

I was too distracted in 2010 to observe any news that didn't directly involve me or, say, the end of the world, like, the aliens have landed and they're super-pissed off and killing us all for organ meat, so make sure your alarm system's on.

But also, I admit to having the old trauma blinders on. Every once in a while one of these news items turns up, usually on CNN, where dad, or sometimes mom, or uncle or caregiver, goes bananas and ices the family, including the kids. And if I happen to see the headline on a ticker at the bottom of the screen or as a ten-point-font-sized bolded header on the website, I won't click; I won't linger to the end of the hour to hear more. I'm not hungry for others' tragedies. I mean, other *kinds* of tragedies, sure—rich-husband-kills-rich-wife, Tinder con men, sex cult stuff—I'll watch however many documentaries Netflix wants to churn out on those topics. I just prefer not to hear about the thing I have firsthand knowledge of.

So this all explains why I have no memory of the name Pearleater or the murders that took place right around the corner in New Jersey. Jim Pearleater found out his wife, Beth, was cheating on him and shot her in the face, then shot the two sons, ages twelve and eight. Then himself, also in the face, not quite between the eyes, as they say, more in the forehead. Apparently the bullet lodged in his corpus callosum, the collection of nerve fibers that connect the right and left sides of the brain, and astonishingly he stayed alive for a couple of hours before eventually hemorrhaging, but I imagine he probably used that time to reflect on what a loser he was, how he couldn't even off himself effectively.

A text from Jonas drops down, and I swipe it off the screen. I can't engage with his premature panic right now. I keep reading.

Apparently the older son managed to survive a single gunshot wound. No other information about where he was shot or how he survived, just that he was sent to live with cousins nearby following the tragedy. And they don't mention his name, or his doomed little brother's. It seems the press could only bother him so much, him being a minor, lucky enough not to have a guardian like my mother ready to whore him out for the tabloids.

The stories run maybe the course of a month or so in *The Star-Ledger*, and then stop. Nothing more substantial about the Pearleaters.

I click on the link for the journalist who reported the bulk of the stories: Kaz Kalaam, and an email opens up with his address in the "To" line.

"Hi, Mr. Kalaam, I am in the midst of treating Will Pearleater and I was hoping to connect with you on some background. He has given his permission for me to reach out to you, but I encourage you to verify with him if you are so inclined."

Sometimes, when you're lying outright, it's best to hit the gas hard and not bother inching along and checking the rearview every other second. If you're going to get caught, you're going to get caught. And I'm extra-confident, because something tells me Kaz Kalaam never had direct contact with young Will to begin with, much less became his lifelong pen pal.

Also, not for nothing, I've always been able to bluff, since I was a kid. Now they train children to do it in games like Two Truths and a Lie, to say nothing of the anarchic free-for-all that is Apples to Apples. I guess the goal is now to prep kids for a life of healthy gambling habits.

"Thanks so much for your time."

I add my signature line, degrees bolded for extra intimidation. Hit send.

I open my texts and read what Jonas sent:

"Det. Marks gone. Det. Jimenez still here. Waiting for you. I said I didn't know where you are. The truth."

I don't respond, not even with a thumbs-up. Also privately thankful we've never been a read-receipt sort of couple. I'd be hard-pressed to think of any method of communication more passive-aggressive than read receipts.

I glance back at Instagram and have another DM from Mateo

including an email address for Will: "Might be old but give it a try. Hope everything is OK."

I briefly consider all caps to write my thanks, but I never use all caps, so I just start typing: "Thank you so much, Mateo," but before I finish, my phone begins to vibrate with a call: 732 area code. Which is Jersey.

"Hello, is this Dr. Caroline Strange?"

"Yes, hello. Is this Mr. Kalaam?"

"Yes, it's me," he says, sounding relieved. "You just sent me an email."

"I did. Thank you for getting back to me. I didn't expect to hear from you so quickly."

"Well, I have to tell you, I haven't heard of Will Pearleater in eleven years—the family he was living with moved and changed their names, and then they changed his name. I mean, I get it, he didn't want that name anymore—I wouldn't, either, but I've always wondered what happened to him, and I know you can't tell me anything because of doctor-patient confidentiality, but is he . . . okay?"

I look at my eyes in the rearview and think about how helpful people are, how good and genuine they are. Not everyone, of course, some people wouldn't shoot you to put you out of your misery, but just today: Mateo and now ace reporter Kaz Kalaam. He just wants to help, which will make teasing information out of him so much easier.

"You're correct, I'm not permitted to say anything specifically, except that I'm seeing him in a professional capacity."

"Which means he's alive," says Kaz. "Which means he has to be somewhat okay."

I utter a small congenial laugh.

"I urge you to draw whatever conclusions you see fit," I say, in the winky-winkiest tone I can affect. "I was hoping, though, that I could ask you a couple of questions. The only reason I reached out to you was because I felt it wouldn't be a conflict of interest for you, since Will was never a protected source."

"That's correct," he says. "We were never permitted to publish his name, which was fine by me, but when I saw your email, it's clear you know him, so that's why I feel it's okay to talk to you." He pauses and sighs. "And I want to be helpful. To be completely honest with you, I think of that house, and those kids, and Will especially, just about every day. I've never covered anything like it. Never will again."

"Of course. Those kinds of things are once-in-a-lifetime," I say.

"Right—and I'm relieved to hear he's alive, and he must be some degree of okay if he's in therapy."

"Again, I can't get any more specific, but I, objectively speaking, I agree with you," I say. "I just wanted to ask—did you ever interview him personally?"

"Oh no. Cops wouldn't let me near him, and then the family shielded him from the public, which was good, ultimately. I mean, I had to try to get up close to him for the story but didn't push too hard. I didn't want to make him retell it and relive it a hundred times."

"Probably would've ended up being more than that," I say, flashing on the interview with Helene Garelick. Studio lights in my eyes so bright I couldn't see anything except the gaping camera lens with tiny warped me inside.

"I'm sure you're right," he says. "I love what I do. I think it's important, but I'd be naive to say there isn't a hugely manipulative side to it."

"Got to make a living," I say, pushing in a Bluetooth earbud so my hands can be free. "I read all the stories, and I'm sure I'll hear Will's version of the events, but the father—Jim—he had a psychotic break because he found out his wife was unfaithful?"

"Yeah, the other man came forward after the fact, said he and Beth Pearleater had been seeing each other for about a year. He said she told him Jim was abusive with her, used to beat her up."

"And the boys? Was he abusive with the boys?"

Kaz pauses, lets out a small sigh. "Here's a situation when I'm not sure if I should tell you. I mean, you're going to find it out, I know that, but there's a lot I didn't write, because I just didn't think it was fair to have it out there."

"I admire that very much, Kaz," I say, setting my phone on the passenger seat. "I don't want you to do anything you're not comfortable with. If you like, we can hang up, you can do your due diligence on me, you'll see my credentials and my experience, and then you can call me back if you like.

"Please understand, what you tell me will not affect my treatment of Will. I've seen some children and teens for therapy," I lie, having never seen children or teens professionally. Maybe a couple of sixteen- or seventeen-year-olds in residence, but really child therapy is for early-childhood teachers on steroids, people who want to play dress-up with dolls and indulge in what is perhaps the freshest circle of hell: improv therapy. But Kaz doesn't need to know these details, so I continue: "In those situations, I'll have a chat with the parents first to get a baseline before I dive in with the kids. I don't take their word as truth—it's a narrative like anyone else's—but it's good for me to see a couple of angles, like what you do in your writing. Please know, more than anything, I want to help this young man, and from everything I already know about him, he may very well be stuck at twelve years old, so any information, just as a baseline, is helpful."

"Right, that all makes a ton of sense," Kaz says. Then he takes a deep breath. "Okay, I'll tell you what I know. CPS showed up—they have to, obviously—and they ran their examination, and like I said, the cops and family wouldn't let me near Will, but I did have a friend in CPS who I talked to later, and she said there was evidence of sustained sexual abuse. Sodomy and STD-related infection in the throat and mouth."

"That poor boy," I say, opening up a fresh email on my laptop.

"Yeah, I just couldn't put that in the story. I couldn't justify it. I mean, I could have sold it to myself like, Oh this is helping other victims, but that wasn't the truth. It just would've been clickbait."

"Well, you have integrity," I say. "It seems fairly rare in any business, but especially yours."

He chuckles sadly, says, "I don't know, my wife thought I was crazy to leave it out—she's a reporter, too, one of those Woodward-Bernstein types, get it all out there. But I saw that kid, Will, and I just couldn't do it."

I hold my fingers still on the laptop keys, say, "What did you see, Kaz?"

"Just a broken kid, eyes glazed over, in shock. He was also—this is weird, I just remembered this—he was sitting in the back of the ambulance, and I couldn't get too close to him, but he was sort of smiling. I mean, he was all bandaged up and probably in shock."

"How hurt was he?" I say. "Your articles say he survived a gunshot wound, but if he's smiling, it wasn't too bad."

"Yeah, it was just below the clavicle, less than an inch away from the major veins. My CPS friend said he basically took the hit and played dead while the dad finished himself off."

"Smart," I say.

"Totally," says Kaz. "Survival mode, you know? But still a kid, still just wanting to default, like desperately, to being a kid."

"What makes you say that?" I say, cutting-and-pasting Will's Gmail address from my Instagram DM into the "To" line.

"The smiling, for one thing, who knows what was going through his head, and he was singing."

"Singing?" I say, my hands freezing over the keys.

"Chanting, really. He yelled it once, and then the cops kind of calmed him down, shit, not Ring-Around-the-Rosie but something like that. From a kid's game."

"Red Rover?" I say.

"Yeah," he says. "How'd you guess?"

"It was always one of my favorites," I say. "A little violent, though—they don't let kids play it anymore."

"Right?" he says. "One of those things we did like riding without bike helmets and seat belts. How did any of us make it through?"

"Just barely," I say.

I thank him, tell him he's done a truly generous and selfless thing by talking to me, and to keep up the good work. I hear him smiling as he says it was his pleasure and he hopes Will continues to be okay, and then we hang up.

Then it's just me alone in my car, a blank email with what could be his—Will Wall's—email address. Do psychopathic kidnappers check their emails? Aren't they terribly busy torturing people and committing evil deeds generally? If Will Wall is checking, I would imagine he doesn't have much time. He may or may not be reading whose name is on the "Sent" line, so I feel I need to write something in the subject line to get his attention. I don't have to even think about it; the words write themselves: "I KNOW WHO YOU ARE."

# Gordon Strong

After everything that happened last night, I fell asleep eventually on the chair after polishing off the bourbon I bought last week and an old bottle of Slivovitz that had been on its side in the back of the cabinet. Woke up to an empty house around eleven this morning, head screaming.

It's Saturday, so I know Evelyn's not at work, figure she's out running errands. Brendan's working at Cousins, Savannah's probably at the pool.

Slowly the night comes back to me: Dirk's call, grabbing Evelyn's wrists, the kids' faces. For a minute I feel like shit about it. But here's the thing about feeling like shit: It gets tiring. I'm fuck-all exhausted by it, every day, making the wrong decision and saying the wrong thing and not getting a job and not being able to cut that goddamn hedge straight. Maybe this is just who I am, and everyone else needs to just deal with it, or at least give me a little bit of a break.

I stare out the window at the hedge. There's one way to make it even, I think.

I go to the kitchen and grab a six-pack and one of the sandwiches wrapped in white paper Brendan brought home yesterday. Then I go out to the garage and get the shears, the new shears, and walk up to the hedge.

I crack a beer and drink about half. Unwrap the sandwich and take a bite, oil and vinegar and mayo squirting out of the bread onto my chin. I wipe my face with the bottom of my T-shirt, the one I slept in, the one I wore yesterday, set the sandwich and the beer on the ground, and I start clipping at the top, back and forth.

It's satisfying, hearing the blades close over the branches. The new shears are sharp as hell and strong, I don't even have to give it too much energy, just scissor the blades closed like I'm cutting newspaper and watch the leaves and twigs fall.

No one's going to miss this anyway, I think.

I finish one beer, start another, keep clipping. I'm working up a good sweat now, realize I didn't bother with deodorant, or it might be the onions from the sub. The air around me is ripe, but who gives a shit? When I get a job to go to, I'll clean up, dress for it. It's Saturday, for chrissake, and I'm the only one around. But I could use some music.

I hoist the shears over my shoulder and go into the house, upstairs to Savannah's room. I grab her portable boom box and click the top open, pop out the CD inside. It's red, and the title is *Gold Diggin' Girls*.

"You got that right, brother," I say aloud, and then I drop the CD and slap my hand over my mouth because it's exactly something my old man would say.

Take a peek at myself in Savannah's full-length mirror. I touch my cheeks, scratch my chin. It's you, I think, or maybe I say it aloud. Not the old man. You, Gordon. This, right now, what you're doing, is what you would do, not what he would do.

I pick up the red CD and hold it out in front of me, then unload the shears from my shoulder and place the disc between the blades. Then snap. The two halves fall and land with no sound on the carpet.

I look around, pick up another CD from the clear bin next to her bed—"The Crying Game." Do the same thing. Snap. Ugly Kid Joe—"Everything About You." Shanice—"I Love Your Smile." "Informer," "My Lovin'," "Check Yo Self." "Connected." Snap, snap, snap.

Soon I'm surrounded by all the halves, like a bunch of little pizzas. I feel pretty calm, too. For a second I think about how I'll explain it to Savannah, but then I stop.

I stand and pick up the boom box, jog back downstairs, and grab the Billy Ray Cyrus CD. Then return to the hedge outside. Pop the deck open and press Billy Ray into place. Turn it up as high as it will go, which isn't that loud, as it turns out. The air eats it all up.

I keep at the hedge, back and forth, singing, sweating, pausing to eat and drink. I listen to the CD all the way through a couple of times. It's heating up, sun's high in the sky and only a few cotton ball clouds stuck in their places. I take a minute to stand and stretch—everything on me's pretty sore, a plinking rubber band nipping at my lower back, but I ignore it.

Then I notice Caroline coming toward me, waving her arms, talking, but I can't hear her over the music. I lean over and press stop.

"I've been calling to you for five minutes," she says. "Asking you to turn it down."

"Oh yeah?" I say, wiping the sweat out of my eyes with the back of my hand. "Didn't hear you."

She examines the hedge, now only about a foot tall, branches sticking out every which way, leaves in a halo on the ground.

"What are you doing to this?" she asks, not in a judgmental way, just curious.

"I don't know," I say. "I'm tired of looking at it. You ever get so tired of looking at the same thing every day you just want it gone?"

She looks at the hedge, then back up at me, shrugs. "I guess so."

"Well, I do," I say, and then I pick up the shears again.

I keep clipping, and Caroline keeps standing there like she has more to say, but she doesn't. She's just watching me, and it makes me feel like I should say something, but it also pisses me off a little, how she's always lurking around.

"You still grounded or what?" I say.

"Kind of."

"Kind of? What's that mean?"

"I have to still check with my dad on a case-by-case basis, but I think he's over it, what happened. He's letting me sleep over tonight, after all."

I stop working the shears for a second, glance up at her.

"Sleep over where? Our house?"

"Yeah, is that okay?" she says, a little nervous. "I thought you knew about it."

I stand up straight again, hold the shears at my side, points down. "Why would I know about it?"

She shakes her head. She doesn't want to tell me something.

"Caroline," I say, trying not to sound angry. "What do you mean, you thought I knew about it?"

She starts backing up toward her house, stammers, "I have to go . . . I have to clean out the garbage disposal."

I walk toward her, watch her eyes get wide.

"Caroline," I say. "What is it? What don't you want to tell me?"

"Evelyn asked my dad," she says quietly, looking down.

"She what?"

"She rang our bell this morning, and I heard her ask my dad if I could sleep over. Said something about how it would be a favor to her."

"A favor?" I say. "To Evelyn, for you to sleep over? Not a favor to Savannah?"

"No, she said she would owe him one, though. Said, I know Caroline is grounded but it would be great if she could sleep over."

Now the rubber band snapping at the base of my spine seems to have expanded and somehow wrapped around my whole body, constricting my gut. I take some short sharp breaths.

"Owe him one," I say. "You sure she said that? Maybe you heard her wrong."

"Oh no, I have exceptional hearing," she says, like this is a fact we all know.

"Is that all?" I say. "Did she say anything else?"

Caroline nods, and her mouth goes all crooked like a lightning bolt. One tear drips down her face.

"I'm not supposed to make any more trouble," she says, looking me right in the eye for a second. "I don't want to upset my dad any more."

"Hey," I say, trying to sound calm. "It's okay. I promise, I won't say anything to your dad or Evelyn. I know everything went sideways before, but this is different, okay? I promise."

She thinks for a second and then nods and says, "He gave her a note and said okay, and she said thank you, and did this to his arm."

Caroline reaches out and gives my arm a squeeze right above the elbow. I know I've been sweating and drinking in the sun for two hours, but somehow her damp fingers manage to give me a chill.

"He gave her a note? What kind of note?"

"I don't know," she says, shaking her head. "It was small. Evelyn didn't read it. She just put it in her pocket."

I stare at the hedge, say, "She's afraid of me."

"I didn't hear her say that," says Caroline, but I'm pretty sure she's not telling me that to make me feel better.

"Yeah, she didn't have to say it."

I squat halfway down to the ground, clamp the blades around one of the thicker branches toward the bottom of the hedge, and apply a little pressure; the branch snaps, and a whole chunk of the hedge comes loose, just basically a few tangles still holding it together, so I keep hacking away at the smaller branches in the center until about a third of the whole thing just tips right over on its side at Caroline's feet.

She steps back to make room for it.

"I don't really know," she says.

"Know what?"

She blinks at me, mouth open an inch or so, like the frowning clown carnival game.

"All that stuff you just said. Secrets needing to get cut out or else a thing dies. You just said it."

"I didn't say anything," I say, staring at the hedge, but don't sound convinced or convincing, even to myself.

"Yeah, you did. You just did."

Now I feel like I might need to drink some water, head's all swimmy.

"I . . . I said it."

"Yes," said Caroline. Then she puts her hand on my shoulder and says, "You should really talk about that stuff with another adult."

"Like my father."

"Sure," she says. "Does he still live up near Eau Claire?"

"Yeah," I say. "I talked to him last week."

She thinks about this, says, "You should call him. He'd probably have better advice than me, you know? I'm just a kid."

# Dr. Caroline

I spend a couple of long hours in the car, searching Google page after Google page for variations of "Will Wall," "Brooklyn," "Gardener," "Landscaper Experience." Also scroll through the dozens of Will Walls or Bill Walls on social media, with no luck, my searches jammed by the volume of hits along with the fact that Will's revised last name happens to also be a word (an issue I have also encountered while searching for myself online), so there are a ton of posts and ads for drywall experts and Brooklyn graffiti workshops because of course that's a fucking thing in this town, and apparently also there is a party yacht that you can charter called the *Honorable William Wall*, named after the famed nineteenth-century entrepreneur and congressman, although from the Instagram posts there doesn't seem to be much business or policy discussion happening, just party girls showing off their tits in low-cut shift dresses.

But not my Will Wall.

I see a call come through from Jonas, but I don't pick up. Maybe Makeda and Miguel gave up on me for now and he's telling me to come home, but I doubt it. It's more likely him climbing the ladder rungs of panic; he's probably crouching in the bathtub with the door locked, whispering. I don't need the distraction right now.

I check my email and refresh again and again, looking for a response from Will, but nothing. Back to Instagram to check for DMs, then sift through more Google garbage, then refresh my email, over and over.

Then my phone vibrates with a call, and I start to swear at Jonas under my breath, but see that it's not him, it's Mateo again.

"Mateo," I say.

"Yeah, hi, ma'am, it's me. Look, I talked to another guy we used to work with at Jackson—Gerard. We were all sort of friendly, but I hadn't talked to him since before COVID hit, and he, Gerard, gave Will a lead for a job a couple months ago."

"A job?" I say. "Do you know where? Did Gerard tell you?"

"Hold on, I wrote it down. Yeah, as a security guard for, like, this workspace company—you know, where people rent their own studios by the month?"

"Right, sure, like artists and musicians, like that?"

"Right—so, Gerard, he works for the same company, and they were opening another building that they were still getting permits for and they needed someone to watch it at night, basically, so Will, he's there."

I feel all the air rush out of my chest and some other concoction takes its place—relief and nausea mixed together.

"Great," I manage to say. "Is there a name? Of the company, the workspaces?"

"Yeah, sorry, I got like ten little Post-its here. Here we go—got a pen?"

I don't have a pen. I don't need a pen. I never need a pen.

"Yes."

"It's called Your-Space-718. Gerard said Will's working at the one in Sunset Park, near the Brooklyn Army Terminal."

"I'll find it," I say. "Mateo, I don't know how to thank you." I pause, and then I just say, "Thank you."

"Ah, no problem, ma'am. I just want to help, you know."

"I do. I truly appreciate it."

"It's my pleasure," he says, and then adds, "But if he's still working nights, he's not going to be there yet."

"That's just fine," I say. "I'll be waiting for him."

# Ellen Garcia

The first thing I do is apologize.

"I'm sorry she killed you," I say, my head on my would-be savior's chest.

Under normal circumstances, I might be a little skittish getting so close to a dead body. But I feel I know this guy; I owe this guy. If I'd just accepted reality as it was, that I'm crispy shrimp toast, and not dragged anyone else into it, he would still be alive, walking the halls of wherever we are, apparently a building with a padlock on the door downstairs.

Then I pat him down, looking for his phone. Stick my hands under him best I can to reach for his back pockets and pull out a wallet and a sweaty bandanna, but no phone, which is not a surprise. If you're holding your phone, and someone stabs you, it follows that you will probably drop your phone. But I do find something, stuffed in his right front jeans pocket—a ring of keys with a small pocketknife. Swiss Army, just like a Boy Scout. I unhook it from the ring, which takes a minute and scratches up my fingertips.

My nails shred as I try to unfold the various blades, but I pull a few out—large blade, small blade, can opener, tiny scissors. This is the gift he has left behind.

I crawl close to his face. There is blood still dripping in a steady stream from somewhere on his neck. Do people still bleed after death, and for how long? The infant CPR class I took while pregnant did not cover this.

I flip open his wallet, squint at his driver's license. Robert Santuzza. Bobby the Saint, his friends probably called him when he showed up at the social club ready for a whiskey and a friendly game of poker.

I look at his face, his lips twitching. I've heard people can twitch and kick and expel gas after death. I am hoping against the latter, but if he does, it's sort of the least I can do to put up with his death farts, seeing he wouldn't be here if it weren't for me.

I wish he'd made it, though. Not just for him but for his family, the missus and all the little Santuzzas. "Delilah" and "Brittany," read his faded script tattoos—maybe his daughters, or wife and daughter, mom and wife. He was a good man, Bobby.

I should have shut my dumb mouth.

"I'm so sorry, Bobby," I say, and I lean my cheek on his chest one more time.

My head is still pounding in various locations, but now there seems to be an almost-audible pulse in my left ear, pressed on Bobby's shirt. The sound is faint, and it doesn't exactly cause a ripple of pain, but I notice it. I lie very still, and it feels like I'm on a canoe or something, riding a slow wave. I think maybe I'm about to pass out, so I force my eyes open, and I see Bobby's feet moving steadily, or rather, I am the one who's moving steadily, slowly, up and down. Because Bobby is moving. Breathing.

I sit up quickly, try to think through the static in my skull, and realize it wasn't my head pounding or ear pulsing—it was his heartbeat. Bobby is alive.

"Shit," I whisper.

I ball up the bandanna I pulled from his pocket and wipe away the blood on his neck, try to find the point of incision. Blood is dripping but not pouring, and now it makes sense: Dr. Caroline's not Jason Voorhees; she might be crazy but she doesn't necessarily have superhuman strength, just got him once with a blade or a pen or a fondue stick.

I'm able to clean off his neck enough to see the wound—it's small, a little bigger than a papercut, on the side of his neck facing me. She can't have gotten any major artery, either; there has to be a ton of tissue and viscera in the neck besides arteries, right?

The bandanna is pretty saturated now, but I ball it up and press it against the cut, apply as much pressure as I can to stop the bleeding. After about a minute, I see movement under Bobby's eyes, going back and forth like he's dreaming. Then a flutter, open to slits.

"Hey, can you hear me?" I whisper.

He opens his mouth and grunts. It's not a gurgle, though, which all my medical training tells me is a good thing. If it were a gurgle, that would mean his throat would be flooding with blood.

"Sorry, you don't have to talk. You're okay," I say.

Also no medical expertise being utilized here. "Okay" meaning not dead; that is my scientific criteria.

His eyes open wider now and blink at the lights; he looks over to me. Then he sits up suddenly, and basically knocks me off him. He coughs and holds his hand to his neck.

"What—" he says.

"You've been stabbed," I say. "Put this on your neck," I say, holding out his bandanna.

He looks at the blood on his hand and then back at me, takes the bandanna, and presses it against the wound.

"My head," he says, his other hand traveling to the back of his head.

"She stabbed you, and you probably fell. Hit the ground."

"She?"

"Yeah, you were going outside to call for help. For me. Do you remember?"

"I got the wrong address," he says. "I thought this was a storage space."

"Where are we?" I say. "My name is Ellen Garcia, and I've been missing for a few days, I think. I've been kidnapped."

"Kidnapped?" he says.

He seems pretty confused and also like he's never heard of me. So much for Chris and Neditor beating the drums and offering rewards for my safe return.

"Yeah, the woman, the person who stabbed you, abducted me."

"My friend Terry, he told me this was his storage space. I was coming to pick up tires."

I nod. This is not key information for me to have, but I have to let him go through it, piece together his day leading up to this.

"I tried to call him, but there was no service. Then I heard you," he says, pointing at me.

"Where are we?" I say. "In the city, where are we?"

He thinks, then says, "Sunset Park. Near the Brooklyn Army Terminal."

"Can you stand?" I say. "I can't really stand."

He tries to get up, but then I watch his eyes spin like he's the Cheshire Cat, and he stays put.

"I don't know, my head."

"She opens the door sometimes to fuck with me," I say. "Next time she does, we have to try something."

I hold up the pocketknife, all the blades fanned out.

He gets pale all of a sudden, begins to sweat, and his pupils go from very large to very small.

"Are you okay?" I say, knowing for a fact he is not.

"Yeah, I just gotta get some air."

"We don't have that here," I say. "Put your head between your knees."

He does like I tell him, but then his shoulders start to convulse, and he's coughing and grunting, and it's like fucking John Hurt on

286

the table in *Alien*, when Ridley Scott didn't tell the actors what was going to happen, he was just, like, Something fucking nutty is about to go down, because he wanted to get all their real reactions when the little alien bursts through the chest and heads for the hills.

Bobby falls on all fours from his kneeling position and keeps shuddering and convulsing, ripples in his back, and he might actually also be turning into a werewolf, but then he opens his mouth and vomits, heaving, rolling vomit. I can't make out any food pieces, but the smell hits me instantly, and I cover my mouth and nose, feel my stomach churning, and I wretch and cough but nothing comes up. The water I drank a few hours ago must have made its way past my stomach, and for this I am thankful. I feel badly for Bobby, though—he's concussed and confused and even though he's a big boy and could probably take down Dr. Caroline with a single head-butt to her Amber Aoud–scented face, he is severely compromised.

He finally stops vomiting and sits up, then falls backward on his ass again, groans, wipes his mouth.

I crawl toward the door, sit next to the frame right where it will open, back against the wall.

"My phone," Bobby says, patting his pockets.

"It's all right," I say.

I think maybe I won't say the next thing, because I don't think I believe it at this point. I mean, *nothing to lose* doesn't even really do the moment justice, seeing that neither Bobby nor I are having a lot of luck bringing ourselves to standing positions.

But then I think I should say it, because even if I don't believe it, maybe there's some magic in there, a consecration buried in the words; maybe something will be activated by my speaking them. Right now nothing would surprise me.

I clutch the pocketknife, my fingers splayed between the tiny blades, and say, "I'm going to get us out of here."

# Gordon Strong

I'm done with the hedge a little before three. I've missed at least half of the Brewers game by now, but I'm out of beer, and the only liquor left in the cabinet is Kahlúa, and I'll be goddamned if I'm drinking that Hershey-flavored piss, so I got one option, and that's to watch the rest of the game at Gator Sam's.

I know I probably shouldn't be driving after a six-pack, but I do just fine, take it slow and park on the street so I don't have to squeeze between cars in the lot. Go inside, and don't recognize anyone off-hand, even though there's plenty of people there for the game. I find a seat at the bar, and I vaguely recognize the kid working but don't remember his name.

"What can I get you?" he says.

"Hey, you remember me? I was in here almost a month ago."

The crowd boos and swears. Tigers got a base hit.

"Sure, you look familiar," he says, not looking at me, washing a glass under the bar.

"I was in here with a group of guys—we sat at that table. We all just got canned from Kinzer."

"Oh yeah, how're you doing?" he says, but I don't think he remembers me at all.

"Sally around?"

"Sally only works weekdays. What can I get you?"

Now the crowd yells.

"Ah, dammit," says the bartender, glancing up at the screen.

Tigers just scored. I know I should be upset about it, but I don't feel it. I kind of don't give a shit right now about the Brew Crew. I mean, they give a shit that I've had a bad day?

"You sure you don't remember?" I say. "We sat over there, ordered a lot of drinks and a lot of wings. Tasker drove me home."

"I said, sure, buddy. What can I get you?"

"How about a Lite and a shot of Jack?"

"Coming up."

I check out the game but I'm having a hard time focusing on it. Looks like the Brewers got out of the sixth alive but are down 10–3.

The bartender sets the drinks in front of me, and I take the bourbon quick, chase it with half the Lite. I finish the beer in a couple of gulps. Not hard to do. Lite's beer-flavored water. Amazing that Miller can actually sell it as an alcoholic beverage for grown-ups. I stare at the can. Fucking Miller.

"One more," I say, holding up a finger.

"Be right with you," says the bartender, pouring Bloody Mary mix into two pint glasses.

My eyes wander up to the screen. People around me ooh and aah, and I look around at them, and I want to ask them, *You think the Brewers care about you? You think John Jaha's staying up late thinking,* I wonder how all those losers at Gator Sam's are feeling? I know I cared enough about the game last night, but now it feels like a waste of time to me. They're gonna lose, they're gonna win, repeat, repeat, repeat.

"Hey, can I get one more?" I ask again, louder this time, so he can hear me over the room of idiots barking at the screen.

"Said I'll be right with you, pal," he says, pinning lime wedges onto the Bloody Marys.

Seventh inning crawls along. Brewers manage not to fuck it up and let the Tigers get any more runs.

Finally the boy wonder gives me my drinks. I take the shot, chug the beer, feel streams running on either side of my mouth, and cough. Bartender gives me a look, suspicious, and hands me a tiny square napkin.

"You okay?"

I nod, wipe my chin, say, "Wrong pipe."

The crowd screams behind me like they're at a horror movie, and I hunch up my shoulders. I look up at the screen, see that Yount's hit it out, left-field line.

"They're back!" says a guy a couple of seats away from me.

He looks to be around my age, this guy, but he looks pretty sporty—collared short-sleeved shirt and khaki pants. Dark hair with gray. Salt-and-pepper, they call it. A woman's standing behind him, her arms draped around his neck. They're drinking the Bloody Marys that took the bartender so long to make.

The woman's got to be ten years younger than the guy. Blond and perky, wearing a visor and a short white tennis skirt.

"Did I tell you, or what?" says the guy.

"Yeah, you did," she says, and she kisses him on the top of his head.

"One more," I say, waving my finger around in a little circle.

The bartender rubs the back of his neck and comes up to me, his face a few inches from mine.

"I can't serve you any more, pal," he says.

I lean back on the stool, say, "The fuck you talking about?"

Salt-and-Pepper and his girlfriend look over at me.

"You've had enough, is all," the bartender says.

"I had two beers, two shots," I say. "Since when is that too much? What is this—a goddamn church breakfast?"

"Pal, you had some before you came in, and you know it."

"You better stop fucking calling me pal," I say, pointing at him.

"All right," he says, clasping his hands together. "I'm going to have to ask you to leave now, okay?"

"I'm not ready to go yet," I say, crossing my arms. "I'm a paying customer, and I want one more round. So I'll make you a deal—you give me one more round, then I'll leave."

"There's no deal, old man," he says, laughing a little. "You're walking out of here, or someone'll walk you out."

"Who's going to do that, you?" I say. "Leave it to Beaver?"

"I am."

It's Salt-and-Pepper, standing up from his stool. The crowd yells; Brewers scored another.

"Who the fuck are you?" I say, standing up.

"I'm a friend of Pete's," he says, nodding to the bartender. "And I don't like people giving him trouble."

"I never seen you in here before," I say. "I been in here a million times. I sat right there not even a month ago, with all my friends. Tasker gave me a damn ride home."

"You're so important," says his girlfriend.

Salt-and-Pepper chuckles, and then I see the bartender's hiding a smile.

"Hey, fuck you, sweetheart," I say.

Salt-and-Pepper shakes his head, says, "Sorry, Pete," and then he throws a punch. I try to block him, but it's like my hands are moving slower than usual, and next thing I'm on the floor of the bar, and Salt-and-Pepper and the bartender are picking me up, one on each arm.

"What the hell'd you do?" I say to them.

I try to pull away, but they both really have a grip, and I try to catch people's eyes on the way out, thinking maybe someone'll know me, say, *Hey, that's Gordon Strong, don't throw him out*, but I don't know anyone, and they're all too busy watching the game anyway.

Salt-and-Pepper and the bartender walk me outside and give me a shove, and I stumble a few steps into the lot but don't fall. Turn around and say, "Last time I come to this shithole."

The bartender holds his arms out and says, "Our loss, pal. Get home safe."

Then they go back inside.

I find my car on the side street and get in and drive, figure I'll go to Discount Mart on Highway 100. They'd never tell a guy he's had too much.

On the way there I guess I cut someone off, because he gives me a long honk, and I flip him the bird but slow down anyway, think maybe my reflexes aren't perfect, but hell, I've driven drunker than this, I'm sure of it.

I make it to Discount, and I'm in and out. Bottle of Jack, six of Lite, and the gal at the register doesn't blink an eye.

When I get home, I see Evelyn's car in the driveway and park behind it, maybe a little too close, but it's fine. Not like she's got any-where to be tonight, right?

I go inside the house holding the paper bag from Discount under one arm. Evelyn's in the kitchen and glances up at me, and then her face opens up into shock.

"Gordon, what happened?" she says, coming around the counter into the living room.

"What're you talking about? I just went to Discount. We're outta everything."

"Your face," she says, getting up close to me. "Your eye. Did you get in a fight?"

I step away from her and sort of fall back onto the couch.

"No, Evelyn, I didn't get in a fight," I say. "Some asshole at Gator Sam's punched me for no damn good reason."

"Gator Sam's?" she says. "You just said you were at Discount."

I sigh, just so tired of explaining myself to everyone. "I was at Gator Sam's first, then Discount."

"What . . . what happened? A man just hit you?"

"Yep," I say, shoving the paper bag off my lap onto the couch next to me.

"But why?"

"Because people are idiots," I say, pulling the six-pack out of the bag.

Evelyn looks at the beer and then back up at me.

"And you drove like this?" she says.

"Yes, Evelyn, I drove like this, and I made it home in one piece, and the car is fine."

I open the beer and take a sip, Evelyn's eyes following the can tip up and down.

"Gordon, do you need any more of that?" she says, sounding pathetic.

"Yes, Evelyn, I need more of this," I say. "I need it so I can put up with you not trusting me."

"Not trusting you?" she says. "You come home three sheets to the wind with a black eye, and . . ." She stops midsentence.

"And what?" I say. "What are you going to say?"

"I just . . . I don't recognize you," she says. "I have no idea who you are right now."

"It's me, sweetie," I say. "Nobody else."

Her lips tremble, and I can see she's about to cry, and it just pisses me off even more, all her pissing and moaning.

"I'm ordering pizza for the kids," she says, her voice shaky. "Caroline is sleeping over."

"That's right, she is," I say. "I heard about your little visit to Chuck this morning."

Now she goes ghost-white, knows she's caught.

"I wanted to invite Caroline for Savannah," she says. "After last night, everyone just needs to settle down a little bit. Have a break."

"Sure, a break. You want the situation to defuse, right?"

"Yes."

"And I'm the situation, right? I'm the bomb that needs defusing?"

Now her lips aren't trembling anymore; they've tightened up like a little purse.

"Could you please at least clean yourself up before the kids come downstairs to eat?" she says.

Then she turns around and heads for the stairs, but before she goes up, she adds over her shoulder quietly, "And please clean up that mess you made of the hedge outside."

Is she sad? Is she scared? I can't tell anymore, and I'm sick of trying to guess.

She's gone, then, and I sit for a minute and finish my beer, pull the bottle of Jack out the bag, stand up, and go downstairs to the basement bathroom.

Flip on the lights and lock the door. Look in the mirror, and as much as I hate to admit it, I see Evelyn's point—I barely recognize myself, too. The skin around my eye's starting to swell and turn blue, which I don't even feel until I bring my fingers up to the lid and press, and it hurts, feels like a burn. Then my vision in that eye starts tunneling just by me becoming aware of it; it's started to close like a Venus flytrap.

My shirt is soaked through with sweat, and there's a big green stain in the middle, I guess from the hedge—maybe I leaned over it at some point. I don't remember.

I open the bottle of Jack and take a swig.

Then I run my fingers through my hair back and forth. Scrub-a-dub. Used to get it trimmed about once a month, keep it about an inch on top and half an inch on the sides, but I'm overdue, and it's sticking out everywhere.

I open the cabinet under the sink and rummage around; there's extra toilet paper rolls and boxes of Q-tips, shampoo and conditioner and sunscreen, a tub of Tylenol, bug bite cream, a ratty hairbrush. In the back I find a plastic disposable razor and an old can of Barbasol, brown at the nozzle. Also some scissors—they're the small ones, curved at the tip, for nose fluff and eyebrows, but they'll do.

First I cut off the wild bits, then get as close to the scalp as I can, all the hair falling in the sink and on the floor. My hair is fair anyway, a dull dirty blond, and the gray just makes it look blanched and burnt—like a sick baby chick. But the more I cut off, the less I see of either color. It's like a blank slate, and I like that.

When it's short enough I rub water all over my head and then the cream, and I shave it. All of it. Cut myself up a lot—the razor's old and dull, so I have to push on it as I drag it from the front of my scalp to the back—but it's worth it.

When I look at myself—profiles and then straight on, my head bloody from the nicks—finally it feels like for the first time in a long time, I know who I am.


I guess I don't realize how long I'm in there.

When I come out, Evelyn and the kids plus Caroline are at the dining table, eating pizza on paper plates.

"Dad?" says Savannah.

"Holy shit," says Brendan.

"What—" is all Evelyn can squeak out.

Caroline doesn't say anything, just stares, mouth open.

"What happened?" says Savannah.

She sounds on the verge of tears, and for some reason that pisses me off.

"Needed a change," I say.

"You're bleeding," she says. "On your head, you're bleeding."

"Yeah, well, that's why God made Band-Aids," I say, striding into the living room and grabbing the cordless phone receiver, the bottle of Jack in my other hand.

"Do you have a black eye?" says Brendan, mouth full of food. "Did you get in a fight?"

"Yep," I say, then announce, "I'm making a call downstairs."

I head to the basement, and I sit on the couch down there, which is our old piece-of-shit couch, so it's like sitting on a stack of phone books. I take a healthy swig of bourbon and dial my dad. He picks up right away—in fact I don't even hear the phone ring on his end. It's like he knows I'm going to call.

"Pop, it's me. Gordon."

"Oh yeah," he says, like he just remembered I existed. "You get a job yet?"

"No," I say. "That one at Miller I told you about fell through, but maybe it was a lucky break for me anyway . . . you have a Lite lately? They taste like piss-water."

He doesn't have any snappy response, so I keep talking: "I'm thinking I might get into liquor. Maybe move the whole family down to Kentucky, get a job at a bourbon distillery."

I hold up the bottle of Jack in front of me, watching the amber liquid catch the light.

The old man coughs and cackles, says, "Kentucky, huh? You think that'll keep the little woman's eye from wandering, you're a damn fool."

"Pop, you don't know shit about what you're saying, okay?"

"I know plenty," he says. "I know every time you shut your eyes, she's probably giving that neighbor of yours his own private striptease in her bikini."

"What?" I say, rubbing my eyes. "How do you . . ."

"How do I know about that? You told me yourself, the last time we talked. How much you drinking there, rummy? No wonder you didn't get that job—they're probably worried you'd suck up all the inventory."

Then he laughs and coughs, laughs and coughs.

"I just forgot I told you," I say.

"I didn't forget," he says, proud of himself. "You give her a talking-to? Snap her into shape?"

I shut my eyes, suddenly the dull light down here's bothering me.

"Nah, there wasn't anything going on. It was just me being paranoid."

"Paranoid?" he repeats, like he's never heard the word. He laughs, says, "You were never the sharpest knife, boyo, but I didn't think you could actually get dumber as you got older."

"Listen, Pop, don't start, things have been great with me and Evelyn," I say, forcing out the memory of the last two days.

"Oh yeah?" he says, in a fake cutesy voice. "They've been great? What she's been doing, giving you head day and night?"

"Kinda, yeah," I say, smiling in spite of myself, thinking of how we were just earlier in the week, her biting me like a little animal.

"She showing you new tricks?" he says. "Where you think she learned 'em, huh?"

"Shut up!" I yell, pressing my fingers against my eyes. "You don't know what you're talking about."

He stops laughing all of a sudden, and his voice gets clearer, like he's in the room, and he says, "Listen, boyo, it's gonna be splitsville just like your mother the whore. She's gonna walk out on you and make you pay her for it while she licks all the dicks in the neighborhood like they're goddamn Popsicles.

"You gotta let her know she ain't leaving, she ain't taking your kids, you'll kill her dead before you let that happen."

"Pop," I say, "what are you fucking talking about? No one's killing anyone."

"That's just fine, boyo. She's already gone. It's already over. I always knew you were stupid. I just didn't know you're also a first-class pussy."

"Pop!" I yell, but he hangs up, so I yell, "Pop," again, and he doesn't answer.

Now my hands are shaking—everything's shaking: the room, the walls. I stand up, look at the bottle shaking in my hands, like when whoever wins the series and they shake up the champagne, but I feel like I can't control it, like someone else is shaking it, so I throw it against the wall as hard as I can, and it shatters.

Then Evelyn is downstairs, looking at the wall and looking at me.

"Gordon, what are you doing?!" she says.

"I was on the phone," I say.

"With who?"

"My dad."

"Gordon."

She covers her mouth, stares at the wall, the glass on the carpet.

"I'll clean it up, for chrissake, Evelyn," I say, rubbing my eyes. "It's not the end of the goddamn world."

"Gordon," she says again.

"What?" I say, losing whatever patience I have left. "What? What? Speak!"

She drops her hand from her mouth and says, "Gordon, your father's been dead for three years."

# Dr. Caroline

It doesn't take long to find the Your-Space-718 in Sunset Park near the Brooklyn Army Terminal, on a dead-end block surrounded by other industrial properties. The website says, "Coming Soon to Sunset Park! Work, Create, Be." But right now there isn't much to see, with this building or any of the others, which look fairly abandoned. Only a matter of time before it becomes hipsterville, before whole floors are bought out and renovated for bocce ball leagues and archery tournaments, a craft beer bar in every corner.

I park at the end of the block behind a truck, and then I walk, the only person on the street, glad I'm wearing sneakers and not heels, which would surely echo, not to mention get shredded by the untreated pavement. I stick close to the wall and pause every minute or so to look around for signs of life, but there's nothing, no one.

In front of the building across from Your-Space is an open multi-car garage on the ground floor, also abandoned, no door. I walk in and stand to the side, next to where the doorjamb would be if there was one, and I hide and wait, sticking only my head out so I can see the glass double-door entrance of Your-Space. A chunky chain and padlock are woven through the door handles but frankly look loose enough for someone to open the door a few inches to squeeze through.

My phone vibrates, and I jump. I pull it from my purse—Jonas calling. I ignore it, then Jonas's name disappears, and I gather he hung up, frustrated I didn't pick up on the first ring. A moment later a text comes through: "PICK UP I AM ALONE. JIMENEZ AND MARKS BOTH LOOKING FOR YOU WHO KNOWS WHO ELSE."

I sigh and tap his name. All artists are drama queens.

"Doctor, where are you?"

"Sunset Park," I say quietly, my eyes on the door across the street.

"They're looking for you. They're looking for our license plate."

"You gave them the license plate?"

"I had to!" he says. "They would've found it anyway."

"What did you tell them, exactly?"

"That you came home, took your laptop, and left. Didn't say where you were going. I let them search the crawl space downstairs, and I told them about the Gowanus space and gave them a key."

"You gave them a key?!" I say.

"Yes, I officially defied your orders," he says, a little snotty (kind of hot). Then his tone softens: "Doctor, now they know we're not hiding anything."

"You sure about that?" I say, poking my head out of the doorway just a little to peer down the block.

"Yes!" he says, exasperated. Then, as if he's just now realized what I said earlier: "Wait, where in Sunset Park are you?"

"Across the street from something called Your-Space-718. Will Wall is a security guard here and should be here any minute."

"Who is Will Wall?"

"Billy. Nelson. Same guy. I did some research and talked to some people and figured it out myself, because I couldn't wait for Makeda to put it together."

"What are you planning to do? Confront him?" says Jonas, distress creeping into his voice.

I'm about to answer but then realize I haven't actually thought about it. What I'll do when I see him, what I'll say. Because, frankly, I've done this my whole life: talk to people and get them to tell me things. Will Pearleater is a fun house of horrors, but that doesn't mean I can't get into his head. I've got a few trick mirrors myself.

"Yes," I say.

"But what if he is as crazy as you say? He could hurt you, he could try to kill you," Jonas says, his voice choking, fighting back tears.

"I love you, Jonas," I say. "But you do have to trust me more."

Then I see a man, on foot. It's him, slender, around my height, wearing white just like me, except with black gloves. White baseball cap. Blue backpack. Standard nonsurgical blue mask.

Jonas is still talking in my ear, his voice reduced to a whisper: "Doctor, you cannot do this alone. You tricked death once . . . you can't do it twice."

I smile, ever impressed and touched by the phrases he can pull out of the air. "Darling, I have to go. He's here," and I hang up.

I watch Will unlock the padlock with a key and pull the chain off, drape it over his shoulder, and open the front door, which doesn't seem to have an additional lock. He could go inside and be gone for the night.

Jonas's concerns have made their way into my head now, my heart beginning a nervous gallop, throat and mouth drying up like a sandbar.

I know I have to get to him before the door closes, so I run out from my hiding spot, into the middle of the street.

"Will," I call.

He stops, turns around slowly. He looks like he's been caught trying to leave without paying the tab, but also doesn't seem surprised to see me.

"Will Wall," I say gently, taking a few steps toward him. "But it was once Pearleater, isn't that right? And Nelson and Billy, too?"

He seems to shrink in front of me, backing up against the door.

"It's all right," I say. "I understand you've been through a great deal. I'd like to help you, if I can."

He looks down, so I can't see his eyes anymore, hidden under the lip of the cap. I take one more step.

"I can't imagine the war going on inside you, Will, that no one else can see," I say, and he doesn't move, frozen in his spot like one of those people in Times Square who cover themselves with silver paint. But just like them, you're not a statue, are you, just pretending, I think. Then it hits me, how I should do this, and I say, "Actually, wait, that's a lie."

He raises his gaze to me again.

"I *can* imagine, because we're a little bit the same, you and I, yes? Very few people went through what we did as kids. So you read about me and the Strongs, right? Then you saw that picture of my mother at Golden Brook, and so you got a job with Jackson Landscapers so you could talk to her? Because you're good with gardens."

He blinks and looks at the ground again.

"What's important is that you found me, and you came to me for help. I know you may think that 'Nelson,'" I say, with just the tiniest least-offensive air quotes I can manage, "found me to taunt me and perhaps implicate me in a crime, and that 'Billy' sought me out to warn me and maybe also confuse me, but I think it was you, Will, all along, who knew that I could help. Not just because it's what I do, but because I understand you.

"I think you're driving, Will, and it's a scary thing, to be in control of one's life, especially when the road behind you is littered with bodies, but that is how you'll find your way out. That's how I've found my way out.

"Whatever you've done, whatever has happened in that building, in those rooms, even if Ellen Garcia is dead, we will figure out how you can move forward, you and I together. I'll help you. But you have to let me in."

He takes off his cap, rubs the heel of his hand against his forehead.

He looks fairly lost in his expression, literally, as if he's trying to discern a map on his phone. Gradually his chin and lips start to quiver, and then he crumples, loses his balance where he's standing, and drops to his knees, buries his face in his hands, and begins to sob.

Now I go to him, rush up the five steps and lean down, hold out my hands.

"It's all right, Will, let me help you stand."

"It all got away from me," he says through his fingers.

"I know it did."

"I didn't mean for any of it to happen. I can show you . . ."

He removes his hands from his face and shrugs his backpack off, sitting with his legs stretched out, bent a little at the knee. He unzips the backpack and rifles through, pulls out a green spiral notebook.

"I wrote it all down," he says, handing me the book.

"That's good, Will," I say. "Thank you for sharing this with me. I'll read the whole thing, if you'll let me."

He opens his mouth to speak but then barks out another sob and hunches over the backpack, trying to hide his face from me.

"But first we need to find Ellen Garcia, right? Can you take me to her?"

He mutters something, but it gets lost in the weeping and the cavern of the backpack.

I squat down.

"I couldn't hear you. What did you say?" I say softly.

He sniffs and snorts into the bag, then takes in a big heady breath and raises his head. His face is wet, tear-streaked, but he seems to have stopped crying rather abruptly.

He looks straight at me with those clear blue eyes and says, "Red Rover, Red Rover, send Nelson right over."

"Will—"

Before I can say anything, before I can reason him out of believing he actually has an alternate identity, he yanks a tiny black bottle from his backpack and sprays me in the eyes and nose and mouth.

It's like my whole head is a matchstick that's just been struck—everything burning, on fire, and I don't even realize I'm screaming until Will grabs me by the hair and shouts into my ear, "Shut up, dummy," and then he pulls me along the ground, and I kick with my legs but can't open my eyes, can't do anything but scream, and the only thing that shuts me up is him hitting me twice, three times in the face until I'm out.

# Gordon Strong

Suddenly I feel every razor slice on my head, each one burning and moving like it's alive and on fire. Then my lower back, like someone's pumping a jack between the bones, the muscles hot and humming. My busted eye is almost totally closed, so I see Evelyn blurry and flat, but with everything on her face, eyes and mouth, wide open and spread out with shock.

"Remember, Gordon?" she says, her voice shaking. "He died. Lung cancer, after the stroke?"

I try to remember. I went to see him at the hospital near the end. He looked like he was already dead, just a pile of bones with some skin thrown over like a blanket. He wasn't conscious, hooked up to ten machines. I held his cold hand. Said, "This is it, Pop. Say hi to everyone in hell."

"We had the service here because he didn't have any friends in Eau Claire," says Evelyn. "So our friends came. All your friends from work, the neighbors."

"Stranges, too?" I say.

"Yes, them, too. Don't you remember?" she says, starting to cry.

We had it at Caldwell Brothers Home in a room with a green carpet, green wallpapered walls, a heart-shaped wreath of pink carnations next to the casket. There were a couple of empty rows but we mostly filled the place. Savannah read, "Those who walk uprightly enter into peace." We let Caroline sit up front with us so Savannah wouldn't feel as nervous.

"Yeah," I say, waving Evelyn away. "I just got confused. Had a few too many."

Evelyn nods like she understands but doesn't mean it.

"A guy can get confused, Evelyn. Give me a break on that, at least."

She stops nodding, says sternly, all of a sudden, like she's talking to the kids, "I want you to stop drinking, Gordon. Tomorrow."

"Come on, Evelyn. I'm just blowing off steam," I say. "Sometimes you like to drink, too, you know—those frozen margaritas down at Botanas."

"It's making you crazy, the drinking," she says. "You shaved your head . . . you're imagining three-hour conversations with your father."

"What if I told you the drinking didn't have anything to do with it?" I say. "The booze just makes me feel good for a change, so I can get away from thinking about you cheating on me."

She opens her mouth and raises her hand to her cheek like I've slapped her. Then she shakes her head, says, "Never once, Gordon. I have never cheated on you."

"Yeah? Then how did Chuck Strange get a picture of you in a swimsuit, huh?"

She crinkles her eyebrows, shakes her head, sputters, "What . . . what picture?"

"Yeah, what picture? How about all that stuff you were doing in bed? All that biting my nipples and licking my chest—you never did any of that before. Chuck teach you that?"

Now she stops shaking her head and tears are filling her eyes, but her mouth is all tightened up in frustration. Women never just get angry—it's always angry and sad.

"I read about it in *Cosmo!*" she yells. "I'm not cheating on you!"

"Oh yeah?" I say, coming up close to her. She doesn't dare move, though. "What about this morning? What did Chuck give you? The note."

She's confused now. "How do you . . ."

"How do I know about that? Caroline told me."

"Caroline?" Evelyn says. "You're asking Caroline to spy for you?"

"No, she . . . she just tells me what she sees. And she told me you went over there this morning to beg your boyfriend to let Caroline sleep over because you'd feel safer."

"Wait," she says, waves of worry crashing over her face. "Did you put her up to writing those letters?"

"No, that wasn't what happened. It was all her."

"You lied," says Evelyn, stunned. "Caroline was telling the truth the whole time. You stood there and watched Chuck punish her."

"No," I say, rubbing my unswollen eye. "I mean, okay, it was both of us."

"Both of you," says Evelyn. "She's thirteen years old, Gordon. You're an adult. You came up with that crazy plan and convinced a kid to help you with it, and you thought this was totally normal behavior."

I hear a buzz in my right ear, a mosquito or a fly, and I bat it away.

"You're just trying to distract me," I say. "What kind of note did Chuck give you, huh? You making plans? He telling you where to meet him?"

She starts huffing air through her nose, wipes tears from her eyes.

"It was the name of a psychiatrist he knows from work," she says. "For you, Gordon. So you can get some help."

"You think I need a shrink?" I say. "Maybe you need a fucking shrink, Evelyn, if you think that's what I need."

"Maybe I do," she says, sticking her chin up toward me, playing brave. "I need to tell someone how you've lost your damn mind."

I grab her shoulders and put my face right in hers, say, "You've made me like this. I wasn't like this before. I can't trust you."

She's closing her eyes, because I guess I'm yelling, and I realize I'm digging my fingers into her skin—she's just so small, her shoulders so bony; I could snap pieces off her like chalk.

She wriggles away from me, and I let her.

"You sleep on the couch down here," she says, sobbing, pointing to the couch. "I don't want you near the kids."

"I'm not near the kids if I'm in our bedroom."

I know what she's going to say. I just want to make her say it.

"I don't want you near me, Gordon," she says.

Then she runs up the stairs, and I'm alone.

I lie down on the couch and shut my eyes, not sure if I fall asleep. Next time I open them, the clock on the wall reads 11:29. I can barely open my left eye now, the skin around it hot, all the small muscles pounding.

I go upstairs, and the house is dark. Into the kitchen, open the freezer and pull out an ice cube tray, wring it out onto a dish towel, and hold it to my eye. Open the fridge with my other hand and pull out another Lite, pop the top, and drink. I don't realize how thirsty I am and suck down the whole thing. I bring my head back down and set the can on the counter, croak out a burp. Then I see Caroline, at the bottom of the stairs. Frozen, watching me.

"It was the number of a shrink," I say. "That was on the note your dad gave my wife. You know what that is? A shrink?"

She nods.

"That's what she says anyway," I say, going back to the fridge.

I take out another beer and open it, slurp the foam off the top.

Caroline's still standing at the bottom of the stairs, looks too scared to move.

"What do you need, Caroline?" I say. "You want a soda or a snack or something?"

"I told Savannah I was coming down to get chips," she says.

"Chips? Sure."

I reach into the pantry cabinet and grab a bag of barbecue Lay's, toss it to her. She catches it. She looks at the bag in her hand and doesn't leave. It looks like she wants to talk.

"You got something to say?" I ask.

She shrugs, still staring at the chips.

"Well, I got something to say," I tell her. "I'm sorry I didn't come clean with your dad about you and me both coming up with those letters."

"It's okay," she says, shrugging again.

"We're good, then, you and me?"

She nods but won't look at me. Then she says, so quietly it's barely even an actual sound, "We're good."


I've finished the beer and the crusty-topped Kahlúa in the back of the cabinet, and I don't feel a thing. Sober and awake. I could drive to Door County. I could take a math test. I'm not going to do either of those things, though.

I've been sitting in the basement, and the fumes from the bourbon have bloomed and filled the room, so I feel it in my throat and nose when I breathe. I stare at the broken glass chunks on the carpet. There's one that's larger than the others, and I pick it up and turn it over in my hand, watch the light bounce around.

It's funny, I feel like I just talked to Caroline five minutes ago, and it's been three hours. Everyone's asleep. Not me.

I stand up from the couch and head upstairs. House is quiet. Then I see something bright out of the corner of my eye, on the floor next to the front door.

There's luggage. Savannah's pink carry-on suitcase, Evelyn's leopard-print carry-on, Brendan's gym duffel.

I don't make the decision to run to the door; it's like I'm being pulled by an invisible lasso around my waist. I tear open Evelyn's bag: blouses, underwear, socks, stockings. I grab handfuls of the clothes and let them fall from my fingers.

I walk up the stairs and stand in front of Savannah's door. Don't hear anything from inside, no giggling or music playing, and I open the door softly and see Savannah asleep on top of her covers, and Caroline in Brendan's old sleeping bag on the floor, wearing headphones.

I close the door and go to Brendan's room. He's in bed, asleep, one leg out, one arm over his eyes. I leave.

Then I open the door to my and Evelyn's bedroom. She's rolled in a ball under the top sheet, facing away from the door.

I step out of the room but leave the door open a few inches.

I walk downstairs, then out of the house to the hedge, where I've left the shears in the middle of the mess. I bend down and pick them up with one hand, hold them up to the streetlight, and watch the gleam bounce off the blades.

Then I go back inside my house, and before I head upstairs I catch my reflection in a small wall mirror. I guess I should be even more shocked at how I look, the cuts on my head scabbed over and my eye completely swollen shut, but all I can think is how I look like a newborn baby before it gets cleaned up, bald and bruised and bloody.

# Dr. Caroline

I'm not actually out, not for more than a few seconds—I don't lose awareness of my existence; it's just that the entirety of that awareness has been hijacked by pain.

I am being dragged by the roots of my hair that I spend one hundred seventy-five dollars every five weeks to color, which doesn't feel great, but that pain is at the very bottom of the step-right-up-test-your-strength column, whereas the stinging, screaming pain of every exposed hole on my face hits the ding-ding bell at the top. My eyes may be the worst, because the tears gushing from my ducts are fire, too, burning tracks into my cheeks.

"Will, Will," I say, over and over. "Will, listen."

"Shut up."

Then he pulls me up some stairs, and I grip his wrists with both hands, and my back and ass scrape and land hard on each step, so as much as resistance seems like a nice idea, I have to *help* him drag me to reduce my own discomfort, so I pump and scrabble with my legs.

"Will, listen to me. You don't have to do any of this," I say, trying to think of something I can say that will buy me time. "Or is it Nelson?"

He stops for a second, and then his breath and voice are in my ear.

"Something none of you understand," he says. "We're actually all here at the same time now. Helping each other."

I tilt my head in his direction and say, "What-the-fuck-ever, Will."

He grunts in disapproval and yanks me even harder—I can feel follicles tearing as he tightens and retightens his grip.

I'm on flat ground now, and I realize I'm making sounds, too, sharp cries as the tears keep gushing like flaming twin waterfalls.

I try to open my eyes but they burn even more when I do, so I squint, and everything is blurry and beige, LED lights every few feet overhead. It occurs to me that if Ellen Garcia is dead, maybe this was the last thing she saw.

But it also occurs to me that she may not be dead yet.

"Ellen," I say.

"I said shut up," says Will. "Don't you ever shut up?!"

"Not really," I say, and then I cough, my throat dry and also burning like I've accidentally swallowed the whole habanero at the bottom of the ceviche. It'll hurt to scream—it'll burn and sting and choke whatever air I have left—but I have to try.

So I take in as much oxygen as I can through my nose and mouth at the same time and scream, "Ellen Garcia!"

# Ellen Garcia

I'm still sitting against the wall next to the door, trying not to breathe through my nose to avoid the vomit smell, clutching the pocketknife.

Bobby's slumped against the wall to my left, and his eyes keep fluttering shut.

"Hey," I say to him. "Don't pass out, okay? It won't be good for you."

"Yeah, yeah," he says, but honestly he doesn't look so hot.

The bandanna ball is soaked through now, so every time he presses it to his neck, blood dribbles out onto his arm and then the floor. There is quite a bit of blood on the floor and his clothes, and so I think maybe I should just let him sleep—between the concussion and the blood loss, maybe he's headed for coma city anyway.

I wait and nod off at some point, shake myself awake as I start to fall to the side, and I see Bobby's asleep but breathing, mouth open, sitting with his back against the wall, so I guess that's a good sign, that he's not passed out lying down?

I start to doze again and then I hear noise from the hallway— talking, then movement—footsteps. Multiple footsteps, definitely more than one person. I open my mouth to yell, but then I hear a woman's voice, screaming my name.

There's a surge in my chest—the relief of recognition. I think I read an article about it—or at least the first paragraph of an article about it—something happens neurologically when you hear your name, brain says, Someone else sees me, so I must not be dead. And I am not.

I pound on the door with my fist and yell back.

"I'm here!"

# Dr. Caroline

I hear pounding and a muffled "I'm here," but Will doesn't like that and hits me in the mouth again, splitting my already swollen bottom lip open like a foiled baked potato, the blood drizzling hot down my chin.

I reel from the shock of it, can't quite register the pain yet; there are too many sources. I'm able to open my eyes a little more, so I try again.

"El—"

Then he brings my head down hard against the floor, and I swear I hear a crunch, like it's just another coconut cracking against a tree.

# Ellen Garcia

I hear a thump right outside the door and then crying, and it sounds female. Then a man's hushed voice, and they're close, both of them, right on the other side of the door. I sit up straight as I can, head still throbbing on all sides, and I'm weak, know I couldn't run even if I tried, but I'm wide awake, goddammit, all the endorphins and adrenaline coursing through my old, tired, boozed-up veins. Amazing when the body knows it's about to die.

I grip the pocketknife and think, Not yet, goddammit. Not quite yet.

Then there's silence outside. The talking stops; the movement stops. All I hear are Bobby's soft groans—he's finally tipped over onto his side now—and my own breath, my rabbit heart pumping away in my ears.

The door swings open, but before I can even lift the knife, a man's face is in my face, blue eyes, a woman on the floor behind him, and it's all over too quick. It's like he knew exactly where I'd be, and then I'm hit, he's smashed my nose, and I hear the crack before I feel it, and I fall onto the floor sideways, but I don't let go of the knife, keep it tucked under my hip.

He drags a woman into the room, and my vision isn't great, hard to focus, my nose starting to swell, but I can see her face, the skin red like she's been burned, blood pouring from her mouth. All in white.

"Dr. Caroline?"

# Dr. Caroline

I hear my name and try to stretch my neck in that direction, but it feels like there's vinegar-dipped gauze that's been stuffed into my mouth. Open my eyes just a little more and see a guy who looks like a truck driver passed out on one side of the room, then near the door there's a woman—I can't see any specific features but can just make out the shape of her face.

"El . . . El," I say.

Will leans down and pulls my head toward his face, says, "Oh, now you want to make friends with her," and just as he finishes his sentence, I see her sitting up, raising her arm, something in her hand that glints in the light.

She brings her arm down fast, and Will screams and lets me go.

# Ellen Garcia

I don't aim for anything in particular, don't have any time to plan, just jab the longest blade as hard as I can into his calf near his knee.

He screams and drops Dr. Caroline's head, and she hits the floor hard. He falls to one knee, reaches a hand back toward the pocket-knife, hurt but nowhere near broken, and I know I have thirty seconds, maybe a minute, to get away, so I start to crawl toward the door, but you've seen this movie—the girl tries to escape, through a window or an air vent maybe, and just at the last second when you think she might make it, the killer grabs her ankle and pulls her back in.

# Dr. Caroline

I'm on my side and can see a little now, but it's spinning, point of focus not staying still—Will is leaning down, and then he's pulling Ellen Garcia back into the room, and she kicks him in the chest with her free foot, which sets him back a second, but he doesn't let go and drags her toward him, and she pushes up off the floor with her hands. He lets go of her legs and throws a punch at her face, lands it on her chin.

She cries out, her arms buckling. Will comes back to me, limping, and he kneels in front of me, reaches his hand back, and pulls something red and silver from his leg, what Ellen must have stabbed him with. A Swiss Army knife.

He presses the biggest blade, already bloody from his leg, against the soft meat of my neck; if he were to stab exactly where he's tracing the blade he may get my thyroid or trachea or larynx. It's a small knife, but he seems like a creative guy. I put my hands around his wrist but don't make any other move.

I see Ellen slowly pulling herself toward the door again. If I can occupy Will for just a couple of minutes maybe she'll have a chance to get to my purse with my phone—I'm assuming it's near the front door; I was not at my most alert when the strap fell from my shoulder.

"You were right about one thing out there, Doc," Will says. "You and me, we are the same. Only difference is I killed my family, and you killed the one next door. Maybe you were just warming up, I get it."

Then he tosses a glance over his shoulder in Ellen's direction and turns his gaze back to me, the blade still at my neck.

"She won't make it far. Front door's locked," he says. "It's you I wanted anyway. She was just the starter."

"Then you don't need her anymore," I say. "Just let her go."

"No way, Doc," he says. "She was so mean to you. She knew what you'd been through and she still wrote what she did. I'm doing all this for you."

He nods toward Ellen in the hallway and to the man on the floor.

"I'm sorry, Will," I say. "But this, just like it was when you took out your family, this is all just for you."

# Ellen Garcia

I'm crawling in the hallway, blood streaming from both nostrils, my nose swelling up under my eyes, and it feels like there's no air around me and I might be passing out at any moment, but I keep my eyes on the end of the hallway, and I keep crawling.

I can hear the voice of the guy, the actual kidnapper, he's talking to Dr. Caroline, and it doesn't sound like the killing part has started yet, and I wish I could help, but I think she would know better than anyone that the only way any of us—me, her, Bobby—have a shot is if one of us gets out.

But being real, that's not the fire under me.

The only way I'm still moving is because I'm picturing Bella and thinking about her breath on my neck when we're hugging like pencil-cling koalas on the couch aka my bed.

I mean, I'm barely moving; my feet got stuck in cinder blocks somehow, so my arms are doing most of the work, and I can see the red EXIT sign with an arrow high up on the wall about fifteen, twenty feet away, and I'm not sure how long killing or at least severely maiming someone would take, but I'm guessing not as long as it will take me to Terminator-crawl to the end of the hallway and out of here.

"Bel," I say, trying to conjure her.

I don't know what I'd say if she were here.

Actually, that's a lie. Even almost dead, I'm a liar. Of course I know what I'd say. The thing that is more important than love.

"Sorry, Bel. I'm so sorry."

But then there is a loud snap coming from beyond the end of the hallway, and then some footsteps, and then it's not Bella coming up the steps, but a big Black woman, and she has a gun.

She holds her finger to her lips, telling me to *shh*. I hold my finger up to my lips to say, *I understand, you got it, lady*. Then I drop to the floor, the wells of my eyes too shallow to hold my grateful tears.

# Dr. Caroline

**E**llen wasn't strong to begin with, not like you," Will says, cupping my face with his left hand.

I don't have a lot of options at the moment. Either he stabs me in the throat right away, or I try to hit him or push him away and he stabs me by accident, so I just keep squeezing his wrist, and I think, Have I always been expecting this since I ran out of the Strong house that summer morning? Have I always been waiting to take my place?

I shut my eyes and let go of his wrists.

"Drop the weapon. Hands in the air," says a voice.

The familiar husky voice of a goddess.

I open my eyes, and there she is: Makeda. I know I'm on the floor and my perspective's off in a number of ways, but she looks taller than Padma from *Top Chef* on roller skates, like she's about to hit the ceiling with her sensible and unmovable chopped layer-pixie cut.

I know it's her job to hold a gun without exhibiting any signs of anxiety, but really there is not an ounce of tension in her fingers or her hand or her face. She looks just as she did when she suggested I stay at the station for questioning, as when she handed me the search warrant, as when she first rang my office doorbell.

"You first, Officer," says Will, turning his head just the slightest bit to look at her.

"Drop the weapon, sir," she says. "Hands in the air."

He is still holding the blade to my neck, but the pressure is not the same as it was. I wonder if Makeda knows this, and then I think, of course she does. She knows that if he is glancing over his shoulder at her and then back to me, his attention will be divided. Easy to lose one's balance that way.

Just for a split second she meets my eye, and I try to imagine what she'd say: *Dr. Strange* (so stubborn never calling me Dr. Caroline), *don't do anything that will jeopardize yourself any more than you already have. Stay still, and let the police handle this.*

I know for a fact that is exactly what she'd do, doling out instructions even at what may be the last seconds of my life.

She should know me well enough by now.

She starts to say it one more time: "Sir—"

I watch his face flood with frustration, nostrils flaring, and as soon as he turns his head once more to her, I try to slap his hand away with my palm, but he only budges about an inch, the blade scraping my neck. He has not let go of my face and turns back to me, only determination in his eyes. So that is the last thing you see. You are just a job to him now.

Then Makeda jumps, cracks him over the head with the butt of her gun, and he drops the knife and falls forward onto me, not unconscious and not quite conscious, breathing into my chest, both hands traveling toward his head in a daze. Makeda squats and pulls him off me and lays him on the ground gently on his side, holding him by the shoulders, then pushes him onto his stomach, pulls his hands from his head, and unlatches handcuffs from her belt.

I touch my neck and look at my fingers and see the blood. Not a lot.

"Pretty sure it's just surface," she says, fastening the cuffs onto him.

I nod.

"Makeda," I say, "thank you . . . you saved my life."

"You're welcome," she says, standing. She extends her hand to me to help me up. "Also I'd appreciate it if you'd call me Detective Marks."

# Ellen Garcia

en in white, more angels, appear, pick me up off the floor, and walk me outside to a parade of flashing lights, ambulances, cop cars, a fire truck. Flashlight in my eyes, back and forth. Do I know my name? IV plugged into my arm, ice pack on my nose, gauze in the nostrils. Bend your knee, bend your elbow. Foil blanket around my shoulders.

"My husband," I say. It sounds better to ask for your husband instead of your ex-husband when you have narrowly escaped death— that's a thing I picked up just now.

There's a gurney in the ambulance, and all I want to do is lie on it, but the guy says, "Don't, you've still got blood running in three separate places inside your nose. They'll cauterize at the hospital."

I watch them wheel out Bobby. He's got an IV, too, bandage wrapped around his neck.

"Is he okay?"

My guy says, "Sure, he'll be fine. They don't give an IV to a dead man."

Then out comes Dr. Caroline, bright white suit drenched in

blood, her arm slung around the police officer who saved us. Another pair of paramedics rush to her and take her from the officer, one of her arms around each of them. They sit her up in the back of an ambulance parked across from mine, and run the same game—flashlight, bend the limbs, IV, foil blanket.

A gurney rolls out: the kidnapper, the guy Dr. Caroline kept calling Will. He's passed out, hands pinned under him. He gets rolled into another ambulance, and the doors shut right away.

Out of the corner of my eye I see movement, someone running, and I jump—I think my nerves are going to be a thing for a while, but then I focus, and it's Bella in a little orange-and-white-checkered dress and sneakers, and Chris is jogging behind her.

I try to stand up from the ambulance bench, and one of the paramedics says, "You should sit down. They'll come to you."

"Gentle, Bella, gentle," Chris calls.

Bella doesn't slow down and then is wrapped around my waist, her head on my chest.

"What's wrong with your nose?" she says.

I'm crying now, pressing my forehead to hers, trying to smell her but can't through my busted nose. But her skin's the same, smooth and warm, squinty eyes always trying to guess the next thing.

"I sniffed one of those exploding flowers," I say.

"Huh? What?" she says.

"I'll tell you later," I say, as Chris comes up behind her.

His eyes are full, and he's shaking his head. "Are you okay?"

I nod, and he kisses my forehead and puts his other arm around Bella, and the three of us are all wrapped around each other, ready for the holiday card shoot.

In the movie version, this whole event is the catalyst for Chris and me getting back together, and even though I don't see that happening in reality, right now it's a place I am happy to visit.

I peer over to Dr. Caroline in her ambulance, one of the paramedics wiping her face with a cloth. Then he starts unpeeling bandages and unwrapping ice packs, and our view of each other is unobstructed, and she and I look at each other.

She smiles first.

# Dr. Caroline

Ellen Garcia waves at me and smiles, hugging her little girl and her dorky but emotionally attentive husband.

"Doctor!"

It's Jonas, and the poor thing looks like he's been up for ten days and ten nights, face sallow with grief, bags under his glimmering eyes. He bends his knees into a partial squat so he and I are face-to-face, puts his hands on my cheeks.

"Are you all right?" he says.

"Yes, Jonas, I'm all right. I'm fine."

Then he kisses me, cheeks and lips and eyes, but I try to push him away—I can't imagine the paramedic was able to wipe away all the pepper spray with a washcloth.

"Stop, Jonas—you'll get burned."

He pulls away, my face still in his hands, and he smiles and laughs, tears springing from his eyes, and says, "This I am used to, from kissing you."

You of course know the rest.

Ellen Garcia wrote her article for *The New York Times Magazine,* the photo of the three of us in black-and-white, her in front, Detective Marks and I flanking: the story of three women. Honorable mention to Miguel and Bobby Santuzza.

I give her permission this time, to write about me and my history, how Will Wall became obsessed with me and convinced himself that I'd committed the same crimes he'd gotten away with, and so he kidnapped Ellen not only to pledge allegiance to me but also to put me a little bit in the hot seat. His goals were a bit splintered—he wanted to have me for himself and also kill me. It was all mixed up, the sex and mommy-daddy stuff and the joy that violence brought him. My personal theory is that he experienced the single greatest relief of his life when he killed his father, who'd been abusing him, and so perhaps he killed his mother and brother because he wanted the feeling to continue, the way a toddler gets swung around by the wrist and ankle for the first time by a kind uncle: Again, again, says the brain.

Not sure how much of that he'll find serving his twenty-to-life in Attica.

Remember what I said about narrative omission? You leave out what might lose your listener, or, more likely, what will make her not want to listen. Too disgusting or confusing, and she'll be gone.

It was horrible, abominable, unimaginable, what I saw in the Strong house. I woke up as I'd fallen asleep at 10:00, with *Check Your Head* on repeat in my ears, which may seem an odd choice of music to doze to, but it always worked for me. I was usually asleep by "Something's Got to Give." It was early, 5:35, according to Savannah's digital alarm clock, and I had to pee.

Savannah's bed was empty.

In the hallway I saw blood spattered on the walls and on the carpet, a thick stripe leading to Brendan's room, and I pushed his door open and saw them, both of them on the floor, dead and still dripping. Later I learned that Gordon stabbed his beautiful, popular girl right in her kind heart until it stopped beating, and Brendan heard her screaming and woke up and tried to stop him, so Gordon first punched him and then sliced his throat open, and then Evelyn woke up, too, and so Gordon stuck the blades into her chest while he finished with the kids.

He dragged the kids to Brendan's room and then went back to Evelyn in the hallway and cut the fingers off her right hand, I guess to stop her from writing flirtatious notes in the afterlife. Then he carried her back to their bedroom, where he laid her on top of the bed. He placed the fingers around her head on the pillow like a halo.

That morning I ran from Brendan's room into their room, and my eyes didn't know where to go first. The blood, the fingers, her face stuck in a grimace forever.

I was screaming, of course, and then I ran down the stairs and out of the house. I did not go into the basement to where Gordon had hanged himself. I ran outside as my father was pulling into the driveway, coming home from work. I remember him getting out of the car, running toward me, saying my name over and over again, in an effort to stop me from screaming, I suppose.

I screamed for a long time.

That's what you want to know, right? All the bloody stuff? That's all anyone wants to know.

Believe it or not, that's not the money shot, not even Evelyn and her doll parts.

Like I said, Savannah and I listened to *Check Your Head* on heavy rotation that summer in addition to the hits that cycled on the radio and MTV. Not to get too Manson-y, but so many of them had genuine violent messaging tucked inside seemingly benign lyrics. Gordon's favorite, for example, "Achy Breaky Heart," and "Everything About You" by Ugly Kid Joe, even sweet little Shanice has a weird dark bridge in "I Love Your Smile." Weird dark bridges for everyone in 1993.

My and Savannah's favorite line was of course from "So What'cha Want," the one I played for Gordon that day to make sure he heard it.

But I'll back up.

I'm not even sure how I got the idea. Inspiration isn't always a lightning bolt; sometimes it's a collection of leaks through a bum roof, dribble here, dribble there, until the whole thing comes down.

One night when I slept over, Savannah showed me the album with all the pictures of her mother in the bikini.

"She's on a diet and takes one every day," she told me. "Not even my dad knows. She's so weird."

I don't know what exactly compelled me to peel one of the pictures off the sticky page while Savannah brushed her teeth. I think I thought Evelyn looked provocative and sexy, her mouth slightly open, lips glistening. I imagined if I looked like that, a boy like Brendan Strong might like me. Not like his mother, of course, but petite and giant-eyed, breasts plentiful but not grotesque, and a flat tummy, perky bottom. I hadn't fully finished out puberty, but at that point I was shaping up to be more of the bigger, horsier type of girl, every surface flat enough to play cards on.

So I'm not sure what came first, me swiping the picture or seeing Gordon out there making a mess of the hedge.

My mother had forbidden me from going to the Field House for day camp like every other girl my age because she didn't want me to get near boys, which was hilarious because boys wanted nothing to do with me. My father didn't argue with her, never argued with her, just let her make arbitrary rules that constrained every aspect of our lives. When I think of him, I think of how much I loved him, but there is also the pity, how I pitied him so much I tasted it in the back of my throat like the excess spill from a bloody nose. Sometimes I was angry at him for this, but more often than not my ire was rightfully aimed at my mother.

And that day in the front yard, when I told Gordon about my dad teaching Evelyn to flip a burger, I had no idea it would light the fuse in his frontal lobe, burning up whatever reasoning and high-level cognition he had left from the years of low-key alcoholism and unchecked PTSD from childhood.

But I saw how much it bothered him, how he kept gnawing away at that one thick branch, trying to twist it in the blades of the shears because he couldn't cut the damn thing. How ineffectual, impotent, he was. Seeing that, it just made me so angry. Cut it, cut the stupid branch. Get sharper blades and cut the damn branch. Be a man.

So I drew the heart on the back of the bikini pic and just started making shit up.

I didn't hate him. I wasn't seeking revenge. I didn't have anything against Evelyn. I had big absurd feelings for Brendan that I knew would start and end with my fruitless attempts at masturbation. And Savannah was, after all, my best friend.

Like most thirteen-year-old girls, though, we had a complicated relationship. We spent hours listening to music and painting each other's nails and prank-calling boys, but she also knew she was prettier than me and would subtly, or maybe not subtly at all, remind me of it from time to time, just so I knew my place. I remember both of us examining ourselves in the full-length mirror that hung on the front of her closet door, and she'd say, "Isn't it funny how some people have certain shapes and other people have other shapes?"

But still, I didn't hate her for it. I loved her, as much as I could love anyone. I was never grinding my teeth in resentment toward her when I began to chip away at her father's sanity and sense of self. I wasn't thinking about her at all.

Who was I so angry at? What could a thirteen-year-old girl be so angry about?

In the beginning, it was that branch. As I've said, I've been through years of clinical psychotherapy as part of my training, so I've talked a lot about that branch. Or rather, I started talking about that branch, but I kept it to myself when I realized what the branch was long before Dr. Ringo had a chance to catch on.

Or rather, who the branch was.

Have you figured it out yet? You've seen how I do this.

It became easier and easier, because old Gordon just kept tumbling on his own. Drinking and talking to himself and hallucinating conversations with his father. Of course I knew his father was dead—I was at the funeral when Savannah read her psalm like a little angel, or so all the adults kept saying.

My father knew I could mimic handwriting—it was a thing I'd already gotten in trouble for the previous school year, when I wrote a note in my father's hand to the PE teacher that I had rolled my ankle and couldn't participate in swimming for the week, when in fact I'd just wanted to avoid wearing a swimsuit in front of my peers. So when the opportunity arose, all I had to do was suggest the scheme with the letters and make Gordon think it was his idea.

I knew that might be the end of the whole thing, and that I might get in a respectable amount of trouble, but it was a little unexpected that Gordon pushed me onto the tracks so readily. That pissed me off. My tears were mostly genuine, especially when I saw how angry my father was.

Even though Gordon was happy there for a brief moment with Evelyn and full of optimism for his new job, I wanted to see how far I could push it.

I know this sounds cruel, but even now, I can't hide the truth: I was enjoying myself, you see. At that point it wasn't about the branch anymore. It became a game, not chess, really, because thirteen-year-olds don't have a lot of foresight. I mean, I'm sure you can't swing a cat on any street corner in Russia without hitting a thirteen-year-old chess prodigy, but even they can't do that kind of planning in real life, only on a board.

It was really a much more simple game with one goal: Red Rover, Red Rover, send Gordon right over.

Then his new job fell through, which was just luck. Even though I couldn't have planned it better, I didn't have anything to do with that. When I saw Gordon clipping that hedge down to stubs, I knew I only had to tie that knot a little tighter.

And then that night, *the* night, I heard him downstairs in the kitchen and told Savannah I was getting a snack. I'd seen what everyone had seen at dinner, with his shaved head and the black eye and seemingly not being in the most stable of moods, and Savannah and I both heard the bottle break in the basement and Gordon and Evelyn fighting. Of course it was scary—that delirious, unpredictable violence. But I was so close. So when I saw him, chugging his beer with an ice pack on his eye, struggling to keep his balance, I knew it would just take one more breath, a puff of air in his direction, to bring him down.

It wasn't hard. I knew they kept their suitcases in the hall closet, and I knew they used the big wicker basket in the bathroom as a hamper. So I threw some dirty clothes in all three bags and set them by the front door. Figured when Gordon came upstairs from the basement he'd see them and lose his last remaining marble, because he was already such a mess of a man. I hesitate to say he was a monster, because that implies he wasn't human. He was absolutely human. If he was anything, he was human. Just like little Will Pearleater, and his father before him. Just like me and you.

Just like my dear old parents. You get it now, right? Freud 101. That thick sponge of a branch was my mother, and weak, useless Gordon was my father, and in that moment all I knew was that I hated them both, and I wanted someone to pay for it.

You can see "So What'cha Want" was not the real top track that summer. Even though it wouldn't be released for another year, there is only one Beasties song that should have occupied the airtime in my head: *Listen all y'all, it's a sabotage.*

I am being as true as I know how to be when I say I had no idea what Gordon would do. That he would go that far. I honestly thought he would devolve into alcoholism and depression like a normal person. I don't hold myself responsible for what happened. But I did learn at a young age that I could break someone in half if I tried, so I've made it my life's work to put people back together.

Now there's a new variant out there; everyone's in masks again.

Now we are all the girl in the movie trying to escape through the window, and the pandemic is the psycho pulling us back in by our ankles.

You can kill people simply by saying I love you to their faces, so yes, I'll do anything I can to help them. I'm *going* to help them.

And I'm going to help you, too.

# Acknowledgments

I am so, so lucky Daphne Durham gave my story an initial read on her phone as she was getting her toes done and was unable to stop swiping. Limitless thanks to her for the heartfelt guidance, for the editorial expertise, and for going to the mat.

I'm also most grateful to Sean McDonald for making me feel at home and for charting a course for this book.

Many thanks to the remarkably talented and generous people at MCD x FSG: Caitlin Cataffo, Dave Cole, Flora Esterly, Brianna Fairman, Nina Frieman, Abby Kagan, Spenser Lee, Alex Merto, Andrea Monagle, Bri Panzica, Elizabeth Schraft, Sheila O'Shea, and Claire Tobin.

My agent, Mark Falkin, continues to be a great guy who gets me and my shit. None of this would ever be possible if he weren't in my corner.

I listened and relistened to many episodes of *Psychiatry & Psychotherapy*, with Dr. David Puder, and they were enormously useful and made clear so many murky topics and terms for a layperson such as me. I am also struck by how kind he and his guests / fellow mental health professionals are, how invested they are in their patients' well-being.

Also *Ask Lisa: The Psychology of Parenting*, with Dr. Lisa Damour, is consistently revelatory and has the unique ability to make me remember what it was like to be an early-teenage girl.

The book *Sybil Exposed*, by Debbie Nathan, was key in forming Dr. Caroline's opinions on that case study and the topic of dissociative identity disorder.

Additionally, the Netflix series *Monsters Inside: The 24 Faces of Billy Milligan* got me thinking about DID in the first place.

Many fragrant thanks to Bill Wei at Saks Fifth Avenue in midtown, who spent more than a few minutes explaining the art and science of high-end perfume to me and spritzing sample cards for me to take home (even after it became clear I was not going to buy anything).

My brother, Zach Luna, is the sole witness to my childhood and somehow manages not to make fun of me for nonsense I've spewed on and off the page for the fifty years we've known each other. I can't tell you how great it is to have potentially the dumbest idea for a book and then call someone so supportive and have them say, "Nice, dude! See where it goes." Which happens to be the thing I always need to hear the absolute most at that moment in the process.

My mother, Sandra Luna, is the toughest, kindest, gorgeous-est woman I know. She makes chiles rellenos and mushroom bourguignon and pasta and bread and donuts from scratch for me to eat. Once she fished my Princess Leia figure out of the crevice behind the back row of the 41 Union bus with a hanger. She's supported me and this whole creative-life thing before I could name it. There aren't enough thank-you candies in the Gratitude Piñata . . .

And lastly—it's strange to think I've never formally thanked them before, but I offer my deepest thanks to the shrinks who've gotten me out of quite a few tight spots over the years: Dr. Roger Lauer, Dr. Susanne Ahmari, Dr. Eduardo David Leonardo, and Dr. Brian Jacobson. I promise I did *not* base Dr. Caroline on any of you.

## A Note About the Author

Louisa Luna is the author of the Alice Vega series: *Two Girls Down*, *The Janes*, and *Hideout*, which won the G. P. Putnam's Sons Sue Grafton Memorial Award at the 2023 Edgars. She has also written the novels *Brave New Girl*, *Crooked*, and *Serious as a Heart Attack*. She was born and raised in San Francisco and lives in Brooklyn with her husband and daughter.